BRACHAN

A Soldier's Secret Mission

Larry Kaniut

D1738090

Paper Talk
Larry Kaniut
Anchorage, Alaska

2015

ISBN: 978-0-9709537-1-1

AUTHOR CONTACT INFORMATION:

Larry Kaniut, 4800 Natrona, Anchorage, AK 99516

Email: kaniut@alaska.net

Web site: www.kaniut.com

COVER PHOTO CREDIT:

Stuart Bennett

ACKNOWLEDGEMENTS:

Daughter, Ginger, for her encouragement,
as well as Bradley and Sarah Risch for their support
Daughter, Jill Kaniut, for her numerous ideas
Son, Ben Kaniut, for the use of his multitude of books
Wife, Pamela Kaniut, for her editing, support and suggestions
Others who have encouraged me to write over the years include
Beverly Roper, Laura Smothers, Les and Laura Lee Smothers,
Steve Phelps, Peggy Merritt, Diane Hartley, Kay Deeter, Pat
Scott, Jim Crawford, Art and Florence Friese, students
and many others
Cecil Sanders, owner Last Frontier Magazine
Jody Winquist, Dennis DeWinter
and the staff at Northern Printing

DEDICATION:

I dedicate this book to those seeking the truth . . .
hoping they find it.

Table of Contents

INTRODUCTION

It has come to my attention that people are interested in the events of my time in Israel...to know the details of these years as I knew them. Whereas some great military leaders postulate their tribulations and victories on the field of battle, I have no such history. Instead I am compiling this comprehensive account from my memory, daily journal and my dispatches while absent three years from Rome.

Some have asked me how I know of future happenings, forgetting that I compiled this report long after the principle events took place. Perhaps my story will tug at your heart strings and encourage you in a positive manner.

--From the written files of A.J. Brachan

Although I wrote this work of historical fiction, I chose to tell the story through the eyes of a Roman soldier and credited him as its author. Information about the translator appears in the back.

--Larry Kaniut

CHAPTER 1 — Mission

"A-lex-y! A-lex-y! A-lex-y!" Thousands of voices chanted in unison, their tribute thundering throughout the arena. Wave upon wave echoed in a near deafening crescendo until the arena rocked with the intensity of the victory. Alexius had won again. Alexius the gladiator. Alexius, the people's choice. Arms raised above his head and fists clenched, he stood as a stately statue, facing the crowd and acknowledging their accolades.

Voices boomed from the lowest to the highest tier. Senators, merchants and wealthy visitors shouted from the seating closest to the arena. Behind them sat the philosophers, magicians and dissidents, the sword-wielding imperial guards keeping a watchful eye for any signs of discord. And from the upper tiers the plebeians and rabble hooted bawdy, if not obnoxious, comments…the cacophony evolving into a thunderous rumble.

As in countless days gone by, the amphitheater sucked thousands of Romans to her breast. Some visitors stayed in tents outside the arena waiting for scheduled events to begin. Countless spectators filled the stone structure in riotous voice.

Now Alexy strode confidently across the sand covered arena, his leather thonged feet kicking up granules. His bronzed body under the residue of perspiration revealed sculpted muscles glistening in the sunlight. This same man is the same who was my childhood companion. We'd grown up together. How many times had I watched Alexius enter the arena? How many foes had he vanquished? Dozens.

He's taught me much about strategy and survival in the arena. After years of camaraderie I'm watching him again, prior to my mission.

Climbing the stone steps toward me he hails, "Hey, old friend. Greetings."

"Congratulations, Alexy. Another victory."

"A hard fought one against a worthy opponent. Do you want to go to the *ludi* before our evening begins?

"Why not?"

"Then, let us go."

Musing aloud, I asked, "Alexy, how much longer do you think you'll challenge the arena's combatants?"

"I've not thought about it much. The glamour of the gladiators is romanticized. As you know, I have no thoughts of fame. Much work goes into my chosen profession. It's not easy, you know."

"Remind me, O Gallant One, just how hard do you work?"

"Survival in the arena requires disciplined persistence—constant effort to condition and to perfect maneuvers."

"Yeh, yeh, yeh."

"You surely remember the face of the gladiator has changed significantly over the years. From slaves or captured prisoners of war those of suitable age and physique and body type were sent to take the oath of the gladiators, the rest put to death immediately or sold as household slaves. As time passed gladiatorial contests did not end in the death of one of the combatants. The crowd decided his fate—thumbs up, he continues his profession; thumbs down, he's killed."

"Yes, I know all that," Alexy. "Why should we not be surprised that many of these free men sold themselves to gladiator schools for money?"

"Indeed. We should not be, my friend."

As we neared the school, I egged on my companion somewhat, "So, 'Lex, I'm guessing you initiate all the new gladiators to give them a leg up?"

"A leg up, yes. A chance to defeat me, no. With them I share mostly our history. That's all."

At that point we reached the *ludi*. A stout young man, barely dry behind the ears, interrupted our discourse, addressing Alexy, "I was told the older gladiators could provide some background about the ludi. I presume you are a gladiator. Would you have time to answer a couple of questions?"

Obviously this kid was new. He didn't recognize Alexius, the true veteran that he is.

With a twinkle in his eye and a wink in my direction, Alexy replied, "Well, now, New Man. How about I first ask a question or two of you?"

Without skipping a beat, New Man looked Alexy in the eye, "That's fair enough. Go ahead."

"For starters, since you might be my opponent one day, what's your name?"

"Laelia. My friends call me Lucky."

"Well, let's not get too informal at this point. Next question. Nowadays free men choose to become gladiators. We both know that some of these men, formerly Roman soldiers, either sought fame and fortune or pursued their only skill. Some were wealthy Romans who wanted adulation and glory. Since they were allowed to keep any prizes or gifts they were given during gladiatorial games, a successful gladiator could improve his financial status handsomely. Others turned to the arena for the money. Successful gladiators could become famous and retire wealthy. Are you a free man, criminal, prisoner of war or slave?"

"Criminal. Recently captured."

"Oh…not so lucky, then?"

"My crime was stealing food for a starving family."

"For that you're sent to the Ludi Gladiatorium?"

"There are two kinds of luck."

"So there are. Okay, I'll answer your questions…as long as they do not undermine my personal strategies and safety."

"For starters, what am I to expect?"

"You will receive excellent training in weapons and combat techniques here. As a new recruit or *novicius* you enter the school and the manager or *lanista* assesses you, right?"

"Right."

"Unattractive men are automatically rejected—spectators prefer beauty. Your physique determines the type gladiatorial training you will receive. For instance, does your body type suggest that you will be suited for heavy or light armor? The lanista's determination goes a long way in   d i r e c t i n g your training."

"Although the manager determines my training, what options do I have?"

"The trainers are often retired gladiators. They specialize in specific styles of fighting and weapons. The Dimachaeri carry two swords while the Samnites carry a short sword, a rectangular shield and wear a helmet; Velites use a javelin and the Sagittarii are mounted horseback and armed with bows and arrows. Each style has its advantages and disadvantages."

"What about injuries or other health issues?"

"A doctor checks you for suitability as a trainee and for medical issues. You look healthy. It would not be good for me to suggest your style because we may battle in the arena. You wouldn't want to trust me on that call."

"Okay. So let's say I pass muster. Then what?"

"Serious gladiators endure a strict daily training regimen in order to achieve the highest skill levels, the best fighters rising to the top. Probably any one of the new recruits could subdue the bulk of outsiders, those who only come to watch us. You are closely guarded but your treatment and need for shackles ease with time served. You may choose to become a highly trained gladiator, an expensive commodity. As such you will be treated with some care. Your training cost is high. You'll be well fed and receive excellent medical treatment. Some of the tattooed veterans are members of *collegia*, a formal association which ensures proper burials that compensation will be duly given to their families."

When Laelia responded, I knew we had a live one, "I'm fond of food. I like all kinds and lots of it. But better than that, I like life. Trust me, I'll train hard." He finished with cocky bluster, "I won't mind the money either."

To that, Alexy responded, "Looks like I'll have to start training harder or make sure we don't cross paths in the arena. Perhaps we'll join ranks and become a fearsome dual threat."

Somewhat surprisingly Laelia next alluded to Spartacus, "I bet some of those wealthy Romans investing in troops of gladiators wish Spartacus had stayed in the school so they could have invested in him."

Alexy admitted, "Yes, Spartacus was a worthy contestant and a crafty foe. After Spartacus turned from soldiering to becoming a gladiator and trained in the gladiatorial school of Lentulus Batiatus, he became an escapee. With the aid of seventy men wielding kitchen utensils they fought their way out of the school and seized several wagons of gladiatorial weapons and armor to become enemies of Rome."

I felt inclined to share my pleasure with my relative involvement, though distant, "It makes me proud when I say that my grandfather was among those soldiers who put a stop to his reign. Many times I've listened to my grandfather tell of the travails he endured chasing Spartacus and his rebels."

Alexy responded, "It's interesting that due to the rebellion of Spartacus all gladiatorial weapons are secured to prevent another such uprising. While continuing to recruit other slaves he trained his followers and they defeated the Roman soldiers on numerous occasions."

And I stated, perhaps the obvious, "It was only a matter of time before the Roman army toppled them. As a message to future insurrectionists, the army crucified the six thousand survivors, thirty or forty yards apart, along the Appian Way, where they were left as examples and fed upon by vultures and dogs."

By now the day was waning and Alexy excused himself, telling the young combatant that we were departing to enjoy the evening.

As we left the ludi, I asked, "'Lex, do you ever wonder about the parallel between the arena and Rome?"

"I've never given it great thought, however I see a definite parallel. The arena symbolizes our society. The masses flock there to watch human suffering and bloodshed—either from beasts or man. Those who come to the arena want to be entertained. Some are merely killing time while others lust for the danger and the killing. And they flood the arena with their perverted sexual displays. Even under the watchful eyes of guards, the masses engage in disgusting behavior from the bottom row to the top of the stadium—from Caesar to the lowliest peasant."

"Maybe some of them should be subjected to the arena where gladiators could address their immorality."

"Good point. How much chance would one of them have against a gladiator?"

"The tone of the nation is set by its leaders. If they are defiled and degenerate, what kind of example is that to the civilians?"

"Like I said, our society screams for personal pleasure and blood lust.

"Speaking of Spartacus and his followers and their quest for freedom from Rome, what are you hearing about the hotbed of anarchy in the south? After Archelaus was removed and when Judaea came directly under Rome's control, the tyranny and extortion of Roman governors and their efforts to introduce heathen symbols and customs almost brought the country to a boil."

"Things are still a cauldron of chaos—clashes of culture, social issues, religion and politics occur daily. Rumblings have reached Rome, rumblings regarding revolution, uprisings or some other controversy in Israel. Endless unrest continues unabated. What else is new?"

"Maybe some of the protestors could come to Rome and my gladiator pals and I could engage them in the arena."

"That's a thought. The Jews aren't the only ones—they're just the loudest...and maybe the most brazen. They complain that the boot of Rome is upon their necks. Their dislike and distrust of Rome has fed their fears and fanned the flames of hatred for their oppressors.

"Can we really blame them? We cherish our freedom. How do you suppose we'd feel if we were in their sandals?"

Laughing, I replied, "Alexy, most of these people don't have sandals—they're barefoot. I know what you're saying. I would probably despise my oppressors too. For seven decades after Rome assumed control of Judaea, growing Jewish opposition to Roman laws has festered under the surface.

"On the other hand, Roman officials have concern because of Jewish nationalism and their religious fervor. The Jews especially despised the Roman imposition of a census of property for tax purposes and what they considered Rome's heathen traditions. Ancestral land held an exalted position in Jewish ideology and many Jews feared that the new laws would lead to Roman appropriation. These concerns fly in the face of their religious beliefs. In the past we've witnessed Jewish uprisings protesting our laws. Those protests led to the crucifixion of thousands of Jewish insurgents and the selling into slavery of perhaps 20,000 more."

"Like you said earlier, 'So, what else is new?'"

"It's bad enough that there's resistance, however the most intense opposition comes from Galilee, which has been considered the center of an armed resistance movement, the Zealots. These rabid citizens are country folk—fishermen, farmers and farm laborers—living on the Sea of Galilee which provides a strong economic base. They are known trouble makers."

"Kind of like Spartacus?"

"I never thought of it like that. Here it is the fifteenth year of Tiberius Caesar's reign. Pontius Pilate is governor of Judaea. Herod's tetrarch of Galilee. His brother Philip is tetrarch of the lands of Ithuraea and of the region of Trachonitis. And Lysanias is the tetrarch of Abilene. You and I both agree that these guys could govern without mayhem.

"Sometimes I think my training and education are a curse. Evidently Herod Antipas has some concerns which he relayed to Tiberius Caesar. My superior responded to their concerns and is sending me to Judaea. I was selected because of my military background as well as my knowledge of Roman law, my expertise in languages and my understanding of the Jewish culture, religion and history. And a bit of medical know-how. I'm guessing my father's military achievements, his command of languages including Aramaic and the Jewish culture in Judaea contributed in part to my selection."

"What do you think will come of your trip?"

"I don't know for certain. As you know, my allegiance is to the Empire and to Caesar. As a Roman soldier I'll do my duty to the Empire, whatever that requires. If by some means a worthy scoundrel is arrested, maybe I'll return him to Rome so you can battle him in the arena. I'm assuming I'll return within a few months. I'll send you a letter to keep in touch. One good thing about Judaea is that I might be able to visit some of my military friends such as Gaius and his wife and daughter in Jerusalem where he's stationed. I'll also attempt to look up some of the others.

"I'm not particularly apprehensive about the journey, just aggravated that I have to go. The trip by sea could take as long as two months but I trust Jupiter and his brother Neptune will favor me and shorten the journey. Hopefully the sailing season will be kind and I'll arrive no worse for the wear. I'm scheduled to make landfall at the deep water port of Caesarea in Judaea, one of many projects built by Herod the Great. And I hope to view many other projects we Romans have completed over the years."

It wasn't long before I embarked on my trip. Since I would start in Ostia at the mouth of the Tiber and one of our largest harbors, I made my way over the cobblestones and through the narrow streets of Rome to the harbor. I could have caught a ride in a naval vessel however in keeping with my cover, I took civilian passage.

I boarded a Corbitas, a round-hulled freighter with a curving prow and stern. The captain told me she was a hundred-ton vessel, not so large as those capable of carrying 350 tons, six hundred passengers or six thousand clay jars (amphorae) of wine, oil, or other liquids, nevertheless a huge ship.

Our manifest included woolen products and tin. The skipper told me the vessel would likely be laden with a combination of wheat or papyrus, timber, spices and purple dye on its return to my homeland.

JOURNAL

I'm off to Israel. We slipped our moorings and eased into the waters bound for Judaea and, in all likelihood, Jerusalem. I've had sufficient time to grow my hair and facial hair longer, avoiding the short hair and beardlessness of Roman soldiers. I can now more perfectly blend in with the travelers along the way which will add to my anonymity.

After meeting with Alexius I determined to document my activities in a journal so that I could keep an accurate account until my return to Rome. I wanted to share more with Alexy but am under strict orders of secrecy. I'll travel as a civilian, ferreting activities that could be detrimental to the Empire. My primary assignment is to monitor a wilderness wild man and to gauge his motives. Since I can't be everywhere at once, I'll have a network of agents keeping me posted on unfolding events in their neighborhoods. My assignment is to investigate the rumors and report the details to my superior.

Knowing that it was safest to travel between May and October, I hoped for decent weather. The journey from Rome to Alexandria was a ten day to two month affair, depending upon the weather. Though my destination was not Alexandria, we slipped out of the harbor under favorable seas in good weather, surrounded by the ever present seagulls and sea birds squawking and wheeling overhead.

Although some passengers grumbled about the arrangements, our days were filled with walking the deck, visiting with fellow passengers or sailors and relaxing. I did not mind the requirement of providing my own food, blankets, mattress and cookware. Nothing exciting was happening, just the usual humdrum rocking of the ship as she glided through calm waters.

One positive I look forward to daily is the always changing patterns of the sky. One day while looking overhead toward the heavens, I saw a flock of elongated white-gray sheep grazing in a pale blue field. How could it be more beautiful?

Ten days into our journey while walking the deck I noticed a flotilla of half-dozen triremes. I wondered what these Roman naval vessels were up to. Perhaps they were either on maneuvers or searching for pirates, one of the significant dangers on the high seas.

It was the great Greek historian Thucydides who wrote about pirates' plundering un-walled villages, causing villagers to build away from the sea to provide further protection from those pirates practicing "an honorable profession."

Piracy had become a highly successful business. Because it might include robbery, kidnapping, rape and/or murder, the Roman senate had established rules to address it. Under the watchful eye of Caesar, efforts minimizing piracy on the Great Sea had worked for a period, however in spite of the enforcement, piracy was thriving.

Capturing and selling people as slaves was lucrative and the pirates showed no mercy. More rewarding than selling people was collecting protection money from villages for the reassurance that the pirates would leave the villages alone. Before the protection money was paid, pirates commonly attacked villages using more than one vessel because more men were necessary in order to repel a village full of armed men.

The following afternoon at the rail and contemplating the navy triremes I'd seen the previous day, I recalled some of their history. Those military vessels comprised 200 men—three tiers of 170 rowers and 30 sailors including captain, helmsman, bow-man, time-beater and lookout.

These ships were normally accompanied by a marine detachment. The trireme, fitted with a smaller and a larger mast and square sails, was capable of a top speed of perhaps 7 knots and a sustained speed of 4 knots while resting half the rowing. They could make sixty miles a day in good weather.

My contemplation of triremes was interrupted when I glanced to the horizon and observed a sail. After watching it several minutes as it drew nearer, it was obvious that it was gaining on our craft causing many of us to wonder what was happening. In due time it became obvious that the approaching ship was a bandit—a boat load of pirates.

I was dumbfounded that this ship continued its approach toward mine. Those aboard my ship became more and more alarmed, no doubt anticipating the worst. *Will I be robbed? Taken captive? Sold into slavery? Murdered?*

As the ship closed, most of the passengers hid in fear while a few men and the crew came on deck to confront the bandits whose ship hove against our starboard rail. Grappling hooks sailed over our side and the bandits ascended the ropes. A few were knocked back by those above but before long some pirates reached our deck.

Though none carried a boarding axe, most were armed with either a cutlass or a dagger sheathed on their belts. Garbed in cutoffs, they vaulted the rail barefoot.

Thinking I could either run through a pirate or push him overboard, I had armed myself with a pike pole. Coupled with the many skills I'd learned from Alexy and my military training, confidence guided me. While others confronted those forward, I challenged one who came over the stern rail. As he squatted preparatory to leaping from the rail, I thrust the point into his chest. He shrieked as I pushed him overboard. Turning quickly I faced another bearded bandit. With no time to poke him I wristed the butt of the pole against the side of his head and he dropped to the deck and lay motionless.

Pandemonium reigned. Cursing and angry threats from both our crew and the bandits filled the air.

Noting that two bandits pulled Ariella toward the rail, I launched myself toward them. That is my last memory.

When I regained consciousness, my head throbbed and I tasted blood. It hurt to open my eyes and when I did, my vision was blurred by something. My head pounded. Warm, sticky liquid ran down my cheek as I tried to sit up. I rubbed my eyes and noticed the shouting and other sounds had ceased. I was finally able to focus my vision and made out a few men near me. Someone had an arm around my back supporting me and another swabbed at my eyes and head with a damp cloth. I slowly realized they were navy men. *They must have rescued our group.*

The captain of the freighter spoke to me, assuring me that I'd been injured by a blow to the head and a stab wound to my back—evidently two pirates struck me simultaneously, one to the head while a mate struck with his dagger. It appeared my falling forward and away from the dagger reduced the injury I would have sustained.

As instructed, I lay back and four men placed their hands under me and lifted me from the deck. Another cradled my head and they carried me to a room. I thought I noticed smoke but wasn't in condition to determine that. The captain charged a man acting as doctor to tend my injuries. He addressed my head and back wounds, applying some sort of herb to a cut on my head. I'm not sure what happened after that as I fell asleep. It wasn't until I awoke the next day that I was informed about the rescue and my care giver.

When I groaned and tried to move, opening my eyes, I heard a woman's humming. Then she spoke, "Easy. You may have a serious head injury. The doctor asked me to keep an eye on you and to alert the captain as soon as you awakened."

She spoke to someone nearby who left. It sounded like Ariella but I wasn't sure. My head throbbed and my vision was blurry. The area around my right scapula felt tight.

Wanting more information about the attack I asked, "Can you tell me what happened…was it yesterday?"

"Yes. Yesterday. You remember the pirates boarding our ship?"

"The last I remember is that two pirates pulled Ariella toward the rail."

"I'm Ariella. They reached the rail with me then noticed three Roman navy ships approaching. Two vessels pulled up outside the pirate ship while the third cut them off by pulling in front of them. A band of Roman sailors and marines vaulted aboard the pirate ship, I think a mixture of men from both navy ships."

"Where did the navy ships come from? They weren't about when we watched the pirate ship."

"The captain said they had lain in wait for pirate action, coming from behind the headlands on the island of Cauda, just south of Kriti."

"That makes sense. Have you any idea how long the battle lasted? And what was the result?"

"I'm not sure. My father said about twenty minutes. I was fighting for my release. When the pirates holding me saw the navy sailors, they released me to fight for their lives.

"I think that's when you were injured. I rushed to safety. My father said after the pirates were subdued, the officer in charge condemned them to the sea, except three men—their captain and two others. The navy commander said he would free them when they were near landfall, expecting them to be witnesses to others as to what they could expect from pirating if caught.

"The navy commandeered beneficial supplies and some sailors fired the pirate ship while others kept the water-bound pirates at bay. Once the ship was aflame and a blaze overwhelmed it, the pirates who clung to the hull swam futilely from it. We sailed away and the three navy ships soon sailed off to the north."

"So, I did see smoke. How did our crew fare?"

"A few were injured but no one killed. I was most concerned for my father but he is okay. During the initial attack I wondered if the pirates might take my father for ransom, perhaps having discovered his line of business. When I saw you fighting the pirates, I was amazed by the way you fought. "

"I learned a great deal from my friend Alexy the gladiator. Perhaps you've heard of him? After his time as a tribune in the Roman army he joined the gladiators as a free man."

"I do not know him but I have seen him. One day my girlfriend and I saw him on a street in Rome and she told me about him. He has some kind of fame."

"Yes, he does. And he's a wonderful friend and man."

"How are you feeling now? You had a nasty cut on your back."

"I'm stiff and sore but I think I'm feeling better. I'm assuming my injuries will heal and I'll be close to normal by the time we reach Caesarea Maritima or shortly thereafter. I'm looking forward to landing and visiting the city. My father supervised the building of the two breakwaters for the artificial harbor during his military days."

By now the captain had arrived and questioned me about my condition, looked at my wounds and assured me that they appeared to be much improved.

He said I would be examined more closely when we reached port.

During those days I continued to improve and developed a more pronounced relationship with those aboard who claimed I was some kind of hero for my daring against the pirates. They expressed their sympathy for my injuries and best wishes for good health. I made it a point to visit with Ariella and her father on a daily basis, learning about his trade and their homes in Jerusalem and Rome. She assured me that after our journey should I fail to contact her, her familiarity with Rome would allow her to locate me.

The final days of the voyage passed quickly. As we came in sight of the bustling town of Caesarea, the first thing I noticed was the northern and southern breakwaters, 275 and 500 meters long respectively. King Herod had built them over a seven year period. My father had told me the material for the moles consisted of lime and a type of volcanic ash that turned solid under water. The building of these moles required serious architectural skills and underwater divers to solidify the foundations for them. Beyond the breakwater lay the port and the city.

When we finally reached port, I was feeling much better. I thanked my well wishers and bid them farewell, noting in my journal directions to Ariella and her father's home should I get the opportunity to visit them later.

CHAPTER 2 — The Baptizer

Considering our history, our place in world affairs and my mission for the Empire, I proudly represent Rome.

Our road system and aqueducts, our culture, our power, our way of life—all superior to any other in the history of man. The Roman way excels all others. We own the world.

We have conquered the nations opposing us…and Romanized the world. Our military is relentless and powerful. We devised the ultimate punishment to deal with our enemies…nailing men to a tree, probably the most painful and heinous punishment known to man. Is it any wonder that nations fear us? Rome is in control. There is every reason for nations to fear us. Ask those pirates who had recently felt the wrath of messing with my ship and the Roman navy. The ones who survived.

Now here I am. Given ultimate authority by my superior to find and follow this Baptizer, to see what he's up to and what he's about. I will find and follow him until I determine whether or not he poses a danger to the Empire.

After reaching port my first objective was to send a dispatch to my superior apprising him of my safe arrival and of my immediate search for the Baptizer. I need to find a letter courier for my report to my superior. That should be no serious task, knowing Augustus Caesar's mail system works well. The service, *cursus publicus*, provides delivery with light carriages called *rhedæ*. Their fast horses can deliverer a letter five hundred miles distant in 24 hours. Additionally, there is a slower service equipped with two-wheeled carts (*birolæ*) pulled by oxen. This service is reserved for government correspondence. A service for citizens was later added. I have faith in our system.

Having dispatched my letter, I found the agent for the area. My supervisor Flavius Diusus Caldus had apprised me before my departure that he had established a network of informants to report to. He had requested Antipas to supply some of his most trusted men. I would meet one now to acquire the information.

Eager to engage the informant when we met, I asked, "So, tell me, friend, when did you last see John the Baptizer?"

"Just before my replacement came, allowing me to come meet you here. It has been about three weeks. I don't think there is need to monitor the Baptist further; he preaches the same message every day."

"What can you tell me about him?"

"I ran into him at the River Jordan, where he was baptizing what he calls believers. I think he initially baptized at Bethany beyond the Jordan. Although I was in the region of Kharrar, it's been said that he travels the river to appropriate areas for baptisms. I had been sent indirectly by Herod

Antipas as part of my duties. As you know, my mission was to observe him and to discover what his objective was.

"I was dressed as a peasant and made it a point to ask him questions that would reveal his motives without arousing his suspicions. I had heard that his entire days consisted of preaching and baptizing. I played the game and even got myself baptized.

"Since we all know the publican's penchant for padding their pockets with inflated taxes, I thought I could trick him into revealing himself regarding taxes a soldier must pay a publican. He turned my question into a pronouncement about the importance of reforming. He said the most important thing a soldier should do was to 'change his ways and make good with God. Do violence to no man, do not falsely accuse anyone and be content with his pay.'"

"So, he preached about God and that soldiers should be happy with their pay while being nice?"

"Yes. Primarily he spoke of changing for God or getting ready to meet God, doing good for others and behaving in a kind manner. He said nothing of achieving power or demonstrating against the government."

"What else can you tell me about him?"

"John the Baptist was an only child, raised in a religious home by aged parents. His father was a priest. John never had his hair cut. He drank no liquid from the vine and did not indulge in rich food. His diet consisted of locusts and wild honey he'd gathered from stumps or rock crevasses.

"He grew up living a simple lifestyle in the wilderness of barren hills. He was accustomed to the harsh wasteland pockmarked by sand, rock, scrub, thorn brush and blazing sun. Talk on the street is that he's probably deranged. He has never married and lives by himself in the desert with lizards, hyenas and wild boar, kind of a desert recluse. He makes his home there among the ravines and caves, drinking from the land's water. For some reason he chose the wilderness as his home, away from the crowds of people haunting villages and cities, forsaking human companionship in a civilized setting."

"Why would he live such a solitary life?"

"I'm not so sure it's solitary any more. People from all lands are flocking to the area beyond Jordan to hear the Baptist. People from Jerusalem and all over the Jordan Valley and every section of Judaea have traveled to the wilderness to hear him. Many consider him a prophet risen from the dead. They refer to him as a 'real prophet' because his words smack with authority. They say it's been centuries since they've heard such power in words. But even though he is strong willed and determined, he defers to another."

"Have you reported this to Antipas and do you think the Baptizer poses a threat to the region?"

"I have reported to Antipas. The Baptist's followers are so enthusiastic and growing in numbers that Antipas is still concerned. I've heard he may have preached to a million in just over a year's time. As I stated, some people think he might be Elijah or perhaps the Messiah."

"I know that the Jewish holy word talks about a Messiah. What do you make of this talk?"

"I don't know what to make of it. The Baptist is either confusing or confused. There is quite a stir over the fact that whereas Jews traditionally focused a great deal of time on washing rituals, John is paying more attention to washing people in water. He denies being the Messiah but claims to be the forerunner to the Messiah and preparing them for the Messiah's arrival.

"He keeps trumpeting about a colleague who's coming to assist him— 'Someone greater than I whose sandals I am not worthy of kneeling and untying.' And if that's not strange enough, John claims this Messiah will not baptize with water but with the fire of the Holy Spirit. Maybe it's some of that Jewish hogwash that's been going on for centuries about a deliverer."

"I'll be leaving tomorrow, heading beyond the river to find the Baptizer and to see what I can learn."

"You can't miss him. Look for a man in camel hair clothes with a big leather belt."

As I left the informer, I couldn't help wonder. It was a festering thought… could this wild man really be a threat to Rome? Four hundred years have passed with no such voice as the Baptizer's—flaming warnings of disaster to Israel…warnings of a coming savior. Could he be the deliverer the Jews have long awaited? I may have bitten off more than I can chew. We'll see.

As I wandered, so did my mind, back and forth from the Baptizer to the continuing Jewish-Roman status. While wondering who he was and what he represented, it was obvious that communication with others would provide information and fill in some of the blanks about him. However the best means of learning about him was personal contact. I would evaluate him when we met.

I had long wondered and wanted to learn more about what the Jews thought about their Roman overlords. *What would it be like to be in their shoes and controlled by others?* To a degree, the Jew-Roman situation is somewhat like a parent and child relationship. In general children adhere to parental authority until they are old enough to branch out on their own.

The Jews, however, are adults and do not need supervision by some foreign power. Is it any wonder the Jews are disquieted?

The citizens' dislike and distrust of the Roman power feeds their fears and fans the flames of hatred for their oppressors. Overpowering taxation and idolatry flies in the face of their religious belief. After the removal of

Archelaus, Judaea came directly under Rome's control, resulting in the tyranny and extortion by Roman governors. Their efforts to introduce heathen symbols and customs resulted in a seething citizenry whose hatred for the Romans teetered the nation on the brink of revolution.

They especially despised the Roman imposition of a census of property for tax purposes. Ancestral land held an exalted position in Jewish ideology and many Jews feared that the new laws would lead to its appropriation by Rome.

Sedition was the order of the day in Judaea. Numerous plots were hatched against the Romans, one such being that of Judas in 6 A.D. when he and a band of revolutionaries captured the city of Sepphoris five miles from Nazareth. The Romans acted quickly in our merciless manner and hanged 2000 of them from trees on the hill on which the city stood, selling perhaps 20,000 more into slavery.

I believe I would have been hard pressed to obey the demands of such a government, wanting my own freedom to pursue my life and goals, to enjoy my culture without intervention. So here we have a captive people as it were, growing in animosity toward Roman authority or those appointed by the Roman ruler.

It will be interesting to see what develops during my stay in their land.

When I reached the land beyond the Jordan to which I'd been directed and saw the Baptizer for the first time, I was momentarily shocked. I hadn't expected to see such a man-of-the-earth looking character. His was the appearance of a commoner, long exposed to the sun and outdoor living. I immediately spotted the leather belt. A shaggy mane of hair tumbled from his head covering his shoulders. I thought he was in his own wilderness. Perhaps in addition to being in a physical wilderness, he was also in a mental one. It was obvious that I'd have to observe him a while before I could make that determination.

The first time I heard him speak, I detected a commanding voice. His eyes flashed with the passion of powerful belief. Courage enveloped him as he tossed out words of urgency. He held nothing back. Pulled no punches. Passion is necessary to live life to the fullest. One must embrace it and live it. I am passionate about protecting the Empire. I will fight to preserve it.

Day after day I listened to and watched the Baptizer work with countless, hundreds of people—baptizing them, encouraging them to wait upon the Lord. His message flooded Israel like an incoming tide turned tsunami.

Pharisees and teachers of Moses' Law refuse to believe and they reject his message and his baptism. My perception was that he was saying "the baptism I offer you supersedes the superficial 'cleanliness' of your washing traditions that you smugly continue in the belief that they will cleanse and save you."

He excoriated them for their refusal to listen to his message, calling them vipers. He offended people. I wondered if they would retaliate in some fashion.

Thousands expected the Messiah to come soon. Countless ones thought John was the Messiah. The topic was discussed everywhere. It was the question of the hour.

This entire business about the Baptizer and his prediction that another would follow him, gave me pause. What kind of situation is developing? It seemed prudent to figure out who this Messiah is. I had heard that the Nazarene was preaching, that he had been commissioned, as it were, to preach some sort of salvation. Was there some connection? I have more work to do.

Finally one day I chose to take a break from the Baptizer's incessant preaching. Having listened daily to his constant refrain—"repent and meet your God," I rationalized I was due time off. A break would do me good. John had indicated nothing of revolutionary consequence against the Empire. *I'll miss but a day or two of his preaching and return before long to take up where I left off.*

While walking along the Jordan River, I stopped from time to time to observe my surroundings. The blue of the sky was comforting and soothing. I was reminded of two of my great delights—black birds and cattails. I found peace in the solitude of the marshy areas producing the water flora like the cattail, which changed so dramatically in seasons. It always gives me a sense of tranquility to watch the ever present blackbirds perched on cattails or flying to and from them.

Amidst my thoughts of peaceful pleasure, I decided I was due a long soak. *It's time to initiate my own personal baptism.* I dropped my grip and rustled through it for the *sapo* a German mercenary had given me. He claimed their soap made of ashes and tallow was the best available. The soak would allow me time to "bathe" not only my body but also my brain, to unwind and to soak in the surrounding flora and fauna.

I chose a secreted spot, removed my garments, folded them and placed them one atop the other on my sandals before picking up the sapo and entering the water. While I made my way far enough from shore where water was shoulder deep, my eyes captured the scene around me and my body adjusted to the water's temperature. After a short time I made my way shoreward to shallow water and sat down on the river bottom.

While trying to lose myself in the moment, I was surprised by the bark of a hyena. *That's strange. Hyenas are nocturnal. Was it a hyena? Yes, there it is on the opposite bank. And it's not alone. Looks like a mother with two pups. Wonder what they're doing in daylight?*

17

Made me wonder about the myths associated with this animal. The striped hyena is a small dog-like creature with powerful jaws. I watched them, unobserved. The mother seemed to enjoy her pups' playfully romping about. All too soon they melted into the undergrowth.

Some minutes later I slowly eased through the water and onto the bank. Moving through the grass to my clothes, I enjoyed the sun's rays warming and drying my body in my place of solitude. Feeling clean and greatly refreshed, I bent over my clothes, shaking each piece briskly to assure the removal of any visiting insects or other critters. I was not interested in a scorpion surprise.

On my way again pointing toward the King's Highway, I looked forward to observing the activity of commerce and day to day living. I slowly and purposely forged ahead, thinking about my next meal.

While walking, I considered the Roman road system. We had built a network of 63,000 paved miles—
    miles connecting cities and cultures;
    miles used by traders, builders, soldiers and government officials;
    miles of great thoroughfares such as the coastal route called "the Way of the Sea" or its Latin name *Via Maris* and, of course, the King's Highway, running north and south.

I was always amazed at my discoveries along the way. Traffic ebbed or flowed depending upon the time of day, the specific roadway and/or the season of the year. As I reached the byway, I discovered a steady drumbeat of traffic. Droves of people dotted the roadway coming and going afoot or aboard various animals.

Although Judaea is primitive compared to Rome whose construction of storm drains, aqueducts and harbors teems with growth, the hustle and bustle around me was evidence that construction carries on much the same as in the days of Herod the Great—harbors, aqueducts and various buildings.

Merchants moved various trade goods and market items—spices, silks and sapphires. Their camel caravans seemed endless. The heavily laden animals were obvious targets because thugs lay in ambush to rob the merchants, hiding before and after their devious deeds. Numerous ox carts loaded with marble slabs, designated for some temple or elaborate government edifice, chugged along. Litters carried the rich.

Beautiful horses pulled chariots. The lowly donkey with its burden of a single person whose feet nearly touched the ground brought a smile to my face. I'd always been enamored to this little fellow that possessed so much character and strength.

Multi-national and multi-racial faces sojourned in all sizes with business or personal activities to attend...
    a yellow face with white goatee and narrowed Chinese eyes;
    a small black face with white teeth, curly hair and happy, smiling

eyes;

an old brown face, topped with white hair and grooved with baked-by-India's-sun wrinkles.

I always found joy when traveling early in the morning, observing the awakening of the day and its people…

sometimes a morning chill;

or a rosy sunrise;

sparkling dew drops on the grass;

animals with glazed-over-half-open eyes contentedly chewing cuds;

people stumbling from tents, rubbing sleep from their eyes;

tinkling bells on bellwether sheep;

sheep dogs barking at miscreant charges.

And in the fading twilight at day's end …

people erected tents;

cooking fires produced rich aromas;

folks fed and cared for their animals;

people settled in for the night.

After a long day on the trail, the demeanor of both man and beast demonstrated less patience than earlier in the day. I could write a book on my observations during my travels, encapsulating the numerous events—some funny, some not so.

While resting under a palm tree, I heard a commotion and looked up the roadway. To my surprise a dromedary camel charged toward me, its lead line bouncing in the breeze. Through the cloud of dust it stirred up, I made out a man running after it, arms aloft and waving. From his lips came undecipherable words. He was more than likely the owner or a driver who was obviously desperate.

The camel was making a mad attempt for freedom.

Thinking I might stop the animal or turn it back to the pursuer, I jumped to my feet and waited as it rumbled toward me, spitting and growling a guttural grunt, *eerrraahhhhhhuunnhh*. Dirt clods kicked up every time a hoof hit the ground. I waved my arms with no visible effect. When it was about to run over me, I lunged for the flopping rope. I grabbed it with one hand, quickly gripped it with the other while yanking it downward and simultaneously jumping to the side. The animal stumbled a few strides yet kept its feet while I clung tightly onto the rein. It was all I could do to maintain my balance and keep from being jerked off my feet. Then the brute stopped.

Coupled with some angry "words" from the camel and my soothing words of comfort, it finally settled down. By then the nearly breathless owner approached me. He signaled his gratitude and when finally able to speak, in a labored whisper, he thanked me over and over. I acknowledged his gratitude and only then discovered that during the melee I'd broken the leather thong attached to my right *caligla*. The owner offered to pay for the repair of my sandal or purchase of a new leather thong, suggesting a tent maker in the nearby village. I gratefully refused his offer for payment.

I'd been in country long enough to know about tent makers and their profession. Because tents were made from skins, the tent maker was by his very nature a leather worker. Reminiscing about the tanning process, I must admit I wasn't overly excited to pay the tanner a visit.

The process of making leather begins when it is first taken as a skin or hide from the animal. Then it is tanned. A solution of water and sumac leaves along with oak galls and dog dung is applied to the hide. Hair removal is accomplished by scraping, soaking and the application of lime. The foul smell emanating from the tannery relegated the tent maker to property on the outskirts of town where the prevailing wind blew away from the population center.

As I made my way to the tent maker's while keeping my sandal from falling off, it was a bit of a challenge. However it was little discomfort compared to the multitudes walking barefoot on the byway.

Thoughts tumbled through my brain and it seemed hardly any time at all and I was at the tent maker's.

I entered the shop, requested a leather strap and noticed an aged man sitting in a corner. I paid the price for the strap and approached the elderly gentleman. I asked about his length of residency in the area. He seemed eager to talk. Thinking I might supplement my knowledge of the religion of the Jews, perhaps gaining more knowledge regarding this Messiah business, I engaged him, "Tell me, Aged One, what says the law of Moses pertaining to the Messiah?"

"We eagerly await the coming of the Messiah's reign. We have been assured that he will come and deliver us from our enemies."

"I understand. According to your holy word it is my understanding that your Messiah will return."

"That's correct. He will restore his people, the Jews."

"Have you any idea where this Messiah might appear?"

"In this land."

"Why do you feel this way?"

"Our holy word tells us that a son named John will announce his coming. Zacharias, John's father, prophesied that John would precede the arrival of a mighty savior. I'm convinced that the man now preaching, teaching and baptizing beyond the River Jordan is this same John."

"I have just come from there. The Baptizer talks about a Messiah. Based on the holy word and your experience, do you think this Messiah will appear in our lifetime?"

"I believe what I've told you. The Messiah of whom John speaks and who was prophesied has to be Yeshua. I believe the deliverer is here now. Yes, he will appear in our lifetime."

"You're saying the Galilean from Nazareth is this Messiah?"

"I believe it to be so."

"I'm looking forward to seeing him. I know some of his history, based on my familiarity with the Jewish religion. It claims that he was born of a virgin. I'm not even sure how anyone could believe that. Born of a virgin. A child born without a father's input. How is that possible?"

"I believe the word of the prophets. I cannot explain the abnormality of such a birth except for the power of Yeshua. This issue is not a matter of reason but rather of faith."

"Perhaps it's prejudice but I've heard it said that people think nothing good can come out of Nazareth. Is that meant to be a joke?"

"I can only tell you what I believe. And that is that Yeshua is the Messiah."

"I suppose as time passes we will know whether your words are borne out."

How was I to translate this conversation? He tells me he thinks the Nazarene is the prophesied Messiah but I wonder if his age has tricked him. Is this old man in full command of his faculties? Is it possible he's a little crazy? Nonetheless I need to catalogue his comments just in case Jesus is the Messiah.

Is it possible the Nazarene IS the savior proclaimed in the Jewish holy scriptures? All the clamoring from the multitudes about this Jesus…and this Aged One believes this man from Galilee is he. Maybe there is something to this excitement. This is getting complicated. *My mission has just taken a new direction. I must now re-double my efforts and keep an ear out for Jesus as well as keeping my eyes on the Baptizer.*

When I returned to observe the Baptizer, days turned into weeks. I followed him from day to day on both sides of the Jordan—the whole while he taught to turn from sin and turn to God.

The message he continues to hammer gets my dander. How can he claim his God is superior? What's so special about this Jewish God? What makes the Baptizer think his God is better than mine? What does his God do that my gods can't? We Romans have our temples, each named for a specific god, such as Temple of Diana or Temple of Jupiter. We do not worship in the temple itself but near it, in the outdoors.

DISPATCH: Superior Flavius Diusus Caldus,

As you know, I have always prided myself in my observational skills and my judgment of character. Perhaps those played into your

21

decision to select me for this mission. I've seen and heard this John the Baptist. He seeks not riches nor wears fancy clothes, just the simple garments of a common man. I've followed him daily from place to place on both sides of the Jordan River—from Bethany beyond the Jordan and primarily at Aenon near Salim.

Crowds seek and follow him, congregating to him as he teaches them to turn from sinning to Godly living. His message is powerful. He pulls no punches and holds nothing back. His words and ways frequently offend people.

Many are baptized. But the haughty Pharisees and teachers of Moses' Law refuse to believe. They reject his message and his baptism. The Baptizer calls them a den of vipers not worthy of baptism because of their haughty ways. From what I can see, the Baptizer has a greater influence among the people than the priests.

His passion is superior, proclaiming to prepare the way and being a messenger of a deliverer to follow him.

It appears that this spirited Baptizer could generate an apocalyptic revolution among the peasants. Because his message consumes Israel like a brush fire, my concern is that he and this Messiah could portend problems for Rome. If the Baptizer is accurate about this Messiah, then we must concern ourselves. In addition to observing the Baptizer, I'll keep an eye out for the Nazarene, the one the Baptizer claims will follow him.

I await your instructions.

Brachan, in your service

CHAPTER 3 — Preposterous Tales

Not long after posting my superior, I heard that the Baptizer had been arrested. While wondering what he could have done to get himself thrown into prison, I remembered the words, "Someone is coming after me who is greater than I am." I did not hear them from a second hand source or from an operative. I heard them directly from the lips of the Baptizer. If Antipas feared John's popularity and growing following, what would he think of the man of whom the Baptizer spoke? Surely this Galilean would prove a greater threat than the Baptizer. Wasn't the Baptizer saying as much?

As stories about the Nazarene and his growing popularity mounted, combined with the Baptizer's imprisonment, I determined to learn more of his whereabouts. I targeted the lake side town of Capernaum in Galilee, an area roughly sixty miles long and thirty miles wide.

Who and where is this mystery man? This is going to take some understanding and serious research. What will my research unveil?

As I followed the valley of the Jordan to Capernaum, I was somewhat amused by its serpentine river. It was roughly one hundred feet wide and up to ten feet deep, flowing through the valley which was three to fourteen miles wide. Although it meandered sixty-five miles, the numerous bends stretched its actual length to over two hundred miles.

The rounded slopes of the surrounding hills framed the silver sheet of water on the valley floor known as the Lake of Galilee. It was fed by underground springs and the Jordan River. The pear-shaped lake 700 feet below sea level isn't a large lake by any means, roughly thirteen miles long, eight miles wide and thirty-three miles in circumference. Depending upon the weather, her waters reflect blue, gray or black.

The lake is a prominent landmark whose shoreline cities are populated by Jews, Greeks and Phoenicians. Her western shore is a flourishing and heavily populated. Tiberias lies midway between the north and south ends of the lake. Capernaum nestles at the lake's head to the north. A plain skirts the shores of the lake with Bethsaida to the east of Capernaum and the beautiful plain of Gennesaret to the west.

The valley's rich vegetation relies heavily on winter rains. The lush land surrounding the lake is known as The Garden of the Gods. Terraced hillsides, pockmarked with farm fields, produce numerous crops. Farmers and their stock animals endure back breaking labor to turn their land into sumptuous produce, fruits and grains such as wheat and barley. My mouth watered while contemplating eating grapes, pomegranates, figs and olives. Palm trees grow in profusion as do brightly blooming flowers. Eucalyptus trees and cedars checker her hills.

Besides committed farmers, commercial fishermen provide the area's major source of income. Whereas beasts of burden with implements worked for the farmer, fishermen use weighted and buoyed drag nets and casting nets to procure flavorful tilapia from the lake's waters. My taste buds spoke to me as I savored the memory of fresh fried tilapia.

Although on a major thoroughfare of travel between the interior and the Mediterranean Sea, Capernaum is a thumbprint-sized berg boasting fewer than 2000 people. Nearby is the retirement village of Emmaus whose spa attracts the aged and sick who travel from all over the country to soak in its healing mineral waters. Tiny towns dot the lake's shore and boats ply the surface of the lake's waters. Inhabitants seem to scurry about with the busyness of life.

I chose a leisurely pace in order to clear my head of this whole Baptizer-Nazarene affair. My goal, a reasonable conclusion. I needed resolution for the many stories piling up in my head about the Baptizer and his cousin. I've made mental notes about some and the more important ones made their way into my journal.

While I trudged along, I witnessed a glorious change in the day. Whereas earlier an overpowering grayness overshadowed the sky, a growing lightness reigned. Couched against an ominous, stark gray sky, a thin, golden-orange cloud layer, laced with silver, radiated brightness. Five vast ribbons of steel gray separated by shades of light blue and framed by dark gray paraded across the sky, lifting my spirits.

Shortly after that while halfway down the lake from Capernaum, I spotted a group of local fishermen on the beach. They mended their fishing nets and appeared to be in a discussion. As I drew nearer, I noticed a couple of them were quite animated. I listened to their story, two things about it capturing my attention right away: 1) the inexplicable incident and 2) the unbelievable response.

A squinty-eyed, crusty old fisherman seemed to carry the story, encouraged by the others. "Some time back I heerd the story. Here it is. Daylight was breakin'over the Sea of Galilee. Fishermen had fished the night away catchin' nothin'. Jesus stood at the edge of the lake probly hopin' to catch some rest away from thet noisy gang what followed neer every day. Hardly no time went by before a big bunch of people pressed again' him on all sides—I seen aged men leaning on staffs, hill country peasants, merchants, rabbis, fishermen, young and old, rich and poor, sick and well. Seemed they was all a tryin' ta touch him.

"About then some fishermen come to shore nearby to clean their nets. A piece down the beach John and James was in their boat with their father Zebedee. The fishermen's nets was tangled and tore up, showing a tough night on the water for these men. I heerd the men a laughin' and jokin' back and forth while mendin' their nets. Their talkin' was colored with the normal fisherman swearin'.

24

"Not long after thet they spotted Jesus surrounded by thet gang of folks. Spottin' two empty boats by the lake, Jesus strode to one. Loadin' himself into it, he asked the owner Simon, to go onto the lake ta get away from thet gang a piece from shore so's he could be seen and better heerd by the people. He then set down and commenced talkin' from thet boat.

"When he had ceased speakin', he said to Simon, 'Move off shore into the deep and let down yer nets for a ketch.'

"Simon was powerful upset. Knowin' he'd spent the night thinkin' about the poor fishin' and John the Baptist was a languishin' alone in a prison cell. He was mad about the malice of the rabbis and priests. He was none pleased with his profession at what he was havin' hardly no success. Here he was tired to the bone, gnarled paws tellin' him how they hurt, hunkered over with bloodshot eyes. It weren't a good night.

"If anyone knowed fishin', this rough man did. He knowed thet night time when it was dark was the proper time ta fish the clear waters of the lake. To cast a net durin' daylight hours made hardly no sense. He no doubt thought thet Jesus was touched in the noggin to suggest such a notion. No fish is caught durin' the day on the lake. How stupid is thet!"

At this point the old fisherman paused, wiped the spittle from his chin with a dirty sleeve and inserted his personal opinion, "I know. I been a fishin' this water fer thirty years."

Then the old gentleman continued, "Through tired lips Simon spoke to Jesus, 'We done fished all night and caught nothin'. You want us to try again? In daylight? If you want us to, we'll let down the nets.'

"Simon and his brother lowered their nets. When attemptin' to lift them nets the boys found 'em heavy with fish near ta breakin' them nets. They hailed their partners James and John to come help 'em. Turns out they filled both boats so full thet they was near sinkin'.

"More 'n a mite surprised with the ketch, Simon fell down at Jesus' knees. He and all the others—James and John the sons of Zebedee —was astonished by the ketch. Simon was speechless. He was dumbstruck by Jesus' capability and humbled by his own feelin' of worthlessness.

"Simon said, 'Depart from me, for I am a sinful man, O Lord.' Still embarrassed by his humanness, Peter clung to Jesus' feet.

"Jesus looked at him and said, 'So, you are Simon the son of John? I'm namin' you Cephas which means Peter. Do not be afraid. From now on follow me and you will be a ketchin' men.'

"And Jesus continued, 'Blessed are you, Cephas—thet means rock in Aramaic and Greek or Simon Bar-Jona! He told Peter 'it twern't flesh 'n blood what revealed this but my Father who is in heaven. And he assured Peter He was the rock onto where Jesus would build his church...and the powers of death would never have no power again' it.'

"Jesus invited them to join him. They dropped their nets, clamored overboard, packed up their fishin' nets and gear and stored it at Peter's house. Then they done took off after Jesus."

Several fishermen spoke up proclaiming their amazement at the turn of events. They'd seen the lousy fishing at night to be outdone by day time fishing predicted by the Nazarene. Some were skeptical but most of the men were astonished at the outcome of the fishing as well as the total commitment of the fishermen to leave their nets.

I, too, was amazed by the results of the Nazarene's instructions—*how could a common man forecast fishing success to a seasoned commercial fisherman? And what kind of men—rough men at that— would walk away from a lifetime livelihood when a stranger invited them?*

What kind of stranger would have the kind of magnetism to achieve such results? Perhaps the fishermen followed him because they wanted freedom from the boot of Rome and they accepted him as the Messiah John talked about...so it became easy to toss aside their livelihood to pursue the much anticipated man of freedom. I've heard many say they've waited too long for freedom from Rome's bondage.

As I stood wondering about their comments, a big, burly Greek fisherman named Kallistos volunteered that he'd been hearing all kinds of stories about Jesus and wondered what he'd meant by "fishers of men." I asked him if he'd seen the Nazarene. He said "no" but hoped to see him some day himself. He turned away to work on his fishing boat and left me also wondering about the fishers of men comment.

Speaking of stories, another one came my way. The story had to do with the Galilean, a wedding, water and wine. Jesus performed a "miracle" which I determined was significant enough to send another dispatch to my superior.

DISPATCH: Superior Flavius Diusus Caldus,

I apologize for the length of this dispatch but want to enumerate the details for your overall perusal. Even though it is preposterous—perhaps completely insignificant—or a rumor, I felt I should inform you.

While I made my way to the north in search of the Nazarene, I heard about his act of converting water into wine. Jesus had returned from the Jordan to Galilee. Three days later there was a marriage at Cana not far from Nazareth. Relatives of Jesus' parents were taking their vows and anticipated several days of celebration as was the custom. Even though Jesus' father Joseph was no longer living, the Nazarene's mother attended and represented the family. Knowing the relatives and being in the area, Jesus, along with his disciples, had been invited.

Mary was pleased to see her son and enjoyed watching the disciples, who call him Master, manifesting their love for him and sharing with her what has been happening with her son. As the assemblage continued to stare in adoring fashion at her son, Mary couldn't be prouder of him.

Mary had assisted with the wedding arrangements and she realized that the wine stores were depleting. Knowing the tradition of showing hospitality with a well stocked supply of food and drink she contemplated the situation before approaching her son.

In due time she informed him that "they have no wine."
Although he was sympathetic and wished to support the happiness of the occasion, he responded, "O woman, what have you to do with me? My hour has not yet come." In essence he calmed her fears with the knowledge that he could take care of the problem, for which she was grateful.

She told the servants, "Do whatever he tells you."

Six empty stone jars, used for Jewish rites of purification and each capable of holding twenty to thirty gallons of liquid, rested upon the ground. After the Nazarene told them to fill all the jars with water and they complied, he instructed, "Now draw out some water and take it to the steward of the feast."

The servants did as he suggested and the steward tasted the water. He was shocked because the liquid was wine. Although he did not know the source of the wine as did the servants, he was truly amazed. He approached the bridegroom to commend him, "Every man serves the good wine first; and when men have drunk freely, then the poor wine; but you have kept the good wine until now."

I assume the Nazarene engaged in some sort of sleight of hand or sorcery...who could possibly do such a thing? Or did it even occur?

I will make every effort to discover what of this event is relevant to the Empire.

Brachan, in your service

It is my intent to monitor the Nazarene until the Baptizer is released from prison at the fortress castle of Macherus, east of the Dead Sea. My agent keeps me apprised about the Baptizer and it seems like he's in safe keeping. The best information I have is that the Baptizer is being held in the fortress of Antipas, a nearly impenetrable castle where Antipas' fear of attack from Arabia motivated him to install military mechanisms to deter enemy approach, things like archers atop his 60-foot thick walled nest with towers rising 90 feet.

However at my next report from that informant, I was surprised to learn that the Baptizer had been killed. In an odd sense he lost his head over Herodias, no pun intended.

As you are probably aware, Herodias is a Jewish princess, the daughter-in-law of Herod the Great. It's no secret that she is a conniving, selfish woman who wants to be in the driver's seat, an overwhelmingly ambitious woman. She is so jealous of her brother Agrippa's authority in Judaea that she wanted more power for Antipas. She also sought to have Antipas receive as much or more than Phillip from Caligula but he would have none of it. And, of course, she yearned for revenge after the Baptizer spoke to Herod about his marriage to her.

Evidently the Baptizer had confronted Herod Antipas about his dalliance with Herodias, his half-brother Philip's wife. As the governor of Galilee and Perea, Antipas had travelled to Rome. It was there that he had seen and become infatuated with her. It was common knowledge that when Antipas returned to Judea, he put away his wife Phasaelis, daughter of King Aretas IV of Nabatea, and married Herodias.

No doubt it was during his time in Rome that Antipas had expressed his concern about the Baptizer which led to my selection and mission.

At any rate, John had excoriated Antipas publically and told him straight up that his taking Philip's wife was sinful in the eyes of God. Although Herod enjoyed John, he probably got tired of hearing Herodias defame the Baptizer. As a result of this and his concern regarding the Baptizer's following and growing popularity, it was just a matter of time before Antipas went after the Baptizer. Thinking it was in his best personal interests, he had John arrested and held at the remote fortress of Machaerus, on the steep eastern shores of the Dead Sea.

Although Antipas feared that having the Baptizer killed might lead to a riot by his followers, it's possible he would have released the Baptizer forthcoming. But Herodias had other ideas. I have it that the Baptizer spoke directly to her, which could be nothing more than a rumor. However, if it is true, it's no wonder she was vehement.

The way I heard it, John looked her in the eye and said, "First you married Philip, your brother-in-law. Then you 'fooled around' with the man who is currently your husband. You've allowed your daughter Salome to dance like a stripper in order to inflame a crowd of half-drunk military officers. You are incestuous, adulterous and a pimp all in one. It's an abomination to God. You yourself are a disgrace. The stench of it looms to the heavens." Evidently that was enough for her to have John's head, on a platter, if you will.

Antipas had thrown himself a birthday party, not only to celebrate his big day but also to honor his courtiers and army commanders for leading the people of Galilee. When Herodias' daughter Salome performed a dance, he and his guests were so pleased that Antipas promised her anything she desired, up to half his kingdom.

Her mother urged her to request the head of John the Baptist. Not wanting to go back on his word and especially with guests present, Antipas ordered one of his palace guardsmen to oversee the task. When he returned with the Baptizer's head on a platter, Salome presented it to her mother.

If John hadn't upbraided Antipas and aroused Herodias' anger, he'd probably still have his head and either still be in prison or preaching. I was left wondering *what kind of man is Herod Antipas, to behead a religious leader at the behest of his daughter and because his adulteress wife wished it?*

Upon reflection of Herod the Great, I suppose I should not have been surprised about anything Herod Antipas did. Herod the Great was a half-Jewish, half-Edomite ruthless tyrant. His modus operandi was to destroy anyone he disliked. Early on he killed. It was he who had all the baby boys up to 2-years of age slaughtered while seeking to destroy the babe in the manger spoken of by the three wise men. Herod the Great had passed a decree giving mid-wives directions to destroy them by any means. My Roman soldier compatriots used sword, dagger, stone, strangulation and even dropped them from bluffs.

But King Herod didn't stop with the killing of the innocents. He feared his brother-in-law Aristobulus' popularity among the people so Herod had the young High Priest drowned in the swimming pool at Jericho's winter palace. Three dozen years ago or so he had his Hasmonnean mother-in-law Alexandria executed. And if that wasn't enough, when he feared her daughter Mariamme, one of his ten wives, he executed her. He then murdered two of her and his sons, Alexander and Aristobulus, by way of strangulation. And only five days before he died, Herod had his oldest son Antipater executed. He had hundreds of people killed during his lifetime. Small wonder he was feared.

However as Herod the Great lived through his six decades on the earth, he had gained considerable weight and was fraught with medical issues. Probably most were a result of chronic kidney disease though other conditions included gout, lung disease, heart condition, sexually transmitted diseases and gangrene that caused his male parts to blacken and rot, actually becoming maggot infested. Not a pleasant thought.

Later while approaching a babbling brook I caught the aroma of cooking food. Bacon (Petaso. Boiled pig with figs, browned and seasoned with pepper sauce). *Mmmmm.* And biscuits. *Oh, it smelled sooo good.*

It wasn't long until I encountered a gaggle of carts and animals lining the edge of the road. Whereas oxen were harnessed to some carts, other carts were drawn by mules. I knew Romans preferred mules over horses for beasts of burden because of their superior strength and intelligence.

A large contingent of Roman soldiers rested not far from the animals. It looked like a troop of eighty or so legionnaires.

Some ate their noontime meal; others attended the animals; some snoozed. I dodged around a few cooking containers before finding the group's Centurion commander and asked if I might join them to eat my lunch and see what news they had of Rome. Even though I did not tell him I was a Roman, he assented.

I made my way to a boulder near some men where I sat and delved into my grip for my food. I had some dates and figs which I normally carried in journey. And, of course, I had an uneaten gyros from the day before, one of my favorite foods in the world. Though it would be soggy, I would relish its delightful flavor.

While digging into my pack I observed the soldiers' various trappings and was grateful I wasn't in my military garb. I recalled the handicap of carrying weapons and gear. What with the breastplate, helmet, shield, javelins, short sword and dagger, water bladder, cooking equipment and shovel, that amounted to quite a load. Add their marching pack, capable of containing two weeks' rations, and you're talking at least fifty pounds. They would get a work out. Fortunately, I would not.

As I munched on a fig, I heard a shout from the area of the animals.

"What's that?" a smiling soldier queried back.

"Oh, don't worry. It's just Muley," a pudgy soldier interjected. "He's such a perfectionist. One of his kids probably kissed him on the face."

Feeling out of the loop, I asked, "What's the story about Muley?"

Smiley replied 'Muley is what we call Tullius. He's kind of the chief mule handler. He acts like the mules are his kids and thinks their care is the most important job in the world. There's no doubt he's completely competent."

"Yeh," Pudgy added, "we get pleasure from giving him a hard time. He's pretty passionate about his beasts of burden. He claims that mules are more dependable than horses. It's no secret they can't reproduce. Mules are half breeds, a cross between a horse and a donkey."

Smiley took up the refrain, "And Muley heralds their unequalled traits. They live longer and are smarter than horses. Mules require less food and don't overeat. Old Long Ears has more strength pound for pound, is more sure footed, has more endurance…"

"And, don't forget," interrupted Pudgy, 'they handle heat and cold better and are less susceptible to disease than any other beasts of burden.'"

"So you see," concluded Smiley, 'mules are more determined when it comes to self-preservation and they require less upkeep.'"

So much for my animal husbandry lesson. "Thank you, fellas, for the information. I didn't know mules were so special."

Several men chatted about the weather and events in general. When I asked about news from Rome, I learned that an abnormally large number of farmers continued to infiltrate the city as slave operated farms had sprung up.

While some poked fun at Jews and their fear of the Romans, one of the men on the edge of the group arose, took up his spear and walked to the roadway where a Jew traveled slowly by sitting upon his burro. The soldier jabbed the animal in its backside with the spear and shouted, "Make haste little burro. Before you know it, the Sabbath will be upon us!"

The animal jumped and kicked and lurched into high gear as its rider shouted in Aramaic to the soldier, raised his fist and held on.

Some of the soldiers laughed and shouted insults to the departing donkey's rider.

Along with Italians, I witnessed men from neighboring countries as well as far flung places—Germany, Spain, the Balkans and Africa. No doubt these men held hopes for their return to their homelands and their families, and they were merely doing their jobs so to speak. It was understandable that some felt their power over the Jew, perhaps holding a grudge. However I noted that some among the soldiers felt ambivalent toward the Jews.

Coming down the road was an ox cart and just about the time it filed past us, a youngster fell from it onto the ground among the stones and dirt. Two of the soldiers rushed to the child, one carrying a medical kit he'd grabbed on the way.

By the time they arrived, the child was sitting up with blood running from his head and shoulder.

The soldiers spoke with an adult who had hopped to the ground. They then administered first aid, wiping the blood away, washing the wound with water and applying a bandage. The shoulder wound looked minor. The soldiers wrapped a bandage around the head wound, spoke again with the adult and assisted the youngster onto the cart and they departed.

It was interesting to note that not all of these soldiers held the Jews in disdain. Made me feel good to realize there was still humanity in some of my warrior colleagues.

Meantime conversation turned to political issues of the day. A tall soldier spoke, "See, we have Romans who are compassionate while some are mean and spiteful toward our enemies and others. No wonder the Jews strongly dislike us. Speaking of their disdain for us, I think some of them dislike their own. I heard recently that Jesus walked through Solomon's Porch in the temple where some Pharisees confronted him and accused him of keeping them in suspense regarding being the Messiah. Then they bluntly demanded, 'If you are the Messiah, tell us.'

"He responded by telling them that he'd previously answered that question but that they had refused to accept his answer. He then gave them a brief answer. He did not lower his head; he did not shuffle his feet but while looking them straight in the eyes with penetrating eye contact and confidence, he proclaimed, 'I and the Father are one.'

"Now, that got their attention. 'Blasphemy! They shouted. You a mere man claim to be God!' And they picked up stones to stone him. They tried to arrest him but he walked through the clamoring crowd and vanished from their midst. I wish I could have been there to see that."

A youthful, innocent looking soldier with fuzz on his face, probably on his first assignment, asked, "I've heard it said that he heals and does other wonders. What of that?"

A man sitting next to me with a scar that ran from his lower left jaw beneath his lips across his face and turned upward nearly to his right ear, spoke of the Nazarene's growing status and activities. He admitted he'd not seen the Prophet perform any exorcisms or healings but that he had heard, "When Jesus healed people and evil spirits came from them, the spirits proclaimed him to be the Son of God. It made me wonder what it could mean if even demons proclaimed him God."

Tall Soldier asked, "So your experience is mostly second hand, like mine. That is, you've heard stories but not seen these things with your own eyes?"

"That is correct. I heard that when John the Baptist's disciples asked Jesus if he were the one sent from God, he told them to 'tell John what you have seen and heard. The blind are recovering their sight. Cripples walk. Lepers are healed. The deaf receive their hearing. The dead are brought back to life.'"

Suddenly a ragtag mutt bounded into our midst, sniffing here and there, aggressively looking for a handout. A bedraggled man huffed up almost out of breath calling his dog. "Whiskers! Stop! Come!" Gasping, he grasped the dog and apologized for his intrusion, backed away slowly while catching his breath, bowed and begged our pardon while dragging his dog with him.

Surly, the man who had speared the burro, started to respond but Scarface spoke over him, words of consolation, "Not to worry, stranger. No harm, no foul. Your dog reminds me of my own back in Rome."

Fuzzy Face revisited the prior conversation, "Before we were interrupted by the dog, we discussed Jesus." Addressing Scarface he asked, "Since you

32

have not met him, your comments are based on the words of others?"

Scarface replied, "Yes, I have wondered considerably about him and his increasing following. His seems to be the name on every lip—either those of his detractors or his supporters."

Tall Soldier spoke, "Why do you think he's so popular?"

The Centurion standing off to one side spoke up, "While on patrol I witnessed Jesus on a couple of occasions, working with people. Essentially I'd say Jesus' good works toward people have endeared them to him. However I think three specific qualities have contributed to his success—he's a perceptive and active listener; he allows or encourages people to celebrate; and he fosters a feeling of self-worth in people.

"He seems to listen intently to others. He treats the speaker as if he were the only person on earth, as though he wants the speaker to know he has his full attention. He seems to hang on the person's every word. He doesn't eagerly await the speaker to finish so he can launch into his own story. He probes the speaker. Jesus addresses the speaker's interest, focusing his undivided attention on him.

"And another thing, when he speaks, it's not only his words but also the sincere and authoritative way he says them."

Fuzzy Face wondered aloud, "Centurion, what do you mean about 'celebrating'?"

"He allows people to be themselves without criticizing them. He permits them to focus on themselves and their activities. Take the story about the Cana wedding. He honored the couple by heeding his mother's request to provide wine for their reception. He let the limelight shine on them and their marriage. He didn't try to upstage them. How many people did he heal or comfort without taking credit for it? He didn't pound his chest or do anything to take the attention away from those he healed."

Scarface chimed in, "I agree with Centurion. It's possible I'm wrong, however it appears that most who come in contact with Jesus go away feeling or being better because of the encounter. I think it's because he gives them a greater feeling of self-esteem by stroking their egos. It's almost as if he treats each one as the most important person alive, giving each his undivided attention. I've wondered what effect it would have on the world if everyone practiced that behavior."

I was somewhat amazed to hear hardened soldiers discuss things so transparently, especially what Scarface said next. "And his ultimate characteristic appears to be love. He seems motivated by a desire for other's happiness, wanting their best. Not their approval or sycophancy but merely to fulfill their joy. It's as if he accepts everyone unconditionally, wanting that person's happiness."

Almost as an afterthought, he added, "On another note, people love listening to the Nazarene. It's not necessarily because of his stories as much as it is the words of empowerment and the new way he presents old Levitical laws. Another way of looking at it is that people love a good story teller and the Nazarene is that except his 'stories' are of common sense ways to put their faith in God into action.

"Furthermore Jewish leaders followed strict rules governing all of life in its most minute detail—their rabbinical laws are contrary to common sense. And the Nazarene does not engage in the foolishness of these ceremonial rules."

Then Centurion concluded the conversation as the men prepared to leave, "He is both engaging and he engages people. They seem drawn by his magnetism which includes his charismatic demeanor. He actually engages them in a positive way and that engagement becomes total. I can readily understand why people want to be in his company."

After the sharing by the soldiers, I felt even more pride in my Roman brothers of the military. As the troops picked up their weapons and packs or boarded their carts, I thanked them for allowing me to eat with them and for their sharing their views.

CHAPTER 4 — Three Bad Men

After John's disciples returned and buried his body, they went to relate the information to the Nazarene. When he heard the news, his first action was to depart to a remote area by boat in order to be alone. As I mentioned earlier, that's when I learned of his departure with his mother and his disciples for Capernaum. I set my sights for that region in order to search him out.

While I traveled, I acquired information that the Rabbi met all nationalities without prejudice. He taught in synagogues with equal acclaim. His fame spread throughout the land and surrounding territories. Huge crowds followed him from Judaea in the south to Galilee in the north and beyond the Jordan River.

The overwhelming conversation centered around the Nazarene and his teachings which paralleled the Baptizer's message of repentance and the kingdom of God. I'm told that he spoke with the same zeal as the Baptizer. That people eagerly awaited his message, amazed that his teaching and words rang with authority similar to the words of the Baptizer. "No man ever spoke like this" was a constant refrain.

On more than one occasion I heard, "This must be the man who will save the world." And, of course, I heard more than once those questioning his identity, "Who is this man?" Made me feel good to know that I wasn't the only one who felt that way. More than ever I needed to find out more about him.

The next thing I knew, I heard the Nazarene was in the country around Jerusalem. I'll check with my agent and stop at Antonia Fortress to get directions to the home of my friend and compatriot Gaius and his family. I'll take a breather there from my mission. Though I'd not been to Jerusalem, the respite will provide me both an opportunity to clear my head and to get a different perspective on this whole Baptizer-Nazarene affair—*to determine once and for all if the Nazarene is a co-conspirator with the Baptizer?*

Meeting Gaius will enable me to discuss the situation with my cool-headed friend, one in whom I share many values. It will be good to compare notes with someone in whom I have a relationship and confidence.

Meanwhile I'll dispatch my supervisor.

DISPATCH: Superior Flavius Diusus Caldus,

From what I've observed so far Jesus doesn't appear to be any kind of threat. John, as you know, is no longer here. His vociferousness tended to be more dangerous than the Nazarene who plays with the children, attends parties and is extremely popular. Through some sort of sleight of hand or magic, perhaps wizardry, he heals people. But other than that he appears to be pretty much a social character laughing, playing and having a good time.

Perhaps I should not be surprised, however this Nazarene is known by many names which include Rabbi, Prophet, Galilean, the man from Galilee, Healer, Deliverer, Master, Savior and Son of Man.

The one concern I have is that of the Baptizer's referral to the Nazarene as "someone coming who is greater than I." Therefore I will make every effort to locate him and keep an eye on him until I receive further instructions from you.

In your service, Brachan

JOURNAL

As I crisscross the countryside, I continue getting all kinds of information about the Nazarene. It seems like everywhere I search for him, he has just left. When I heard he was on his way to Jerusalem, I set my sights in that direction, allowing me to visit my friend Gaius ...and, of course, I'll try to look up Ariella.

The trip covered nearly one hundred miles as I climbed up from Capernaum to Beth-shan the first couple of days. My mid-journey took me to Tirzah and Shechem where I saw Mt. Gerizim at nearly 3,000 feet elevation. And the final stretch through the Ephraim hill country brought me to Bethel, Mizpah and Ramah just prior to Jerusalem. Mt. Scopus towered above at nearly 2700 feet.

While traveling along I recalled another story about the Nazarene—one which created more angst among the Jewish leaders and concern for me. He and his disciples encountered a man who was blind from birth. The disciples asked, "Rabbi, since this man is blind, who sinned, he or his parents?"

"Neither he nor his parents sinned. He is in this condition so that the works of God may be shown. I must do the works that I was sent to accomplish while it is still day because the night is coming when no man can work. As long as I am in the world, I am the light of the world."

When the Nazarene finished speaking, he spat upon the ground and made a paste of his spit and the dirt. He then applied it to the eyes of the blind man and said, "Go and wash in the pool of Siloam." So the man went off and washed and was able to see.

His neighbors and people who had previously seen him and knew he was blind asked, "Isn't this the man who used to sit and beg?"

Some answered, "Yes, it's the same man."

Yet others said, "No, it only looks like him."

The blind man answered their doubt, "I am the one who was blind."

The crowd asked, "How, then, did you get your sight?"

"A man named Jesus made clay, smeared it on my eye lids and said, 'Go to the pool of Siloam and wash.' I went to the pool. I washed. Lo, and behold! I could see!"

"Where is he?"

"I don't know."

Because it was on the Sabbath day that the Nazarene healed the blind man, people took him to the Pharisees who asked him how he received his sight.

He explained the procedure and the results.

The Pharisees were angered because the Nazarene had healed on the Sabbath, "He can't be from God. He doesn't keep the Sabbath. How can a man who's a sinner produce signs like this?"

The Pharisees were divided among themselves. Some asked the healed man, "Since you are the one to whom he gave sight, what do you have to say?"

"He's a prophet."

The Jews didn't believe the healing had taken place and argued that they wanted to know if he was actually born blind. They summoned his parents and asked, "Is this your son who was born blind? How is it that he can now see?"

"We know that this is our son who was born blind. We don't know how he is now able to see. He's old enough to talk. Ask him. He can speak for himself."

His parents feared the Jews and chose this method of answering the questions. They didn't want to be expelled from the synagogue which was the Pharisee's stated punishment for acknowledging Jesus as the Christ.

The Jews called the healed man and stated, "We know that this man Jesus is a sinner therefore give God the praise."

The healed man said, "I don't know whether he's a sinner or not, but I do know that I was blind and now I see."

"How is it that you received your sight?"

"I can only tell you what I told the religious leaders, the same answer I gave others who asked me…I don't know. Once I was blind but now I see. Jesus did for me what no other man could do. I will always know him as Master. He's the master of the universe."

The outraged Jews asked, "What did he do to you? How did he open your eyes?"

"I've told you already but you wouldn't listen. Why do you want to hear it again? Do you also want to become his disciples?"

"You are his disciple but we are disciples of Moses. We are concerned to discover where this man came from."

"He opened my eyes. This is a wonderful thing. And you're wondering where he is. Since the beginning of the world no man opened the eyes of someone who had been born blind. If this man wasn't from God, he could not do anything."

The Jews were fit to be tied, "You were born in sin and you're teaching us!" They drove him out.

When Jesus heard what they had done to the healed-blind man, he found him and said, "Do you believe in the Son of Man?"

"Who is he, Lord, so that I might believe in him?"

"You are looking at him. And it is he who speaks to you."

"Lord, I believe."

And the healed man worshipped the Prophet who stated, "It is for judgment that I've come into the world, so that those who cannot see, might see and those with sight, might be made blind."

Some of the Pharisees were upset with his words and asked, "Are we also blind?"

Jesus answered, "If you were blind, you would have no sin, but because you say 'we see,' your sin remains."

The Jews were totally out of sorts. They blind! They called him a liar for referring to himself as the light of the world. They claimed he was a fraud. He defended himself by saying that he was from above and they were from below. He indicated that he was not of the same world as they and stated, "When you have killed the Messiah, you will realize that I am he." He completely baffled them and they remained confused as well as frustrated.

I was also confused and wondered what the future held for me and for him.

About that same time I heard about a robbery on the Jericho road, part of the most important east-west routes from the coastal plain to the Jordan valley. It was a known fact that villainous persons with ill intent inhabited the byway. I was positively amazed when I heard about a victim to a beating and robbery where the victim was left half-dead. Three men passed by the victim after the fact. The first man was a Jewish priest. The second was a temple assistant. But only the third one stopped.

He rendered aid, transported the victim and paid for his care. The man rendering aid was a despised Samaritan. He left two denarius as payment, one being equal to a day's wage. In spite of Jewish rhetoric, the two religious Jews ignored the injured victim's needs. There seemed quite a contrast between words and action—the Jews spoke; the Samaritan acted.

For the life of me, I can't imagine how the Rabbi could be fomenting a revolution when he's preaching peace. He's trying to get enemies to become friends. Seems like his is a revolution of peace, understanding and love. I have yet to hear an utterance indicating the Galilean plans any kind of takeover whether it be of the Empire or his homeland. Is it possible this is a ruse to confuse?

I will dispatch my superior from Jericho.

Jericho lies a few miles from the Jordan on the western edge of the valley. The luxurious city's lush gardens and palm trees are fed by springs, in sharp contrast to the limestone hills and desolate ravines surrounding her. Jericho is a center of traffic with many Roman officials and soldiers as well as strangers from various parts of the world.

While contemplating customs collecting—which necessitates numerous publicans, most of whom were Romans, I dispatched my superior.

DISPATCH:

Superior... Whereas the Baptizer had a large following which concerned our Roman leaders, his was not an uprising against Rome. Likewise it appears the Nazarene is a revolutionary....but only in the sense of his new message—instead of the tired, ancient, staid customs and beliefs held by the sanctimonious Jews, where rules dominate their daily lives, the Prophet suggests a daily commitment and personal accountability to the God of Abraham. He teaches that a man can know God in a personal way through prayer, living the Holy Word and personal responsibility to that God and his fellow man. Out with the outdated, hypocritical rules and in with common sense and common decency, serving God and man. I find no threat to the Empire in this.

Nevertheless, that may change as I learn more of this man from Galilee.

In your service, Brachan

Considering the roadway ahead and hopeful of seeing Gaius and his family, I was reminded of my informer's report about the Nazarene's fondness for children. He had told me of his amazement when observing the Nazarene contentedly playing with children. A young boy around seven years of age tugged at the Prophet's tunic and said, "Come play with us, Jesus."

The informant was close enough to observe Jesus as he feigned a scowl of mock disgust and spun around to face the youngster in a fighting stance, bent knees, hands raised in boxing fashion in front of his chest and replied, "I'm too old."

"No, you're not."

"You don't want me."

"Yes, we do."

"Okay. Okay. But you have to promise not to hurt me."

"We promise."

"Remember, I'm pretty fragile, you know."

"We promise not to hurt you."

The boy, tagged Jesus and said, "You're it," then ran. During the conversation several children had gathered in a loosely arranged circle and the Nazarene then ran among them feinting toward one then the other. At length he reached out to a girl and tapped her on the shoulder, "You're it."

After that the game gathered momentum with the children tagging one another, all trying to get close enough to tag the Nazarene. He dodged this way and that evading the tag and laughing the harder each time with bright eyes and smile. Periodically he dived to the ground and rolled away from the tag or jumped to the side.

In a short time the game evolved into a game of leap frog, initiated, the lookout shared, by the Rabbi. A line of children positioned themselves on all fours and he hopped over each in the row until he reached the first. He was immediately followed by the child behind him who followed his example. The emissary lost count after the first time through the line and didn't know how many times they repeated the leaps.

At any rate, before he knew it, they were playing follow the leader, the leader being Jesus. He gathered them in a group, spoke to them, placed his hands on either side of his head like ears on a camel and hopped along the ground a dozen times before stopping, each of the children hopping along with glee. Next he stuck his arms out to his sides shoulder high and moved in a semi-circle to his left while dipping his left shoulder and raising his right arm; he then repeated the movement to the right while taking long steps. After a few minutes he relinquished the lead to a youngster who took the group on a somersaulting journey before surrendering his lead to another.

The emissary recounted that as he watched, it seemed numerous adults viewed the activities in happy contentment, almost as if they wanted to join the fun. In the end, the children gathered in a group around the Galilean and cheered.

His playing with children made me smile. I tried to imagine him playing leap frog in a tunic. Might be a bit of a challenge at that.

These thoughts passed through my mind as I trudged along, enjoying the travel, even though I knew I'd be in for a climb of nearly six thousand feet—from a few hundred feet above sea level up to an elevation of just over six thousand. About then I heard a cacophony of caterwauling and recognized the sound as that of those mourning for the dead. Now what?

While villagers walked en masse toward a burial plot, I found myself joining them. As the funeral service continued, I learned the dead man was the Aged One who had spoken to me when I purchased my sandal strap at the tent maker's shop. I assume he died of old age. This event reminded me of my conversation with the Aged One and renewed my commitment to learn more about the Nazarene and I continued on my journey.

I had some knowledge of the route and looked forward to the outing. One thing I was not looking forward to was the traffic. Three times a year Jews filled the roadway on their pilgrimage to Jerusalem to observe a succession of feasts—Pesach and Mazzot (Feast of Passover and Unleavened Bread), Shavuot or Pentecost (Feast of Weeks) and Sukkoth or Tabernacles (Feast of the Booths). And each year leading up to Passover week the population burgeoned with thousands of pilgrims coming to worship their God, especially in Jerusalem's Temple, their center of worship.

The Passover feast was about to begin. It commemorated the Jews' liberation from Egyptian slavery and was the biggest event of the year. The entire population of Judah, the region and distant lands would be traveling to fulfill the ancient sacrifices of the Jews. Beginning on the fifteenth of the Hebrew month Nisan, it would last seven days. Pilgrims would jam the roads from every corner of the world.

Along with the human traffic would be the myriad animals to be sacrificed in commemoration of the Jews' safe arrival from Egypt. Of late I'd been hearing about the Feast of Passover, a celebration of God's protective care and love for the children of Israel. It was often called The Bazaars of Annas since the former high priest and his sons controlled the affair.

At night the Temple and its court blazed with hanging lighted lamps. Music and waving of palm branches and shouts of "hosanna" filled the air. Priests were dressed in their finery. It would be something for me to behold. However with all the worshippers, their sacrifices, animals of burden combined with regular travelers, the roadway was going to be a nightmare.

I knew I'd have to keep an eye out for chariots. Periodically the goofy guys at the reins drove at reckless speeds. Made me wonder if these battle taxi drivers were practicing for the popular chariot races. And if those daredevil charioteers weren't bad enough, there was the ever present challenge of looking for beast of burden blessings thoughtfully left behind. These little treasures were compliments of the animals—donkey dung, camel caca, mule biscuits, ox offerings and horse muffins.

I reminded myself that the Roman authorities always get a little nervous during this time because of the increasing numbers in Jerusalem and the growing unrest among the Jews…a very delicate balance regarding the tenuous relationship between the Jews and the Romans—a sure opportunity for revolution. Rome paid close attention to Temple activity.

Any threat to Roman power over the Temple--even a symbolic threat--was dealt with harshly. I recalled an incident where a group of about forty young men climbed to the roof of the Temple and began chopping down a golden eagle, seen by them as a symbol of Roman control; the men were arrested "with considerable force." Those observed on the Temple roof were burnt alive and the others merely executed.

I left bright green forest on the valley floor and ascended into the foothills beyond. Anchorite caverns, sweet oleander—varying from white to red— and strips of cane met me as I moved up the grade to the rugged hills beyond, I overlooked the dizzying, nasty gorge of Waddy Kelt, truly amazed at the variety of beauty that met my eyes. I passed through sandstones lower and moved on to red clay formations.

I enjoyed the journey and gained a new appreciation for those barefoot peasants snailing their way over the dust and hot stones of the roadway. The walking also gave me some insights into the physical conditioning it would provide the man from Galilee who spent his entire life walking.

Nearing my destination, I observed numerous round topped hills stretching off into the distant wilderness of Judea—almost like soldiers, one behind the other. Olive trees covered the terrain and shepherds tended their flocks. Made me wonder if springtime was a nightmare for shepherds as that was the peak of lambing season.

That's when I noticed three figures coming my way a short distance ahead. Knowing of the notorious section of roadway, I was ever on my guard. The figures approached, morphing into men. My gut told me they spelled trouble.

There was nothing unusual about them. Their clothing was non-descript. They wore sandals and mantles over tunics. Their hair was brown to black in color. Each manifested a countenance of meanness. The only major difference I discerned was that one was larger than the other two.

When these men, who appeared to be Egyptian, were mere yards away, they brandished knives. As strange as it seems, what popped into my mind was my last visit with Alexy at the gladiatorial school. Time and action seemed to slow down as I remembered gladiatorial weapons of choice. Sagittarii were armed with bows and arrows which would be useless to me now. I could use one of the javelins chosen by the Velite or the standard 2-foot Roman sword and shield carried by the Samnites. But here I was armed like the Dimachaeri with my dagger.

My mind's screen filled with days of training with Alexy, practicing the art of self defense, knife skills, footwork and strategy. Alexy had schooled me well and I had acquired survival skills of which I was ever confident.

And thus I was about to put those skills to yet another test.

For some inexplicable reason I was almost giddy with thoughts of the arena—

her violence,

her gladiators engaged in intense battle,

her life or death aura.

I was reminded of the crowd's salivating and unusual disregard for human life. They often determined a man's destiny with gestured thumbs—thumbs up or thumbs down.

Thumbs up, they approved.

Thumbs down, they disapproved.

Thumbs up, I win.

Thumbs down, I lose.

Thumbs up, I live.

Thumbs down, I die.

But I wasn't playing to the crowd. I was playing to myself. I mentally gave myself a thumbs up.

The big man spoke, demanding my money. Telling him I had none and held little hope of ever getting any, I tried to reason with them. I set my grip down and explained that they, no doubt, had more earthly goods than I had.

Completely confident in my training and my skills, I decided to have some fun with these louts. "I don't suppose it would interest you to know that I am a visiting gladiator with numerous kills to my name?"

"Not a chance," one of them blurted.

"What if I told you I was a highly trained military man with several personal victories to my credit?"

"You're bluffing. We're not interested in your lies."

One final effort, "Suppose I said I was robbed within the past hour just a few leagues down the road before meeting you?"

"Enough. You're wasting our time," shouted the big man.

They would have none of it. Big Man commanded, "Throw down your purse."

My quick appeal to Jupiter was fraught with sincerity but I wasn't sure he heard me, *Okay, Jupiter, what have you now for me? The pirates weren't bad enough...they were a warm up?*

It seemed my destiny was to go through with this event. Thinking I could stall no longer and unable to come up with a better response and with all confidence in my ability to handle the situation, I said, "Whatever I possess, belongs to me. There are two ways you can acquire it—one, I give it to you; two, you take it from me. I'm not giving it up. If you want it, at least one of you may die. It doesn't' matter to me which of you I kill. Is my purse worth a life?"

By now they had moved into a triangle with me in the center. The one before me lunged at me, knife held overhead. He thrust it downward toward me. I launched myself at his right shin, driving my right foot against it. I heard a snap as the fibula broke. He dropped his weapon and rolled to the ground clutching his leg while simultaneously gasping in pain.

Attempting to rise to his good knee, he shouted, "Kill him!"

I had executed a front summersault, gaining my feet and facing my other two assailants, one on my right, one on my left. The smaller one said, "Take heart. We'll kill this man and get you help." Holding his knife in his right hand, waist high, he lunged toward me while exhorting this companion, "Help me kill this man!"

By now I had loosed my blade from its sheath. When he was within three feet, I jumped into the air, spinning to my left and slicing my blade across his right chest and shoulder as he passed. He shrieked in pain and blood colored his garment as I landed on my feet facing the third man.

It was obvious that the man with the broken leg would do me no harm. The one with the sliced shoulder, a look of fear on his face, dropped his knife, stumbled to a boulder at the road's edge and sat down on it, a look of chagrin upon his brow.

Big Man seemed to lose interest and asked his friends, "What shall we do now?"

The tables had turned.

Broken Leg said, "I need help."

Bloody Shirt agreed, "As do I."

Now it was my turn. Completely in charge and knowing it was but a short way to Jerusalem and the Roman garrison at Fortress Antonia, I commanded, "Drop your blade. Now, get your friend with the cut to help you raise your friend with the broken leg. Each of you put an arm over your shoulders. With your support your friend will have to hop on his good leg."

Knowing that the men needed medical help and wouldn't be moving very fast and that Antonia bordered the Temple Mount in Jerusalem with Roman soldiers who would be only too glad to intercede with these lawless men, I decided to leave them on their own. With an eye on them, I bent over and picked up the three knives and my grip. I left them and journeyed onward, planning to report them to the garrison commander.

Topping out on the roadway after what seemed like an endless, rocky staircase-like path, I beheld rolling hills as far as I could see and the beautiful snowcapped Mt. Scopus beyond. I knew I was within striking distance of the city.

Historically Jerusalem had been an isolated fortress on a hill. Her value was in her location, not her splendor. Called the City of David. After the return of the Jews from captivity in Babylon, Herod the Great restored the city during his 33-year reign. He built a theater, amphitheater, viaducts, palaces, citadels and public monuments, increasing the city's importance to the Roman Empire.

Rounding the Mount of Olives, I suddenly caught sight of unparalleled beauty. Beyond the Kidron Valley in the distance stood the gold-embellished dome on the Temple a striking landmark, standing high above the old city in the center of a huge white stone platform. For the first time I was to visit the center of Jewish trade.

A wall of thick, gray stone roughly four miles in circumference surrounded the city, perhaps 25,000 people within her walls. I guessed it would not be long before I encountered a publican at one of the large gates where publicans awaited at customs stations to collect taxes on all goods.

Inside the walls I was met by dusty streets and alleyways running up and downhill in every conceivable direction. Clustered about the roadway market were craftsmen of every sort—tailors, potters, weavers, carpenters and metalworkers. Amidst the clatter of hooves and babble of voices arose the cooking odors where I encountered the bazaar and merchants selling vegetables, fruits, clothes, perfumes, jewelry and dried fish.

As I passed taverns and restaurants, my taste buds tickled my memory, causing me to consider asking Gaius about a good place to eat when the time arose. And, of course, that would include the most delectable locale for local wine or imported beer. The Upper City's white marble villas and palaces of the rich, appearing almost like snow patches, beckoned me.

Excited about seeing Gaius, I hastened toward the Fortress. After reporting there and describing the three bandits to the captain of the guard, I inquired about my friend Gaius. Turns out the captain knew Gaius Vesuvius Marcallas well and gave me exact directions to his home. On the way I composed a poem highlighting my trip.

JOURNAL

Not much of a literary person...I composed a little poem along the journey:

On day one I left Capernaum

My ultimate goal Jerusalem.

Between these two cities I would find

Many folks and beasts of every kind—

from local folk to foreigners

they travelled the road, mostly strangers;

oxen, donkeys, camels and horses

each doing its part to move the forces;

carts, chariots and countless caravans

from market goods to construction plans.

It was quite the trip I must admit

And I'm very glad I'm over it.

CHAPTER 5 — I see Jesus

The narrow streets gave me an opportunity to observe homes and other buildings.

As I walked, I recalled a comment about the Baptizer, that his influence being greater than that of the priests.

Remembering some of the Temple history and numerous stories I'd heard over the years, especially about the priests, I should not have been surprised. Traditionally priests required sacrifice of thousands of animals in the Temple. With typical religiosity they insisted that God's blessing required a pure animal. Although many worshippers arrived to provide a sacrifice to the Most High God, others appeared without an animal. The faithful, however, were prepared to purchase such an animal in the outer courts of the Temple. Some stories mentioned the more perfect animal was available at the priests' conveniently jacked up price.

And then there were the money changers, joining the priests in graft and feeding upon innocent worshippers. Pilgrims were expected to pay the Temple tax of a half shekel to the Temple treasury. Because Temple requirements necessitated foreign money be exchanged for the sanctuary coinage, called the Temple shekel, money changers thrived in their efforts to exchange monies with people from all classes and cultures of the Great Sea world. The exchanging of the money provided ample opportunity for fraud and extortion, a disgusting tradition that became a source of revenue for priests.

In addition to the priests and money changers were the dealers in animals. These greedy merchants robbed the pilgrims. They demanded exorbitant prices, sharing their profits—a commission, so to speak—with the priests. Thus pilgrims became victims of the trilogy of priests, money changers and dealers.

I could easily imagine these representatives of the people and intermediaries to God. The priests had the power and the responsibility to clean up the idolatry and the abuses, but they ignored the misdeeds of the Temple. They were part of it.

Feast attendees included distressed and desperate people, people wanting solace—blind, lame, lepers, some on beds. Many poor were unable to purchase the expensive sacrificial animals, even too poor to purchase food for their needs. Whereas the priests boasted of their piety and their role as guardians of the people, the people were distressed by their greed. The poor, sick, suffering and dying found no solace in the hearts of the priests.

A cauldron of corruption reigned.

Some 30,000 corrupt and parasitic priests and helpers trafficked in bamboozling the people each year, bilking the faithful of their money, possibly

35 million dollars annually. My investigation assured me that Caiaphas and pals have a great deal going. Caiaphas pretty much runs Jerusalem where deceptive high priests feed upon the worshippers to the victim's disdain and the priests' financial gain. No wonder the Jews want to get rid of the Nazarene.

I'd heard many stories of pilgrims—sordid tales of grief and graft. For decades pilgrims had made the difficult journey to Jerusalem only to be compounded by the avarice of the temple authorities. One woman told of the time she'd taken a lamb, raised with dedicated devotion as a sacrifice to be borne to Jerusalem only to have the scornful priests mock her and tell her to purchase a purer lamb from the dealers. A white haired, wrinkled old man saved money for months to purchase his gift only to have the money changers convert his provincial currency into temple coin at a robber's rate.

In spite of the dismal thoughts about the men who were supposed to be aiding the worshippers, it was difficult not to notice my surroundings. It was a beautiful cosmopolitan city. Countless open air markets dotted her cobblestone streets and merchants hawked their diverse wares—from live creatures to breads, milk, vegetables and fruits. I decided to stop to purchase a few items for Gaius, including a pomegranate for his daughter.

Before I could accomplish that task, however, I was surprised by the din of voices and footfalls on the roadway just beyond the temple.

That was my first time to see the Nazarene. I heard before I saw. The steady drumbeat of voices and sandals on the cobblestones gave warning of an approaching throng.

I saw him from a distance. But as the gap narrowed, the stories I'd heard about him piled up in my mind. He took on a different, if not more meaningful, appearance. I'm not saying I was mystified but I was pretty impressed.

I was struck by his bearing, military-like in posture. The things I'd heard about the him and his message were starting to jibe. They say there's an edge to his words. That he speaks as no man before him.

I'm beginning to believe the people are right.

Further he proclaims he has a new message—one not of contradiction nor condemnation but rather one of completion. Is it any wonder people flock to him? No one has ever heard such words nor this kind of logical, easy to understand message.

I'm beginning to understand.

Clad in his long mantle, striding erect, gazelle-like in his robust gracefulness, Jesus occupied the forefront. Each step brought him closer to the Temple, allowing me to more fully assess his features.

He wore dusty, leather sandals. Tanned arms extended from his tunic and his hands were those of a skilled tradesman.

Dark brown, somewhat wavy hair, brushed away and back from his face and forehead, framed his face. It was two to four-inches long, in places the tips seemingly bleached and tinted blonde by the sun. His healthy cheeks and lips were somewhat hidden by his well groomed and symmetrical full beard, one to two inches long with corresponding shorter mustache. Bold, dark and thick eyebrows highlighted his clear, greenish-blue happy, bright eyes.

His eyes. There was something about his eyes. They spoke volumes…of knowing, of suffering, of experience. And I must admit, compassion.

He looked peaceful enough but somehow his appearance belied my assumption. He walked upright, eyes ahead, his gaze missing nothing. And his features—the healthy look of cleanness shone from his face. His motions were robust, demonstrating a physical power, a rawboned toughness developed by his hours in the building trade and his miles of walking.

There was something about this man—a presence, an overpowering magnetism. That presence commanded my attention, causing me to focus on him and to question the source of his power. A silent calm gripped me where I stood. A silence greater than a canyon full of empty.

Everything about this man compelled me to notice him and to question his comportment and bearing. I've observed military men. I've seen businessmen throughout the "new east"— in caravans, in tight spots, in tough times and in plenty—but I've never observed so complete a man, so accomplished and confident, so stalwart in stature and in control.

Try as I might, I couldn't put my finger on it. As monumental as it appeared, my job was established…my mission became sharper edged, more suspenseful and more significant…even more urgent. Who is this man?

The Temple's ivory majesty, pure white marble walls, gleamed, rising fifteen stories, accentuated by gold capped columns. Corinthian pillars rose a hundred feet in the air. Near the entrance was a vine of gold and silver with green leaves and clusters of grapes depicting Israel as a prosperous vine.

The crowd entered the building, providing me firsthand experience in observing this man from Galilee and I entered with the others.

Promiscuous throngs filled the temple courts. A chalky haze of dust rose above beasts in the outer courtyard. Cattle contentedly chewed their cuds. While caged doves and pigeons cooed in the background, an occasional ox bellowed and sheep bleated.

An increasing murmur intermingled with the din of animals and the hubbub of their movement coupled with the angry altercations of traffickers permeated the atmosphere. Merchants and money changers haggled over prices. Boisterous chatter and clamor rose to fever pitch. Words addressed to the Most High were obliterated by sounds and the uproar of avarice. Drawn away by lust for money, the Jewish leaders had become estranged from the worship of Yeshua.

The word on the street was that the Galilean knew all too well that centuries of abuse had taken place, that the priests had no intention of meeting the needs of the worshippers. There was no effort by the priests to inform the worshippers as to the particulars of the process of worship.

When I next saw the Prophet, I read disgust and anger on his face. The peaceful, joyful countenance he'd exhibited outside the Temple vanished. I also noticed he had acquired a cord. As I watched him surveying the scene, he braided the cord in his hands with controlled movements, weaving it into a whip of sorts.

Next he confidently strode toward a Temple merchant. The startled seller saw Jesus in time to avoid the swirling swish of the whip. The Nazarene's eyes flashed. He raised his whip and as he swung it, his opened sleeves disclosed his rope-like muscled forearms.

His demeanor reminded me of a disciplined military man determined to see a job through. I was impressed with his bearing. His movements were precise—every move calculated, not a single wasted motion.

Girded with the love of his God and sheathed in muscles groomed over years, eyes afire, the Nazarene's muscled arm lashed out with the whip. He then overturned heavy merchant tables of wares, the whip in constant motion as he told the money changers they were a disgrace to the God whose Temple they desecrated.

He was thorough in his mission. One after another he upended table after table, reaching his hands under each and twisting it over…all the while berating the violators for corrupting the Temple and themselves. Thrusting his whip overhead his right arm rose again and again, wielding it against the spineless swine at the table. No one seemed willing to rise against him. I wondered what kind of challenge that arm and body would present to my friend Alexius in the arena. *Could be interesting.*

He moved among the stalls of penned animals—bleating sheep and cattle and doves… releasing or driving them from their pens and cages. The air filled with flapping and fluttering doves, the dust from the stampeding sheep rising to co-mingle with them.

A look of righteous indignation overshadowed his brow. He shouted to the pigeon dealers, "Take those things out of here. Don't you dare turn my Father's house into a market."

He drove out the animals and upbraided the priests with words of wrath, "You will not make this Temple, my Father's home, a trading center! Get these things out of here." He tossed bird cages and sacks of coins and trading tables out onto the courtyard.

Pandemonium reigned. The scene was electrifying.

Unbridled fear shook some of the priests to the core. They wondered if Beelzebub himself had come in the form of this mad man…or if he were a demon. Others shuddered in anger toward this man who threatened their positions, their power and chances of advancing their agenda, not to mention their wealth.

Above the melee I heard their angry shouts: "What gives him the right to act this way in the Temple, affecting an age old tradition?" And, "Who does he think he is?"

After witnessing this performance, I was dumbstruck to say the least. The Rabbi left the building. I followed him directly but lost him in the crowd. Knowing I could catch him eventually if I pursued, I chose rather to continue to Gaius' to relate this event and, again, try to gain a perspective as to this Galilean and my mission.

My military connections with Rome provided much access and made me privy to the Roman records including scuttlebutt about various Roman leaders as well as many subjects, accounting and business matters.

CHAPTER 6 — I See Gaius and Ariella

The first thing I did was stop to purchase the items for Gaius and his little girl. Then, lost in a trancelike mood, being free to let my mind rest to some degree for the first time since leaving Rome, it seemed hardly any time at all before I reached the home of Gaius where he greeted me warmly. After a joyous reunion at the door, he ushered me inside where he introduced me to his wife and little girl. He insisted that I stay for the evening meal which I gladly accepted. Then we reminisced about our days of military training, work in the field and our long-lasting friendship. We laughed as we reminded each other of the numerous goofy situations we'd experienced.

Before we knew it, the meal was prepared and we sat at the table to a wonderful feed. After a delightful dessert we retired to the sitting room and continued our revelry.

Wanting more information about Jerusalem and her citizens, I asked Gaius to tell me about the city, as I leaned back and took it all in. He said that "most folks live in one and two story houses packed together in the Lower City with the narrow streets. The Upper City, however, boasts wide streets arranged on an orderly grid much like the elegant cities of Rome and Greece, housing the rich, powerful Jewish families and Roman administrators. They dwell in white marble mansions and palaces surrounded by courtyards with pools and gardens.

"In the upper market you'll find booths in the court surrounded by three walls, where gold and silversmiths sell wares, ivory, incense and precious stones and perfumes. Merchants include master tailors and silk merchants. Commonly, household slaves run errands for their masters. Wealthy Jews attend popular Greek and Roman plays in the open air theater built by Herod the Great.

"And the Temple. It is revered by Romans and Jews, Pharisees and Sadducees. The Romans have spent inordinate time, energy and money in rebuilding and refurbishing it. They are proud of it and pleased with its beauty. They would be incensed with its destruction. Although the Romans have contributed much to the pleasures of the Jews, traditional Jews scorn everything Roman.

"During feasts the city swells to four times its normal population, many staying with friends or relatives or in inns or tents outside the city."

When he'd entertained my ears and my mind long enough, the mood changed to a more serious nature when Gaius asked me if I'd seen the Healer.

"Yes, as a matter of fact, I saw him for the first time just today in the Temple. Perhaps you heard about the hubbub."

"Yes, I did. I wish I'd been there to see it. It sounds pretty amazing."

"I must admit, it was spellbinding. It gave me a sense of wonderment

about this Galilean. I'd heard many stories but never seen him until then."
Wanting more information about Jesus and hoping Gaius would provide it, I
asked, "What do you know of the Nazarene?"

"Like you, I've heard many stories. My wife Livia and I had a personal
experience with him that has left me wondering. We recently took our
daughter Carisia to him. We had heard he was in the neighborhood and hoped
he could help with her illness. And he did."

"What exactly did he do?"

"We're not sure. Livia and I had no idea that he could actually help. The
way he looked at us and at Carisia made us feel that he was doing the greatest
good on earth...that he was wanting to bring joy to our lives. We know that
he relied upon some power because when he saw her he merely placed his
hand on her forehead and spoke kindly to her. And her health was restored.
We were thankful beyond words. We told him how grateful we were and told
him we could never repay him. He said his recompense was in seeing her and
us happy. Then he said something that puzzled me and I've not been able to
get it out of my mind."

"What did he say?"

"As we left him, he merely nodded his head and responded, 'We'll meet
again under less favorable circumstances.' I keep wondering, when would
we meet again? How could he know that? And what could the less favorable
circumstances be?"

"What kinds of things have you heard others say about him?"

"The usual stories. I'm guessing they're probably some that you've
heard. He heals all sorts of illnesses, makes the blind to see and the lame
to walk. He works with demon possession and exhorts people to come to
God. Most people seem pleased by his presence and his activities. I can find
nothing harmful in this Galilean. In fact the only complaint I've heard about
him is from those hypocritical religious leaders accusing him of being the
head of demons. My perception is that they just can't handle his revealing
their phoniness."

"On a related subject, what's your take on the Baptizer?"

"His was quite the following. Some thought he was laying the groundwork
for a revolution but that's not so. I know he lived a humble life away from
the cities, preaching the love of God and telling men they needed to repent.
The Healer spoke of him saying 'there is no man ever born greater than John.'"

"Brachan, what kind of news do you bring from Rome? We get dispatches
and verbal communication, but nothing of any import recently."

"About the only recent news I have is about the Baptizer, not about
Rome. You probably heard about his death?"

"Yes. I guess it does not pay to inflame the wife of a tetrarch."

"Gaius, I was sent to monitor the Baptizer. Now he's dead. Because of his message about the Messiah, I'm wondering about this man from Galilee... whether he might cause trouble."

"I don't think I can help you much there. I haven't heard anything involving him and a revolution. If I do, I could let you know."

"Okay. That's fair enough. I'm going to keep an eye on him until I receive further instructions from my superior in Rome. But don't let it be known to others what I'm about."

"You can trust me, Brachan."

"I know I can. So, Gaius, how are things with you here in Jerusalem?"

"All in all, quite good. I can't complain. I look forward to the end of my soldiering days. There was a time when I enjoyed my job, when I relished it. My defense was that I did it for the Empire."

"Some accused us of barbarity, considering our methods ruthless and unmerciful. However, we Romans pride ourselves in bringing justice to those who deserve it."

"That's what I told myself. I mutilated so many men that I became callous to my job. But that has changed. What am I actually accomplishing? I'm just torturing people, many who may actually be innocent."

"You provided a service to the Empire. I've seen my share of your scourgings. You did Rome proud."

"Livia and I have talked. I have recurring nightmares, more so lately. I've taken to drink more than ever. If I can fulfill my service and retire, there is a chance the nightmares will end."

"You are the master of the flagrum."

"I know. I wielded that tool as a pure sculptor wields his hammer and chisel. Sometimes someone preceded me using his flagrum consisting of lead balls. I then brought out the one with mutton bones woven into the leather, called plumbatae. He bruised; I sliced."

"Yes, I know."

"The two tools are identical except for the bones. To the 8-inch wooden handle are attached three leather thongs which include two lead balls, in line and secured with a knot above and below. In order to keep the balls from striking each other and to provide more damage to the victim, the thongs vary in length—11, 12 and 13 inches. The balls cause bruising and softening of tissue and result in torn flesh. Both instruments cause severe injury. But the bones bite deeply into the muscle structure.

"Sometimes mutton bones are replaced with shards of metal or glass. I prided myself in the process. I learned to come down with each stroke and, as the bones struck flesh, to twist my wrist downward almost simultaneously snapping my wrist backward and up, tearing out chunks of flesh. My work was so good that I often saw my victim's internal organs. Can you understand what I've become?"

"To a degree. Since I've not walked that pathway, it would be hard to completely understand. I witnessed some of your work. Truly brutal. The large, deep bruises and broken skin from subsequent blows, leaving the skin of the back hanging in long ribbons and the entire area an unrecognizable mass of torn, bleeding tissue. I know your work. But I've never wielded the whip. So I can't project myself into your situation. I can only say that I understand to a degree."

"Well, I know you know I serve the Empire."

"Yes, I do, Gaius. No truer soldier ever served Rome. I justify your work because you are loyal to Rome. You punished countless parties, weakening them to the point of non-resistance to the cross. In some ways, your work was so efficient that they suffered little on the cross as a result of blood loss, being in a state of shock or both."

"Let us hope that those days are coming to an end. I dread the thought of another flogging."

"For your sake, Gaius, I also hope you are not required to perform any more. Speaking of uncertainties, another question. How do you think Pontius Pilate is working out here?"

"I think we can agree that Pilate idolized his friend Caesar Tiberius. Also about Caesar's being a tyrant and that both men shared feelings for each other."

I agreed. "Yes. A few years back Caesar was fond of him enough to commission Pilate to rule the government of Judaea, one of Rome's most trying provinces. Caesar even allowed Pilate's wife to accompany him, a rare treat for governors."

"Wonder of wonders, although well educated and cultured, Pilate detests the Jews because of their legalistic policies and behaviors. He's had more than a little trouble with them in the past. He considers them narrow minded. Even Philo says Pilate excels in venality, violence, unlawful appropriation of property, continued executions without legal proceedings and incessant and unbearable cruelty. Have you heard that he has had Galilean pilgrims butchered in the temple. His insolence and cruelty has given way to murdering innocent as well as guilty without a trial."

"Yes, I have. He seems to be building some kind of track record. The Jews have a long history of hating Herod the Great: the slaughter of male infants, suppression of their allies, his disregard for the *Torah* and other sacred Jewish traditions. His son Herod Antipas fared no better in Galilee than his father in Judaea. Antipas built Tiberias by the Sea of Galilee on top of a Jewish cemetery, creating additional distaste among Jews because it was unclean. Can you blame them for feeling that way?

"Way before I left Rome I heard Pilate incensed the Jews further by his idolatrous actions. He had his troops outfitted with a silver insignia of the emperor. Jewish tradition forbad idols and other gods. Pilate made himself an instant enemy, if you will, of the populace. In time he respected the wishes of the priests and had those idols removed. He further angered the Jews by taking private tablets into his home, another violation of the Jews as they served as votives for his god. They sent representatives to Rome to complain which put him in a bad light with Caesar."

"And," added Gaius, "He also further angered the people by having an aqueduct diverted and installed Roman baths in order to enjoy his personal pleasures…another mistake in the eyes of the Jews. When they began complaining, Pilate sent soldiers among them and cut them down. His tactics silenced the vocalizations to a point but set him at great odds with the populace—the priests especially loathed him."

"Sometimes you have to wonder if our leaders learn much from their experiences."

"Brachan, with the religious leaders plotting to do away with Jesus, do you think there's a chance they will call for his execution?"

"On what grounds?"

"They could manufacture something. They are long on tradition and short on common sense. They could probably conjure up some ridiculous charge and pay informers to lie for them."

"From what I've heard and seen that wouldn't surprise me. But would they have the authority to execute him? When my grandfather helped put down Spartacus and his gladiators, there was just cause. Spartacus and his men were insurrectionists and were hanged upside down on the Appian Way. We both know too well the history and the severity of Roman execution. There is a time when both flogging and the tree are necessary."

"Having studied and witnessed hanging from a military perspective, I can assure you that if the Jews hatch a plan to execute him, it will not be pretty. If, for some reason, Roman law is followed—allowing any number of lashes—the Rabbi probably will not survive the flogging. If this man is to be executed, Jupiter forbid that I'm the one to swing the whip."

"For your sake, Gaius, I hope you're right. That your days of stroking for justice are over."

After spending the night with Gaius, he all but begged me to stay longer but I wanted to try to look up Ariella before leaving Jerusalem. I also wanted to post a dispatch to Alexy in response to the one he'd sent me in care of

Gaius. Gaius gave me directions to a postal office and I was on my way, planning to take up my quest of the Nazarene as soon as I visited with Ariella.

I found the dispatch office and sent a letter to my gladiator pal. I answered his questions, especially the one about my delay in returning to Rome. Since I'd previously informed him about my trip, the pirates and Ariella as well as meeting the Baptizer, I told him I missed his action in the arena. Then I brought him up to date on the Baptizer's arrest and subsequent beheading. I mentioned the Jews still objected to their Roman overlords and my run in with the bad guys and ended with some of the weird things I'd witnessed. I explained my return appeared imminent.

After posting the letter to Alexy, I started for Ariella's home. Walking through the streets and alleyways reminded me of the confusion of city life compared to country living. In the city people haggled in the marketplace; smoke filtered skyward co-mingled with aromas of roast lamb and matted sheep wool; hooves clopped on cobblestone. Though these things also occurred in the country, they were easier to live with.

Country offered pastures where sheep and goats nibbled grasses; calm, soothing breezes whispered through orchards and vineyards; multicolored flowers blossomed and burbling brooks enchanted; and gray-white limestone buildings did not blot out blue skies. The hubbub of the city drowned out the peacefulness of nature's pastoral life.

The contrast between confusion and calm was profound. It just seemed an overpowering oppression hung over the city where plans and projects demand harried attention and completion. Kind of a hurry up and get it done mentality. There was little time to relax and to reflect. The heavy feeling of city life made me want to hasten back to the country.

While continuing toward Ariella's, my plan was interrupted when I came upon yet another group of the Galilean's followers.

As we approached the Sheep Gate, I noticed the pool called Bethesda (in Hebrew Bethzatha). It was a rectangular building divided in the center of its length by a fifth leg. Each leg consisted of a walkway above which rose columns supporting a roof. Basically I was looking at five porches that enclosed two pools. The porticoes sheltered hundreds of sufferers—from the heat by day and from the cold by night.

Like a magnet, the pool's magical powers drew crowds of people with physical needs—blind, paralyzed, maimed and ill. They gathered under these porticos awaiting the water's movement, hoping and trying to reach the water.

The pool is somewhat of a mystery. At certain seasons a supernatural force moved the water. Some claim the movement is caused by the angel of the Lord who goes into the pool and disturbs the water. For ages people have come here from miles around hoping to enhance or improve their health. Traditionally the first person into the pool after it is disturbed was cured of any disease so they awaited their opportunity.

When the occasion of the water's movement occurs, it is difficult for the weak or seriously afflicted to reach the water at all, let alone before anyone else. It is common for people to be trampled. Many who reached the edge of the pool died there.

While thinking about this and watching the masses, I was surprised to see Jesus approach the pool. He saw the sad sufferers. He realized it was the Sabbath, that many were at the Temple for worship and that any act of kindness or healing would launch a tirade from the Jews. It appeared to me he intentionally chose to confront the baseless Sabbath tradition of the Jews, maybe even to pick a fight he knew he'd win. In so doing, he specifically chose to deal with a helpless cripple even though his disease was a result of his own sin. This particular health seeker had never been able to reach the water even though at times friends were prepared to carry him to it. He had lingered at the pool forever.

He came.

He waited.

He wanted.

But it was in vain. On that day he lay beside the pool, hobbled by his paralysis. How was he to know that help was on the way? Help as he never expected it.

The Rabbi walked up to the invalid and asked, "Would you like to get well?"

"Sir, I don't have anyone to put me into the pool when the water is disturbed. Someone always beats me there while I am attempting to reach the water."

"Get up. Pick up your sleeping mat and walk."

The man was immediately healed. He stooped to pick up his mat and blanket. When he looked up to see his Deliverer, the Healer was gone, having melted into the crowd. The healed man tried to catch the Nazarene, fearful that he'd forget what he looked like if he didn't catch him. In the process he ran into some Jewish men who reminded him that it was unlawful to bear burdens on the Lord's day, "You aren't allowed to carry your sleeping mat on the Sabbath."

"The man who cured me told me to pick up my sleeping mat and to walk. I obeyed him."

Another Jew bombarded him, "Who told you to 'pick up your mat and to walk?'"

"I have no clue. The man healed me and departed. I lay beside the pool for thirty-eight years. No one helped me get well. Even though friends tried.

This stranger healed me. And you come along and tell me it's unlawful to carry my bed. Give me a break! He didn't condemn me. What makes you think I care about your rules and regulations? What, exactly, have those regulations done for me?"

With those words he departed.

I'm thinking, maybe the guy was excited…wouldn't you be after a 38-year illness!

I'm seeing more evidence that the religious Jews live in a land of unreality. I'm believing more and more that they have perverted the law into a yoke of bondage. They invented so many traditions and restrictions—even to the point of not lighting a candle or building a fire on the Sabbath—that they are the laughing stock of many nations.

There was more to the story as I learned later in the Temple Jesus found the man he'd healed at the pool and said, "Now that you are well again, sin no more, or something worse may happen to you."

When the former invalid left the Temple, he identified the healer as the Nazarene.

So much has happened I believe I'll spend a few more days in Jerusalem. Maybe I'll hear more talk of the healed man and the Prophet while I'm trying to catch up with Ariella. Perhaps I'll receive some sort of instruction from my supervisor by way of Ananias; then I'll take up the trail of the Rabbi again.

Almost before I knew it, I found myself at Ariella's. And she was home. She welcomed me and said she had wondered if we'd ever meet again. I reminded her that I told her I'd try to make it happen. When she showed me inside, her father greeted me warmly and told me I was fortunate to catch them at home as they had been traveling on business and were about to leave on another trip.

She ushered me into the sitting room where the three of us sat on cushions to catch up on the past several months. She said she had wondered about me and hoped that my injury had healed, leaving me with no ill effects.

I replied in jest and with a smile, "I'm okay. Maybe the knock on the head did me some good."

We spoke about events of the months gone by. I spoke in general terms about my actual business and shared my months in country and my pleasure with its beauty and its people.

When I asked if she'd had time to follow the events of the past several months, her eyes lit up and she smiled. "Father and I had an interesting and unexpected encounter recently on our return from a business venture. We had stopped to visit one of father's old time friends, one whose time on earth is not long. He owns a tannery and makes tents among other things."

"That's strange. Some time ago I visited a tannery to purchase a leather strap for my sandal. There a very old man spoke to me of the Messiah."

"Do you remember the town?"

"Actually, I do. It was el Maghtas."

"El Maghtas? That's where our friend lives. I don't suppose you remember his name?"

"No. He sat off to one side. I didn't know he owned the shop. Because he looked so old, I referred to him as Aged One."

"It would be some kind of coincidence if he's the same man we know. His name is Reuven ben Judah."

"I'll make a note of it so I can stop next time I'm in the area. And you mentioned an unexpected encounter…what was that?"

"We ran into the man rumored to be the Messiah. We were traveling south between Samaria and Galilee when we came upon a group of folks gathered on the roadside outskirts of a small village."

"That's interesting. Your friend told me he thought Jesus was the Messiah."

"That is interesting. Not unlike Reuven at all. Hardly had we come within hearing of the crowd when we heard proclamations, 'Unclean! Unclean!'

"And then, 'Jesus! Master! Have mercy on us!' Father and I were surprised to be in the presence of the rumored Messiah. We had heard about him and his works but certainly had no intentions of meeting him. Nor had we expected to be in the midst of some lepers."

"So, you were surprised to meet Jesus?"

"Yes. Even though we had heard stories about him and his activities, it was a surprise and a shock."

"What about the lepers, were you afraid?"

"Only a little concerned about being in their proximity. But things happened quickly. The Messiah, if that's who he was, responded to their plea by curing every single one of them. It was pretty amazing.

"These lepers were a sorry sight—various parts of their bodies were covered with rotting flesh or evidenced missing fingers, toes, hands, feet, noses or ears, their disease gradually eating away at their body tissue. Their disease dooms them, transforming their healthy bodies into emaciated skeletons with abnormally deformed or missing limbs. Although most try to keep clean, they are shunned and degraded. Their deformity often reduces their travel to crawling or dragging themselves along the ground as a means of ambulation.

"Perhaps you know they are not permitted into the town proper. By the very nature of their illness they are rejected by society and their solo lifestyles force them to beg or scrounge for food away from population centers. Isolated. Alone. Subjects of total ostracism. Sometimes they band together in their suffering, seeking sustenance in whatever manner available to them. They pursue life daily, a life unknown to those not afflicted by leprosy. It is so sad."

"Ariella, I saw the Nazarene recently for the first time at the Temple where he excoriated the priests and money changers. When you saw him with the lepers, how would you describe his demeanor?"

"He seemed pretty serious but it was a serious situation. I felt there was a certain charisma to him, as though people were drawn to him. He acted with the utmost concern for the lepers and seemed to care deeply for them. He even seemed to care for those who criticize him and appear to be his enemies."

"I missed the friendly side of him in the Temple. He was extremely serious and business like during his time there. However I did see him working with a blind man at the Pool of Bethesda and he showed considerable compassion. He cured the man's illness and he instructed him to avoid future sinning."

Thinking perhaps with tongue in cheek, it seemed as if she were cross-examining me when she asked, "Did you wonder about the connection between illness and sinning?"

"I suppose it crossed my mind. I know the Jewish religion considers illness or poor health a result of sin." Then it was my turn to cross-examine. "Were you thinking he had some kind of agenda?"

"The only motivation I detected was what you said about compassion. He just seemed to care for the men beseeching his help. And once he'd helped them, he went on his way. He didn't ask for recompense or praise, just left them. He did instruct them to 'go show yourselves to the priests.' Normal process called for the person to approach the priest for confirmation of the disease's disappearance before an offering could be accepted. I don't know if you know, but the only time a leper approaches a priest is to evidence his healing. One leper was a Samaritan who stood no chance of seeing a priest since Jews do not intermingle with Samaritans.

"The poor man was still estranged from communication with the 'religious' community, however he knew that he was healed.

"They departed but the Samaritan turned and praised God at the top of his voice. He returned to Jesus and fell before him on his face.

"I assume Jesus wondered about the gratitude of the healed men."

"Why's that?"

"He raised the question to the Samaritan, 'Weren't there ten of you made clean? Where are the other nine?' Then he acknowledged, 'It appears the only one returning to praise God is you, a foreign Samaritan. Stand up and go on your way. Your faith has made you whole.'"

"So, then what occurred?"

"My father and I were both dumbfounded. About then Jesus and his men departed. It happened so fast and was so unbelievable that it almost seemed as though it never happened. They were there then they were gone."

"This entire business regarding instant healing is new to me. I've heard some stories about miracles but I don't think I ever expected to see one. I didn't have a chance to talk with the blind man yesterday at the pool or to the Healer. However I wondered how such healing could occur."

"I felt the same. My perception is that Jesus listened…

> to the words of their wants;
>
> he heard the longings of their hearts and
>
> he heard the cries of their souls.

"But he did more than listen. He did more than hear…

> he responded to their words,
>
> he addressed the longings of those hearts and
>
> he rewarded the cries of those souls.

"He called it faith. In nearly every case—if not all—he told those he healed that they were healed because of their faith."

At that moment Ariella excused herself, stating she was going to the other room to get some foodstuff. I tried to object but it was in vain. Her father and I discussed his upcoming plans and in no time at all Ariella had returned with a platter on which were figs, grapes, pomegranate sections and a pitcher of wine with some glasses.

After the fruit and wine and not wanting to wear out my welcome, I told them that I must be on my way. When they asked me where I was going, I said that I would continue scouting business opportunities and try to learn more about the Galilean.

CHAPTER 7 — Mysterious Events

Some days before the Passover Feast, the apostles whom the Rabbi had sent out to preach and heal returned and gave him an accounting of their ministerial activities—where they'd gone, what they'd done and taught. The Rabbi took them in a boat to the other side of the Sea of Galilee and to a quiet place belonging to the city of Bethsaida. Even then many saw them and followed along the lake shore. Not wanting to be lost in the crowd, no pun intended, I hustled along until we all ended up on a hillside.

Jesus seemed touched by our presence since we appeared like a ship without a rudder and he began teaching. As the day wore on, he felt pity for us and wanted to feed us. The disciples suggested that since they were in the country, they go to get something to eat, perhaps from the neighboring farms or villages. However the Prophet suggested the disciples feed the crowd. Not wanting to spend the money, the disciples remonstrated.

When the Rabbi asked his disciple Philip where they could buy bread, Philip responded that "two hundred denarius worth of bread isn't even enough for them each to have a small piece."

Jesus suggested they check to see what they had in the way of food. He told them to "give them something to eat" and asked, "How many loaves do you have?"

Simon Peter's brother Andrew said, "A small boy here has five barley loaves and two small fish. But what is that between so many unless we go and buy food. We have no more than five loaves and two fish."

"Bring them to me."

He instructed them to have the men sit on the grass in groups of fifty and one hundred. People complied—the men alone numbered five thousand. Looking to the sky, the Master took the five loaves and gave thanks. He broke the loaves and gave them to the disciples who distributed them to the crowd. He then did the same thing with the two fish and the disciples divided the fish among them. Everyone had plenty of food.

When they'd been filled, the Galilean said, "Gather the left over pieces so that nothing is wasted" and when the disciples had completed their gathering, they had twelve baskets of fragments from the barley loaves and fish. The crowd agreed that he was truly the prophet who came into the world. Many had witnessed another remarkable, surprising event.

Then he spoke to the group, "I am the bread of life. I tell you truly unless you eat the flesh of the Son of Man and drink his blood, you have no life in you.

"Haven't I chosen you? My time is not yet come. My teaching is not mine, but comes from The One who sent me."

I mingled among the crowd attempting to understand his message but more specifically wondering how in the name of Jupiter he could produce enough magic to feed these many people and have food left over when he started with a couple of fish and some bread.

The Healer perceived that the crowd wished to make him king so he hastily told the disciples to get the boat and precede him to Bethsaida on the other side while he dispersed the crowd. The men approached the lake, boarded the boat and began towards Capernaum.

It wasn't long and I was left among the crowd, thinking he'd not have left if he was interested in fame and glory. The Rabbi, like so many times previously, had disappeared. Someone told me later that he had gone into the hills to be alone and to pray.

While he was so engaged, his shipboard disciples approached the beach about three miles distant. As it grew late, the Nazarene left his cloister, headed for the lake and observed the boat in the middle of the lake, the men straining at the oars, rowing into a strong head wind. Coupled with the rising wind and the roughness of the heavy seas tossing their boat about and their exhaustion, the men must have been terrified for their lives.

They looked out upon the lake during their struggles and saw someone or something walking toward them on the lake surface. In panic mode they agreed they saw a ghost, stating, "It is a spirit!"

As strange as it sounds, the Healer had left the beach and walked on the water's surface. He approached them on the fourth watch of the night. He could see that they were worn out from rowing into a strong head wind.

But they were in for a surprise. Not a ghost…but rather the Master strode toward them and consoled them, "It's all right. Be of good cheer and take courage. It is I. Don't worry or be afraid."

Too frightened to believe their eyes or their ears, they stared dumbfounded until Peter finally asked, "Lord, it is you? Tell me to walk across the water to you."

"Come."

Peter climbed overboard and began walking towards him. As soon as a gust of wind hit Peter, he got frightened and started sinking. He cried out, "Lord, save me!"

Jesus immediately stretched out his hand, caught Peter and said, "Man of little faith, why did you doubt?"

The boatmen agreed, "Truly, you are the Son of God."

The Galilean climbed aboard the boat and the wind dropped. But the men were still scared out of their wits.

However they were no more confused than I who remain mystified. How could anyone walk on water unless it was a frozen body? What kind of magical trick is that?

After the Galilean and his men departed, I began the journey around the lake to follow them. The people who'd witnessed the disciples' departure the day before were surprised to learn that the Nazarene and the disciples were not there. Some had seen the disciples leave but knew that the Healer was not with them. Other people arrived by boat but they, too, discovered that the Rabbi had left. Several had boarded boats to cross over to Gennesaret to search for him.

Meanwhile a group of people waited on shore in Gennesaret and when Jesus and his men secured their boat, they immediately recognized him. The word went out rapidly and men carried the sick and maimed on stretchers to the Healer and the disciples.

Not long afterward the crowd that had sailed in search of the Galilean arrived to join the others.

As he and the disciples moved throughout the country, people took up open places and streets so that they might be healed.

By the time I caught up with him he was in the synagogue in Capernaum. People asked him when he had come to Gennesaret and what was required for them to labor for the Lord.

And they wanted to know what sign he would show them. They alluded to God's feeding their forefathers manna and asked what sign he would show them. He told them that they sought him not because of signs they'd witnessed but because of the food they'd eaten. Then he said, "Moses did not give you bread from heaven; my Father did. He gives the true bread from heaven. His bread is the one who comes down from heaven and gives life to the world. You should not work for the food which does not last but for the food which lasts on into eternal life. This is the food the Son of Man will give you, and he is the one who bears the stamp of God the Father."

They responded, "Lord, always give us this bread."

"I am the bread of life, the person who comes to me will never hunger and he will never thirst. You have seen me but you still do not believe. Everything that the Father has given me will come to me and I will not turn away anyone who comes to me because I have come from heaven to do the will of the One who sent me. It is His will that everyone who sees the Son and believes on him will have everlasting life and that I will raise him up on the Last Day."

As I pondered these words, some of the Jews complained because the Galilean referred to himself as the bread come down from heaven, "Isn't this Jesus the son of Joseph. We know his father and mother, so how can he say 'I came down from heaven.'?"

The Healer answered them, "Stop grumbling among yourselves. No one can come to me unless he is drawn by the Father who sent me. And I will raise him up at the Last Day. It is written in the prophets. Every man who has heard and has learned of the Father comes to me. No man has seen the Father but the one who is of God. I assure you that everyone who believes on me has everlasting life. I am the bread of life."

Then the Jews argued even more. Some laughed out loud and asked, "How can this man give us his flesh to eat?"

He tried, "I tell you truly. Unless you eat the flesh of the Son of Man and drink his blood, you have no life in you. Whoever eats my flesh and drinks my blood has eternal life and I will raise him up on the Last Day. For my flesh is real food and my blood real drink."

Even his followers were shocked, some responding, "What he's saying is intolerable. How could anyone accept it?"

The Galilean knew intuitively what the disciples were thinking and asked, "Does this trouble you? What if you were to see the Son of Man ascend to where he was previously? It is the Spirit that gives life, the flesh offers nothing at all. The words I speak to you are spirit and are life. That's the reason I said that no one can come to me unless my Father had given it to him to do so. But there are those among you who will not believe." He knew who believed him and who would betray him.

That was a turning point for many as several left him and no longer walked with him. The Nazarene asked the twelve, "Are you going to leave me too?"

Peter responded, "Lord, who would we go to? You have the words of eternal life. We believe and are sure that you are the Christ, the Son of the living God."

"Haven't I chosen you? Yet one of you is a slanderer."

There was no response. However I wondered about that statement. What did he mean?

Furthermore, I wondered more and more about people, things and concepts. In the first place, my assignment was to monitor this strange John, gallivanting around and preaching. Not just preaching but preaching an unfamiliar message. After John, my assignment evolved into shadowing the Baptizer's cousin. In addition to the Baptizer and the Rabbi, I also faced the questions about other concepts—some old, some new, that caused me concern.

Take sin, for instance. What is it? How do I respond to it? And what about the concept of heaven? And what about this bread of life business and eating his flesh and drinking his blood?

After these things Jesus remained in Galilee because he knew the Jews in Judaea were out to kill him. Galilee's rugged terrain was inhabited by large numbers of war-like Zealots, so called because of their zeal against Rome. As far as the Romans were concerned, Galilee was all but unconquerable.

With the Jewish Feast of Passover drawing near and Jesus' brothers, who did not believe in him either, said, "Why don't you go to Judaea if you want your disciples to see the works that you are doing. Nobody does anything in secret if he's personally interested in being publicly recognized."

The Galilean said, "My time is not yet come. But your time and season are always at hand. The world can't hate you, but it does hate me, because I give the testimony about it, that the things that are done in it are evil. You go up to the festival; but as for me, the season when my time has fully ripened is still to come."

After the Rabbi said this, his brothers went up to the festival while he remained. The Jews were on the lookout for him at the festival. So he departed discretely for the festival so as not to draw attention to himself.

Many of the people murmured among themselves and some said, "He's a good man."

Yet others disagreed, "He's leading the people astray."

Most feared speaking openly about him because of their fear of the Jews. Halfway through the feast Jesus appeared and entered the Temple to teach. The Jews were astonished and said, "How can this man read? He's never been taught."

The Healer responded, "My teaching is not mine, but comes from the One who sent me. If anyone is prepared to do His will, he will know of the teaching, whether it originates of God or whether I speak of myself. When a man speaks of himself, he is seeking is own glory. But when he is working for the honor of the One who sent him, then he is sincere and no unrighteousness is in him. Didn't Moses give you the Law? And yet none of you keep the Law? But you criticize me for breaking it. Why are you trying to kill me?"

The crowd answered, "You must be mad! Who is trying to kill you?"

He alluded to their accusing him while being in violation themselves, "I have done one thing and you are all amazed at it. Moses gave you circumcision and you will circumcise a man even on the Sabbath. If a man receives the cutting of circumcision on the Sabbath to avoid breaking the Law of Moses, why should you be angry with me because I have made a man's body perfectly whole on the Sabbath? You must not judge by the appearance of things but by the reality!"

Some of the people of Jerusalem heard him and said, "Isn't this the man whom they are trying to kill? It's amazing—he talks quite openly and they haven't a word to say to him. Surely our rulers haven't decided that this really is Christ! But then, we know this man and where he comes from—when Christ comes, no one will know where he comes from."

In the middle of his teaching the Healer called out, "So you know me and know where I have come from. But I have not come of my own accord; I am sent by One who is true and you do not know Him! I do know Him, because I come from Him and He has sent me here."

I'm wondering if I should turn my attention to this person the Nazarene said sent him. *Maybe I should be monitoring that person.*

Many people said, "No man ever spoke like that."

But the Pharisees refuted them, "Has he pulled the wool over your eyes too? Have any of the authorities or the Pharisees believed in him? But this crowd, who know nothing about the Law, is damned anyway!"

I later learned from an agent that during a meeting of the Jewish council, Caiaphas the High Priest expressed wanting to be rid of Jesus. Some thought it was not yet time while others agreed with him. One of their number, Nicodemus, rose to speak on behalf of the Galilean. He was one of the most highly educated and influential members of the Pharisees. Because the Rabbi's authoritative manner and message had intrigued him, he had met with the Rabbi secretly one evening previously. And even though Nicodemus was a religious leader, he had questions about such things as heaven. Jesus had explained the difference between Jewish tradition and the new meaning of real living to Nicodemus.

In a clear, calm voice that echoed throughout the marble hall Nicodemus raised the question, "But surely our Law does not condemn the accused without hearing his defense where he is allowed to call reputable witnesses in order to determine the facts?"

Caiaphas, a sneer upon his lips emanating from the evil in his black heart, mocked Nicodemus, "Are you, too, a Galilean. We know nothing good comes out of Galilee. I'm surprised at you, sir. Perhaps you are suffering from some September madness."

They took a dig at Nicodemus, sarcastically slamming Galilee, "Look where you will—you won't find that any prophet comes out of Galilee." They laughed him down, broke up their meeting and went home, while he went off to the Mount of Olives.

The priests and rulers regularly tried to entrap the Rabbi and sent spies to report their findings to them.

It had become obvious to me that Jesus might be replacing the Baptizer and I decided it was time to meet with one of my informants. Perhaps he could shed some light on the Healer. As predetermined, I made my way to the local inn to dine and discuss events.

It was a strange day in a strange place and a strange event. Highlighted by a bedazzlingly bright rainbow and ushered in by a strong southeast wind, a low weather system enveloped the valley. Wanting to avoid getting soaked, I took shelter beneath the outstretched limbs of a giant oak tree. Every blast of *whooshing* wind rattled it. Hail pelted the red-brown earth, bouncing upward like so much popping corn, turning the ground white.

While the day wound down, the wind worked its magic—orchestrating the dark, ominous cloud cover. It was almost as if one of our storied Italian fresco painters teamed up with Apollo, producing a masterpiece for the ages. While heralding out the day, our god of the sky charged his chariot across the heavens, stopping long enough to dip his finger in a paint pallet. He nudged his horses slowly onward while mischievously running his hand across the canvas of sky, creating a mosaic that showcased the very pageantry of the heavens.

As the sun tiptoed to bed in the west, the passing storm morphed into a dazzling apricot sky, presenting a glorious pattern. Thirteen zebra-like ribbons of orange-gold-apricot clouds, bordered on either side by shades of blue sky, paralleled the valley.

Above my head a dark, steel gray lid stretched as far as the eye could see north and south. Adjoining that dark cloud, a cobalt blue sky embraced an apricot cloud. Beyond that cloud a brighter, lighter blue touched yet another cloud of silver-laced apricot. The pattern repeated itself till the sky met the earth in the west. As if by an out-of-control fire, the horizon lit up, spilling brilliant orange across the sky as the sun sank from sight.

The painted scene, if set to music, would be an anthem to the day. There was a certain wholesomeness—if not holiness—to this masterpiece.

This display of beauty amidst the storm kept my head swirling as I reached the inn. After we ordered our meal, I asked my snoop if he could tell me anything about the Nazarene."

"I guess the most amazing thing I can tell you is an unusual event I witnessed recently."

"How so?"

"I happened to be in the area, heard the Healer was about and sought him out. He was surrounded by a few thousand people on a hillside where he spoke to them. He mostly spoke about a coming kingdom."

"What kind of kingdom?

"He referred to it as the kingdom of God. He said it was a 'kingdom not of this world'."

"More specifically, what kind of kingdom?"

"All I can figure is that he meant a mental or spiritual kingdom. Something related to personal responsibility or being accountable for personal choices. He indicated they could become better people by practicing more loving behavior. Some of the concepts he addressed were simple while others were hard to understand."

"Give me an example."

"He said they should obey the government and respond kindly to anyone who persecuted them."

"Why would anyone be kind to someone who abused him?"

"I don't know. That's what seemed hard to fathom."

"Did he mention revolution or any sort of resistance against Rome?"

"No. He talked about being kind to everyone, but that's not all."

"Go on."

"The Healer showed kindness as people came to him with different ailments and he healed them."

"How so?"

"I have no words for it. A blind man received sight. A leper's body was restored. It was like magic. Some were healed when he spoke to them while others received healing when he touched them. The way he dealt with people in touch and manner reminded me of a mother. His concern and care for them was that of a loving mother for her ailing child, a mother who would do anything to see her child well. The key difference is that he was not a mother but a man...a man "mothering" the hurting.

"Did he speak unfavorably about the Romans?"

"Not at all. He made no mention of Roman governorship."

"Okay. Continue."

"The most unbelievable part to which I referred at the beginning was how he fed these people."

"What do you mean?"

"His disciples were hungry and wanted to dismiss the crowd and to eat. But he told them to feed the mob. They had but a little food, a few fish and loaves of bread. They remonstrated, whining about having nowhere near enough to feed the crowd. Claiming they would need to go to town to purchase food in order to feed that many people."

"And just exactly how did he plan to perform this task?"

"The Healer told them to arrange the people in groups of fifty. After that he looked up to the sky, mumbled some words and dispersed it. When the crowd finished eating, there were a dozen baskets of food left over."

"How do you explain this phenomenon? How could he feed that many people out in the country"

"I don't know. I can't explain it...unless it was an act of God."

After our delightful meal and update, I thanked my operative before he departed. I retired to my room and tried to sort through my thoughts about the Healer. The more I learn of him, the more puzzled I become. This singular god thing is confusing. I question the Prophet's claim to be the Son of God. How is this God different from the Roman gods?

Having grown up in a polytheistic culture, this one god concept is a whole new wrinkle for me—somewhat confusing if not troubling—and will take some thought and time to comprehend.

And this business about praying. When I heard about Jesus' recommended method of praying, I wondered about its meaning. He talked about "our Father in Heaven." I didn't know about his heaven. My people believe in immortality. After death we are buried with precious possessions including food and jewelry. Always a coin with which to pay Charon after Jupiter's son Mercury delivers us to him. The coin pays Charon to ferry us across the river Styx which flows nine times around the underworld.

Pluto rules the underworld where Minos, Aenaeus and Rhadymanthas judge the people, sending them to one of three destinations:

the Fields of Elysium for warriors or heros;

the Plain of Asphodel for average citizens;

or Tartarus for citizens who committed a crime—where they are tortured by the Furies until their debt has been paid to society.

Besides the differences in his god and mine and the praying, other preposterous, if not bizarre, activities surround this man. Things like a virgin birth and other things such as turning water into wine or converting a few loaves of bread and a couple of fish into enough food to feed thousands of men, not to mention women and children. I'm not sure if I'm getting closer to solving the puzzle so the search goes on.

The Nazarene travels with his twelve disciples and a few women who provided for him out of their own pockets—Mary Magdalene whom he cured of seven demons; Joanna, the wife of Herod's steward Chuza; Susanna and others.

His focus seems to have shifted a bit—from preaching extensively to the crowds to training the twelve. Because the twelve expected the Nazarene to deliver them from Rome, I guessed he was training them for that outcome. He asked them what they were hearing on the street about who he was. It sounds secretive to me, as if he is ratcheting up his revolutionary plan.

Nevertheless many consider him a prophet. Others think he is the Messiah. When he asked them who they thought he was, my interpretation was that he was going to instruct them in ways they could arouse the crowd to rebel against the Empire, removing those shackles from them. I figured I needed to re-double my efforts and to apprise my supervisor. I will renew my efforts to ferret who is meeting with him and what they're discussing. And it's time to dispatch my superior. I keep wondering what he thinks of all this unbelievable information I'm funneling to him.

While contemplating my dispatch I encountered Ananias, my carrier of choice and told him I would promptly have a dispatch for him. He seemed pretty excited and told me about a recent dispatch he'd taken and another he'd carried back. Both involved Jesus. Naturally he had my attention *post haste.*

He told me, "It seems the whole world is talking of this Jesus. Only recently I delivered a message from King Abgar of Mesopotamia to him. The king was overwhelmed that the Rabbi healed the sick and lame and gave eyesight to the blind; and he was excited to have the Rabbi treat him. Abgar let it be known that he believed Jesus was either God or the Son of God. The king has suffered from a lasting illness and, having heard of Jesus' reputation, requested an audience with the Nazarene. The king was excited about the possibilities of improving his health and being made whole.

"When I delivered the letter to the Prophet, he had me wait to return his reply to the king. And when I returned to Abgar with the Rabbi's response, the king let it be known that Jesus was unable to attend him but that he would send another in his place directly."

"How is it that you learned the contents of the dispatch?"

"The king was so convinced the Healer could treat him, that he told me his hopes as I prepared to leave to find the Healer."

"And?"

"When I returned the Healer's dispatch to the king, he shared his disappointment that Jesus was unable to come but that his hopes were renewed. The bad news was that Jesus couldn't comply but the good news was that he would send a representative to cure the king's illness as well as his family's." (see Appendix 1)

This account left me wondering yet again. The Master claims to help but here chooses not to. *What could his refusal mean?* Ananias took my dispatch and I moved on.

CHAPTER 8 — Strange Encounter

Before I reached the northern shore of the lake of Galilee, I heard from one of my informers a story that had considerable social, political and religious ramifications. It was no secret that the Jews and Samaritans disliked each other. Hated might be a better word. Contemptuous of the Samaritans whom they considered crude and immoral, the sanctimonious Jews traditionally avoided Samaritan country, walking around Samaria so as not to defile themselves. Jews never spoke to Samaritans. Whereas they didn't want to risk "catching" anything from the Samaritans, it appeared the Galilean would go to any lengths to help.

For whatever reason, Jesus purposely chose the north road from Judea to Galilee, taking him directly through Samaria. Took all morning to walk the hot, dusty road. Walnut and olive groves surrounded the group and red anemones carpeted the ground as his group trudged toward Sychar. They looked forward to cool, fresh drinking water from the Well of Sychar, water spoken of highly by the locals and sojourners. And they anticipated the reward of rest in the shade of trees near the well.

Although my contact was not privy to the conversation, he managed to get a reasonable understanding of what took place; he learned the Rabbi told the lady things that he would not have known unless he knew her or were privy to her doings. And he summarized the event.

Around noon the Rabbi and his band reached Sychar, tired, thirsty and hungry. While his followers went on into the village to purchase food, the Galilean waited by Jacob's well, 150-feet deep and dug 150 years previous. It never ceased to flow, providing spring fed wonderful water. Expecting someone to come extract water from the well, the Rabbi rested comfortably upon the ground in a tree's shade.

The columned temple stood atop Mount Gerizim, a robin egg blue sky beyond while shimmering heat waves rose from the surrounding earth. There was no human traffic until footsteps announced to the Rabbi that someone approached. It was not long before a Samaritan woman appeared, a traditional large clay pot balanced upon her head. She wore common clothing of the community, nothing special nor eye catching: an outer tunic with fine multicolored needlework, colorful silk belt and headdress and soft leather sandals.

Social mores demanded silence between strangers of the opposite sex. In addition to the gender deference was the Samaritan-Jew divide. Nevertheless Jesus surprised the woman by requesting that she provide him water—a Jew asking a Samaritan woman, no less, for a drink. It was absolutely taboo…and shocking.

My operative had knowledge of the woman's character and speculated the Prophet was there to do business with her, the kind of business she was known for. Whereas women came to the well in the cool of the evening, she had come during the mid-day no doubt to avoid association with the decent women of the town. Momentarily surprised by the discovery of Jesus, she continued toward the well. It was then Jesus engaged her, "I wonder if you might give me a drink of water?"

What an odd thing to ask.

She readily recognized him as a Jew; she was a Samaritan.

He was a man; she a woman.

Recognizing both situations highly unusual and stunned by the Galilean's request, she asked him, "How is it that you, a Jew, ask a drink of me, a woman of Samaria?"

"If you knew who is asking you for a drink, you would have asked him instead. Then he would have given you living water."

"But sir, you have nothing to draw with and the well is deep. Where do you get that living water? Are you greater than our father Jacob who gave us the well and drank from it himself, as did his sons and his cattle?"

"Everyone who drinks this water will thirst again, but the water I offer quenches all thirst. It brings eternal life."

"Sir, give me this water, that I may not thirst, nor come here to draw."

"Go, call your husband, and come here."

"I have no husband."

"That's true. You have had five husbands and the man you now live with is not your husband."

The Healer allowed her to lead the conversation and replied to her concerns, awaiting the opportunity to meet her needs.

All the more amazed by this stranger, she said, "Sir, I perceive that you are a prophet. Our fathers worshiped on this mountain. Jerusalem is the place where men ought to worship."

"Woman, believe me, you will worship the Father neither on this mountain nor in Jerusalem. You worship what you do not know. We worship what we know, for salvation is from the Jews. But the hour is coming, and now is, when the true worshippers will worship the Father in spirit and truth, for such the Father seeks to worship him. God is spirit, and those who worship him must worship in spirit and truth."

Because she'd never heard such things from the priests of her own people or the Jews, she was impressed. She recognized that this man knew her, yet he did not condemn her. He merely told her past and presented her with concepts previously unknown or unacceptable to her...

that a Jew could share the same well with a Samaritan;

that he could know her past as no man had;

that he could offer her living and eternal water.

*Hmmmm…*she wondered…*could this man be the Messiah?* She stated proudly, "I know that the Messiah called Christ is coming. When he comes, he will show us all things."

"The man speaking to you now is he."

Before she could respond and with no little surprise to her understanding, the disciples arrived. Although they were somewhat startled to see the Healer speaking with a Samaritan, a woman at that, no one said anything or asked him any questions about her.

Leaving her water jar, the woman returned to the city.

In her absence the disciples asked him to eat but he told them he had food. When they wondered how he had acquired it, he told them his food was to do the will of Him who sent him.

Meanwhile the lady reached the city, a crowd gathered and she eagerly shared, "Come. I just met a man who told me all that I ever did. Is it possible he is the Christ?"

Her words touched them. Those who knew her and her reputation observed a changed countenance about her. They read a new beginning in her body language.

They wanted to meet the man and followed her back to the well. Many of them believed in the Galilean because of her words. Many more believed because of his words and told her, "It is no longer because of your words that we believe, for we have heard for ourselves. And we know that this is indeed the Savior of the world."

They invited him to stay with them, which he did for two days. More people believed when they heard for themselves. Samaritans believed the Messiah would restore the world.

I wondered how this Jew from Nazareth could justify entering a Samaritan village, entertaining a Samaritan woman…but mostly I wondered how in the world he knew her past.

Contrary to established Jewish tradition, it was patently obvious that Jesus chose to deal with situations using a common sense approach, much different from the staid ways of the Jews. I deduced that he had demonstrated considerable intellect and cunning.

The lady must have been totally dumbfounded when she told the Galilean she expected the Messiah and he told her he was he! And I caught myself wondering about this "living water" and the "Father's will as food." Seems like I am taking more notes in my journal about concepts than I am about events. I'm forced to ask myself again, is it possible he is the promised

Messiah? And if so, militarily?

DISPATCH: Superior Flavius Diusus Caldus,

I recently heard of the Galilean's presence in Samaria. An amazing circumstance in light of the Jew-Samarian situation. But of a more serious nature was his message. He suggested a trade—he would give a Samaritan woman something in exchange for the water she provided him. For the water she gave him to drink he would give her what he called living water. How could he when he had nothing with which to fetch the water?

She was intrigued. I was intrigued! Then he began to air her dirty laundry about the five men to whom she was not married. And he mentioned the sixth man with whom she was living.

When I heard about this, I marveled yet at another example of his success in human skills. It has become quite obvious to me that a portion of his success lies in the fact that he is a listener. And he speaks the language of the listener. He relates to people either one to one or in group settings. He speaks simply yet profoundly. He engages people through is magnetic personality, his charisma and his sincerity. In his way he provides them a platform from which to evoke their personal pride and/or happiness. He seems to find joy when they are happy. And they seem to be happy when he accepts them and showers them with his attention.

Not long after hearing about the Samaritan woman at the well, I had a most interesting and what could have proved fatal experience. Threading my way through the carts, camels and sojourners one mid-morning while walking the roadway I heard a shrill scream and bolted up a slight incline on my right to investigate.

I'd barely covered half dozen yards, the tune of more wailing serenading my ears, when I topped the knoll. My peripheral vision caught movement. A soldier sailed through the air covering some ten feet before hitting the ground in a dust cloud. Then I noticed a large male lion. Fifteen yards beyond me another soldier approached the lion face-on with a spear in hand. Another spear lay on the ground a dozen feet away and between the downed soldier and me. *Must be the other soldier's* I thought.

At any rate the lion stood over the man on the ground, mouthing his head and trying to close its jaws on it. A great relief must have flooded over the soldier as his helmet protected his head. Nevertheless the lion continued its attempt to grip his head while the man moaned and called for help. Drawing his knees to his chest, he attempted to roll away from the cat. A drumbeat of mixed roaring and shouting filled the air…"Dinus! Dinus? Help me. Dinus!"

Amidst the din, time slowed considerably. So slowly that I noted every action.

Something was unusual, almost out of place. Normally a lion kills by suffocating its prey, often by swatting to stun the prey then placing its mouth over the animal's. However this one seemed skittish by comparison...almost reluctant.

For some reason, perhaps the presence of three men around it caused it concern. Or maybe the cat was injured. In all probability it had never suffocated a man. It was obviously in poor condition.

Tail twitching, the scrawny cat stopped its efforts to bite the soldier and looked quickly from the other soldier to me, then back at the soldier...and, again, at me. It then returned its attention to the man on the ground, trying to gain purchase on his head. The victim continued groaning and yelling for help, curling into a fetal position and trying to fend off the cat with his fisted arms.

Simultaneously the soldier with the spear and I moved—he, toward the lion...I, toward the spear on the ground. With a roar of defiance the beast launched itself toward the spearman. Somehow the man ducked as the cat sailed over him. The soldier quickly turned to face the animal just as I reached the spear. By now the cat had recovered and started to turn. At that moment the soldier tossed his spear at it. The animal roared as the blade sunk beyond its full length into its side. Immediately the soldier pulled his sword from its sheath.

Having moved closer to the beast, I prepared to meet it gripping the spear in both hands at my right waist, left hand forward on the shaft. I rushed the lion, ramming the spear's blade behind the brute's left shoulder. I struggled while holding onto my spear and hoped to keep the lion as far from me as possible.

The cat reacted like a single 200-pound muscle, thrashing and roaring. Although it was still full of fight, its strength ebbed noticeably. It spun around, trying to pull free from my spear. The other spear, sticking in its side, struck the standing soldier, the impact sending him spinning.

It was difficult to hang onto the spear and keep my balance so I let go and pulled my blade with my right hand. I was determined to dodge the cat's charge, grab a handful of mane in my left hand and swing onto its back as if mounting a horse. I could then thrust my blade into its neck or side at will.

The mangy lion glowered at me, tail lashing back and forth. The injured man lay close by. Escaping the cat's notice, the soldier with the sword arose. At that moment with me as a distraction, my fellow rescuer raised his sword and brought it down onto the lion's back, severing the spinal cord and effectively paralyzing its hind quarters.

Blood flowed from its spear and sword wounds as muted roars escaped the beast's throat. Though it tried to reach its antagonist with its forepaws clutching the earth and pulling its immobilized rear quarters, it bled out and in moments we heard its death rattle.

By now the ruckus had aroused troops on the road and some came rushing to check out the commotion. A couple of them turned and ran back. Before long, help arrived in the form of more soldiers.

My fellow rescuer Baldinus and I rushed to the injured man. By some miraculous means he was still alive and conscious though wounded and bleeding. I was surprised by his minimal injuries. There was no arterial bleeding. Puncture wounds on his chest, back and legs oozed blood.

My compatriot spoke with his friend and I was pleased that more soldiers arrived. They came to a halt near us and a couple of men ran toward the injured man, carrying materials to be used in stanching the blood or bandaging his wounds. One was a medic who took charge and attended the injured man while others stood nearby prepared to carry their mate to the roadway on a litter they'd brought.

Thanks to the great Greek medical doctor Hippocrates who said, "He who desires to practice surgery must go to war," we have learned from the Greeks. We adapted and surpassed their medical system which rivals our military.

Realizing the value of healthy legions, Emperor Augustus had established the first military medical school. Our medical personnel learned that boiling water sterilized forceps and scalpels. They learned the use of tourniquets, catheters and clamps as well as sedatives and painkillers in the form of opium and henbane seeds.

Over the years we developed sterile services where our men were treated by *optio valentudinarii* at legion fortresses (medical people who ran hospitals).

Our wounded soldiers were cared for by *capsarri* or medics who carried bandage boxes. No doubt when the mauled man reaches the fortress, a *medicus* or medical officer will oversee his treatment.

While considering our medical supremacy and soldiers, it was interesting to note that our foot soldiers were nicknamed Marius' mules. So named because they resembled those pack animals in that they, too, carried their equipment on their backs in "T"-shaped packs. The animals were spaced after every eighth soldier and carried gear for the group. They were quite the sight, reminding me of some of my former forays into the country. So here was a group of men and mules on their way somewhere, which worked out well for the attack victim.

A few others and I observed the dead lion. I was saddened to see the king of beasts in this deplorable condition. It was half the size of a mature male. Something was seriously wrong. Its two upper fangs were broken as were some lower teeth. The remaining teeth were worn to the gum line. I had no doubt the non-fatal injuries sustained by the soldier were greatly attributable to the animal's damaged teeth as well as several broken and/or missing claws. It was missing tufts of hair and had a couple of long unhealed gashes on its shoulders and other lacerations emitting puss. That was the first time I noticed the rank smell of the animal, no doubt its injuries partially caused its condition. The lion seemed to have attacked from hunger.

The medical man quickly examined the wounds, establishing they were not fatal, then dabbed and wiped blood from them. He cleaned them and applied the antiseptic acetum, some healing herbs and bound the worst ones with a poultice of either fenugreek or figs to counter the bleeding and pain and to induce healing. Once the medic had him stabilized for transport, his fellow soldiers placed their hands palm up under him and raised him while two others slid a litter beneath him. The bearers gently lowered him onto the litter and all six took a grip and walked in march step toward the roadway.

I followed and observed their loading him into an ambulance wagon. Baldinus wanted to cut off a lion's paw as a souvenir for his friend and stayed behind to accomplish that task. Meanwhile my thoughts turned to the Galilean.

It seems the more I see and hear about him, the more I wonder about his ancestry and his motives. He does not impress me as an arrogant ego-maniac trying to rally against the Empire. It was becoming apparent to me that he polarizes people—either they love him or hate him. It appears the haters are mostly numbered among the religious leaders.

He speaks simply and directly. People relate to his words. He meets people on their own ground. The Galilean gets results. He doesn't flap his lips to hear himself speak; he acts.

Speaking of acting, I recently took action to assist my hunger, dropping into an inn to have a noon meal. I had learned to be a little more selective in my choice of eating places. I had come to experience a vast difference between reputable inns and what I called "slaughter house" inns. The former did not house animals next to the inn proper. I realize there is nothing wrong with that arrangement, I just felt many an inn with adjacent animal lodging bore the smell of the animal, often on the hands or attire of the host or cook.

While awaiting my meal, I caught myself thinking about the Nazarene. There is something about him…something I can't explain. But I'm processing it. I had taken a table next to two Roman soldiers. I'm guessing they had taken time out from their patrol to have a bite of food. As usual I found myself eavesdropping and hoping they might discuss the Rabbi. I might add, it was most interesting.

Here they were, Roman soldiers, eating Greek food, drinking fruit from the vine and—as it turns out— discussing the Nazarene. The one with the gruff voice acknowledged, "Even if he ain't the Messiah the Jewish religion eggspects, this man's teachings are astounding. He tells listeners if they are abused, mistreated or put upon by others, their reaction should be to change their natural bent for revenge and pray for those what persecuted them. Even to love them abusers. How unusual is that?"

His companion, a slight man with a big nose responded, "It seems unusual. Definitely unnatural."

Gruff Voice continued, "When an oppressed person responds in a kind, loving manner, it totally disarms the abuser. I actually seen it work. Remember that obnoxious, foul mouthed soldier what nearly killed the young recruit a while back?"

"You mean the Animal?"

"Yep. He ain't none too smart."

"That guy is heartless."

Gruff remarked, "One day on the byway I come across a woman with a young kid. She had just picked him up offun the ground. She examined him, discovered he was uninjured, brushed dust from his clothes and spoke to him. Seems the Animal had kicked their donkey as it passed and the burro bucked and kicked, pitching the kid from its back.

"Although he was unhurt physically, the boy wondered out loud about the soldier's action. The kid wanted justice. I heard the mother say, 'We must practice the teachings of the Master. He told us to pray for those who are mean to us and to find love in our hearts in order to treat them lovingly.'

"She then approached the soldier, a look of smugness upon his face, and apologized to him for upsetting him. I watched him as he noticeably softened and explained that it weren't her fault. And, get this…he apologized to her."

"That had to be a first."

"It was pretty amazing. I've never knowed that soldier to do nothing but prod and provoke others. I can't explain his actions no other way."

Here was yet another second hand story I needed to add to my growing list of considerations regarding the Nazarene.

When I first came to Israel, I tried to be objective, to take in the language and activities of the area, to catalogue them without making any snap judgments. It became increasingly apparent to me that the Pharisees despised the Prophet's simplicity.

They ignored his miraculous activities demanding some sort of sign from him to prove to them that he was the Son of God. On the other hand, the Samaritans asked for no sign. They believed that the Messiah would come as the Redeemer, not just to the Jews but for the entire world. I struggle to understand what this salvation game is all about.

The Rabbi's compassion, understanding and tolerance to all whom he met began bridging the divide between Jew and Gentile, diminishing the Pharisaic customs of Israel. He ate at their tables, slept under their roofs, taught in their streets and treated them kindly.

He was familiar with the Temple at Jerusalem since childhood, where the low wall separated all other portions of the sacred Temple from the outer court. That wall contained inscriptions in diverse languages declaring that only Jews were permitted beyond this wall. He knew that Gentiles who trespassed into the Temple would defile it and pay with their lives. Jesus' work among the Samaritans drew them to him, availing his salvation to them—the very salvation that the Jews rejected.

His activities among the Samaritans was an eye opener to the disciples who labored under the Jewish tradition of bias toward the Samaritans. His followers thought they were to be loyal to their nation while demonstrating enmity toward the Samaritans.

Realizing more and more that He addressed them as no other could or had, people flocked to hear him. His words reflected his knowledge and understanding of the laws and institutions of Israel, exceeding that of the priests and rabbis. He addressed the realities of life today and in the future, breaking through barriers of formalism and tradition.

Because he spoke with the authority of the Law, his stories were new and different and people related to them. He shed light on the teachings of the patriarchs and prophets and the holy word came alive. They'd never been taught nor perceived the depth of meaning in the word of God.

They were rejuvenated at the possibility of living, not just existing. Hearers were impressed with the way he preached.

Since hundreds sought the Healer's help, it was common for many to be turned away at the synagogue on the Sabbath when he appeared.

One day as the Galilean spoke in the synagogue of the kingdom he had come to establish and the plan to set the captives free from Satan, a man caught in the grip of an evil spirit rushed forward shrieking, "What have you come to do with us, Jesus of Nazareth? Have you come to destroy us? I know who you are, the Holy One of God."

People stared, awestruck by the situation. What was going on?

The Rabbi cut him short speaking sharply, "Hold your tongue and get out of him."

The man's body shook and he fell to the ground, writhing and thrashing in the grip of the demonic spirit. He screamed with a loud voice and the spirit left him. The man rose, free from the demon's bondage. He praised God for his deliverance, he who had of late demonstrated insanity now appeared intelligent and beaming with joy.

I wondered, *what in the world is going on?* And others stood amazed. Dumbfounded might be a better word for it. In an effort to understand they asked each other questions—"What is this, a new teaching? The results are amazing." They marveled that his authority commanded even the unclean spirits which obeyed him. I had to wonder about the unclean spirits and even how in the world they could know perfectly well who this man was.

As I approached the village of Cana, people flocked to the Healer, seeking his succor. It turns out that a Jewish nobleman, a courtier of the king's court in the locale, sought out the Nazarene. The man's son hovered at the point of death, suffering from an incurable disease.

The man was a member of society's upper crust. A rich man of great assets with access to the best doctors in Capernaum, a town noted for its medical men and a health resort known throughout the Middle East for its mineral springs. Also available were the latest medications and health prescriptions.

Physicians had given up on the child, knowing that his eventual healing was out of their hands. However when the nobleman heard that Rabbi was near and having tried all else, he sought him out to cure his son, trudging cross country in search of the Healer. Eventually he found a throng surrounding the Galilean.

Pressing through the crowd, he beheld the Rabbi and wondered if a man dressed so plainly—disheveled and weary from travel—could accomplish the task the nobleman sought. He doubted the Rabbi could heal his son. Nevertheless he secured an interview with the Miracle Worker.

He told Jesus of his need and requested the Rabbi to accompany him to his home.

The nobleman was totally unaware that the Prophet knew his needs and his son's situation even before the official had left his home. And that he knew the official expected a sign as essential to accepting him as the Messiah.

The Deliverer wanted both to heal the child and to bring his healing balm to the man, his household and community. The Rabbi asked the man if he needed a sign or an omen before he believed. Possibly he was trying to teach the crowd that there was more to him and life than performing miracles.

The nobleman realized immediately that Rabbi saw through him. He knew that his reticence might cost the life of his son. He hastily requested of the Nazarene "come or my child will die." He wanted desperately for the Healer to accompany him to Capernaum.

But the Healer told him to "go home; your son lives." The nobleman believed that his son would be restored, but also he trusted the Rabbi to be the Messiah. His word of assurance was enough for the man. He needed no further proof.

While the nobleman was with Jesus, those beside the child's bed continued watching for any sign of improvement. It was during that time that they noticed a change in the child. His face changed from the darkness of death to the light of life. During the heat of the day the fever-plagued face evolved into a soft glow of healthfulness. The dim eyes brightened. Strength returned to the emaciated body. His fevered flesh became soft and moist and he fell into a healing sleep.

The next morning while walking home, the nobleman met his servants and asked his people when the fever broke. They told him that his son was healed at the very moment the Galilean announced to him that "your son will live."

That day when he reached home, he rejoiced with his son. The nobleman wished to learn more of the Rabbi and in time his entire household became followers of the Prophet. And the healing and transformation of that family laid the groundwork for many wonderful accomplishments in Capernaum for the Master's ministry.

CHAPTER 9—Eliazar

Traveling religious men stopped at the local synagogue, the community meeting place where children studied the *Torah*. Thus it was that the Nazarene visited his hometown and read from the holy scroll in the synagogue. He had gained considerable attention and decided to return to his hometown, no doubt thrilled to visit old shops and to see old friends and acquaintances.

When he arrived in the village where he had grown up, he probably went to his childhood home to greet his mother and she greeted him warmly. And his brothers and sisters came to see him, talking about his many exciting activities since he'd left…the rumors they'd heard and the things that they knew. They wanted to know what he'd done and where he'd been.

The next day he appeared in town where tongues wagged over his rumored activities. Some felt they'd let him down. Others were unimpressed with this son of Joseph the carpenter. They expected him to be bigger or dressed better. He did not meet some expectations; and surpassed others'. Human nature prevailed—the complainers complained; the optimistic were positive.

The Rabbi went into the synagogue on the Sabbath to teach his mother, brothers and disciples. The congregants were amazed as his words rang with authority unlike the scribes. The elders and scribes labored with cold, formal lessons resembling rote learning. They felt the word of God held no vital power. They substituted their own traditions and ideas, professing to explain the law. But no inspiration from God stirred them. Consequently the people were unmoved.

But it was different with the Rabbi. Many acknowledged, "No man ever spoke like this." An elder read from the prophets, exhorting the people to hope for the Coming One who would banish oppression. He encouraged them of the Messiah's near arrival. Customarily, when a rabbi was in the synagogue, he was asked to present a sermon. Consequently they asked Jesus to do so.

He stood up to read and was given the scroll of the ancient prophet Isaiah. He carefully unrolled it until he came to the sixty-first chapter and read, "The Spirit of the Lord is upon me, because He has anointed me to preach good news to the poor. He has sent me to proclaim release to the captives and recovering of sight to the blind, to set at liberty those who are oppressed, to proclaim the acceptable year of the Lord."

A great hush fell upon the congregants, every eye riveted to this child-become-man whom they knew.

The Galilean continued, "Doubtless you will quote me this proverb, 'Physician, heal yourself; what we have heard you did at Capernaum, do here also in your own country.' Truly, no prophet is accepted in his own country. I tell you, there were many widows in Israel in the days of Elijah, when the heaven was shut up three years and six months when there came a great famine over the entire land. Elijah was sent to none of them but only to Zarephath, in the land of Sidon, to a woman who was a widow. And there were many lepers in Israel in the time of the prophet Elisha. None of them was cleansed, but only Naaman the Syrian.

"I come to my own and my own would not have me. I call to you but you will not come. You simply don't believe in me. In a word, you have no confidence, no faith."

He concluded, his final nine words slicing like a sharp sword, "Today this scripture has been fulfilled in your hearing."

He returned the scroll to the attendant before sitting down. The eyes of the congregants followed him.

They were moved as the Nazarene spoke. He assured them that the Messiah would liberate the captives. He would heal the sick and restore the sight of the blind. He would bring the light of truth to the world.

His message was brief but to the point. Pregnant with meaning. Those in attendance were spellbound—in awe and full of wonderment by his words. They had never heard words that rang with such conviction.

These Israelite children of Abraham let his words sink in. Words of their bondage as prisoners trapped in the darkness of evil and to be delivered into the light of truth. But their initial amazement gave way to doubt.

Their fears were aroused and their pride offended. They wondered aloud...

"Who is this Jesus?"

"Isn't this Joseph's boy?"

"He's a neighborhood kid who grew up among us."

"He claims to be the Messiah yet is the son of a common carpenter."

They questioned his words. They knew him. He had grown up right here in Nazareth. They knew his brothers and sisters. More questions arose...

"How could he be the Promised One?"

"How could he be the Messiah?"

"What special consideration should he get, wasn't he a carpenter?"

Though his life was spotless, they could not see him as the Promised One.

They concluded that he had no real credentials.

Their amazement turned to anger. They were indignant, realizing that they had departed from God thus forfeiting their claim to be His people. They cried out against the Rabbi, their voices rising as one. These who prided themselves in keeping the Law were offended.

They rose up in fury and pushed him out of the synagogue. This must have been a far cry from the joyous days he'd had as a youth contemplating sunsets, playing with other children, the sensual experiences of freshly sythed hay on the breeze with spring flowers blooming nearby and rain falling on the newly turned soil.

A roar ascended from the crowd. Some threw stones. They cursed. Some kicked at him. They jostled and shoved him up the street toward a cliff on which the city was built, planning to throw him from it.

Suddenly he was gone. Vanished from the mass. He passed through the midst of them and went away ghostlike. Like a lion among jackals, the Lion of Judah WAS among them. Had they understood what he said about a prophet's rejection in his own country and that this was his final visit to his birthplace, perhaps some would have reacted differently.

Two days later he departed for Galilee. Having been at the wedding feast in Jerusalem and seen all that he had done there, the Galileans welcomed him.

Another interesting story I heard involved a leper. Traditionally leprosy was considered a direct result of the leper's sin. I recalled my conversation with Ariella. Lepers were considered unclean and shut out from other human companionship and they were required to announce their disability to others they approached, "unclean, unclean!" Customarily people avoided a leper with no desire to be so afflicted.

However a leper who had appeared before the Pharisees and doctors many times approached Jesus. Because they considered his illness a direct result of sin, they refused his pleas, considering him incurable.

When the leper saw the Deliverer, he fell to his face on the ground and beseeched him, "Lord, if you want to, you can make me clean."

The leper showed typical signs of his illness. He was unkempt, his filthy and ragged clothing covering his body. Rotting skin and open wounds pockmarked his body. And he smelled foully. To say he was in wretched condition is understatement. How could anyone stand to be around him? Essentially the Pharisees condemned him where he stood, having nothing to do with him. However the Galilean was another story.

Perhaps surprising everyone present except himself and with a voice that sounded full of pity, the Master reached out his hand and placed it on the leper. In response to the leper's "if you want to," he simply stated, "I want. Be clean."

In the twinkling of an eye the leprosy left. Immediately the leper's skin changed, a soft glow similar to that of a healthy child, took its place.

The Healer told the leper to tell no one about his healing and instructed him to "go show yourself to the priest and offer for your cleansing what Moses commanded, for a proof to the people." Once he'd been accepted, the leper would be able to return to his family with no further uncleanness of body or community.

Overjoyed, the man left and talked freely of his experience, telling everyone his story. The effect was so great that the numbers of people in the city looking for the Healer increased and he was forced to remain on the outskirts healing in the less crowded areas. After he had healed many, he withdrew into the wilderness to be alone in prayer.

He knew the Pharisees criticized him because his teaching was contrary to their traditions and the Jewish leaders had hired spies against him, yet his response demonstrated his compassion, his respect for the Law and his power to deliver from sin and death. And when Jewish leaders criticized the Prophet, the crowd defended him by asking, "What do you expect the Messiah to do that this man hasn't done?"

Coming into Capernaum one day at the height of his popularity, he was nearly mobbed. As time passed, larger and larger crowds wanting to see him flocked from all over the known world—Libya, Egypt, Arabia, Persia, Mesopotamia, Greece and Rome. Roads and byways were clogged with people, clamoring to hear Jesus or to entreat him to heal their illnesses.

The disciples regained hope. Until now the Galilean had been rejected and even threatened with death. Yet here in Capernaum things were changing.

Some time later while in the marketplace I bumped into Eliazar. Our meeting brought to memory our first encounter some months previous. That's when I found myself one evening in an ale house listening to him and his friends discuss affairs of the world, so to speak. Although I'd guarded my drinking in order to preserve my identity and I chose not to become chummy with anyone, Eliazar's charismatic nature captivated me. Almost in spite of myself I was drawn to him. Although his given name was Eliazar, his buddies called him Eli. So Eli became a drinking acquaintance. I had occasion to see him a few more times in the ale house and to learn a bit about him.

He had come from a family of some affluence. Gotten tired of the home life and wanted to see the big city. He talked his father into giving him his inheritance and though his father loved him dearly, he granted his little boy his freedom. Albeit his older brother made him the laughing stock and was jealous and angry with the father's decision.

Eli had come to the city and enjoyed the high, nightlife with new found friends. One evening Eli bemoaned his choices and admitted that he wanted to go back home and hoped that his father would understand and accept him. He swore that he would go home but he wasn't ready to return just yet.

On more than one occasion I'd seen Eli leave the ale house to find ladies from the street. Although he always seemed in good spirits and good health, it was my understanding that he'd just about spent all his money. He seemed most content every time I'd ever seen him, even the night I saw him engage a woman on the street and they entered a nearby building. You'd have to be blind or stupid or both to not know what was going on in the streets—with brothels and the like. That's the last time I saw Eli so I was eager to hear his story.

Here in the marketplace he greeted me warmly and asked how I'd been. He admitted he'd experienced a new beginning since our last meeting. He eagerly launched into his story about encountering the Nazarene.

"I had sunk to the lowest I'd ever been. Seemed like I was living in a bottomless pit. It got so bad that I was slopping hogs and even eating their food at times. I wanted to go back to my homeland. I was disgusted with myself and wanted to regain my self-esteem. I was at rock bottom. When I thought I was at my lowest, it got even worse. One morning I awoke and couldn't move. I didn't know what was going on but I had my suspicions. No one seemed to want to have anything to do with me except my friends. They came by that day and found me paralyzed.

"The pompous scribes claimed to know both my ailment and its cause. They figured I got what I had coming to me—that I'd sowed the wind and reaped the whirlwind…that my promiscuous living had finally caught up with me, culminating in my just desserts.

"They denied me help when I sought it.

"They offered me neither sympathy nor hope.

"They told me I suffered the curse of God for my sinfulness.

"They pointed their fingers at my evil nature without recognizing their own—without taking into account that they were no better than I."

I asked Eli if it were possible he'd been misdiagnosed or if he may have suffered a temporary paralysis.

"All I know is that I was incapable of movement for several days. Doctors' treatments did nothing for me. I was desperate and completely dependent upon others. I had heard about Jesus and pleaded with my friends to take me to him, hoping the things I'd heard about him were true and that he would take kindly to me.

"They carried me in my bed to the house of Peter where Jesus was preaching. We learned Jesus' disciples were inside clustered around him while Pharisees and doctors of the law sat nearby—representing every town throughout Galilee and Judaea, even the city of Jerusalem. Some of the religious leaders were spies, seeking an accusation against Jesus. Whereas the Pharisees and doctors felt no sense of need and that the healing wasn't for them, others from surrounding nations clamored to get inside. But it wasn't happening. Unable to push their way through the crowd, my friends wondered what they could do.

"I was devastated. I was so close...so close to the Master and his healing touch. But it seemed even more hopeless. I couldn't let it end like this. I looked about in frustration and disappointment. What could we do? We discussed the dilemma and decided on a daring maneuver. At my urging, my pals carried me up the outside stairs, prepared to remove tiles from the roof. I was desperate enough to try anything.

"One by one, they removed tiles. They rigged a rope to my pallet and, once they'd created a hole large enough to gain access to the room below, they lowered me and my pallet toward Jesus.

"As they lowered me into the room suspended from ropes, my senses heightened. Things slowed down. People inside chattered away, excited to be with Jesus, oblivious of the activity above. When they saw me, their chatter ceased. A cataclysmic change occurred. Jesus commanded the situation.

"In that moment I knew that Jesus saw what no one else saw. He seemed to know more about the cause of my paralysis than anyone in the room. Having grown up in Nazareth where wild living was common, he knew that such living had its consequences. In this world of prodigals and prostitutes Jesus knew about the young girls sucked into the skin trade. And He knew that young men followed them. Yet he did not condemn me nor did he question me. As I suspected, if my condition was contracted from a venereal disease and was incurable, what hope had I other than Jesus?

"When Jesus saw my faith, he demonstrated his power—not only to heal my body but also my soul. He was only too eager to instill this power on my behalf. With compassion he broke the muted silence. He spoke unapologetically...loving and healing words, 'Take heart, my son, your sins are forgiven.'

"Shocked beyond belief, I lay there in blissful silence, too happy for words. Tears filled my eyes. Joy filled my heart. It had happened. To me a worthless, wasted life.

"Then, as surely as the crowd stood watching in disbelief as to what was happening before their eyes, I stood up. Never had this crowd witnessed such a recovery. They—as I— puzzled at the meaning of his words 'your sins are forgiven.' I can't explain it, but I was healed outside and inside.

"A mild uproar occurred among the religious leaders who questioned Jesus' words and behavior, 'What? Why does this man speak this way?' They accused Jesus of blasphemy, claiming only God could forgive sins. They were hot because Jesus spoke on his own authority, not theirs, not quoting some human authority but the authority given him by God!

"He used the term *abba* in reference to his father, a term denoting intimacy between a child and his father—meaning Father dearest...even,

Daddy, if you will.

"Boy, that got their blood boiling. Several responded adamantly.

"'It is blasphemy! Who can forgive sins but God only?'

"'Who is he trying to fool?'

"'What does he mean, playing God Almighty?'

"'What's he trying to prove?'

"However Jesus saw things through different eyes. He read their thoughts and said, 'Talk's cheap. Let me put it another way. Why must you argue in your minds? Do you suppose it is easier to tell a paralyzed man his sins are forgiven or to tell him to get up, pick up his bed and walk?'

"After giving them some time to think about his question, Jesus addressed their concerns compassionately to me, 'But that you may know that the Son of Man has authority on earth to forgive sins, I say to you, get up. Pick up your bed. Go home.'

"And that's exactly what I did. I picked up my bed and moved off through the multitude carrying my pallet as if it were a pillow. And I blessed God at every step.

"I had renewed physical strength—a spring in my step, my arms working in unison, my lifeless gray skin now fresh and ruddy. I was full of joy. I AM full of joy. Surely others must have been as shocked as can be imagined when they observed the change and the countenance on my face.

"At first the crowds were afraid and then glorified God. Awestruck by the event, people made room for me and whispered among themselves, 'We have seen strange things today. We have never seen anything like this.'"

Happy for his healthy condition but still pursuing the possibility of Jesus' being a threat to Rome, I asked, "Eli, what is your best guess as to the Nazarene's motive?"

"I think he revels in people's happiness. He seems overjoyed to help others. He is not paid nor does he seek payment."

"You're saying he's content to provide healing. Nothing else?"

"He's shown no other inclination."

"So, what are your plans now?"

"I will be going home as soon as I earn enough money to purchase clothing and other items to freshen up for the trip."

As I left him in the marketplace, I said, "I wish you well, my friend."

I heard later that Eli returned to his father and was gladly reunited.

The more I see and hear about this man from Galilee, the more I wonder about his ancestry and his motives. He does not appear to be an arrogant ego-maniac trying to rally against the Empire. He is gregarious and loves people. He enjoys their company. He seems to want their happiness and well being.

The traditional rabbis expect a religious teacher to study at rabbinical schools. The Nazarene had not, nor had John. Both were regarded as ignorant. Yet people wondered how the Prophet was able to explain things without the rabbinical training.

Those who heard him were as spellbound as those who preceded them. Nor had they heard such words. With such power. Even those who were most violent toward him felt powerless to harm him. Day after day he spoke to them until finally the last day of the Feast of Passover dawned, a day in which most were wearied from the long celebrations.

The courage of the Galilean continued to impress me. He confronted the Jewish leaders and said, "Their entire lives are centered around a façade. The scribes and Pharisees quote the law of Moses essentially forcing others to comply with their instructions. They preach but do not practice. They burden you with impossible requirements which they ignore. They increase the size of their phylacteries. They love to be seen and fawned over and excel in promoting themselves. Do not follow their example."

Furthermore he reminded them that healing and providing for others' happiness was good—even if done on the Sabbath, explaining that even the hypocritical churchmen worked on the Sabbath turning their oxen or donkeys to water…or that they would rescue such an animal if necessary on the Sabbath.

He also reminded them that Pharisees sought the limelight—best seats in the house and proudly flaunted their prayer beads.

He was fully aware that the priests and rabbis sought his demise…that they'd sent messengers all over the country warning people against him, calling him an impostor.

CHAPTER 10 — Lives at Risk

One day as I stood on shore, I watched the Nazarene and his young fishermen friends shuck their sandals and push off from the beach. They hoisted the sail and set the oars in place and their voices, fortified by good natured ribbing, carried across the water to me...

"Hey, Pete, before you go out next trip, you might want to check out these oars. A couple could use some help."

"I know a guy who has some good used ones. I could probably get you a good deal."

And Peter's ready response, "Ahh, come on you knuckleheads. You'd complain if you had a net full of fish."

They carried on until they were out of earshot.

I continued relying upon my trusted liaison to provide me accounts of the Rabbi's activities—sometimes the details were vague. For instance, when he left with his followers across the lake, I heard them for a while but later acquired some of the information from a fishing friend of the Sons of Thunder with whom they shared their scary and unexplainable trip in the storm.

Knowing I had no means of following them, I contemplated retiring from the lake to go have a meal. It looked like I'd have to wait for more information about his activities until I heard from my informant on the far side of the lake. I should have realized others would follow Jesus. Before I knew it, a half dozen skippers prepared to follow his craft. As it turned out, one of those was the Greek fishermen I'd met previously on the beach. I hailed him, "Kallistos!"

He didn't seem to recognize me but I reminded him about the strange catch and the fishers of men.

"Oh. Right. I remember."

"I'm guessing since you're putting out following the Nazarene that you've seen him?"

"Yes, I have. I'm wanting to get to know more about him so I'm following him while hauling passengers, kind of killing two birds at the same time."

"So, may I be one of those passengers?"

"Hop aboard, my friend." How was I to know that decision would nearly cost me my life? With that I settled in and he took control of the vessel as we hove out into the lake. We trailed some distance behind the boat that carried the Rabbi.

I figured I'd be able to land some distance from the Rabbi and remain undetected among the crowd, thus continuing my observation of him and his men. As the boat sailed gently across the lake, a storm came up, one of huge magnitude. As we sailed into the teeth of the monster, she snarled, bared her teeth and snapped her growling jaws.

With little warning, the ugly sky and sea cascaded upon our craft. A cacophonous cauldron of wind and waves met us. Rain poured from the darkening sky accompanied by shrieking winds. In the distance other boats rose and fell upon the turbulent waves, thrashing amidst the howling winds. It was not looking good for any of the sailors.

Wave after wave pounded the hull. Visibility measured a dozen yards. Violent winds rocked the boat from starboard to port, the mast nearly touching the waves on either side. The aged sail ripped apart and without power we were dead in the water. We were at the sea's mercy. More water enveloped us, to the point of rendering our craft unmanageable. We were taking a shellacking. We lost flotation. Freeboard became zero. Before we knew it, the boat swamped . . . and within minutes, sank. Swirling water swept people and items overboard and the boat's mast and sail descended slowly into the depths. It was a case of every man for himself.

Surreal is the only way I can describe it—what had been frantic, fearful yelling turned to muted voices in the water. The whistling wind, relentless rain and reckless waves overpowered the people. All around me they struggled to stay afloat. I watched as some sank beneath the pummeling waters. Wailing waves dispersed us quickly.

Before being flushed into the water, I noticed some floating debris in a trough some yards off to the right. *Perhaps I could reach it?*

Heads bobbed about me as men sought to stay afloat. As I kicked out toward the flotsam, hoping it would stay above water, others followed. I've been in any number of tight spots during my thirty years but this could top them all. *Was this my reward from Jupiter for standing up for the Empire? Pirates, brigands, lions. Now this!*

My garments hampered my ability to swim, however while riding cresting waves I was able to keep the debris in sight. Suddenly something yanked on my left leg, pulling me under. What was it? The waves pounded from above and something pulled from below. *No way to breathe. Rope. Secured to some sinking object. My blade. Got to get it. There.* I grabbed the rope in my left hand and cut with my right, striking repeatedly through the strands of rope until the final strand released my leg. I didn't know how far below the surface I was but I kicked as hard and fast as I could for the air above.

Shooting out of the water, I gasped for life giving air. *Aaaarrrrrhhhhhgggg!* I sucked it in as never before. Gasping. Sighing. Glad to be free of the rope and the weight. Glad for the air. But now I faced the problem of finding something to keep me afloat. Cresting wave after wave, I paddled and fought to keep my head above the water.

In the damp, death-like jaws of the water's grasp I bumped into a piece of floating debris and managed to maneuver my arms and shoulders onto it, keeping my head above the water and resting for a brief time. Eventually I managed to haul myself onto it to a degree. Although I was delighted that it supported my weight, it took all my strength to hang onto it. It dawned on me that my lifeline was a portion of the boat's mast.

I clutched it as if my life depended upon it, as it surely did. Two or three other men clung to the boom and we held on amidst the pummeling. Time passed slowly as we clung to the boom, looking for land, knowing our survival depended upon the respite from the storm, reaching landfall or having other boaters rescue us.

Fingers became numb, making it more difficult to cling to the mast, I must admit I tired. I was cold. Feeling was leaving my hands and feet. It seemed my body's energy seeped from me. I struggled to stay afloat. I wondered what would happen next, thinking about my homeland, my family and friends. *What if I never see them again?* I determined to keep fighting until my energy was spent.

In the midst of all this it was almost mind numbing to observe the lake's surface flatten out. The rain stopped almost as if someone turned off a waterfall. And the wind ceased. For the first time since it started, the roaring sound in the air was absent. Silence prevailed. It was almost as if a magician commanded it.

We then discovered we were not terribly far from land. Deciding we could kick our feet to propel the boom toward shore, we worked in unison. The effort was demanding but with renewed hope we pressed on. That's when we noticed a boat moving in our direction. Almost before we knew it, the boat and the mast met.

But when we did, I was exhausted....

my legs cramped;

my fingers and hands tingled;

I suffered piercing chest pains;

my arms were rubbery and weak and my toes were numb. Nevertheless I was extremely grateful to be alive.

The skipper directed the others to haul us aboard and with great difficulty they managed. He gave orders to secure the boom so that my Greek friend could use it if possible.

Chilled to the bone and shaking, I tried to warm myself but it was of little use. Most of the passengers were in the same condition. We could only wait to reach shore and hope for some warmth from clothing or fire.

When we stepped ashore some time later, Kallistos was among a gaggle of the passengers. Some of them had already departed. Although chilled and exhausted, I had recovered to some degree but still wanted warmth. Fortunately my purse was intact and I could replace my clothes and other items.

I told Kallistos of the salvage. He was pleased and invited me to his home for food and rest. I thought briefly about it and agreed to accompany him. After enjoying warm food and a pleasant evening, I accepted his offer to stay the night. Might as well enjoy as much warmth as possible.

The following morning, having breakfasted on a sumptuous meal, I bid him a fond farewell. My goal was to discover what had become of Jesus.

Just a day or so later I received word from my man across the lake in the country of the Gerasenes (Gadarenes). He reported that he had joined a group of townspeople who hurried to the cemetery. It was just after I'd seen the Prophet disappear over the water, just before the horrendous storm lashed the lake. My informant told me, "A group of herdsmen stormed into town proclaiming that the local madman had a confrontation with the Rabbi.

He recalled the event announcing that, "Various folk commented":

"'Come.'

"'You've got to see it to believe!'

"'It's beyond comprehension!'

"Because the madman was known to the townspeople of Gadara and they feared him, they always made it a point to bypass the cemetery where he lived. Witnesses stated they'd heard him screaming and that they'd seen him cutting himself with sharp rocks. It was normal to see blood on his body from self-inflicted wounds. Coupled with the dried blood, scabs and scars on him, he was easily recognizable.

"This man had been bound many times with chains and shackles but these restraints could not hold him. He broke them every time and disappeared into the wild. He raged through the night. Did I mention that he was nearly always naked?

"The herdsmen's candor and our curiosity compelled us to return to the cemetery with them. Imagine our surprise when we neared the cemetery and saw hundreds of dead swine on the lake shore and floating in the water. Must have been a couple of thousand.

"Anyway, when the Nazarene's boat reached shore, the madman rushed from out of the tombs, raced for the boat, screaming at the Rabbi, beseeching him to leave him. He'd suffered enough and shrieked that the Prophet had no right to torment him further.

"The Galilean asked him his name to which the madman responded, 'Legion. There are many of us.'

"Jesus recognized that the man was possessed by demons and he commanded them to depart into a grazing herd of swine on the distant hillside. The herd stampeded down the hillside and ran over a cliff, tumbling into the lake where they all drowned.

"As we approached the Healer, his group and the madman, we saw the previously possessed man sitting there properly clothed and perfectly sane. The villagers were so surprised and frightened that they pleaded with Jesus to leave the area.

"Respecting their wishes, Jesus boarded the boat to leave with Legion asking if he could go with hm. But Jesus told him to return to his home and declare what God had done for him. The Gadarene departed stating that he would tell his story throughout the Ten Towns."

While listening to the story, my puzzlement was rekindled. *Would nothing about this Rabbi surprise me?* My senses and intellect confounded me when it came to trying to understand the events of the Gadarene and the calming of the water. *I could easily imagine the joy of freedom from shackles. But to be free from demonic bondage, how could that be? And how did the storm suddenly stop?*

Hardly had my mole finished the story of the madman when he told me what he had heard of the storm-tossed boat the Rabbi had arrived on. The disciples eagerly shared their fearful experience on the water which my informant overheard: He said, "I heard the story from one of the fishing brothers, the loudmouths called the Sons of Thunder. It was James."

In great detail the agent related the following:

Above the lake to the east lay desert regions. The hills baked under the desert sun, painting her landscape khaki-gray. Scattered thorns and dwarf scrub brush eked out a living in the dry soil where wild asses and Bedouin goats roamed. Nighttime captured the haunting cry of wild jackals and yipping foxes under the starlit skies.

Free from the oppressive crowd aboard the boat and exhausted from the previous days' efforts, Jesus sought a place to lie down. He found it in the stern. Hardly had they left the beach before he fell fast asleep on a cushion.

Because of the lake's location, cupped beneath the Galilean hill country which radiated extreme heat, sudden squalls and storms were not uncommon. In minutes the water's surface could change from calm to chaos, churning waters into a foaming fury. At those times the sailors' only hope was to race to shore to escape the thundering whitecaps waging war against their small craft.

Although the evening had been calm, darkness overspread the sky and a wind came up.

Before long the wind changed into a violent squall. A somber sky evolved into dark, ominous clouds, blocking out the sun. Shimmering bright, blue waters metamorphosed to steel gray, then a scowling black. A sharp clap of thunder added its voice to the storm, reverberating from the water's surface. Lightning flashed, lighting the sky and illuminating the shadow-filled boat and silhouetting the distant, dark hills above the lake.

Winds whipped the air and the lake into a frenzy as a full blown storm hammered the vessel. Whooshing and shuddering, the winds increased their velocity, shrieking through the shrouds and pummeling the mast. Wave after wave pounded the boat, exploding against the sides—wind driven spray sliced through the air like so many knifelike pellets.

Sheets of rain slashed horizontally, slapping fishermen relentlessly. Ripping winds popped the sail, furling and unfurling it, whipsawing it back and forth against the mast. The sail's staccato *Pop! Pop! Pop!* cracked like a powerful whip as the wind threatened to rip it from the mast.

The sailors fought to keep the boat afloat, bailing water and manning the sail. Their efforts wrought little. The boat wallowed in the troughs and waddled up the ensuing waves to their crests before falling off and slamming into another trough, only to be repeated again and again. The lake was in turmoil. Paniced pandemonium prevailed. The fishermen shouted directions to each other, yelling at the tops of their voices to be heard. Although they'd spent their lives on the water, they'd never experienced anything like this. They could do little to stay above water. Absorbed by their efforts to stave off the impossible, they had forgotten their leader. But now, they remembered.

"Where's Jesus?"

"We've got to find him!"

"Where is he?"

Beside themselves with fear, near hopeless with the prospects of their safety and realizing they were doomed, the sailors sought Jesus. But they could not find him in the dark.

Although the howling wind and the hammering waves coupled with the confusion aboard overshadowed their voices, the men caught bits and pieces of their shipmates' shouts…

"…the mast!"

The winds intensified, whipping wildly, lashing the sail.

"Lower…sail!"

"Row together…!"

The lake's waters piled up.

"Watch…curling leeward wave!"

A maelstrom of confusion continued.

Fears fed their thoughts…

Have you forsaken us?

Where have you gone?

You cured disease and cast out demons, can't you help us now?

As the shrieking winds and the roaring waves increased, their cries became mute. It was an exercise in futility. The boat listed and began to sink. A micro-second separated them from safety and certain death.

Suddenly a flash of lightning illuminated the one who'd brought them here. He slept undisturbed partially covered by a replacement sail.

Amazed, they rushed to him. They jostled him awake, "Master! Master!"

"Don't you care?"

"Don't you care that we're drowning?"

He rose from his nest and steadied himself against the wind and rain that tore at his body and clothes. He must have concluded that the sailors' wondering whether he cared was indication that they still did not understand his purpose. Why did they suppose He was with them? He had no fear of the storm. Steeling himself against the driving rain and deafening wind, he decided to have some fun with the boys.

Laughing he joked, "You're supposed to be hard core fishermen. I'm the landlubber here and you wake me to help you? That's too funny. It's only a storm. What's the matter with you guys, don't you have any faith? Relax and watch this, boys."

Addressing the sea, the Galilean commanded with authority, "Hush now! Be still!"

In that moment it was almost as if life ceased to exist. Silence reigned... not a stirring, not even a whisper of water or wind. The world about them stood still. The sailors stood speechless.

He laughed and challenged them. "Hey, what happened? I don't see any waves. Come on, guys. What were you afraid of?"

They had no response. Each man held thoughts about the storm. And even more thoughts about he who had slept peacefully before calming the sea. They were fascinated and in awe all at once at what he had done. They wondered aloud, "Who can he be?—even the wind and waves do what he tells them."

At the conclusion of his story, I thanked my informant and laughed inwardly about the "don't you care that we're drowning" question. Jesus must have wondered if these knuckleheads would ever get it. And I made an observation ...*not only did he calm the physical storm, he is able to calm the storms—every one—in our lives.*

And so, the disciples survived the storm...as had I. I'm wondering...*the calming of the sea occurred simultaneously for the disciples and me. Is there some significance to that?*

CHAPTER 11 — Strange Healings and Happenings

I was hearing so many stories. I had to jot information so that I could follow up on the more significant ones. One was about Manilus Novius Adventus, a Roman Centurion whom I knew. His input could shed considerable light on the Nazarene and his motivation.

It was several days before I made my way to meet Manilus. I'd heard he had an encounter with Jesus. I knew him to be of excellent character and, militarily, impeccable. His story was one I had to consider in evaluating the Rabbi. He told me that on a day when the Rabbi entered Capernaum, a group of Jewish elders approached him and asked him to intervene on Manilus' behalf.

I asked Manilus to tell me what he thought of him.

He stated, "I found it interesting that the Jews had learned from childhood the Jewish customs, traditions and religion, yet many saw nothing in this man. Juxtaposed, here I am a Roman, born and educated into what some consider heathenism and an idolatrous culture. I am of a different nationality and I am trained as a soldier. Yet I saw more in Jesus, a Jew, than his own countrymen.

"Although I had never met the man, I'd heard about him and his miraculous teachings. I believed I had overcome the barrier of nationalities and the hatred of the conquered for the conquerors. Because of these things and what I'd heard of Jesus, as well as my urgent desire to see my servant well, I had asked the elders to represent me before this man. Though my prayers to Jupiter were unanswered, I wasn't down playing my religion; it seemed the Rabbi could provide the necessary healing and it was expedient to do so.

"I asked the elders to tell him that my servant was lying in my home paralyzed and in great pain, hovering at death's door. They told him my servant had been a slave whom I'd purchased. They explained that whereas many servants were abused and mistreated, I made every effort to treat my servants with respect and kindness. I held great regard for this particular servant.

"Jesus' response was that he would come and heal him. Thus he immediately followed the elders to my home. However because of the large crowd pressing against him and the travelers on the roadway, he found the going slow.

"Part way to my home, Jesus met a messenger sent by me. I requested that Jesus not trouble himself to come to my house, explaining that I was unworthy of his presence in my home. I also knew my status as a gentile would defile Jesus should he come under my roof. Therefore my request to him was, 'Merely speak the word and my servant will be healed. I am an officer and obey my superiors. I also have men in my command. I know the ramifications of commanding and taking orders. If I order a man to do such and such, he obeys and carries out my command. As I represent the power of Rome, my men know that I speak with authority. In your case, you represent your Infinite God and you have the authority to deliver your promise. All created things obey your command. Only say the word and my servant will be delivered.'

"I'm told that Jesus was amazed by my commanding presence and my faith and stated, 'I tell you not even in Israel have I found such faith.'

"Jesus sent word to me, 'Return to your friend as your faith has caused your servant to be healed.' The servant was instantly healed and when the petitioners reached my home, he was well."

I asked Manilus, "Can you explain how the Nazarene healed your servant? Did he use herbs or some sort of magic?"

"I can't explain it. I just know that my servant lay dying and without even going to see him or touch him, Jesus healed him."

Again, I found myself wondering if it were some magical trick. To take it a step further, I commented to Manilus and asked him, "I find this seriously puzzling. We both know these Jews hate the Romans and their dominance over them. Yet this nomadic Prophet—a Jew—is not only being kind to a Roman but also heals his servant. Can you explain that?"

"Actually, Brachan, I can't. I know that he honored my request to heal my servant from a distance, that he is, in fact, a Jew and his kindness is definitely hard for me to understand in light of the Jewish hatred of the Romans."

The more I see and hear about this man, the more I see a parallel between him and the prophesied redeemer from the Jewish *Tahakh*. The parallels are striking. Maybe, maybe he is he. Wouldn't it be something if I came on a mission turned sideways to follow a different threat to the Empire?

It is my understanding that not long after this, the Nazarene and his followers encountered a large crowd. Among those who greeted them was Jairus, a synagogue president and a prominent person of Capernaum. His wealth was such that it elevated him above fraternizing with the local common folk. I had heard of him earlier, that he had been present in the synagogue when the Rabbi cast out the demon. He had also been impressed by the Galilean's handling of the sacred scroll which, no doubt, gave him confidence in approaching Jesus. He believed that the Healer could heal his daughter who lay near death. The thought of losing her tore at his heart.

In his frantic searching he must have mourned the loss of his child and wondered what his life would be like without her. He continued his search until he found the Nazarene. Then he threw himself at the Rabbi's feet and proclaimed, "Please, I beg you. My twelve-year-old daughter is lying at the point of death. I beg you, come to my house and lay your hands on her so that she can be healed and live."

The Galilean immediately joined Jairus en route to the home of this synagogue director, followed by his disciples and a large group of people. Their pathway was jammed with folk wanting to get close to the Rabbi. Jairus was desperate, thinking that his daughter would surely die if they did not reach her in a timely fashion. They pushed on. But the crowd was nearly impassable.

Suddenly the Rabbi stopped. Somehow he knew that someone with a severe disease had touched him as he felt energy leave his body. While looking about the crowd, he asked, "Who touched me…who touched my clothes?"

His followers wondered about the strangeness of the question. They were shoulder to shoulder, all about him. Dozens of people could have touched him. Why would he even ask such a question?

Everyone denied it and Peter and his companions asked, "Master, how can you ask 'who touched me?' when so many hem you in? You've probably been touched by any number of this crowd."

The Healer continued looking among the faces in the crowd.

A woman among the group had been afflicted with a flow of blood. Like thousands of others who heard about the Galilean, she sought him out. Thinking *if I could just touch his clothes, I will be healed*, she had come up from behind him and touched the hem of his garment.

As soon as the woman touched his clothing, the source of her bleeding dried up and stopped and she felt that she had been healed of her condition.

Realizing that she had not escaped notice and that she had been healed, the woman trembled with fright. She fell down before the Rabbi and told him of her guilt and the reason for her touching him, and how she had been instantly healed. "I did. I've had a hemorrhage for twelve years and have seen many doctors. I've spent massive amounts of money and gotten no help. In fact my health is getting worse. When I heard about you, I thought you might be able to help me. I am so destitute that I thought maybe it would help if I just touched your clothes."

He said to her, "Daughter, it is your faith that has healed you. Go home in peace and be free from your trouble."

By then Jairus was near panic. Time was of the essence.

Abruptly some of his servants jostled their way through the crowd, sweating and panting, eyes dilated. They saw Jairus and proclaimed, "It's too late. Your daughter has died. No use expecting the Master to help now!"

Jairus was speechless. He turned to the Rabbi. The Nazarene had overheard the servant's comments and spoke, "Now, don't be afraid. Just go on believing."

Jesus took only Peter, James and John with him and continued toward Jairus' house. As they neared the president's home, they heard wailing and screaming. The paid professional mourners were in fine fiddle. They'd begun their lamentation. Flute players and people mourned the child's death. Women beat their chests and men moaned through their beards, chanting and groaning lamentations. They held their heads in despair. The finality of death shackled them and gripped them with pain and sadness.

At the point when the Healer reached the mourners, he spoke to console them, "What is the problem? Why all the grief?"

They were shocked at his pronouncements. They wondered how anyone could be so stupid! Is he mad?

Then he spoke, "The little girl is not dead. She is sleeping."

He brushed aside their derision and went into the house. With firm, quiet authority he requested the people to leave the house.

Of course, they laughed at him and ridiculed him because it was obvious that she was dead. After they left the house, he took the child's mother and father as well as his companions to the child's bedside. He reached out and clasped her tiny hand while speaking softly, "Little girl, get up." Holding the twelve-year old girl's hand, he spoke in Aramaic, "Tal-i-tha-cu-mi" (*Talitha Kum*), which means "Little Child, I tell you to get up."

Her eyes opened wide and she was puzzled at the presence of strangers. At once her spirit returned and she jumped to her feet and walked around the room. She walked to her parents who stood wide eyed and amazed, sighs of relief and joyous smiles upon their faces. The others went wild with joy. He told them not to let anyone know what had happened and told them to feed the child.

Then he was gone.

When I heard this story, I was again reminded that the Nazarene healed and did other kinds of good among the people. One of the strangest things about this story was when his disciple Peter asked the Master how he could question that someone in the vast crowd had touched him, his response was that he could feel healing power go out from him. I wondered what he meant. More confusion to my mind.

One late afternoon knowing the following day would be a long one and wanting to get a good night's rest, I dropped into an inn *(pandocheion)*. My belly overpowered my consideration of the inn's quality or that of the inn keeper. I hurriedly procured a room for the night and hustled to catch a bite before turning in. I hoped they'd have my favorite Greek food on their menu.

More than a hint of mint, dill and cilantro assailed my nostrils as I jostled my way through the crowded dining area. Tantalizing aromas triggered my imagination—pork, chicken, herbal seasonings and baked bread.

I battled my nose to a corner table where I could let my hair down so to speak and have a view of the surroundings. My mind fought a pitched battle: pork chops bedded in asparagus spears, chicken boiled in olive oil with a delicate thyme sauce or maybe some cheese. *Is my hunger running away with my mind?* But one thing was certain—regardless or whatever I ordered, I would have fresh bread…and probably Katiki cheese dip for it. And a glass of white wine. Of course, I envisioned a breakfast of sausage and cheese.

While glancing around the room I spotted a man who had a familiar look. Try as I might I couldn't put my finger on who he was. Then I was certain he was the victim of the lion attack to which I'd responded. He sat between two other men and all seemed in good spirits, drinking and laughing the afternoon away.

My curiosity aroused, I made my way to his table to ask if I might join them, "I'm not wanting to impose but I'm pretty sure you're the soldier I helped rescue some months back… from a lion."

The man to his left, seemingly amused, responded, "Yes. He's Muttonhead alright."

Somewhat surprised by the response I asked, "Why do you call him Muttonhead?"

Then the man on his right smiled, looked at Muttonhead and said, "Simple. We tell him the lion probably thought he was a sheep, thus the name. We've called him that ever since."

The victim of the lion attack laughed and said, "Yes, they have. I'll probably never live it down. Since you saved my life, it would be rude of me to refuse your request. And we're always up for a visit. Have a seat, stranger."

"Thank you. So, you survived the attack and seem to be in reasonable shape?"

"Yes. I have some scars but I healed up pretty quickly. Doctors feared an infection which could have been disastrous but they told me my youth and attitude were in my favor. Since the cat couldn't gain purchase on my head, most of the injuries were puncture wounds to my legs and arms along with some claw marks on my chest."

"I'm glad to see that you're up and about. It was quite an adventure intervening on your behalf. Wasn't sure what the outcome would be but I wanted to do what I could. The other soldier showed extreme courage and we managed to beat back that cat."

"I'm mighty glad you both came to my rescue. And I'm glad I had my helmet on. The funniest thing is that we had left the troop to go off to the side of the road to respond to a call from mother nature. Were we surprised when the lion jumped from the bushes and attacked. Since my bout with the lion things don't always fall together right for me. Sometimes I don't remember things from day to day. Sometimes I wonder if things happened, perhaps in another life."

"I'm sorry to hear that but hopeful you'll make a full recovery in time."

"I think so. It's getting better."

As the evening wore on, I learned that he was celebrating mustering out of the service with two civilian friends he'd made. Seems he'd healed from the lion mauling but his forgetfulness and other factors caused him to consider his usefulness to Rome. He'd been given a medical discharge and looked forward to his return to his homeland. After an enjoyable evening with him and his two friends, I wished them well and retired for the night.

The next day I learned of another event involving the Galilean. On his way to Nain, he and his disciples encountered a large body of people wailing in procession to a burial. As they drew closer, the Healer observed an open bier upon which rested the deceased, the only son of a widow lady. It appeared that all the townspeople accompanied the sad lady comforting her in her bereavement. When the Nazarene saw her trailing the procession, he had compassion on her and spoke to her, "Do not cry." He reached out and touched the bier than spoke, "Young man, I say to you, arise."

Shocked by the result, the crowd stood in awe as the young man opened his eyes, noticed his grieving mother and clasped the Healer's hand. The Nazarene helped him to his feet where the young man embraced his weeping mother. The crowd was speechless and amazed for among them stood a man like no other they'd ever seen.

I knew from agent reports and personal observation that the Nazarene surrounded himself with a dozen close associates. Because of reports I'd heard, I continued seeking the nature of this group, still thinking his selection of these men might indicate a step toward organizing for an uprising.

His work with these close associates as well as his appointing five dozen or so to do his bidding troubled me. I've heard he walked the beach and the byways selecting men to work with him and that they are a bunch of louts—coarse, crude, common, rough, unorganized, uneducated and, possibly, cheats. They are all outside the mainstream.

He knew their makeup—their nature, humor or lack thereof, sense of loyalty and industry. And he knew their strengths and weaknesses. I could not differentiate between each one but the most well known to me were Peter, James, John, Matthew and Simon the Zealot. They appeared the most outspoken and most well known among the Jews. Their credentials are questionable.

Take for instance the two brothers James and John, known as the Sons of Thunder. They are headstrong, fiery, hotheaded and rough, though John seemed more vocal. Their father is Zebedee and their mother Salome. These boys, called the Thunderers, are strongly opinionated.

Peter comes across as a loudmouth. He is impulsive, abrasive and never at a loss for words—which he usually eats. He is powerful, crude and coarse, a fisherman from Galilee who can cuss with the best of them. He often acts without thinking and regrets it later. Peter is the natural spokesman for the twelve. He is fiercely loyal and a native of Bethsaida, a coastal fishing village and twin city to Capernaum, the center of the Nazarene's activity.

And this Matthew fellow. A tax collector and a public servant of the Romans. Why would a Jew trying to establish a following and attempting to gain favor among the religious Jewish leaders recruit a tax collector?

The Jewish publicans collect taxes on behalf of the Romans. The existing taxes burden the people beyond belief—personal taxes, property taxes, poll taxes, road taxes, trade taxes, temple taxes. The Jews detest taxes, especially those imposed by a foreign power. And they hate the publicans working in concert with Rome. Their countrymen regard such men with utmost contempt, considering them traitors and less than dog dung,

Through threats and blackmail the publicans collect the required Roman taxes. Then they tack on additional fees. They are aware the locals know they skim off money for an exorbitant profit.

As for Matthew, it's a strange thing. One day along the seashore a huge crowd gathered around the Deliverer on the beach while he taught them. I lost myself in the group as we walked on and the Rabbi stopped at a toll booth where Matthew, the son of Alphaeus worked either directly or indirectly collecting taxes for Herod Antipas. By that time I was within earshot and heard the Nazarene speak to Matthew, "Follow me." To my astonishment, Matthew arose and obeyed, never looking back.

Matthew was a Capernaum customs official taxing imports and exports based on his judgment. He was an accurate record keeper who gave up a fortune and financial security to follow the man from Galilee into uncertainty. I heard later that he knew the human heart and longings of Jewish people and that he was loyal to the Prophet. He turned from a greedy man to a loving follower.

Choosing to leave his past behind, he threw a celebration party, inviting family, friends, cronies and peers. You might say they were society's worst—tax collectors and their enforcers, prostitutes, pimps and other degenerates.

He also invited his new found Master to the party. The Prophet and his disciples attended.

Not the least of Matthew's guests were numerous swindlers. Jesus fit in not because he was a swindler but because he loved people.

When the Scribes and Pharisees learned of the Galilean's partying, they sought to distance his disciples from him. In their pomposity they asked,

"Why is he eating with tax-collectors and sinners?" With little thought of their condemnation and failing to see that they were in worse spiritual condition than those they condemned, the Pharisees failed to see themselves for what they were...or at least failed to admit it to themselves.

The Nazarene overheard their conversation and responded, probably with some sarcasm, "Those who are well have no need of a physician, but those who are sick. I came not to call the righteous but sinners."

The man did not disappoint. He demonstrated his compassion toward the attendees, expressing his jovial humor and immersing himself in the gaiety of the occasion. He regaled them with stories and his good humor, topped only by his complimentary words to those in attendance. They wished for his acceptance and approval. He availed himself and his teachings to bring them hope and a new life.

I heard later that Jesus was the life of the party. One of the party goers explained that the Rabbi was laid back and comfortable, so relaxed and amiable that the guests took instantly to him. The partygoer said the Nazarene listened to anyone speaking, treated each person with respect and seemed to accept each one which created an atmosphere of ease and friendship.

Interestingly, one of the criticisms laid at his feet is that poor people flock to him...basically ignorant commoners. However well educated, aristocratic followers mingled among the crowds. The religious leaders refer to him as a wine bibber and a glutton. I say, "What's wrong with good food and drink? The man has good judgment. I pass it off as religious leaders' jealousy."

Of these followers of Jesus, as I pointed out earlier, I knew fairly little— Andrew, Philip, Bartholomew, Thomas, James, Thaddaeus, Simon and Judas:

Andrew was a quiet fisherman from Bethsaida and Peter's brother. I believe he's the one who introduced Peter to the Master.

Philip was one—if not the first—of the Rabbi's followers. He introduced Bartholomew to Jesus.

Bartholomew, after hearing the Rabbi was from Nazareth, asked if anything good could come from there.

Thomas was skeptical, tended to be moody, some considered him a doubter.

James was the son of Alphaeus.

I knew nought of Thaddaeus.

As for Simon the Zealot. When I heard he was a member of the Zealots who hated Rome and openly opposed us, my ears perked up. Images of eagles on Roman coins caused him to seethe and a storm of indignation flooded this zealous patriot. I wondered if he might be a liaison between the Galilean and the Zealots.

And Judas Iscariot. He was the treasurer for the band. The only Judaean among them, he was crafty and cunning. His greed caused him to slip funds from the coffers of the group.

While considering this idea, I was reminded of another tax collector, the little fellow the Nazarene chose for a dinner companion. He probably had much in common as this Matthew. His name was Zacchaeus, a Jew detested by his countrymen because of his line of work. And he was a chief tax collector.

When Zacchaeus heard that a holy man known as Jesus was passing through Jericho with others in a caravan bound for Jerusalem, he joined others clamoring to see the holy man and to learn more of this rabbi's teachings. As the caravan approached, people flocked along the way in hopes of getting a glimpse of Rabbi.

Because Zacchaeus was small of stature, he hustled ahead of the crowd and swung his frame up into the branches of a sycamore tree so that he could get a better glimpse of Jesus.

Before long the Master came into view and stopped beneath the tree, peering over the heads of the boisterous crowd at the publican. He then spoke, "Zacchaeus, hurry down from there. I'm going to your house."

Zacchaeus was stunned to think that he had been all but banned from the Jewish places of worship because of Jewish leaders' claims that he was a sinner; yet Jesus accepted him at face value without condemning him…and went directly to his home, accepting him unconditionally. The experience shed more light on the Jewish leaders' hatred for Jesus—he demonstrated with his words, his actions and his life that love, not rules, changes men.

I heard murmurings among the crowd, complaining that the Nazarene had really overstepped his bounds by engaging a tax man. They were truly repulsed. The more I experience about Jesus, the more I understand the reason that men are compelled to him.

In due time the Rabbi sent messengers before him and began his journey to Jerusalem. I learned he had not sent the men to recruit disciples but rather to warn them of their need for God and to encourage them. He sent them ahead of him into the towns he planned to visit and told them to go among the people where there were few helpers. He said they would be prey to all kinds of torment. He instructed them to travel lightly, carrying no purse, bag or extra pair of sandals. Also not to dilly dally but to express to the occupants, "Peace be to this household!" He assured them if one of the occupants loved peace, he would accept their words of blessing. He instructed them to stay in the same house, not to move from one house to another and to eat and drink what was provided.

He told them, "Wherever you are welcomed, eat the meals they offer and heal the ill. Tell them, 'The kingdom of God is very near to you now.'

But where you are not welcomed, go into the streets saying, 'We brush off even the dust of your town from our feet as a protest against you. But the fact remains that the kingdom of God has arrived!' I assure you that it will be better for Sodom in 'that day' than for that town.

"Remember, whoever listens to you is listening to me. He who has no use for you has no use for me. And the man who has no use for me has no use for The One who sent me!

"Alas for you, Chorazin, and alas for you, Bethsaida! For if Tyre and Sidon had seen the demonstrations of God's power that you have seen, they would have repented long ago and sat in sackcloth and ashes. It will be better for Tyre and Sidon in the judgment than for you! As for you, Capernaum, are you on your way up to heaven? I tell you that you will go hurtling down among the dead!"

Sounded like pretty strong words to me. I wondered how he proposed to accomplish this.

As his messengers traveled, they stopped at a Samaritan village to prepare for him. But the people refused to welcome him because he was going on to Jerusalem. When the town rejected the group, the two hot-headed brothers James and John were steamed and asked Jesus if they could call down fire from heaven to punish the Samaritan villagers. The Galilean reproved them and they bypassed that town and went on to another.

Again I wonder *what kind of powers does he possess?*

Later the seventy-two returned and reported to him, rejoicing and proclaiming that "Lord, even evil spirits obey us when we use your name!"

He agreed with them and said, "Yes, I gave you power to tread on snakes and scorpions and to overcome all the enemy's power. There is nothing at all that can do you any harm because your names are written in Heaven."

It was time to dispatch my superior an update.

DISPATCH:

It was recently reported that the Nazarene proclaimed, "I did not come to be served but to serve and give my life as a ransom in place of many." My thinking is that this statement is either totally egotistical or...he may be what he states. If it's true, he does not seem to be coming from a revolutionary position but rather a meek and mild surrender to servant-hood. From my observations he teaches respect for Jewish and Roman government and respect for citizens of all nations, even though he constantly rebukes the religious Jews for their hypocrisy.

I'm still struggling to ascertain his true motivation. He sends people out with a message of peace, but I can't help wondering if he's building an organization and laying the groundwork for revolutionary action.

CHAPTER 12 — Adulteress and Lazarus

While listening to the Nazarene in the Temple on the Mount of Olives, I was surprised by the Jewish leaders and Pharisees. They made a show of bringing in a woman while Jesus was teaching. They paraded her right in front of the assembled crowd, creating quite a stir. Temple-goers murmured, no doubt wondering, as did I, what was happening.

Having caught her in the very act of adultery, they accused her of being an adulteress. They questioned him regarding her demise, referring to Moses' law. The penalty of her violation was death by stoning. I found their motive pretty obvious—they were attempting to trap him with his words juxtaposed to their traditional teaching.

At that point he stooped down and wrote in the dust with his finger. The entire time they clamored nonstop trying to make their point while awaiting his answer. He rose and stated that they were justified in stoning her but suggested that whoever among them had never sinned, be the first to throw a stone.

He then stooped again and continued writing in the dust with his finger. While he was so engaged, the eldest leader slipped away, head bowed in what appeared to be shame. One by one all the accusers followed his lead until none was left.

It was almost surrealistic…seeing the accusers disperse because of the Nazarene's simple explanation. They probably wondered if he were writing their names in the dust. If so, perhaps they felt guilty and, rather than be condemned, left like dogs with their tails between their legs.

Next the Rabbi stood up, looked the woman in the eye and asked her where her accusers were, "Did any condemn you?"

"No, sir."

"Neither do I. Go on your way and sin no more."

It seems to me that rather than stone her, he performed an even greater action by reasoning with her and offering her a second chance. Shouldn't we all get a second chance, an opportunity to turn from whatever destructive behavior we have and to act more positively?

I've always considered myself a thinker. I analyze and consider variables then come to a logical conclusion. Was the Master saying that there was not a sinless man among the accusers? Was he demonstrating by not throwing a stone himself that he was also a sinner? Or was he implying that although he was without sin, the only such man present, that even he would not condemn the woman with stoning?

If the Jewish *Torah is* accurate in prophesying the Son of God and this Nazarene is he, what the Galilean has just spoken is overwhelming in its theological implications. If he is the Son of God, he is the one without sin. If anyone in the group were in a position to condemn her, he was. HOWEVER he did not condemn her nor cast a stone but rather forgave the woman of her sins.

As I left the Temple, I was reminded of the constant drumbeat of chatter about the Nazarene. Evidently word of mouth spreads like wildfire about his miraculous activities. As Jesus made his way toward Jerusalem, I wondered about my experiencing his behavior the past couple of years. I contemplated the information from the Jewish *Torah* as well as some of the rumors I'd heard. Something is in the air. I believe it is a showdown of sorts. Possibly the Prophet and his people going head to head with the Jewish leaders?

Their fear is that the Galilean is a threat and could topple the religious leadership and traditional religious customs of the Jews.

It is more than hearsay that he is targeted for removal. Removal from his preaching position possibly by some religious edict. Or removal from the planet by the scoundrels who have sought his demise from the beginning.

One of the Rabbi's most ardent followers is a fellow named Lazarus. He lives with his two sisters Mary and Martha whose home is the Nazarene's residence of choice in Bethany.

He often sought respite here where he was always warmly welcomed. Normally Martha prepared a sumptuous meal to honor him. And a number of distinguished guests, the disciples and the host and hostesses crowded into the ornate home and shared the evening with him. He could relax and regain his stamina as well as solace and some semblance of social interaction—a place where he could unwind among friends outside the prying eyes of the religious leaders. Their home represented his southern headquarters in as much as Peter's home by the Lake of Galilee seemed to be his favorite headquarters in the north.

In recent days, however, Lazarus had taken a turn for the worse. He suffered some illness and his health declined. His sisters did what they could to ease his pain and nurse him back to health, however he grew weaker and weaker, sicker and sicker. They agreed that if the Rabbi were here, one touch of his hand would restore Lazarus' health. However the Healer was not around.

As time ran out for Lazarus, the sisters decided to make every attempt they could to get word to the Healer. They sent one of their most reliable servants to find him. Word on the street was that he was in the hills east of Jordan. The servant spent several days following word of mouth information and eventually reached Jesus and his pals, proclaiming, "Lord, he whom you love, Lazarus, my master, is very ill."

Jesus heard and replied, "This sickness will not result in death, but for the glory of God so that the Son of Man might be glorified by his illness."

The servant could not believe his ears. He had expected the Rabbi to drop everything and rush to Bethany to rescue Lazarus. He returned immediately to report to Mary and Martha.

They had to wonder, *could it be true? He's not coming to rescue our brother?*

And so it was, two days after the servant returned from his mission to the Healer, Lazarus died. His remains were interred in a mausoleum carved from limestone behind their home.

The sisters' hearts were burdened by the loss of their much loved brother. What would they do without him? And yet, their hearts ached that the Galilean had not come to save him.

Although the Galilean loved the sisters and brother, he remained where he was until the day of Lazarus' death. He told his disciples, "Let's go into Judaea again. There are twelve hours of daylight in every day, during which a man can walk without stumbling. Only at night is there danger of stumbling because of the dark. Our friend Lazarus has gone to sleep, but I must now go to awaken him."

They were comforted in the fact that Lazarus' sleeping well as a sign of his improving health. What they didn't pick up on when Jesus cited "sleeping" was that the Rabbi meant Lazarus had died.

As they journeyed to Bethany, the disciples feared going to Lazarus' because the Jews might catch and hurt them. Thomas the twin wanted to go to Lazarus, stating they could all die with him. The disciples reminded the Nazarene that "the Jews have lately tried to stone you. Why do you want to return?"

The Rabbi and his followers arrived in Bethany a couple of miles down the road from Jerusalem where Lazarus had been entombed four days.

By then Jewish leaders had arrived to pay their respect and to console weeping and moaning Mary and Martha. Amidst the grieving, Martha slipped into a pair of sandals and sped down the hill to meet the Rabbi. Racing along, she confidently expected the Rabbi to save her brother, even now.

When she finally reached him, breathless, mournful, broken hearted but still hopeful, words tumbled from her mouth, "Oh, Master, if you had been here, my brother would have never died. And even now it's not too late. I know that God will bring my brother back to life again, if you will only ask Him to."

The Rabbi replied, "Lazarus is dead. I am glad that I wasn't there for your sake. This will provide you yet another opportunity to strengthen your faith in me. He will rise again. Let's go to him."

Assuming he meant something else, she stated, "I know that he will rise in the resurrection on the last day."

Assuring her as they strolled toward the burial site, he continued, "I am the one who raises the dead and gives them life again. Anyone who believes in me, even though he dies like anyone else, shall live again. He is given eternal life for believing in me and shall never perish. Do you believe that, Martha?"

Standing there on the hot, dusty Jericho road with hot tears streaming down her face she answered, "Yes, Master, I do. I believe you are the Messiah, the Son of God, the One we have awaited for so long. You are the Savior of the world."

With his assurance and the expression of her faith, she hastened home to alert Mary. Up the road she raced, excited to share the news with her sister.

Martha burst into her home and found Mary. She pulled her aside from the mourners and gasped, "He is here and wants to see you."

Immediately Mary left the mourners and rushed down the pathway. She eagerly anticipated seeing their friend where Martha had left him.

Assuming she was going to her brother's tomb to mourn, the Jewish leaders followed her.

By this time the other mourners had reached them and they joined Mary in her wailing.

Jesus saw her weeping, joined by the Jewish leaders and seemed moved with indignation and troubled by their lack of confidence in his abilities.

When Mary reached him outside the village, she fell at his feet in frustration and humble expectation, "O Lord, if you had been here, my brother would still be alive." She was incapable of stopping her weeping and wailed in great sorrow.

"Where is he buried?" he asked.

With the reply, "Come and see," they reached the tomb, a cave with a heavy stone rolled across its entry way. The Rabbi wept. The leaders noted his tears. Realizing that he and Lazarus were close friends, the crowd was moved by his love for his friend. They thought the Healer was sad to see his friend dead and buried.

He wept not only because he loved Lazarus, but, more importantly, it seemed, because he did not wish to call him back to this earth. He also knew that Lazarus would be a target for the scribes and Sadducees because the Sadducees did not believe in the resurrection of the dead. Lazarus would proclaim his resurrection and be under bitter attack.

Some, however, criticized the Rabbi and wondered aloud, "He healed the blind man, why couldn't he keep Lazarus from dying?"

Mary and Martha stood anxiously by wondering about the situation and its possibilities.

Partially due to the smell of a human corpse, Martha was concerned and stated, "By now the smell will be terrible, for he has been dead four days."

The Healer stated, "Didn't I tell you that you would see a wonderful miracle from God if you believe?"

He told them to "roll the stone away."

They rolled the stone away and the Rabbi looked heavenward and said, "Father, thank you for hearing me. You always hear me, of course, but I said it because of all these people standing here so that they will believe you sent me." Then in commanding voice he shouted, "Lazarus, come out!"

Who would have thought it possible? Who would have anticipated, much less, expected what happened next?

Lazarus came—bound up in the grave cloth, his head muffled in a head swath. The Rabbi smiled at the sisters and others close to Lazarus while saying, "Remove the grave wrappings that bind him and free him." Mary and Martha rushed to their brother as tears of gladness flowed.

At that point many of the Jewish leaders finally believed in Jesus. Some, however, went to report to the Pharisees.

As for me, along with my increasing knowledge of him I was growing more perplexed by his activities. I've heard about and/or I've witnessed firsthand his restoring hands, healing leprosy, casting out demons and now, bringing Lazarus back to life. *How can this be?*

As soon as the Sanhedrin, supreme Jewish council, composed of high priests, legal experts and leading citizens, learned of his healing of Lazarus, they knew that the Nazarene had control over death and the grave. The very act of bringing Lazarus back from the grave further inflamed many Pharisees' hatred for him. There was now no way for them to explain away Christ's true person. They must work harder than ever to destroy him whom they could not control.

The resurrection of Lazarus went against all the Sadducees believed. The Pharisees and Sadducees were more fiercely united than ever. But what would be the most efficient way to remove the pretend Messiah?

CHAPTER 13 — Deception and Devotion

After that the Galilean left for Ephraim, a village near the desert, and stayed there with his disciples. As the time of Jewish Passover drew closer, many people from the surrounding countryside travelled to Jerusalem to purify themselves in Passover observance. Chief Priests and Pharisees had given the order that anyone seeing the Rabbi should report him so that the Jewish leaders could arrest him.

I learned that at least on one occasion when Temple police were sent to arrest him, they refused because they believed his teaching was inspired by God, proclaiming, "We've never heard anything like it."

Many on their way to the Passover and while waiting outside the Temple in Jerusalem, looked for the Deliverer and wondered, "What do you think? Will he come to the festival or not?"

The past few days have been a tumult of developments. Things are happening at a fever pitch. It seems like something's in the air. Stories are piling up, including one I just received from an insider about Simon the Pharisee, the Nazarene and a woman. I'm wondering if the contact made some assumptions or, perhaps, generalizations. He indicated that Jesus could easily have been the first man who had never exploited this woman and that his earlier encounter with her evidenced a love for her that changed her life.

I had heard of this woman with whom he had dealt several months past. She'd made a living working the streets. Rumor was that he saw through her exterior and reached out to her, setting her free from her downward spiraling lifestyle. Supposedly he had released her of demon possession. Some say as many as seven demons.

Now he had come to Simon's. Although Simon the Pharisee despised the Rabbi, he reasoned that having this popular person in his home would be a feather in his cap. He could gloat over having this wonder-working mendicant on display, something to brag about among his peers, giving him more attention and more importance. Consequently Simon invited the Rabbi to dinner.

The Nazarene accepted.

When he entered Simon's home, his host did not offer the customary water and towel for washing and drying his feet. As the meal commenced, servers busied themselves waiting on their guests who reclined comfortably conversing on couches or pallets arranged around the table. While the Galilean, Simon and notable guests ate a sumptuous meal, it was not long until a silence fell over the room. Whereas the guests had previously focused on the Galilean, they discovered an interloper.

Raven locks framed her clear complexion. She moved with grace, motivated by great love, embodied by a sense of remorse and compassion.

Her eyes spoke of deep adoration. She approached the Rabbi from behind with a wrapped parcel and knelt at his feet. Tears streamed down her face and her body rocked with sobs. Tears dropped from her cheeks onto his dust covered feet, bathing them. She dried each foot with her long locks then leaned forward and kissed them tenderly in an act of total adoration and contrition.

Her boldness in displaying such open emotion before those who'd known her former life was overwhelming. If this is the same woman he forgave caught in adultery, it is all the more telling that her great joy overpowers her past. Perhaps this was her way of thanking him.

She slipped the ornately embroidered wrappings of an alabaster box of rare and very expensive, amber colored Indian nard known as Jatamansi. With trembling fingers she gently opened the pure nard, a costly perfume that some merchant had transported hundreds of miles over blazing deserts in a camel saddle. The contents of the bottle would cost at least 300 pence, 300 times the wage of a working man, equivalent to a year's wages. She poured the spikenard over the Master's feet, demonstrating her total submission to and respect for him.

The nard's fragrance permeated the entire house. A hush fell over the diners. Every person's eyes were riveted on her as she knelt before the master.

He turned to Mary whose eyes expectantly returned his gaze. His words were more fragrant than any perfume, "You are forgiven. You are remade. Go in peace."

The tears she'd shed were tears of joy, joy that her life was changed. Undoubtedly Jesus' compassion to her was the reason for her joy.

The guests were appalled by her antics and low murmurings of dissatisfaction rose in the room. People talked against her.

Someone stated in indignation, "For what purpose was this ointment wasted?"

The disciples were furious with the woman's actions, the Rabbi, the waste and their frustration—the money wasted on the perfume could well have been converted to the purchase of foodstuffs.

Another voice broke the silence, "This ointment is worth a fortune. Why wasn't this perfume sold for 300 pence and the proceeds given the poor?" The sacred scene where everyone was in rapt attention was broken. Shocked and wondering, the revelers looked to the voice. It was Judas Iscariot. When he questioned Mary's action, was he really concerned about the poor?

Judas Iscariot was from Kerioth in southern Israel. He was the only one of the Rabbi's companions not born in Galilee, from that standpoint, an outsider. Judas wasn't concerned for the poor rather he was a thief. His protest that funds for its sale could be placed in the band's treasury was merely a ruse. It was common knowledge among the Rabbi's followers that Judas managed the finances of the group and felt no shame in periodically raiding the kitty for his personal use. The Rabbi had spared his life on at least two occasions when the men were in danger of drowning. Even the Galilean had to pay taxes on one occasion with a coin from a fish's mouth. And he didn't even have enough money for a change of clothing. Judas had just embarrassed the group and shamed Mary. For what?

Although he had never taken Judas to task for his thieving behavior, his rebuke of Mary provided the opportunity. The Galilean admonished without mincing words, "Leave her alone. Mary has done me a high honor in preparation for my death. Why are you making problems for her? What she has done for me is indeed a good work! It was for the day of my burial that she kept this scent. You will always have the poor with you and you can be kind to them whenever you want to, but you will not always have me. She has done what was in her power to do. She has come beforehand to anoint my body and prepare it for burial. I tell you most sincerely, whenever this good news is proclaimed throughout the world, what she has done will be told also, in remembrance of her."

With the Rabbi's eyes piercing his, Judas dropped his gaze to the floor.

In the aftermath of the moment Judas was embarrassed and deeply angered. Judas' response was the turning point in his relationship with the Master, probably his best friend. Judas was hurt and his pride injured, and he wallowed in self-pity. Hostility, if not hatred, seethed within him and he determined to do something about it.

No one in the room could help notice the goings on. Simon smugly interpreted Mary's action as scurrilous, thinking it obvious that the Rabbi was not what he proclaimed or he would have known her history and not associated with her, much less allowed her to make a fool of herself over him—*If this man were a prophet, he would have known who this woman is who's touching him and what kind of woman she is because she's a sinner. The Deliverer would not have permitted this kind of woman to touch him. His very inaction to her makes a fool of him. Any dolt would know better.*

When I heard the story, I had to wonder if Simon knew Mary. *Is he one of her former clients, one of many men to do business with her on the street? Maybe she was not the only woman he had paid for her services.* Just wondering.

Simon's piety was all for naught as both Mary and Jesus knew and saw through him.

With his eyes on Mary the Prophet spoke to the host, "Simon, do you see this woman? Do you see her now as a sinner or a saint? You, of all people, being an educated Pharisee, a religious teacher of the law, should have known who I am and what I'm about. Yet you chose to think of me as a bumbling man, unaware of her past. You invited me here in order to impress your friends and colleagues.

"I came to your home, an invited guest. Yet you offered me no basin of water nor towel with which to cool and refresh my tired, dust covered feet. That courtesy is the least you could have extended. But you intentionally snubbed me.

"You did not embrace me nor offer the traditional welcoming kiss as I entered your home. You are too proud and it would not bode well with you were your friends to see you or hear about your extending such a gesture to me. You save your kisses for favored friends and their favor.

"You did not provide olive oil with which I could refresh my face with a mere drop or two.

"Where you failed to provide me water for my feet, this woman has washed my feet with her tears and wiped them with the hairs of her head. And the kiss you failed to give me was more than completed by this woman has not ceased to kiss my feet. Where you did not anoint my head with oil, this woman has anointed my feet with ointment. For this reason I tell you her sins, which have been many, are forgiven because she has shown much love. She accepts me for who I am.

"But to the one whom little is forgiven, the same one loves little." But then he turned toward the woman and looked deeply into her eyes, "Your sins are forgiven."

The guests wondered who this man was who forgave sin.

Simon, I have something to say to you."

"Yes, Rabbi. Go on."

"Once two people owed money to a creditor. One owed him five thousand denarii and the other owed him five hundred. Neither was able to repay the creditor and he forgave them both of their debts. Tell me, therefore, which of them will love him more?"

"I suppose the one he had forgiven the most."

"Exactly."

The Rabbi continued. "Your intellectual training apprises you of the differences between the publican and the Pharisee. And yet you have not learned the lesson. The Pharisee stood on the street corner, dressed in finery, where everyone could see him. His station was superior to others'. He was the epitome of success and religiosity. He stood there looking down his nose at others, knowing that he was better than they. He was the prime example of intellectual superiority. He prayed to himself, thanking God that he was not like other men—extortionists, unjust, adulterers and like the tax collector nearby. He extolled his fasting twice a week, tithing on all he acquired.

"Nearby stood a publican. As you know the Jews hate such men because they work in conjunction with the Roman government. The publican felt so unworthy of God's love and grace that he did not even raise his eyes heavenward when he prayed. With a contrite and humble spirit he addressed God and said, 'Lord, forgive me. I'm a sinner. I'm not worthy of You or your kindness.'

"Whom of these two do you think God would honor more—the proud, haughty Pharisee or the prideless, humble publican?"

When Simon did not answer, the Nazarene stated that the tax collector would be immediately forgiven but the Pharisee would not...that he who humbled himself would reap greater rewards than he who exalted himself.

With no response Simon's gaze fell toward the floor.

Although she remained silent throughout the entire affair, Mary's actions spoke volumes. The looks on the guests' faces reflected the greatly divergent effects her actions had upon the Galilean and Simon.

CHAPTER 14 — Jesus Visits Jerusalem

One of the great advantages of walking is the time given to thought. I've had much time to do that. When I took on this assignment of the Baptizer, thinking and telling Alexy I'd see him in a few short months, I never dreamed my mission would go on and on. Although it was taking longer than I'd assumed and at times I felt I was in over my head, I wasn't about to give in until my task was completed. Fatigue of following plagued my efforts yet there was a fascination that fueled my days and kept me going.

Shadowing Jesus, always trying to figure him and his motives, I added to the skeleton of his character. I was intrigued by his fondness for children. Made me wonder on numerous occasions who created this love in him. Was it his mother? His father? Perhaps his numerous siblings or another family member?

He lets the kids climb all over him, laughs with them, picks flowers for them, teases them. I remember a time when a couple of young girls, probably ten or eleven were on either side of him playing with his hair, running their hands through it like combs and fashioning it. It crossed my mind that they mimicked their mothers or other ladies who braided their hair high atop their heads, intertwining jewels.

I knew the adornment of their hair with gold, pearls and precious stones like rubies, emeralds and sapphire presents a showcase — so elaborate as to be a sensation, one enhanced by their costly attire—a definite abandonment of rules for righteous living among the Jewish culture.

Other youngsters sat on his lap or ran about him laughing and playing, trying to get his attention for they seemed to feel his love and approval.

And when he laughed, it wasn't a giggle. He roared real belly laughter.

I've watched him with adults, acting much the same way as with children. They might be having a celebration, party, general conversation or other activity. He seems to always have a good time, whether he's engaging run-of-the mill folks, prostitutes and hard core or sophisticates . . . unless, of course, he's being hounded by the persistent Jewish leaders.

Although some of my thoughts about him were pleasant, even satisfying, others were troubling, or, at least, gave me pause for more concerned analysis. Whereas Roman theology revealed that all go to the underworld after death, the Nazarene's way divided people into two groups, one eternally damned and the other eternally blessed.

And when I heard him proclaim, "I am the Way, the Truth and the Life," I was thunderstruck. Let's examine that concept for a minute. If I break down each of these—way, truth, life, is he claiming to be the gateway, the portal? What about Allah or Buddah? And what about Jupiter? How many paths are there to God? Was he saying that the only way to his Father was through him?

If he is the way to the father and he is equally the truth, his claim indicates that he is life. Do I have it correct...following his path of truth leads to life? And how, exactly, does that work?

Jesus departed Bethany for Jerusalem determined to celebrate Passover there. Hundreds of thousands made the annual pilgrimage and stayed in households, nearby villages or tents outside city walls. And it was customary for people to stay with friends. Pilgrims usually came a week early to observe purification rites. Unrest accompanied the crowd. Roman troops patrolled temple roof porticoes on the lookout for trouble.

Jerusalem teemed with both Jews and Gentiles who had a bad taste in their mouths. Whether oppressed by Roman soldiers or crooked Jewish religious leaders, they wanted an emissary from God to turn their fortunes around. They expected, hoped for and anticipated the Messiah to deliver them from Rome's oppressive rule. They clamored for the deliverer whom their ancient texts prophesied and the climate in Jerusalem was rife for a revolution.

Rumor was that the Messiah was en route to join in the celebration.

Of course, the Pharisees and Jewish leaders hoped that he would appear so that they could condemn him. Many inquired, "Where is he?" But no one knew. As usual he was the topic of conversation throughout Jerusalem as well as throughout the adjoining countryside.

Had he chosen to travel with any of the Jerusalem bound caravans, he would easily have been discovered and feted with wide acceptance and jubilation. However he chose to travel a lesser route to avoid the clamor.

The Rabbi arrived among the celebrants with much more on his agenda than the normal celebration. When he and his followers were on the outskirts of Jerusalem the next day, in sight of Bethpage and Bethany on the Mount of Olives, he sent two disciples on ahead, telling them, "Go into the village facing you and as soon as you enter it, you will find the foal of a donkey that no one has ever ridden. It is tied there. Untie it and bring the colt to me. If anyone says to you, 'What are you doing? Why are you untying the colt?' Tell them, 'The Master needs him for a while, but he will send the colt back when he is finished.'"

The Galilean followed Jewish custom for royal entry. The animal chosen was that ridden by the kings of Israel and prophetically foretold that the Messiah should thus come to his kingdom.

The disciples left to obey his wishes. As they departed scratching their heads, they wondered how the Master could have known about the colt. Everything was exactly as he'd stated. They found the colt as he'd said and began untying it when its owner asked, "What are you doing untying that colt?"

"The Master needs it."

The owner was a Judaean stranger. It was not common in Judaea for people to let their possessions out of their sight. But this man was sympathetic to the Prophet from Galilee. The animal's owner didn't even request a fee.

He agreed to let the disciples take his donkey for their purpose.

While returning to the Rabbi with the colt, they must have wondered why he hadn't chosen some glistening stallion so that he could arrive in splendor. Perhaps they had momentarily forgotten that the ass is symbolic of suffering service, which was the Deliverer's reason for coming to Jerusalem and the world. The lowly animal was also a symbol of judgment—traditionally Israel's judges rode donkeys. Could the Nazarene, in fact, be the Judge of the world?

When they returned to the Rabbi with the colt and he was prepared to mount it, they threw their tunics over the colt's bare back. The frisky colt never flinched, another strange event. Normally such a beast would toss its head and kick its heels, knocking the garments to the ground. Bystanders were amazed at the colt's passivity and at the Rabbi's mastery. Many men removed their tunics and placed them onto the roadbed. A crowd developed and people cheered, climbed trees and clapped their hands.

Even though the joke among the people was that nothing good could come out of Nazareth, the Rabbi came forth riding a donkey, the symbol for peace. He was not dressed to the nines in finery. As he rode through the streets of Jerusalem arriving from the Mount of Olives, from whence the Lord's Anointed was to come, the crowd of hopeful believers laid palm branches and articles of clothing in his pathway. Some waved victory palm branches.

The disciples began chanting in unison, "Blessed be the King that comes in ecstasy. Peace in heaven, and glory in the highest."

The crowd was electrified, some shouting, "Hosanna to the son of David!"

Still others wondered who the man on the donkey might be, "Who is it?" they queried.

They were told, "It is Jesus, the prophet from Nazareth, up in Galilee."

Children ran along beside the colt, laughing and giggling, yelling and waving sticks. Still the colt was undeterred by the commotion and people were amazed.

Many went to see him because they had seen his resurrection of Lazarus or had heard of it.

As he neared the lower slopes of the Mount of Olives, the entire group of disciples joyfully rejoiced with praise for God.

As the event unfolded before me, I recalled Jewish prophesy regarding the Messiah's coming on a lowly animal, not on a white horse in kingly fashion. I'm wondering if the prophecy is being fulfilled before my very eyes.

In Jerusalem crowds, hearing of the Deliverer's approach, took palm branches and went to meet him. Crowds went before him and all shouted...

"Hosanna to the Son of David"...

"Hosanna"...

"Blessings on him who comes in the name of the Lord"...

"Blessed is the Kingdom of our father David"...

"Blessings on the King of Israel who comes in the name of the Lord"...

"Hosanna in the highest heavens!"

The throng increased in size and their excitement swelled. Many gawkers came to witness this man about whom others had spoken.

Somewhere in my recent past my cynicism regarding the Nazarene boiled forth to its peak. Up till then I would have questioned what was happening before me. Here's a man expected to free the Jews from their oppressor...to bring forth an army to slay the bad guys. That kind of man would arrive on a white war horse as a military leader. He would be sheathed in armor from head to foot and wearing a majestic sword. More than likely he'd have a troop of soldiers armed with shields and spears.

But no. He shows up on a burro, the symbol of a servant. He wears no armor, doesn't even carry a weapon. How does he plan to overpower the enemy and to lead these Jews against their oppressors? What's with that?

While I contemplated these things, a nearby stranger shouted, "Jesus the deliverer will save us from the heel of Rome. He will lead us against the Eagle and root them from our land. I'm sure of it."

I turned to him and asked, "How so?"

"Look at what he's done so far—healed the sick, restored the dead to life."

As the throng progressed, more people beheld the Nazarene, frenzy developed and others shouted...

"Jesus the Deliverer comes!'"

"The Deliverer lives!"

"He will save us from our Roman masters. Look what Moses did against Pharaoh. Jesus will do even more—rid us of the chains."

But Jesus was a paradox: people honored him, displaying their joy even though they failed to understand him. And their great city, Jerusalem, failed to understand. Her religious leaders, by rejecting him and his plan, doomed Jerusalem for all time to come. He mourned the loss of Jerusalem much as a mother's loss of a beloved son.

He rode into the heart of the city and on to the Temple. The Rabbi called for man to put God first, to "strive for the kingdom of God" and refused to take his focus from that exhortation. He was a thorn in the side of the religious leaders and the Roman government, arousing the ire of both because he taught that man should be free to worship God in truth. The corrupt leaders did not want to hear that.

He wept over Jerusalem and said, "Eternal peace was within your reach and you turned it down. Now it is too late. Your enemies will pile up earth against your walls and encircle you and close in on you and crush you to the ground and your children within you; your enemies will not leave one stone upon another for you have rejected the opportunity God offered you."

The seasons of the Jewish celebration in Jerusalem always regenerated Roman authority's nervousness. Increasing numbers of people arriving and the tenuous relationship between the Jews and the Romans provided a tightrope of balance—a sure opportunity for revolution. The threat of mayhem was sufficient enough to cause Rome to enforce its military might. Troops at the fortress normally numbered about a thousand, including support personnel; but this celebratory season those numbers would swell into the thousands.

Although Pilate dwelled in Caesarea on the coast, during this time he chose to be in Jerusalem to monitor possible problems and to negate their development. Among the vocal Galileans who tended to be more aggressive, as well as other possible revolutionaries, he thought it prudent to keep a lid on activities.

His soldiers kept a watchful eye from the Fortress Antonia which overlooked the temple courts. The fortress was the home of the 10th Legion, Fretensis, which occupied Jerusalem and surrounding Judaea. In Judaea legionary troops not stationed under procurators would be a military cohort consisting of one thousand men—seven hundred sixty infantry and two hundred forty cavalry.

As I followed the crowd in Jerusalem, I noted people wondered about the Nazarene's lack of interest in attending the religious festivities. Even his brothers questioned his attitude toward the religious leaders. They, as others, wanted a Messiah to free them from bondage to any nation.

The Deliverer's name and wonders had spread and people hoped to at least catch a glimpse of the miracle worker acknowledging who some thought might even be the Messiah. His reputation reached across the nations and thousands travelled to see him, hoping to be cured of illness or to witness in person the man who would free them once and for all.

At the height of the excitement and expectation of his appearance, he entered the Temple court before the gathered crowd. All were surprised by his presence. Minds wondered.

How could he have the courage to present himself?

How would Pharisees and Jewish leaders respond?

What would they do to him?

Entering the Temple that Monday morning with his disciples the Rabbi again found The Bazaars of Annas doing a booming business, accompanied by a bedlam of activity.

He took in the scene at a glance. The Temple was in worse moral condition than it had been the first time he cleared it. Oxen, sheep, dove-sellers and usurers, along with cattle, occupied the tessellated floors beneath the pillared colonnades of the Court of the Gentiles. The tinkling of coins changing hands—money from Egypt, Greece, Persia or Tyre, in exchange for the accepted Temple half-shekel—continued.

Worshippers and scoundrels alike saw the Rabbi. Every eye was on him—priest, worshiper, Pharisee, Gentile—waiting to see what he would do. Every sound ceased. Ever explosive, unbearable silence reigned. Overcome with awe, the assembly awaited—some in trepidation, others in eager anticipation. All read the authority, indignation and power in his glance. His countenance spoke more than his words. His angry scowl registered disgust.

The worshippers witnessed a deliverer; the scoundrels saw an enforcer. The eyes of both groups riveted to his demeanor. They viewed a man

who read their minds,

who knew what they were thinking,

who knew how he would respond to their individual circumstances.

The guilty trembled in fear. The innocent trusted in favor.

The poor thought there would be no forgiveness of their sin without the shedding of blood. However the Prophet had come to change the ancient message of the blood sacrifice of animals. He was the final sacrifice to fulfill the prophecies.

Wide eyed, mute hopefuls, mouths agape, wondered what was happening. They had a hero... someone who was not afraid to face the priests. Someone who took on the avaricious money changers and dealers. But who was he and what would become of him? The simmering silence erupted into a cheer from the crowd that swelled around him as he strode through the Temple.

He had spent a lifetime in synagogues and observed the priests. I wondered how their deceitful actions flew in the face of the God they served.

Incensed by the callousness of the priests, he grabbed the bottom of a money changer's table, lifted it and tossed it to the side, spilling its wares onto the floor. Quickly he stepped to the next table and repeated his previous action, miscellaneous items, silver and bronze coins sailed off and clattered onto the marble floor—shekels, as and denarius rattled and rolled in all directions across the floor.

He passed from one table to another, upsetting each one.

He displaced the benches of the pigeon sellers. And then after an interminable hush of human voices, he spoke with a power unknown to the crowd, "My house shall be called a house of prayer. You have perverted it to a den of thieves." One fat money changer, his face full of smugness changed to fear, cringed behind a table.

Then Jesus strode to the cattle pens, shouldered his way past some dealers, ripped off the bars from the pens and drove the bellowing animals through the crowd and into the street.

He would not allow anyone to carry anything through the Temple.

Surprise and anger registered on the bland faces of the keepers of the tables.

It was a cauldron of calamity.

With all eyes upon him, he confidently descended the steps, approached the greedy merchants, cattle traders, sellers of sacrificial animals and priests and said, "Take these things away. Make not of my Father's house a house of merchandise." He cleared the Temple of the corrupt—priests, money changers, cattle traders and other sellers of animals.

He forced them from the Temple. When he had confronted them previously in the Temple, they were more brazen. Now they fled in fear, driving their bawling cattle, braying burros and bleating sheep before them.

Each person in the Temple had his thoughts about this Galilean, a carpenter whose authority overshadowed even that of the priests who fled in fear. They knew they were cheats and extortionists. Temple guards stood helplessly in awe.

As the priests fled, they encountered more people coming to receive the Healer's ministrations—weak, blind, sick and maimed.

Later that night I heard numerous people telling others about the near revolt in the Temple. More than one spoke.

"Did you hear about what happened in the Temple today?"

"A stranger and holy man named Jesus literally cleaned house. "

"He whipped a few thievin' dealers and money changers. They had it comin' to 'em."

"He used to be a carpenter from up around Nazareth."

"I heard panicked pandemonium prevailed."

I considered the Galilean's healing on the Sabbath and the Jews determination to persecute him, seeking to kill him. I remembered his rebuke of their criticism and his explanation that relieving the afflicted was in harmony with the Sabbath law. He also addressed and denounced the ridiculousness of their made up traditions that had nothing to do with the scriptures. He stated simply and powerfully that "My Father goes on working and so do I."

Thus they became more greatly inflamed, not only because he had broken Sabbath custom but also because he claimed to be equal to God. When they'd finished their futile attempt to condemn him, he said, "I tell you most sincerely the Son can do nothing of himself but what he sees the Father do. The Father loves the Son and shows him all the things that He Himself does and He will show him greater works than these so that you will marvel. Just as the Father raises up the dead and gives them life, so the Son gives life to whomever he will. For the Father has entrusted all judgment to the Son, so that all men should honor the Son as they honor the Father. Anyone who does not honor the Son, honors not the Father who has sent him.

"Don't be surprised because the hour is coming in which all that are in the graves will hear his voice and will come forth—they that have done good into the resurrection of life and they that have done evil to the resurrection of condemnation.

"Of myself I can do nothing. As I hear, I judge and my judgment is just because I do not seek my own will but that of the Father who sent me. If I bear witness of myself, my witness is not true.

"The Father who sent me has borne witness of me. You have never heard His voice at any time, nor seen His shape and you do not have His Word living in you, because you do not believe the one whom He has sent. You think that you have eternal life in the scriptures. These scriptures testify of me and you still refuse to come to me so that you might have life. It means nothing to me to have approval from men, but I know you; and you don't have the love of God in you.

"Even though I have come in my Father's name, you refuse to accept me. If someone else comes in his own name, you will accept him. How can you believe when you constantly look to each other for approval and refuse to seek the approval that comes only from God? Do you think that I will refuse you to the Father? There is one that accuses you, even Moses, in whom you trust. Had you believed Moses, you would have believed me because he wrote of me. If you don't believe his writings, how can you believe my words?"

For six days the Galilean and his close associates commuted between Bethany and Jerusalem where he taught daily. At night they stayed at Lazarus' place or in an olive grove where they gathered around a small campfire in the evening hours.

It has become a priority for me to monitor the undercurrent of deception woven by the high priests in order to ascertain whether they violated Roman law. What was their plan? Where would it end? I hear his words and watch the almighty "holy ones" and marvel...*he's the bravest man I've ever seen. He IS worthy of doing battle with Alexius.*

CHAPTER 15 — Jesus Excels; Judas Fails

The Galilean knew that he had definitely upset the ruling priests and their society and that his time was nearly over.

The Pharisees were jealous of his reputation with the people and angry over his humiliating them. They chose to challenge his authority and to belittle him in front of the people. Fearing for their safety because every day more people heard his message and believed in the Nazarene, the Chief Priests and scribes schemed to come up with a way to belittle and destroy him without upsetting his followers. They figured it was only a matter of time. They would get him.

As the evening trumpet sounded at the Temple to alert worshippers, few appeared. The Pharisees looked at each other and stated, "We've lost. Look— the whole world has gone for him!"

The setting sun reflected from the white marble walls of the Temple looking like a monstrous pile of snow. Highlighted by gold capped pillars it presented a golden visage with green foliage in the background.

As it was late, Jesus went to Bethany with his twelve disciples where he spent the entire night in prayer.

Once again I was reminded about the Jewish elders and their concerns regarding the Nazarene. Their spies shadowed him his entire time in Jerusalem. Many tried to silence him. They told him, "Master, tell your disciples to stop!"

But he replied, "I tell you, that if they were to keep silent, the stones would start to cry out."

While he instructed others, Jewish leaders monitored his every move, calling for yet more spies. There were enough unscrupulous people around who would do about anything for money. Under constant surveillance day and night, everywhere he went someone was watching him. High priests had long been known to bribe ruffians to do their bidding. It would be nothing for those brigands to integrate amongst the passersby and influence an outcome.

Throughout Palestine priests and rulers looked for any opportunity to ensnare him. They knew it. The Nazarene's followers knew it. He knew it. Word had gotten out.

The Nazarene carried on his teaching, either purposely or by coincidence, avoiding his accusers who orchestrated his removal. Things seemed to be coming to a head.

The next day the Rabbi returned to teach in the Temple where the religious leaders awaited his arrival. The priests feared him because they knew he saw through their deceptive Temple trade which would be compromised if people believed him. Even though the Jewish leaders feared that with his increasing status among his followers would cause an uprising that the Romans would suppress, the Rabbi was not afraid of them and their charlatan ways. With deception in their minds they approached him and asked, "By what authority are you doing these things, or who gave you this authority to do them?"

He knew their game. He read between the lines and stated, "I will ask you a question. Answer me and I will tell you by what authority I do these things. Was the baptism of John from heaven or from men? Give me your answer."

The hecklers frantically discussed the question among themselves, knowing that they had trapped themselves. They argued, "If we say it is from heaven, he'll say, 'Then why didn't you believe him?' If we dare to say it is from man, we will have the people to contend with and we fear them. They will stone us, for they are convinced that John was a real prophet. We can't tell him where it came from."

At length they answered, "We do not know."

His response was bold and revealed his craftiness, "Then neither will I tell you by what authority I do these things." He then told them a story involving a man with two sons. "What do you think of this? A man with two sons told the older son, 'Go out and work on the farm today.' The son answered, 'I won't.' Then the father told the younger son, 'You go.' The boy said that he would. As it turned out the older boy changed his mind and worked whereas the younger did not. Which of the two obeyed his father?"

They rapidly stated, "The first, of course."

Then he explained his meaning, "Surely evil men and prostitutes will get into the Kingdom before you do. For John the Baptist told you to repent and turn to God and you wouldn't. But the evil men and prostitutes did. And even when you saw this happening, you refused to repent."

Yet again, I was astounded by the Galilean's courage and straightforwardness. He is really laying into them here! His chutzpah amazes me. He reminds the Pharisees they are guilty of puffing up themselves. As I witnessed the Pharisees and Sadducees try to trick him, it was pretty laughable. They asked him...and he responded by getting right in their faces—a truthful, thoughtful answer that merely inflamed them. They wanted him in their mold. They were staunchly rooted in their belief that nothing new is good—man must rely on traditional bunk. But he merely told them the he represented the fulfilling of the old. He taught the Jewish faith but he took it a step farther.

He told them a story about a vineyard owner who sent his agents to collect the earnings from farmers who sharecropped his grapes. The farmers attacked his agents, killing one, stoning one and beating a third. Then the owner sent a larger group with the same results. So in the end he chose to send his son. These crafty sharecroppers decided among themselves to kill the son so that they could acquire the vineyard. They dragged the son from the vineyard and killed him. Then the Rabbi asked them what they thought the owner would do to those farmers.

"He will put them all to death and lease his property to more responsible men."

He reminded them that the "Stone rejected by the builders has been made the honored cornerstone. The Kingdom of God will be taken away from you and given to a nation that will give God his share of the crop. All who stumble on this rock of truth shall be broken, but those it falls on will be scattered as dust."

The Rabbi explained their need to acknowledge the importance of instruction and fatherhood when he said, "You, however, must not allow yourselves to be called rabbi, since you have only one master and you are all brothers. You must call no one on earth your father since you have only one father who is in Heaven. Nor must you allow yourselves to be called teachers for you have only one teacher, the Christ, the greatest among you must be a servant."

The Chief Priests and other Jewish leaders realized that the Rabbi was talking about them—they could not escape his truthful portrayal of them and their anger burned hatred for him.

I find it more than amusing—almost beyond comprehension—that the laundry list of accusations and charges against the Nazarene is so absurd. Most of his accusers are caught up in rules with no real basis for their claims. Their religious teachings disallow a number of activities practiced by Jesus. And another thing, he called the religious leaders hypocrites while pointing out their burdensome demands and their hypocrisy as play actors—unwilling to follow their own teachings. Their defense of the indefensible gets their goat. To watch him upbraid the Pharisees and other religious leaders for the façade of their attire and attitude is enjoyable.

I've now followed the Nazarene for over two years and the more I see of him, the less he proves to be anything but a threat to the Empire. It seems to me were he planning an earthly kingdom, two factors would have prevailed by now: one, he would have made his plans known; and two, he could have initiated some kind of uprising among his followers to oppose Rome. He would have and could have initiated such a movement had he so chosen.

These Jews can't find him guilty because he's telling the truth. They revile him because he puts a dent in their plans; he speaks to the heart, mind and soul and they are not willing to compromise their selfishness, their access to power nor their goals of riches. They challenge him to prove that he is God. They mock and denigrate with little substance to support their theories. They do not want him ruling their lives. They can do so rather nicely, thank you very much. Jewish authorities want to make him a scapegoat. I need to get word to the Roman authorities to stave this lunacy.

The problem is that both the Jewish leaders and Pilate distrust the other to the point of near hatred. Pilate knows Caiaphas and his associates were not Pilate's friends and would relish his demise. On the other hand Caiaphas knew that he was treading on shaky ground as his father-in-law Annas had recently been deposed. He did not want to suffer the same fate.

Jewish leaders argued among themselves about the most productive means of ridding themselves of Jesus. He does nothing to raise a finger against the Empire. He is not attacking the Roman Empire per se but rather he is attacking what makes man evil. He's confronting the Pharisees, Sadducees, scholars and priests for their convoluting the Law and for their hypocrisy. I must concisely report this to my superior, providing him the truth.

As people gathered around during the days while he taught in the Temple, the Chief Priests, Scribes and the Elders of the people assembled in the palace of the high priest, Caiaphas, to make plans to arrest the Nazarene by some deception and have him killed.

They reminded each other they couldn't make their move during the Passover because of the tremendous number of people who would be attending the festival. Any action against the Prophet could be detrimental to them.

They decided the best means of carrying out the Rabbi's destruction would be under cover of darkness. They could execute their plan before his followers and his adoring crowds discovered what had happened.

Meanwhile he spent his nights on the hill called the Mount of Olives, I learned from a contact he reminded his disciples, "As you know, in two days time it will be the Feast of Unleavened Bread, called the Passover and the Son of Man will be betrayed and handed over to be executed."

Though unknown to most everyone, this betrayal marked the end of the Galilean's public ministry and the preparation of his final acts upon earth.

I gather from his comments that he expects to be accused and executed. If this is the case, it points undeniably to the holy word of the Jews that prophesies in Isaiah that a lamb will be led to the slaughter, that the lamb will be innocent and die for mankind's transgressions against God. More and more this Nazarene puzzle is coming together and making sense, even though I'm not sure "making sense" is the correct phrase. The holy scriptures and the deception of Jewish leadership tend to confirm the Master's fate.

The Jewish council was called. Because both Joseph and Nicodemus had previously blocked the way for them to remove the Deliverer, neither man was called. Although arguments were presented, the members of the council were not in agreement. Some felt that by attacking Jesus the powers they now held and further favors from the Romans would be withheld from them. Even though they were united in their hatred for Jesus, the Sadducees felt much the same way. They feared that people would turn to Jesus because of his miracles, fearing the Romans would respond by taking away their place and nation.

At the height of the perplexity Caiaphas, the high priest, rose. His family connections included many Sadducees whose reckless and cruel nature was hidden under the cloak of pretentious righteousness. A proud, overbearing and intolerant man, he prepared to address the issue.

Although his knowledge of the prophecies was devoid of any understanding of their meaning, he was held in high esteem. Relying on his reputation he intimated scapegoating Jesus in order to save Israel stating, "It is expedient for us that one man die for the people not that the entire nation perish."

Caiaphas felt that the resurrection of Lazarus would likely cause the Galilean's followers to revolt and reminded these men, "If that were to happen, the Romans will quell the revolt, close the Temple and abolish our laws, effectively destroying our nation."

I recalled their deception when they had asked, "Master, we know you're an honest man. You say that you teach what is right. You're not afraid of anyone because a man's rank means nothing to you. You favor no one. You teach the way of God in truth and in all honesty. Under God's Law are we allowed to pay taxes to Caesar or not?"

It seems that on every turn, the Nazarene outwitted them. As usual, aware of their conniving ways, he saw through their trickery and said, "You hypocrites! Why are you trying to set this trap for me? Show me the money you pay taxes with, hand me a denarius and let me see it!"

They handed him a denarius and he said, "Whose head is on this coin and whose name is on it?"

"Caesar's?"

"Very well. Give back to Caesar what belongs to Caesar and to God what belongs to God."

Unable to trip him up and amazed by his response, the Chief Scribes and Pharisees immediately left him.

These men planned to use the Rabbi's words against him. They sent their disciples and the Herodians to the Nazarene and waited their opportunity. Posing as devoted men of the Law these men were to find something in his words to turn him over to the governor.

The same day some Sadducees who did not believe in the resurrection of the dead came to him and asked, "Master, Moses wrote to us that 'if a man who is married dies and leaves his wife without giving her any children, the brother of the dead man is supposed to marry his sister-in-law in order to raise up children for his brother. There was a situation wherein a man died leaving his wife childless. And as it happened each of his seven brothers married her before dieing. She outlived all and had no children with any of them. When they rise in the resurrection, which one of the seven brothers will be her husband?"

"It is because you do not understand the scriptures or the power of God that you're reasoning is so faulty. The children of this world take wives and husbands, but those men and women who are judged worthy of a place in the other world and in the resurrection from the dead will neither marry nor be given in marriage when they rise from the dead because they can no longer die. They are like the angels in heaven. Being children of the resurrection, they are sons of God.

"As for the resurrection of the dead, Moses wrote that the dead rise again. Have you never read in the book of Moses in the passage about the bush what God said to you? God spoke to Moses saying that he was the God of Abraham, Isaac and Jacob. He is not the God of the dead but of the living, and to Him all men are alive."

A Pharisee who learned that Jesus had silenced the Sadducees decided to confront him. This Pharisee was an attorney who asked Jesus, "Which is the first and greatest of all the commandments?"

Without hesitating Jesus responded, "This is the first, 'Hear, O Israel! The Lord our God is the one and only God. And you must love him with all your heart and soul and mind and strength.' The second is, 'You must love others as much as yourself.' No other commandments are greater than these.'"

The Pharisees had no response.

Where the Rabbi spent most of his time speaking in public, the priests employed their most learned minds to try to trick him with their theological and political questions, all the while trying to retain their proud and pompous attitudes.

The Jewish leaders feared the prospect of losing their power, prestige and positions of prominence. They were terrified. Their growing fears led them to the conclusion that they'd have to destroy him, at whatever cost. Their options were based on religion and politics. They must convince the leaders that the Nazarene was blasphemous or they would have to convince the Roman rulers that he was a threat to them.

The Pharisees, scribes, elders, Chief Priests and Sadducees seethed with rage and hatred, humiliated by the Prophet's ever growing crowd of followers and believers.

They had set three traps for him: 1) political: "is it lawful to give tribute to Caesar or not?" 2) spiritual: if a woman married and widowed seven times, which husband would be hers in the resurrection of life?—a stupid question in light of the fact that the Sadducees did not believe in the resurrection and the leaders were ignorant of what God did to restore his own after death. 3) Legal and moral, "What is the greatest commandment?"

He withstood their nonsense and added a question of his own. "What do you think of Christ…whose son is he?"

"He is the son of David."

"If that is the case, how did David call this One, the Christ, Lord?" And taking it a step further, "If David called him Lord, how then can he also be his son?"

They were stumped. They knew they were stumped. And they knew that he knew they were stumped. They had no response. From that day forward no one challenged the Master again.

Not only did the Rabbi speak openly about the Scribes and Pharisees, but also he confronted them, "Everything they do is done to attract attention— wearing broader phylacteries, longer tassels and walking about in long robes, wanting the place of honor at banquets and in the synagogues. They love having you bow to them as they pass by. Even when they pray, they scheme how to prey upon the widows. These men are to be damned.

"They occupy the seat of Moses. Obey these teachers in their teachings of God's word. Do what they tell you and listen to what they say; but do not be guided by what they do—since they do not practice what they preach. They tie up heavy burdens and lay them on men's shoulders, but they lift nary a finger to move them.

"They are a disgrace to the God they pretend to represent. They are a disgrace to themselves. Their words are a travesty to their God. In their presentation they are angels; in their lives, scoundrels and deceivers."

"Hypocrites, you shut up the Kingdom of Heaven in men's faces. Not only are you NOT going there, you prevent those who are on their way from entering. You devour the property of widows even though you make a display with lengthy prayers. Because of this you will receive the greater damnation. You travel over land and sea to convert one person and once he has been converted, you make him twice the child of Gehenna as you are."

He told his followers that the first would be last and the last would be first, something about "the greatest among you will be your servant." What king or leader would be a servant? I wonder *how can the Nazarene be plotting to form a kingdom, one of servants without a king?* And too, he talks about dispensing with all your wealth and following him in order to have life forever. *Why would a man bent on kingship tell a follower to dispense with his money—that money would be invaluable for the kingdom?*

Interestingly, he made the point that only total commitment by his followers would assure them of eternal life. There is a striking parallel to Rome, which demands total commitment of its subjects—just as any successful venture demands the same in order for total achievement.

He even tells people not to call him king nor to refer to him in an exalted position.

While the Galilean was in the forefront of the activity, Judas worked behind the scenes. Ever since his time at Simon's when the Rabbi rebuked him for squabbling about Mary Magdalene's perfume, Judas had thought about his options. From then on he looked for every opportunity to betray the Rabbi without being detected by the people.

Money seemed to be of great significance to him, if not his number one motivator.

Maybe Judas had expectations that did not develop, things that he thought Jesus would or should have done differently. Perhaps it rankled Judas that the Rabbi didn't ask him to act on behalf of churches in a profitable manner. Maybe Judas saw himself like the rich young ruler and the camel's eye in the story told by the Rabbi. Perhaps in some ways he felt he was smarter than the Master. Maybe he reasoned if the Rabbi was going to die, it would be of no consequence that Judas betrayed him...*I might as well gain financially from it.*

On the other hand, perhaps he thought if the Rabbi were to establish a kingdom, his followers would wrest him from death. Judas could turn the Rabbi over to the priests and bring the event to its high point.

It was now time to enact his plan.

He made his way to a group of Pharisees, willing to deliver the Rabbi in exchange for money. Judas asked, "How much is it worth to you for me to deliver him into your hands?"

They were delighted

The men stroked their beards, wondering if Judas would actually betray the man he'd been with for nearly three years. Wondering if he was stupid enough to accept the sum of a slave. They toyed with him. One of the priests, with phony smile and yellowed teeth, withdrew his purse from beneath his robe and suggested, "Thirty pieces of silver."

Judas was pleased. Quite pleased. He'd made a deal and come out on top. A certain smugness overcame him as he savored his craftiness.

All of Jerusalem had expectantly awaited Passover. Worshippers prepared to present their sacrificial animal, firewood was gathered for roasting it, wild bitter herbs gathered or purchased from street vendors, unleavened bread baked throughout the city...preparing and eating the sacrificial lamb and washing it down with wine must be accomplished before midnight.

When the first day of Passover came, Jesus told Peter and John to make the preparations. They asked him where he wanted to celebrate the feast. He sent them into Jerusalem, telling them, "When you enter the city, you will meet a man carrying a vessel of water. Follow him into the house and tell the owner of the house he enters, 'The Master says his time is near and that it is your house where he will celebrate the Passover with his disciples. Where is the dining room?' The man will show you a large upper room furnished with couches all prepared."

What the heck, they thought, *a man carrying a water pot? Women carry water pots, not men! So, we're supposed to find one man in a million carrying a pot?* They, however, obeyed and left in search of the man they sought.

Before long they found a servant from the home of John Mark's father. The home owner owned a large home capable of housing a number of people. As they were directed to a room above the main living quarters, John and Peter were amazed. Provisions for their celebrations had been made and the room was furnished with a table, couches, cushions and pillows. Outside a young lamb awaited its historic place. The facilities and arrangements were more than adequate for the thirteen to celebrate.

Later when the disciples approached with the Nazarene, I followed, watching with growing curiosity and took up a post in hiding outside the place they entered, awaiting their re-appearance. I had heard they were going to eat a meal.

Quite some time later I noticed Judas exit the building alone and disappear into the night. It was much later that I learned about the events that had occurred inside.

CHAPTER 16 — Jesus "Surrenders"

That evening it was with interest that I learned about the Galilean's time with his cohorts. When he and the others arrived, they made their way to the appointed room and arranged themselves on the low couches. Chattering voices filled the room along with the aroma of freshly baked bread and the sweet fragrance of roast lamb. Captured by the festive mood, the men joyfully shared in it. They broke the unleavened bread cakes and dipped them into the steaming dishes of bitter herbs. They ate unsparingly of the roast lamb and drank wine in the candlelight.

However as the evening hours lengthened, there was some discussion as to which disciple should be most important. Scowls and tempers flared. They argued about who should be the greatest. When the Nazarene reminded them that the greatest among them would be a servant, his words effectively deflated their egos and addressed their selfish attitudes.

He took some bread, gave thanks, broke it and passed it among the disciples telling them it represented his body which would be given for them. He encouraged their eating it as a memorial to him.

Likewise he took a cup, gave thanks and told them to drink from it because it symbolized his body's blood, the blood of the New Covenant; his blood would be poured out for many for the forgiveness of sins. He told them he would "not drink from the fruit of the vine until the time he would drink it in the new Kingdom of my Father with you."

Because he knew Judas was about to betray him, the Rabbi was troubled in spirit. In the midst of the good hearted banter he announced, "One of you will betray me."

Mortified and mystified, the disciples wondered who it could be. There was doubt among the disciples. Each responded individually, "Is it I?"

Peter leaned against the Rabbi and asked, "Lord, who is it?"

"It is one of you sitting here. And it would be better for him if he had never been born. The one I am going to give this piece of bread to after I have dipped it in the herb dish."

Acting innocent and knowing full well that blood money lay beneath his robe and that the Rabbi spoke of him, Judas asked, "Rabbi, is it I?"

Jesus handed Judas a piece of bread, saying, "You have said it. What you are about to do, do quickly."

Rabbi then told the disciples that they had faithfully stood by him and that he would be with them only for a short while before leaving them. That they wouldn't be able to follow him.

Peter objected and asked where he was going, stating he wanted to go with him and that he'd lay down his life for his master.

The Galilean told Peter that Simon would denounce him three times before a rooster crowed.

Philip said they would be satisfied if Jesus showed them the Father.

The Nazarene asked Philip if his presence with the disciples these many months hadn't revealed who he was. He went on to explain that whoever has seen him has seen the Father because the Father lives in the son.

He reminded the disciples to keep a new commandment, later to become known as the great commandment: love God with all your heart, mind, soul and strength; likewise love your fellow man as you do yourself. He told them that the spirit was willing but that the body was weak. And he warned them that they would be persecuted if they pledged their allegiance to him.

The hour grew late. The men left the upper room slinking eastward along the city walls, moving silently through the shadowed streets. Furtively looking behind them, they wondered if they were being followed as they hiked toward the Mount of Olives. When they finally reached the limestone ridge of the Mount of Olives, the men breathed a little easier. They dropped down into the Kidron Valley preceding a short climb toward Gethsemane and the place of the olive press.

The disciples had noted a stark change in the Rabbi. Never had they seen him so melancholy. As they approached the garden and their normal place of repose, Jesus moaned and walked with some difficulty as if greatly troubled by something.

Later that night John Mark fled into the night when Judas and the Jewish leaders pounded on his door. He raced to the Mount of Olives to alert Jesus that his enemies sought his arrest.

Meanwhile the Rabbi left his men behind except for Peter and James and John, the sons of Zebedee. As they walked along, he was overcome with a sadness and great distress and he told them his soul was sorrowful to the point of death. He asked them to stay there and watch with him, to pray to be strong against temptation. Perhaps he wanted their companionship, but more importantly, their safety.

He withdrew from the three a little farther, perhaps a hundred feet or so, threw himself onto the ground. Falling to his face he prayed that if it were possible this hour might pass from him. He wrestled over his desire to live versus his desire to do the will of the Father. Anguishing.

Imagine having a great, urgent desire for companionship or release from a troubling concern, only to be forsaken. Here was the Nazarene, knowing he faced a great dilemma—a life or death situation—completely alone. No one to share his burden. Knowing his very life would be challenged within possibly hours.

He did not wish to die.

He did not wish to suffer the pain of death.

He did not want to undergo what lay ahead.

Was it possible to forego his mission? Was it possible to minimize it—to consider and to claim an alternate path that would provide the same results? Was it possible to follow God's way in a less costly manner?

No. It wasn't. That was the reason for his plea, even though he preferred a less discomforting path. He chose to follow is Father's plan.

He returned to his friends to find them asleep. When he asked them the reason for their sleeping, they had no answer for him. He repeated his warning and went to pray alone two more times with the same results—they slept on.

During his final time of prayer, he prayed so intensely that his sweat fell to the ground like great drops of blood, the result of haematodrosis, an abnormality in which a rush of adrenalin prompts the heart rate to increase. Constricting blood vessels then dilate. His blood sugar levels would have spiked, causing panting to increase oxygen intake followed by physical tiredness then exhaustion. His heart rate would slow, accompanied with sweating. Then blood rushed back into the capillaries near the sweat glands, rupturing and causing great drops of blood.

By the time the Rabbi returned to the disciples the third time, he had determined his course of action. As the disciples lay sleeping, he noticed distant flickering torches far below.

It was around 2 AM, the darkest hour. He awakened the men and pointed out it was time for him to be betrayed, "Look. The man who betrays me is close at hand."

Rubbing the sleep from their eyes, the disciples were on their feet, wondering what was happening.

When Jesus next noticed, the torches wended their way up through the olive grove, beneath the twisted trees, moving towards him. A low murmuring of voices reached him. The torches became brighter and closer. Men's mingled rough voices grew louder.

To escape the mob would have been easy but Jesus seemed resigned to meet the group head on and to address their agenda. This gang was made up of Jerusalem's worst—low-life goons and ruffians, street toughs hired by the religious leaders who chose to maintain their legalistic Pharisaical façade— the hypocrites who could not shut up the Nazarene were too upright to soil their own hands and had hired others to do their dirty work.

Onward they came.

He knew their game.

They had no shame.

He was to blame.

Having earlier learned of the plot to arrest him, I wanted to be present to observe the outcome. I had it on good authority that Judas was about to lead this band to Jesus and to finger him. I had joined the group, following them from their starting point in Jerusalem.

In moments footfalls and a noisy hubbub announced the arrival of officials. They hove into view wielding rope, clubs and swords. The oily torches cast dark and eerie shadows that danced across the figures of the shady interlopers.

Beside them marched Judas Iscariot, intending to point out the Galilean to the soldiers with his previously agreed upon kiss, the traditional gesture of a student approaching his teacher. Judas knew the place well since he had been here often with the Rabbi and his disciples.

Well armed, the group, including a detachment of Roman soldiers under the direction of Jewish leadership, carried lanterns and torches. One was a captain from the Sanhedrin; others included Jewish police officers who enforced the Jewish ecclesiastical hierarchy and their abusive ways toward the people, captains of the Temple guard and various religious leaders.

Chief Priests led them.

From a distance I watched the leaders approach the Nazarene. He calmly and confidently stepped forward. He had no fear. In fact, he was stoically serene. It was then that I recognized what I thought a slight smirk I'd come to observe when the Rabbi held all the cards. It was obvious to me that he knew exactly what was going on.

Judas approached him, "Greetings, Rabbi." Judas threw his arms around him in a phony embrace, kissed him on the cheek.

I found it somewhat confusing that Judas chose to betray his friend and could only wonder about this situation.

It was my belief that they had been friends for nearly three years, since just before I arrived in country. I don't believe the Galilean ever failed Judas. I wondered if the Rabbi wanted him to face his failure as a man and his success as a traitor. Perhaps the Galilean hoped that his salutation would register with Judas—perhaps his offering a last opportunity for Judas to come clean before him, to recant his deceitful decision.

The Rabbi spoke, "Judas, would you betray the Son of Man with a kiss. My friend, why did you come?"

Judas did not answer.

Knowing exactly the outcome, Jesus boldly approached the band of brigands. Standing between his disciples and the mob and asked, "Whom do you seek?"

Like a pack of rabid, snapping dogs, they encircled him, their orange torches casting weird shadows across the assembled and the nearby ground and trees. They responded as one, "Jesus the Nazarene."

Without skipping a beat, he stated, "I am he."

At that moment a blinding light appeared, illuminating Jesus' face. Unable to stand in this light's presence, the throng fell to the ground as if dead—priests, elders, soldiers and Judas. Moments later the light faded away and an angel withdrew.

The disciples stood in awe, aghast at the scene before them.

At length the fallen arose.

Again the Rabbi asked whom they sought.

"Jesus the Nazarene."

"I have told you that I am the man you seek." He gestured toward his disciples and said, "If you seek me, let these others go.

He spoke to the group, excoriating them for their gutless behavior, "What? Am I a robber to be subdued with your swords and clubs? When I sat among you teaching in the Temple day after day, you never moved a hand toward me. You had plenty of time to arrest me then without coming out in the black of night under the guise of legality." The implication was all too apparent—they feared his followers in the daylight but the darkness and corrupt ruffians emboldened them.

His eyes sought out and focused on the Chief Priests, Captain of the Temple guard and Elders. With eyes momentarily piercing theirs he stated, "But you need to know that all that has transpired is in order for the scriptures to be fulfilled. This is your hour and the reign of darkness. Evidently not believing or caring about his comments, the captors pressed forward.

In the name of Jupiter! Will this man never cease to amaze? His band responded to defend him. Never one to shrink from a fight, the Big One, brawny and impulsive Peter, in an effort to save his friend shouted, "Master, shall we fight? We have the swords."

Peter brandished his sword in a smooth, swift movement and swung at Malchus' head. However the servant of the high priest saw the action and dodged. Peter's blade sliced off Malchus' ear. Malchus screamed, holding his hand to his head, blood running between his fingers, his severed right ear lay on the ground at his feet. I thought I saw it falling to the ground as the sword flashed.

The Master quickly commanded the situation, speaking sharply to Peter, "Resist no more. Put your sword back in its sheath. All who live by the sword will die by the sword." He bent over, picked up the severed ear and placed it onto the ear stub. The blood stopped. The man's ear was completely restored.

In seconds it was as if it had never been removed. *How could this be? Another instantaneous healing.* More confusion for me.

Speechless and wondering what their next move was, the gang stood before him.

I thought I heard threats from the mob, but they were muffled. I had to wonder if he ws thinking of all the abuse and mistreatment he'd endured.

With an air of control and to acknowledge their shenanigans, the Galilean taunted them, "Here you are with your swords and staves and ropes to place me under arrest like I'm some kind of common criminal."

He continued, "Don't you think that I could call upon my Father and He would send more than twelve legions of angels to my defense?"

I quickly did the math. At his slightest utterance he could command seventy-two thousand angels. (* Footnote: *Holy Bible*, II Kings 19:35, one angel killed 185,000 Assyrians single handedly)

I wasn't sure about this angel business and I wondered how that would turn out. I don't think these guys get it.

He continued in total control, "Am I not to drink the cup the Father has given me? This is not the place for this kind of action."

Still unmoved the crowd wondered what to do. The Rabbi continued, "However, in order for the ancient prophesies to be fulfilled, I cannot and will not call upon my Father for help. You are free to take me captive."

The guard, their captain and Jewish officers, took hold of him. Others immediately rushed to him and grabbed him, manhandling him and trussing him with ropes—placing his hands behind his back and tying them together.

Some of the remaining men turned toward the eleven men who had come with him but now lingered in the shadows. To a man they fled. The young man John Mark escaped by spinning away from a man who grabbed his clothes—running away naked.

The mob who witnessed Peter's sword outburst and the calm healing of the Nazarene, were speechless. They had to wonder, *how could the man they came to arrest do such things?* I'd seen and heard of other healings and this was right up there with the others.

As the throng started past me, Jesus caught my eye. Our eyes locked and he never faltered in his gaze or his stride. Although the guards forcefully pushed him onward—trussed up as he was, within a few feet of me, Prophet stopped before me as if in control of all the power in the world. I saw it again in his eyes.

His penetrating demeanor seemed to look into the depths of my soul. He called me by name, "Brachan, you are not one of my accusers. I've known from the beginning of the spies sent against me by the priests to find fault in me. I know that you are not one of those scoundrels. You will soon return to report to your superior in Rome. My work here is nearly complete." He then turned and walked on, the crowd shouting and crowing in victory. He never looked back.

What had just unfolded was an astounding thing. I'd watched Alexy fight in the arena dozens of times, always the victor. He'd beaten men on every occasion, and sometimes, animals. But this performance by the Nazarene was a wonder to me.

Not only did he make eye contact with me, but he knew my name. He knew about my superior. Truly he is more than people think. Can he be the Son of God as he claims?

As the throng hurried along, their combined noises echoed through the night. The guard then, with their captain and Jewish officers, disappeared with Jesus past gardens and olive groves, down into the Kidron Valley, across the brook and into the silent city. It was well past midnight as Simon Peter and John Mark followed the procession at a distance.

Holy Jupiter. These Jewish priests brought him up on charges. What charges! What has he done? Let's see. He has healed the sick. Cured the blind and the lepers. Sown joy and a stronger sense of community. Brought encouragement. Turned people to a better way of life. He's returned the dead to life.

Oh, wait. Did I mention he did some of this on Jewish Sabbath days?

For nearly three years the priests have monitored him. They've watched him more closely than I have.

Yes, they should bring him up on charges. And just what have they done these past three years? Oh, yes. They've played with their prayer beads, ripped their prayer shawls and condemned him for doing good. Of course… the lot of them are pretenders!

I followed the crowd until we reached the palace of Annas, the High Priest and possibly the most powerful man in Jerusalem.

As late as it was, I momentarily debated stopping at the home of my friend Gaius. This was not a normal occasion so I decided against convention and made my way to his home. I wanted to share the evening's events which would be of interest to him and, to my way of thinking, could have major consequences upon current and future events.

No doubt befuddled by my arrival, rubbing sleep from his eyes, he welcomed me into his quarters. It took him a bit to awaken and realize the gravity of what I told him. Then I related my most recent experience in the Garden and told him the Nazarene had been taken to the home of Annas.

CHAPTER 17 — The Council Decides

"Gaius, tell me what you can about Annas."

"You probably know as much as I. The position of high priest is one by appointment and demands little in the way of qualifications. It is common knowledge that the priests are chosen not so much for their piety as much as belonging to a hereditary caste, the Sadducees—they, more or less, inherited different administrative posts for their families from generation to generation. They were installed by the Herodians and Romans since the time of Herod the Great. I'm sure it's common knowledge that Chief Priests weren't necessarily qualified to lead spiritually, or, perhaps, any other way.

"Annas was the recognized Jewish high priest. He obtained the position himself before maneuvering three of his sons into that office. Annas was the father-in-law of Caiaphas, whom he also finagled into the high priesthood.

"Annas was the richest citizen of Jerusalem. Having been gripped with fear since the Rabbi first cleared the temple three years previous, he was not happy about the possibility of losing his riches as a result of the Rabbi's status and his activities. You know what he thought about ridding Jewish leaders of the upstart Messiah. He could hardly wait for the Prophet's demise to play out. No doubt the old bird was the chief instigator of the mob's activity and awaited their return with Jesus."

"Either Annas or Caiaphas."

"You've known the divide between them and the Prophet. They can't tolerate his putting them in their places, humiliating them in public, questioning their practices—he calls them actors of righteousness who misinform others so badly that they could not know the truth. It seems their resentment toward him intensifies daily.

"They've noodled this for months if not longer and come up with a scheme to eliminate him. If they can't do it through normal channels, they'll resort to a higher authority…let's say the reigning high priest Joseph Caiaphas. No doubt he would be greatly interested in their ideas."

"Without a doubt. Those two priests are the most recognizable. And stand to lose a ton."

"Yes. They run the commercial operation of money laundering. Their staff includes Chief Priests, lesser priests, scribes, animal tenders and slaughterers, stokers, maintenance workers, money changers and others."

"Right. I pretty much figured as much but wanted your confirmation."

Then we discussed the possible results of the arrest of the Rabbi. We concluded that the Jewish law could be trumped by the Roman law— in order to rid themselves of him, the skanky Jewish leaders could appeal to Pilate, but that wasn't likely. The Nazarene has done nothing wrong…except to rankle the religious legalists parading as learned ones. If punishment involved

155

scourging, would Gaius be involved?

And I reminded Gaius, "Let's suppose we're wrong and the Galilean is found guilty. What do you s'pose his punishment will be?"

We discussed the various forms of punishment, wondering whether it would involve the flagrum. If so, would it be the one with shards of metal and bone or the lead-balled one?

We agreed that people differed in their opinions of him. Some thought he was a prophet preceding the Messiah; some thought he was the Messiah; yet others agreed the Messiah couldn't come from Galilee because the Messiah was to come from the royal line of David.

I didn't spend much time at Gaius' home because I wanted to see what would happen at the high priest's. I hurried back to the residence of Annas to observe the proceedings.

Around 3 AM the mob passed through the gates of the palace, jostling the Rabbi to his appointed meeting with Annas. They bantered back and forth, congratulating themselves for their capture.

Twice Jesus had escaped the mob's attempt to destroy him—once after he preached in the temple in Nazareth and once in the temple courtyard in Jerusalem.

I could almost hear a witch-like cackle emanate Annas' mouth as he rubbed his hands together. I could almost read his mind...*now, Mister Jesus Man, it's my turn. I will have my revenge. You are about to become toast.*

The plan by Annas was to expedite the "trial" and achieve the Galilean's removal.

Since he had done nothing wrong, the priests worried that unless they delivered him swiftly for condemnation, they faced considerable wrath. They reasoned if they could get him condemned immediately, the mob and rabble of Jerusalem would work in their favor. However if enough time were available to arouse those who would defend and testify on the Galilean's behalf, their plan would fail.

When Annas began interrogating the Rabbi about his disciples and his teachings, the Galilean easily saw through the pretense and answered Annas' questions.

The Prophet allowed, "I have spoken openly for all the world to hear. I have always taught in the synagogue and in the Temple where all the Jews meet together. I did nothing in secret and committed no subversive activities. Ask those who heard me. They know what I said! I have said nothing in secret. You don't have to question me. My activities are common knowledge."

Annas did not understand his cryptic answers. Assuming he was being disrespectful to his master, Annas's servant guard smacked the Nazarene in the face and said, "Is that the way to answer the High Priest?"

With no apparent fear of the perpetrator the Rabbi addressed his accuser, "What I have stated is a fact. If it is a lie, prove it! If I have told the truth, you have no right to abuse me. You will have to produce witnesses to prove your accusations. But if there is no offense in it, why did you strike me?"

Annas spoke again, "I charge you by the living God to tell us whether you are the Christ the Son of God, the Son of the Blessed One."

Some in the crowd were angered. Pandemonium developed with the crowd's fever pitch. Temple policeman demonstrated typical Temple police behavior used to intimidate. Coached witnesses bantered in loud voices, prepared to lie in support of the crooked priests.

It was pathetic watching Annas' position of power crumble around him, causing him to strike out in violence.

The Temple police mocked the Rabbi, blindfolded him and hit him with their fists then asked him to prophesy who had done it. They rained insults on him. Guards mocked him after the interrogation. They must have felt powerful condemning him while he was bound.

As Annas questioned Jesus, his disciple named John Mark, who had acquired clothing and was known by the high priest, followed the Prophet into the palace. Familiar with the priest's residence, John gained entry from the servant girl at the door. Peter followed but stopped at the door because the slave girl did not know him. However John Mark intervened on his behalf and she allowed Peter to enter.

In the process, she asked Peter if he wasn't one of the Rabbi's followers.

He flatly denied being an associate.

John made no attempt to hide his identity. Avoiding mingling with the rough crowd who reviled the Rabbi, he moved to a corner in order to best observe the ongoing events near the Galilean.

Because it was cold, the servants and guards gathered thorn brush materials and built a fire in the courtyard outside. Some rubbed their hands together as the fire crackled in the chill. Some stood drowsily trying to stay awake. Peter bulled his huge frame through the crowd toward the fire where he could warm up and sat down in the courtyard with the servants to see what would develop.

As Peter enjoyed the warmth of the fire, the servant girl appeared in the courtyard and saw him again. She told the bystanders, "This man was with Jesus of Nazareth. This man is one of them." Turning to Peter she asked, "Aren't you also one of his disciples?" Before he could answer, she claimed, "You are another of them!"

Swearing vilely—so much so that it shocked a soldier standing nearby—Peter emphatically denied it in front of the group, "I am not! Woman, I don't even know him. I don't understand what you're talking about!"

Before long the eastern sky lightened, a slit of silver slicing the sky and guaranteeing sunrise. Peter wondered what was taking so long inside and wanted results.

At that point a relative of Malchus approached Peter. The man appeared angry and hostile when he demanded, "Didn't I see you in the Garden of Gethsemane with Jesus?" His accuser stated, "Your Galilean accent gives you away."

Surprised and confused and with the eyes of the company upon him, Peter blurted a string of profane oaths. He raised his voice and renounced his association with the Nazarene a third time, "You're mistaken. I never knew the man." Hardly had he finished speaking when a rooster crowed.

Peter immediately realized his failings. But he wasn't alone.

Annas was caught red handed too. Instead of trying the Rabbi, Jesus had turned the tables on him. Annas realized immediately that the Galilean was onto his game and that there was no way he was going to trap the Prophet whose words silenced Annas. The high priest thought better of asking further questions for fear of indicating himself or other leaders. He still had other options…perhaps the Sanhedrin or acting high priest Caiaphas, would be up to the task. Annas could wash his hands of the Rabbi and get himself out of hot water. He would take every opportunity to destroy Jesus.

Annas dismissed the still bound Galilean and sent him to Caiaphas.

Moments later the great doors of Annas' living quarters swung open and the Rabbi ushered out. His face was swollen and dry blood flecked his lips. Still bound and in the grasp of his mis-handlers, he spotted Peter and looked into Peter's eyes.

Then he was gone.

Peter burst into tears and wept bitterly before fleeing the area.

Annas and Caiaphas each had living quarters separated by a courtyard in the high priest's house, a spacious and handsome palatial building. It was but a short walk through the courtyard to the high priest's. Both Caiaphas and Annas shared unscrupulous behavior and favored keeping the Roman status quo in order to continue with their fraudulent behavior.

Soldiers and multitude of citizens had gathered in the courtyard, anticipating the outcome. As the soldiers led the Rabbi across it to Caipahas' quarters, those lining the route abused the Rabbi, taking their cue from the council's ill treatment of him and mirroring it—they mocked and jeered as he passed. They spoke blasphemous things against him and the servants slapped him.

Caiaphas cut quite an impressive figure, dressed in ceremonial finery including a violet robe adorned with bells and tassels, a special miter with a golden plate in front inscribed with "Holy to the Lord" and a breastplate with the names of the twelve tribes of Israel. His job description included keeping himself pure from defilement such as contacting dead or dying persons, including his relatives. He was the seventh member of Annas' family to be appointed as high priest.

He was a member of the aristocratic Sadducees—the religious elite of the day— and a man accustomed to owing his future to his own political machinations. He found the Galilean's ideas both disconcerting and anti-traditional, no doubt because Caiaphas avoided the truth.

Caiaphas had pulled some strings, applied his political prowess and orchestrated his colleagues to fulfill his wishes. Even though Jewish law forbade the Sanhedrin's trying someone at night, Caiaphas had organized a nighttime hearing. He took his plan a step further by calling the meeting in his palace, rather than the official premises of the Sanhedrin council. Nor did he invite the entire assembly of seventy councilmen. Rather he invited the "apparatchiks" who were henchmen under his thumb—they could be jockeyed into deceitfully coercing the others to embrace and enact his plan to destroy the pretend Messiah. No witnesses were permitted to speak for the defense. Council members present, acted in secret. Deviously dishonest men accomplish their darkest deeds under cover of darkness.

It was under this deception that Caiaphas engineered his cronies to do his bidding. He knew that Jesus' earlier claim of Godship would not stand without the full council's presence. And he knew that the Roman tribunal would not approve of the death sentence without a full council's approval of the charge. So he laid the groundwork earlier in order to trap the Prophet with a seditious political claim. The priests and leaders had prepared for this interview.

It was apparent to anyone with a modicum of Jewish knowledge that there were but two possibilities for convicting him: 1) the Sanhedrin could conjure up charges or 2) the Jewish leaders could accuse him of blasphemy, the only charge they could possibly make stand for conviction—and that's a stretch for anyone who's followed his movements.

The priests worked rapidly. They knew that time was short in lieu of any reprisal from the Rabbi's followers. Before long they achieved their goal and sent the Prophet before the full council.

Later that morning as dawn broke, the Elders of the people, the Chief Priests and Scribes led the Rabbi before that council. They had been summoned at that early morning hour in an effort to conduct the treacherous plan before his followers could learn of it. Because they feared the Rabbi's followers as well as the Romans, the Jewish leaders knew garnering Roman support demanded craftiness.

Traditionally the Sanhedrin had power over a man's future—they could find him innocent or guilty and punish him appropriately. Knowing that Roman law ruled the land and only they could condemn a man to death—a power denied all other courts, the council, such as it was, plotted to prove the Rabbi blasphemed, which would set the Jews against him. They reasoned if they could make the blasphemy charge stick, the Romans would likely sentence him with a criminal offense which would allow Roman law to prevail—granting them their wishes for capital punishment, followed by his execution.

Both Pharisees and Sadducees were aware of the political ground that each must cover in order to keep from upsetting the other group...while achieving approval of the Romans.

Pharisees believed in miracles, angels and resurrection of the dead. Sadducees rejected all of these.

Pharisees traditionally touted the importance of outward conduct, ritualism and formalism. Sadducees focused on economic prosperity and political power.

As the mock trial began, the august body sat in a semi-circle with the Galilean at the center and the high priest led the proceedings. On either side of the hall sat judges and others interested in the hearing. Caiaphas sat at the seat of the presiding officer. Below the throne stood temple guards with their prisoner the Prophet.

Such proceedings provided for the accused to defend himself with a solicitor and with witnesses. Yet the Galilean chose to take on the Sanhedrin alone. He faced the sham with quiet confidence.

His teachings and the people's desire to learn from him planted a seed of jealousy which grew out of proportion in Caiaphas. He marveled at the Rabbi's dignified bearing. Momentarily Caiaphas felt Jesus was akin to God. But he immediately demanded Jesus perform a miracle.

The Nazarene did not comply.

When the Prophet had alluded to destroying the Temple and raising it in three days, the Pharisees took his words literally. They decided a great starting point for gaining Roman support would be to use that concept to proclaim he blasphemed. Some declared that the Rabbi lied when he said that he would raise the Temple in three days after they destroyed it.

Although the thugs provided by the Jewish leaders to testify against the Rabbi provided false statements, their statements conflicted with each other.

The trial was going nowhere. Frustrated and amazed at the way things were going in general and the fact that they could not trip Jesus in specific, the leaders wondered if they would be outdone yet again. Finally two witnesses, one paid to lie, spoke against the Rabbi.

One proclaimed, "This man said, 'I am able to destroy the Temple of God and rebuild it in three days.'"

Caiaphas asked, "How about it, did you say that or didn't you?"

The Prophet remained quietly resolute amidst all the claims and accusations. In the midst of all the confusion, lies and condescension He alone remained the most calm and collected.

In his case, however, it was a foregone conclusion by the Jewish leaders that he was guilty, a common criminal with no right to a fair trial even though no charges were laid. Caiaphas called him a deceiver when, in fact, it was Caiaphas the High Priest who won that title.

Silence prevailed over the gathering.

Attempting to control the situation, becoming vexed that the Prophet would not respond to any of his questions and wishing to expedite the proceedings, Caiaphas raised his right hand toward heaven and demanded, "I adjure you by the living God that you tell us whether you are the Christ, the Messiah, God's anointed."

Men hung on the edges of their seats. When was such a question asked under these conditions? How would he answer? Surely he would say "no." What if he said "yes"?

No one stirred. All ears awaited his response.

If the crowd was quiet before, a deathlike pall now prevailed. You could hear a falling feather hit the floor.

The brevity of his answer was almost as powerful as his claim, "You said it. I AM. From your own mouth comes the truth, I am! Nevertheless the time is coming when you will see the Son of Man sitting on the right hand of the power of God and coming in the clouds of heaven."

The assembly recoiled in shock.

Then in unison they burst forth, "Are you claiming to be the Son of God, the Son of the Blessed One, God very God?"

Then their anger rose to fury and triumph as they figured they had him.

"Blasphemy!" some shouted.

Others proclaimed, "Your words will hang you from the cross."

More shouted, "You're a blasphemer!"

In a display of righteous indignation Caiaphas tore his robes.

Being fully aware of the Jewish law, Caiaphas knew a high priest was not to rend his garments. Levitical law required the death sentence for such behavior. Jews customarily tore their garments on the occasion of a friend's death. However priests were not to observe this tradition. A priest's garment was to be pure and without blemish. Any priest who did not wear beautiful garments and engaged in tearing them, was considered cutting himself off from God and not fit to represent God. Of this Caiaphas was guilty. Whereas Caiaphas accused Jesus of blaspheming, Caiaphas was the blasphemer... tearing his robes in a sign of piety proved symbolic of the Jews tearing themselves away from Egypt.

As Caiaphas misbehaved, people marveled at the agitated and animated behavior displayed by both him and Annas, compared to the calm demeanor of the Prophet. They wondered whether the Nazarene might, in fact, be God in human flesh.

The thought of the Rabbi's words and past actions refuted Caiahas' belief in no resurrection, no judgment and no future life. *Who does this Jesus think he is? Assailing my most cherished theories?* The Prophet's answer set him back on his heels. He was terrified with the thought of a resurrection of the dead and that all would stand before the judgment of God. He envisioned the graveyards yielding their dead for judgment. And the buried secrets revealed.

Caiaphas perceived the crowd's feelings and hastened the trial. "He has blasphemed! We don't need other witnesses! Why do we need any further testimony? He has condemned himself with his own lips. What is your judgment?"

His behavior was not hidden from them; however, the facts were. They all gave their verdict, "He deserves the death sentence!"

And so, the men of the Sanhedrin found the Galilean guilty of blasphemy and sentenced him to death. Jubilant, they turned him over to the street ruffians, their chosen police, in an attempt to celebrate their victory and to repay the thugs for their participation.

Those guarding Jesus mocked and beat him. After they'd blindfolded him, they struck him. One smacked him on the face and shouted, "Prophesy! Tell us who hit you!"

Angry and frustrated by his composed behavior, the council sent the Rabbi under armed guard to Pilate, the Roman governor.

The crowd of cowards and malcontents continued to serve the purposes of the Jewish leaders. All the while the followers of the Rabbi were unaware of the Council and its farcical fancies.

In the meantime Judas witnessed the charade. He must have envisioned a totally different outcome, perhaps that the Rabbi would perform a miracle to save himself from any harm. Throughout the ordeal Judas squirmed, watching his friend subjected to humiliation and anguish. Judas had failed to understand the meaning of the Master. Judas had his silver. The mob had Jesus. Neither Judas nor the mob would ever be the same.

At this point Judas, realizing that his Master had been condemned, was filled with guilt. He realized he'd made the biggest mistake of his life and his tall form rushed through the throng, his face pale and haggard. With a dulled and pained shout he approached the throne of judgment to return the blood money. He was remorseful, devastated and heartsick.

He tossed the pouch of coins onto the floor before the priests and elders, shouting, "This man has done nothing worthy of death. Release him. He is innocent!

Momentarily stunned, the Jewish leaders were speechless.

Judas continued, "I have sinned. I have betrayed innocent blood."

When they spoke, their response was, "What is that to us?"

Judas had served their purpose. That's all. They didn't care about the money or about Judas. The leaders merely laughed in his face. They had the pretend Messiah.

The Rabbi watched the proceedings, looking pityingly at Judas.

With an agonized moan Judas lunged from the building shouting, "It's too late!"

It wasn't about the money which had served Judas no purpose whatsoever. It was his character—his lack of loyalty, his unwillingness to compromise. And he fled in shame.

Knowing that it was against their law to deposit the blood money into the treasury the Jewish leaders discussed its use. Wanting nothing to do with the money, they bought a piece of property where potters obtained the rich red clay of the area. It was known as Potter's Field, called Hakeldama. It was used as a cemetery to bury foreigners. It later became known as the Field of Blood, the place where Judas hanged himself.

CHAPTER 18 — Before Powerful Rulers

By now the Chief Priests, the Elders, the Scribes and the members of the Sanhedrin had reached the palace of the governor, Pontius Pilate. It was the seat of government of the Procurator of Judaea. He had been appointed four years previous by Caesar.

I arrived a short time later and observed the Rabbi, battered and bruised, dehydrated and exhausted from a sleepless night. He stood among them in the Lithostroton courtyard.

Having been roused from his bed chamber at that early hour, Pilate was not pleased. Obviously the Jews had a captive they wanted dealt with severely. When the assembly approached him, these haughty Jews refused to enter the Judgment Hall for fear of defiling themselves which would disallow their participation in the Passover feast. Therefore Pilate stepped outside to engage them.

He looked them over. His eyes fell upon Jesus, trussed up, bedraggled with a dried-brown blood-stained tunic. Surely, soldiers surrounded him. The hall filled with gawkers and worse.

Wanting this affair over, Pilate asked, "Who is this man and what charge do you bring against him?"

"This fellow has been leading our people to ruin by telling them not to pay their taxes to the Roman government and claiming he is our Messiah, Christ the King."

"Bring him over here to me," Pilate ordered. He asked, "Are you really King of the Jews?"

The Rabbi looked him in the eyes and asked calmly, "Who told you this? Do you ask this of your own accord or have others spoken to you about me?"

"Am I a Jew? It is your own people and the Chief Priests who have handed you over to me. What have you done?"

"I am a king. But my kingdom is not of this world. If it were, my followers would have fought to prevent my being delivered into the hands of the Jews. But as it is, my kingdom is not from here. I am here to bear witness to the truth. All who side with the truth hear my voice."

Ever the student of philosophy, Pilate found his statement about truth interesting. With a shrug of his shoulders he asked, "What is truth?"

But the clamor from the outside mob and the priests gave Pilate no time to await the Prophet's answer. Pilate returned outside to the noisy crowd and stated, "Look, I'm going to bring him out to you so that you can try him …I find no fault in this man and I have no case against him."

The Jewish leaders did not want Pilate to hear from the witnesses of the Galilean's works because they would contradict theirs. Knowing that Pilate commonly signed the death warrant against others brought by the Jews to him, the leaders banked on Pilate's vacillation.

Pilate beheld something in the Prophet that held his attention. The Procurator was reluctant to please the Jews. Pilate had heard of this Rabbi. Who hadn't? His wife had told him of the Galilean and his marvelous works. He recalled hearing about the Prophet's recent raising of Lazarus. He wondered about this Rabbi. Was it possible that the Jewish leaders were plotting? He wanted to confirm the charges against the man.

The uproar from the mob increased, bordering on hysteria. Where there is a mob, the loudest voice is heard and acted upon. This mob wanted blood. They wanted to see Jesus punished. They echoed the Jewish leaders' laundry list of his crimes:

he was perverting the nation;

he forbad the payment of taxes to Caesar;

he claimed to be a king.

The priests pulled at their beards and robes, yelling and spitting on the ground.

"He incites this whole nation!" They blared.

"He has spread his views from Galilee to Jerusalem."

"If he weren't a criminal, we wouldn't have brought him to you."

Pilate found their charges amusing, almost laughable. He had numerous spies imbedded among the Jewish populace for the very purpose of reporting any such damaging information to him. It was laughable. *Surely this mob must realize they are dealing with the governor. I wasn't born yesterday. I'm not some dumb new kid on the block who believes this nonsense.*

He responded, "If your judgment is sufficient, why are you bringing this man to me?" He played some head games with the Jews, "Go ahead. Judge him by your laws."

Knowing Pilate was having fun at their expense, the priests were infuriated. They loudly denounced Pilate, threatening him with censure of the Roman government. They accused him of failing to condemn the Prophet and fiercely persisted.

Unable to hold their anger and frustration in check, they began yelling and screaming, demanding that Pilate judge the Rabbi.

He wondered at the contrast between these crowing priests and the calm demeanor of the Rabbi who took it all in as if watching a boring side show.

Because he was confused by the outcry and in light of the fact that the Prophet made no defense on his behalf, Pilate invited the Rabbi to defend himself, "In lieu of all the accusations have you nothing to say in your defense?"

Pilate spoke, "Aren't you going to say anything? What is it that these men are testifying against you?"

The Nazarene spoke not.

I noticed his demeanor was the same as when I watched him in the Temple—no nonsense, all business, stoic and resolute. Once again I noticed that knowing smirk…that tell-all look on his face when he knows that he's dealing with bogus people. He confidently surveys the situation and waits for the deceitful to implode on their own words or actions.

Unruffled and unmoved by the stifling roar from the mob, the Rabbi remained mute. Thousands of voices rose as one and the Galilean's silent eloquence shouted louder than their words.

Pilate was amazed by the Prophet's bearing. He wondered if the Rabbi disregarded the activities and refused to defend himself because he was disinterested in saving his life. *Does he not wish to save his life?*

The Chief Priests stated their case, "We have already sentenced him but need your approval in order to render his condemnation valid. According to Roman law, we are not allowed to put a man to death by hanging."

When Pilate returned to the Praetorium and called Jesus to him, the governor heard an accuser shout, "He is causing riots against the government everywhere he goes, all over Judaea, from Galilee to Jerusalem!"

Learning the Nazarene was from Galilee, Pilate gave himself an out. Knowing that Herod Antipas was visiting Jerusalem and had jurisdiction of the region, Pilate reasoned he could send the Rabbi to Herod and let him deal with him. The tetrarch of that province had craftily handled the demise of John the Baptist. It would also garner a little political favor from Herod if Pilate deferred to him, smoothing an old dispute between them. Pilate told the mob to take the Galilean to Herod. And so, they filed into the street and proceeded to Herod's headquarters.

Herod Antipas is a cruel and cunning impostor from the Arabian desert and a failed leader. When he first heard of the Rabbi, he thought John the Baptist had come back to life. Herod trembled with fear. When he realized he wasn't the Baptizer, Antipas was delighted to meet him for he had heard much of the Miracle Worker and waited a long time to see him.

Hoping to see him perform a miracle, Herod Antipas put numerous questions to the Galilean. The Rabbi had answered questions put to him by Annas and Caiaphas. He had answered the Sanhedrin. He had answered Pontius Pilate's question about truth. However he did not answer one question from Herod.

In a mocking gesture Herod treated him contemptuously. Why not have some fun? He commanded his soldiers to garb the Rabbi as a king, in a purple cloak. When they'd completed their task, the soldiers taunted and tormented the Rabbi—a few struck him. Some bowed, mocking his claim to be the Son of God. Others rushed forward but his demeanor changed their hearts and they retreated.

Herod addressed the people, "This is the king of the Jews. Give him a crown."

At Herod's pronouncement, they grabbed the Galilean and dragged him about.

The result of the Rabbi's bearing transposed Herod. At the very time that the Prophet's mockers and attackers had their way with him, Herod felt a wave of guilt. In spite of Herod's wickedness he knew that the Rabbi was a good man, an innocent victim of a scam. He also knew that John the Baptist had been a good man. He understood goodness but he did not live it.

So Herod proclaimed him innocent and sent him back to Pilate, the Roman judge.

Thinking that he had seen the last of this man from Galilee, imagine Pilate's surprise when the Prophet was brought before him a second time. Although both Herod and Pilate had judged him innocent of the charges, which created a bond between the rulers, the Jewish leaders still clamored for his demise. That intensified Pilate's desire to free him. He had no dog in the fight and didn't want to face whatever might befall him for punishing an innocent man.

He mistrusted his minion Caiaphas. The religious activities were outside Pilate's authority and his reputation in Rome was tarnished.

The morning had dragged on. It was noon. Tiring of the game, Pilate brought the Miracle Worker in front of the crowd again and ordered him seated on the Chair of Judgment outside the Antonia Fortress. It was the Day of Passover Preparation, the day of preparing the Paschal Lamb. Whether Pilate was being sarcastic or actually attempting to arrive at a reasonable solution, he addressed the crowd, "Here is your king. Do you want to hang your king?"

Perhaps he knew the crowd consisted primarily of paid protestors and malcontents. Maybe he was aware that many of the Nazarene's followers were not in the audience. Even so, he no doubt knew that the bulk of the crowd consisted of those opposed to Rome's rule and it was his way of trying to placate them and the Jewish leaders.

The crowd responded instantly,

"We have no king but Caesar!"

"Take him away."

"Kill him!"

Pilate tried to sidestep the situation again by appealing to the leaders of the Jews, "You have brought this man to me as a political agitator. Look, I have gone into the matter myself in your presence and have found no case against him. Neither has Herod or he wouldn't have returned him to me. I will have him scourged and release him."

Their overwhelming response was, "Away with him. The deceivers cried for Jesus' death, "Hang him! Hang him!"

Praises of "Hosana to the King" six days previous had metamorphosed into ugly cries calling for death. How could that be? Was it the makeup of the crowd? Whereas faithful followers shouted hosannas to the King, now protesters called for his death.

When Pilate heard what they were saying, his fears increased and he re-entered the Praetorium and asked Jesus, "Don't you hear how many charges they have brought against you? Aren't you going to say anything?"

Since he had spoken little to Pilate on the first go around, Pilate should not have been surprised that he remained silent. Pilate asked, "Are you refusing to speak to me?" When he did not reply, Pilate voiced his authority, "I have the power to release you or to have you hanged from the tree."

Jesus spoke of a higher authority, "You could have no power over me unless it had been given you from above. That is the reason that the one who handed me over to you has the greater guilt."

So, here we have Pilate, the governor and controlling authority. And we have a wandering preacher. The ruler alludes to his personal power. But the preacher tells him he has no power except that which his Heavenly Father provides—in effect, "You are powerless to proceed, to prosecute, to even breathe without my Father."

Was he toying with Pilate?

Another interesting thought. *I'm here on behalf of Roman authority. My objective is to discover whether that authority is undermined. Does the authority the Rabbi represents parallel the authority of Rome? Are the two in conflict or are they compatible? Can both co-exhist?*

A messenger now compounded Pilate's dilemma. He bore word from Pilate's wife Claudia. She was the youngest daughter of Julia, the daughter of Caesar Augustus and had had a disturbing dream. Her message stated that the man Pilate judged was innocent and that Jesus should be set free. Furthermore things would not go well for Pilate if he harmed the Nazarene whom she judged a righteous man.

But Pilate reasoned that freeing the Prophet could jeopardize his position with Caesar Tiberius. *What if the Jews filed another complaint with the Emperor? If Caesar so chose, I'd likely and easily be stripped of my position.* The Jewish leaders echoed his fears, continuing to whip the crowd into a frenzy questioning Pilate's loyalty to Rome, "If you set this man free, you are no friend of Caesar's. Anyone who makes himself a king is defying Caesar."

The Jewish elders' cries increased to the point that their supporters chanted more and their shrill cries increased in intensity. They wanted Christ eliminated before the entire city became inflamed.

More than likely it crossed Pilate's mind that he could play his hole card. Having recognized the kangaroo court's frame up and hoping for his escape by providing a time honored substitute, he would suggest releasing a prisoner in exchange for the Rabbi. He might still spring himself from this duty by offering the crowd a choice. He held the political prisoner bar Abbas. The man was a condemned murderer, robber and violent revolutionary. He had achieved hero status among those crowing for freedom from Rome.

To the Jewish leaders Pilate suggested an alternative, "According to your custom I am under obligation to release one prisoner at the Passover. Would you like me to release the King of the Jews? He has done nothing to deserve death."

They weren't having any of it...and continued to clamor for the death of the Rabbi.

I wondered about the similarities of Jesus and this insurgent. He shared the name Jesus with bar Abbas, which I found ironic as the temple prostitutes referred to their sons as Abbas. These women did not name their sons but rather called them Abbas which meant son of the father. Both men were considered revolutionaries and political enemies of the state. And both had a following of men and could be equally considered a threat to the Empire.

Pilate reasoned he could offer the religious leader which would coincide with the time of Passover. On the other hand, if he released bar Abbas, Pilate could have the Prophet flogged. He assumed that flogging him would appease his accusers. Though there was no basis in law to have him flogged, Pilate stated, "I will discipline him and release him."

Pilate stood before the mob and asked them, "Who would you like me to release, Jesus or bar Abbas, the political prisoner?"

Their overwhelming response was, "Release bar Abbas!" They cried out for the Rabbi's death, "Hang him! Hang him from the tree!"

Overwhelming chants of "bar Abbas! bar Abbas!" filled the air. They wanted the murderer released. Pilate was surprised by their response.

Pilate was torn. If he freed the King of the Jews, it would take Pilate out of the equation. However the Galilean's release would also fly in the face of the Jewish leaders whom Pilate hated. Pilate had jumped from the frying pan into the fire.

Pilate asked yet again, "What evil has he done? What is your sentence?"

"The death sentence." They asked him to take their word, enforce their sentence and they'd be responsible for the results.

Pilate refused their request.

He saw through their smoke screen. He did not believe that the Rabbi had plotted against the government. He could not believe that his mild manner painted him as a rebel. He perceived that the Jews were condemning an innocent man.

The situation bordered on riot. The maddened mob was whipped into a frenzy. The paid protestors pounded their chests, more than likely ignorant of the sham. Men on every quarter shouted, "Hang him! Hang him from the tree!" They rabidly shouted down those who favored the Nazarene. I wondered how many of those were bar Abbas' supporters, probable fellows in arms. It appeared a likely presumption that Jesus' followers did not know he'd been arrested and brought here. Whereas the followers and compatriots of bar Abbas had no doubt where he was and the intended execution that awaited him.

The hostile crowd continued the "hang him!" chant. That was followed by "his blood be upon us and our children!" Their clamor evolved into a near maniacal tremor rumbling across the square.

It was in response to their cries that Pilate ordered bar Abbas released. He condemned Jesus to scourging and turned him over to the praetorium guard—an entire battalion—with orders to flog him. They took him into the inner parts of the palace where they gathered around him, stripped him and flogged him.

Pilate fought a losing battle while catering to the crowd. In allowing the crowd to have its way and by handing over his leadership to others, he lost the argument and failed to save the supposed Savior.

Seeing that his argument was useless and fearing a riot, Pilate requested a vessel of water, washed his hands, symbolically refusing to be part of the fiasco, and declared, "I wash my hands of this matter. I am innocent of the blood of this righteous man. It is your concern."

I lost track of time, my mind contemplating the entire process of hanging. I was somewhat consumed by it and wondered about the turn of events regarding the Nazarene.

I recalled other hangings and thought about this hanging business as an end in itself. The first known practice of hanging from a tree was by the Persians. Alexander and his generals brought it to Egypt and to Carthage. My Roman countrymen learned the practice from the Carthaginians and, as with almost everything we do, rapidly refined the skill with a very high degree of efficiency. Hanging showcased our fine tuned execution practices. Our primary victims were slaves, rebels and especially despised enemies and criminals. With the exception of high crimes against the state such as

171

treason, condemned Roman citizens and Senators were usually exempt from this tortuous punishment.

Hanging was considered an ignominious way to die and was performed only to provide a particularly painful, gruesome and public death, usually causing a slow demise. The public execution reminded people of their need to behave.

Hanging involved stripping the condemned of his clothes and nailing him to a tree, forming a cross consisting of a vertical post (stipes) and a horizontal crossbeam or transom (patibulum in Latin). The crossbeam weighed 100 to 110 pounds. Part of the prisoner's penalty included carrying the patibulum, his death instrument, on his shoulders from the prison to the place of execution where he was secured to it. Customarily the instrument of hanging was either a Saint Anthony's or a Latin cross. The former consisted of the upright stipes which housed the patibulum and resembled a capital "T". The crossbeam on the Latin cross intersected the stipes, usually in a mortise, about a third of the way down from the top.

Customarily the execution paraphernalia included the prisoner, execution team, crossbeam, spikes and hammer. Each had a specific function: the condemned carried the transom to the place of execution; the team carried out the execution; the beam held the victim to the tree, attached by nails.

Execution was typically carried out by specialized teams, consisting of a commanding Centurion and four soldiers per each condemned person. When it was done in an established place of execution, the vertical beam was sometimes permanently embedded in the ground. Spikes were tapered iron five to seven-inches long with a square shaft three-eights inch across. A titulus, or small sign, stating the victim's crime was usually placed on a staff, carried at the front of the procession from the prison, and later nailed to the cross so that it extended above the head. And nailed to the top of the cross. That gave it the characteristic form of the Latin cross.

And each of the soldiers had his specific job. They were trained killers, subject to death should a prisoner escape. They made sure victims of the cross were dead, very dead, because they didn't want death to befall them.

Since the flesh of the hands cannot support a person's body weight, the Romans drove spikes through his wrists between the radius and the ulna. In some cases the condemned was held to the cross by ropes around the arms. The victim's feet were usually within a couple of feet of the ground.

Death could come within hours or days, depending on exact methods, the health of those crucified and environmental circumstances. Typically cause of death was asphyxiation. With the body's weight supported by the stretched arms, the victim had severe difficulty exhaling, due to hyper-expansion of the lungs. The condemned would therefore have to draw himself up by his arms, or have his feet supported by a wood block pedestal or by having them secured by rope.

The Roman practice of scourging preceded hanging a victim from a tree. This inhumane torture weakened the victim, preventing resistance to the final execution. Normal procedure called for the victims to be tied to columns with their hands above their heads, resulting in few, if any, lash wounds on the arms or forearms. Many flogging victims never made it to the cross.

Hebrew law was strict on the number of strokes applied to the condemned, limiting it to 40. The Pharisees, in order to make sure that they never broke the law, gave only 39 lashes. However the Romans had no limit, except for the fact that the victims should be left with just enough strength to carry their crosses to the place of execution.

While contemplating this, my mind's eye pictured soldiers ripping off the Nazarene's white tunic, leaving him in his nakedness and revealing a well proportioned, barrel-chested body. They secured the Rabbi's wrists to a column, his hands above his head, which would hold him erect and prevent his falling away from the lashes. The soldier assigned the flogging duties prepared himself for the task. With a nod from the Centurion the legionnaire picked up his ox hide flagrum and stepped forward.

He raised his muscled right arm above his shoulder, cocking it, then swung forward, the whip hissing towards its mark. Again and again the full force of the flagrum was spent against the Rabbi's shoulders, back and legs, to the ankles. At first the thongs cut only through the skin. Then, as the blows continued, they cut deeper into the subcutaneous tissues, producing first an oozing of blood from the capillaries and veins of the skin, and finally spurting arterial bleeding from vessels in the underlying muscles.

With folded arms across his chest, the Centurion stood by, counting to himself. When he reached the count of one hundred ten lashes, he showed the first signs of expression. He determined that the Galilean was near death and shouted, "Enough! Be done." Three soldiers stepped forward, two holding up the Deliverer and one untying his wrists. Half-fainting, the Rabbi slumped to the cold stone floor, wet with His own blood and sweat. He was then yanked to his feet and led outside.

One soldier thrust a reed into His hand for a scepter. Needing a crown to make their travesty complete, another soldier deftly crafted spiny stems from the *Euphorbia Milli* shrub, plaiting them into a circle. Knowing the sap was poisonous, he deftly maneuvered the half-inch thick stems, avoiding being pricked by their brown-mustard thorns. While avoiding its two-inch thorns, he plunged it onto Jesus' head then pushed it down. The thorns pierced the Rabbi's scalp, front and rear, evoking laughter from the soldiers.

The soldier and his comrades saluted the Rabbi. Some fell onto their knees before him in mock worship while others spit on him or slapped him. Some struck him with reeds, driving the thorns deeper into His scalp. In mocked reverence they cried out, "Hail, King of the Jews." Finally, they tired of their sadistic sport and returned his clothes to him.

He was then led by two soldiers standing nearby, one balancing the transom of a cross on the floor—it was the patibulum that had been prepared for bar Abbas. It would serve as the Rabbi's hanging tree.

The two soldiers showed no signs of mercy as they lifted the splintered 110-pound oak transom onto the Nazarene's shoulders. Splinters riddled the crossbeam and stabbed Him like wooden spikes, piercing his raw muscles and open wounds of torn flesh. His forearms wrapped over it so that his wrists and hands were on top-forward of either side. Raw, open wounds on his back exposed ribs and lungs.

When Pilate presented him to the crazed crowd, he carefully chose the words to be placed on the titilus, or small sign, which would precede the Latin and Hebrew: "Jesus of Nazareth, King of the Jews."

The Chief Priests were furious with the placard and demanded the sign be changed to read, "He said he was the King of the Jews," but Pilate defended his original placard, "I have written what I have written." Jewish leaders then preceded him from the hall. The crowd glimpsed the thorn crowned Savior for the first time—blood spattered and patibulum burdened.

Pilate announced, "Look at the man."

Handing the Deliverer to his soldiers, Pilate surrendered the Nazarene to the mob. They saw a great joke in this provincial Jew claiming to be king. Not only had he been subjected to a mock trial and falsely accused, but also he'd just endured a shameless flogging. There was no respite from their ridicule. Made me wonder what they'd do if they got their hands on him.

CHAPTER 19 — Things Get Ugly

Turns out the Nazarene would face execution with two others. Now he and his two condemned fellows maneuvered down the marble steps and onto the cobblestone courtyard. All three began their final journey to their execution. Each of the condemned men was accompanied by five executioners, dispatched at the front and rear. The procession moved slowly along the Via Dolorosa, the Way of Sorrows. A Centurion led the group.

Carrying his own cross to the execution site signified to the populace that the condemned no longer had anything to do with them.

Leaving the courtyard of Pilate's palace the group moved through the Gennath Gate. On either side of the street merchant tables and stalls beckoned consumers. Vendors sold dates, figs, water, roast lamb, olive oil. People and their activity dominated the surroundings—some stooped with age, children's voices shrilly reverberated off buildings, beggars tapped their sticks on the cobblestones, merchants carried baskets of vegetables or lemons or almonds, others moved casks of wine.

The processional moved along toward Golgotha, the Place of the Skull, the place of hanging. Here the Jewish elders anticipated with joy the pretend Messiah's death. Golgotha's rocky hill northwest of Jerusalem lay a lifetime away if you bore a crossbeam upon your battered back—650 yards of brutal agony, every step riddled with ribald scoffers and accusers as well as sympathizers. Six-hundred-fifty yards from the flogging at Fortress Antonia to the place of death.

As I followed along with the crowd behind the soldiers, I heard women wailing and lamenting the Deliverer. I found myself concerned about Gaius and how this turn of events might affect him.

I observed one woman offer the Prophet a cloth to wipe his face. But the Centurion pushed her away. Other onlookers made similar offers, only to be rebuffed.

Momentarily the crowd noticed a tree. Beneath its branches lay the body of Judas. At his own hanging his body weight had broken the rope around his neck and he had fallen to the ground, a mangled body—which dogs now devoured.

The Nazarene struggled over the cobblestones, staggering under the crossbeam's weight. Leaving a trail of blood.

Although I've witnessed many floggings, I had not seen this one. I followed him and his crossbeam as closely as possible, contemplating injuries inflicted upon him. Not just beaten beyond belief…but mutilated. His back one huge, open wound. I guessed he was scourged as badly as any man I've seen who lived.

I found it amazing that he could even walk, much less carry the beam.

It would have taken most of his energy in that condition just to walk, yet he struggled onward with his burden.

Some whom he'd healed or helped trailed at a distance, powerless to help. Some of those broke into tears; others mourned.

When weeping women stepped forward, he told them not to cry for him. I recalled what he'd said to women hinting of the future destruction of Jerusalem, "Daughters of Jerusalem, don't weep for me. Weep rather for yourselves and for your children. Look, the days are coming when the people will say, 'Happy are those who are barren and the womb's that have never borne, the breasts that have never suckled.' Then they will say to the mountains, 'Fall on us!' and to the hills, 'Cover us!' For if men do these things to a green tree, what will happen to a withered, dry one." And I wondered exactly what he meant.

His gruesome form looked barely human. In spite of His efforts to walk erect, the weight of the heavy wooden beam, together with the shock produced by copious blood loss, was too much. Exhausted and at the end of his strength, he stumbled and fell, the cross falling from his grasp. He lay there in his own blood and sweat, the crowd jeering, mocking and laughing. Some spit on him. Some made fun, asking him how it was that the two thieves could carry their burden but he couldn't, challenging him to get up.

But this time he couldn't rise. His damaged muscles had been pushed beyond their endurance, his injuries crippling him. He lay there momentarily. He did not whimper. He did not seek assistance. He just lay there.

For the first time I tried to analyze the intricacies of the execution process. I thoughtfully wondered about the indescribable pain of the flagrum. I found my mind racing ahead to the hanging and wondering about the spikes... jabbing into and through flesh and muscle. And what about the nerves and ligaments of the arms and feet? What would it feel like to have metal pounded through your extremities...plastering you to a hunk of wood?

Watching him struggle with the post—covered in his oozing blood and with flesh hanging from his back—I'm forced to wonder. It's my fortune, or perhaps misfortune, to monitor the activities of this Jew. It is not my duty to defend him. However something is terribly upside down here.

Based on the beating he endured, he should be dead. How could this injustice have occurred? We have an innocent man dying for nothing—nothing that he did and with nothing to be gained from his death. What's to be gained by his accusers? Why should his death matter to me? In light of the Jewish *Tanakh*, I am living in what must be the very decisive time of the Holy One, born in Bethlehem, come to mankind. Can it be much clearer?

Yes, he's a Jew. And I'm a Roman. Still, I'm a man. I know courage. I know honor. I know loyalty. And I know injustice. As a Roman patriot I know a real man when I see one.

The Roman Centurion in charge, eager to get on with the hanging, hawk-like, scanned the masses of people on either side and noticed a great, burly black man. With leather banned wrist the Centurion thrust his arm, pointed an index finger at the stalwart North African onlooker and commanded, "You. Pick up this crossbeam and carry it for the King."

The man, a Cyrenian named Simon, moved forward. Simon had heard of the Messiah. Although his sons Alexander and Rufus believed in Jesus, he did not. Simon hefted the transom onto his shoulders and followed the Centurion. Somehow the Galilean arose, stumblingly following Simon…still bleeding and sweating the cold, clammy sweat of shock.

Onward went the procession, toiling up the hillside toward the summit. Three men to be put to death on its brink. When they reached the appointed spot, the criminals dropped their beams onto the ground, heavy thumps ringing from the solid wood against stone. The Centurion commanded Simon, "Over here. Drop the patibulum here."

Well regimented soldiers set about the process of dispatching the three. While the two sets of five soldiers attended the two criminals, the Savior's five addressed him.

Amidst those mourners, I heard the Centurion barking out commands, "Stand back. Clear!" He didn't need nor want gawkers in the way.

It was 9 o'clock when the well regimented soldiers began the process of dispatching the three condemned men.

Preparatory to execution it was standard practice for soldiers to strip the executed. The rationale of stripping prisoners to their nakedness was to humiliate the condemned as much as possible. That humiliation included the inability of the condemned to control his bowels either in approaching or in actual death—thus he was powerless to control defecation and urination. The humiliation of being hanged nude in a prominent place added to the punishment's intended deterrent value. Stripping also allowed executioners to divide the victim's clothing and other small possessions among themselves.

Two soldiers grabbed Jesus and roughly thrust him backward, slamming his shoulders against the wooden crossbeam, his head snapping whip-like aft. With two soldiers holding each of his arms, the legionnaire felt for the depression just above his right wrist, being careful not to pull the arm too tightly but to allow some flexion and movement. Placing the point of a spike in position between the arm bones, the legionnaire drove the seven-inch heavy, tapered, wrought-iron spike through the wrist and into the wood. A second blow, followed by a third bit deep into the wood, securing the arm to the beam. Methodically, the legionnaire moved to the other side and repeated the action on the left wrist.

Throughout the activity near inhuman screams of pain riddled the air as the condemned three received the same treatment at various times.

Next, four soldiers, two on either side of the patibulum, lifted it in unison as the Nazarene reached his feet momentarily. Then it was on up and positioned above the stipes. On command they simultaneously released their grip and the beam rattled into place with a jarring *thud*. The weight of Jesus's body and the immediate stop, tore at his wrists and dislocated his shoulders and his elbows, stretching arms six inches longer than normal.

With Jesus perched on the tree, hanging from his wrists, his five soldiers gathered at its foot. Two secured his left leg and two held his right as the fifth prepared his spikes and hammer. One man stood off to the left and placed the Rabbi's left foot flat against the pedestal, toes down. He then grasped the leg at the ankle in both hands while his partner reached from behind-off-to-the-side of the cross and grasped the Prophet's left shin in both hands. Keeping the leg bent at the knee nearly ninety degrees, he pulled back on the shin. The soldiers on the right leg repeated the process, placing his right foot near parallel atop the left foot.

As the four "leg men" at their joint task strained their minds and muscles to master the moment and restrict the feet's movement, the executioner centered the tip of a spike on the top of the right foot over the instep and swung briskly against it, driving-stabbing into the flesh and ligaments of the top foot. Another rapping on the spike drove it through the foot and into the bottom one. The soldier kept swinging until the metal met wood, the nail bisecting both arches and securing his feet to the cross. When he was satisfied that the spike secured both feet to the pedestal, the soldier stopped striking.

Although the rhythmic ringing of metal against metal stopped with the final blow, the ringing seemed to hang in the air like a nearby echo. Perhaps it was only in my mind.

The soldiers gathered up their tools, stood back and admired their work.

On either side of Jesus soldiers completed their job and they, too, gathered their tools. They had conducted a well orchestrated execution, punctuated by the normal agonized screams and mourning of the executed.

Even though this situation was strange to say the least, it was just another day at the office so to speak for the Roman soldiers.

They were used to this business—boring, mundane.

They were used to listening to the moans of the sufferers on their crosses.

They were used to looking about for something to do.

They were used to dividing the victim's belongings.

When they noticed the King of the Jew's himation and tunic, they grabbed them—in spite of the bloodstains and dirt covered condition, they were glad to have both. They sliced the white mantle into four parts and decided that the tunic was too nice to sever. Since it was seamless and one piece, they elected to cast lots to see who would receive it.

Through glazing eyes Jesus looked down upon his mockers, gambling for his garment. He rose enough to gather air into his lungs before uttering through parched lips, "Father, forgive them, for they don't know what they're doing."

Many women including Mary the mother of James the younger and Joseph, Salome and the mother of James and John, whose father was Zebedee, watched from a distance. Other friends of the Rabbi had joined them.

Near the cross stood a woman purported to be Mary the Nazarene's mother, his aunt, Mary the wife of Clopas and Mary Magdala. In extreme anguish Mary symbolized motherhood at its finest. How could anyone not respect and pity her at this, perhaps the saddest moment of her life? Her husband was dead and now her firstborn taken from her. When she and a man, Jesus' friend John, approached the cross, I struggled to hear him speak to them.

Looking down at the terrified, grief-stricken mother and adolescent John, Jesus spoke with compassion, "Behold your mother." Then, looking to His mother Mary, "Woman behold your son." It seemed the Nazarene's way of assuring them that she was to be under John's care thereafter.

Others continued watching the proceedings. There was no let up of abuse from the Chief Priests, elders, scribes and others as they continued mocking and taunting Jesus…

"He trusted God, let Him deliver him now…"

"Let him save himself if he is the Christ of God. Let Christ, the King of Israel, come down from the cross and we'll believe in him…

"If he is the King of Israel, let him come down from the stake and we'll believe.

The three condemned men were slowly perishing. Two criminals— Dismas and Gestas— joined mockers shouting to Jesus. Even though the criminals had heard Pilate claim no fault in the Rabbi, Gestas, the one hanging on his left shouted, "If you are King of the Jews, save yourself and us as well!"

However Dismas, the one on his right, observing the strength and attitude of Jesus, saw through the crowd's mockery and realized he was a special person. He rebuffed his fellow criminal, "Seeing that he got the same sentence we did, don't you fear God. But we deserved it. This man has done nothing." Speaking with penitent heart, Dismas asked, Jesus, "Lord, remember me when you come into your Kingdom."

Struggling to breathe, the Rabbi rasped a reply, "Trust me. I promise that today you will be with me in paradise."

I can only assume he meant in the afterworld, wherever that is. It seems extremely ironic to me that the priests and people, even the disciples, have either made fun of or deserted the Deliverer, yet this lowly criminal recognized him as Lord. Strange times.

I kept running through my stockpiled memories of nearly three years in country. I had expected my absence from Rome to be but a few short months at best. The time has gone quickly and I have observed so much. It seems to come down to this. I assume my work is now complete. I'll gather my stuff and make my way to Caesarea and my return voyage home.

Looking up at the titilus above Jesus' head and the words proclaiming "This is Jesus of Nazareth, the King of the Jews," I couldn't help wondering if this were Pilate's backhanded way to mock the Jews who dearly hated him.

As he slowly sagged, producing more weight on the nails in his wrists, excruciating pain shot along his fingers and up his arms to explode in his brain—the spikes putting additional pressure on his median nerves. Pushing himself upward to avoid this stretching torment, his full weight rested on the spike through His feet. Searing agony accompanied the nail's tearing through the nerves between the metatarsal bones of his feet.

The crowd continued to crow. Soldiers scoffed. I caught numerous sarcastic comments coming from the crowd:

"You claim to be able to rebuild the Temple in three days but you can't save yourself..."

"If you are the Son of God, step down from the cross..."

"He saved others but he can't save himself..."

"If God will have anything to do with the Healer, let him rescue him."

As the morning wore on, so did the intense thirst and pain of the condemned—sinews screamed, hearts heaved and lungs labored.

Many who believed in him had witnessed his grueling effort with the crossbeam en route to Golgotha. But they were powerless to help him.

My mind played over a few of those the Nazarene had helped and I imagined their thoughts had they been here:

> The blind man named Bartimeaus would behold with perfect vision the Healer who had taken away his blindness.

> Legion, the madman from Gadara, would be struck with the notion that the Nazarene had freed him from his demons and his shackled life but he could not free himself.

> Jairus and countless others would watch the man who had responded on their behalf, delivering them from their personal prisons...and they would weep and wonder why he could not or would not free

himself from this one.

At this point the Savior's arms fatigued, great waves of cramps swept over his muscles, knotting them in deep, relentless, throbbing pain. Coupled with these cramps came the inability to push himself upward. Hanging by his arms, the pectoral muscles were paralyzed and the intercostal muscles unable to respond. He drew air into his lungs but he could not exhale. He fought to raise himself in order to get even one short breath. Finally, carbon dioxide built up in his lungs and in the blood stream and the cramps partially subsided. Spasmodically, he pushed himself upward to exhale and fight for the life-giving oxygen.

Three hours into the execution, near noon, darkness of night enveloped the entire countryside. Daylight morphed into blackness. It was as dark as the inside of a donkey. Darkness spread as far away as Rome and Athens and other cities along the Great Sea. Even though darkness was total, each successive hour seemed to grow darker, if that were possible.

Deep in the bowels of the earth beneath the Judaean hills and Galilean valleys a tremor developed. Her trembling turned into a groaning earthquake. The earth rolled like ocean waves then split open. She tossed boulders about like matchsticks. Rock ridges disintegrated. Tombs rattled against each other. The earth cried out, belching bodies from her bosom. Corpses sprang to life as tombs and mausoleums opened and many holy men who slept the death sleep left the cemetery and strode into Jerusalem. Walls cracked and barricaded doors flew open.

I wondered about the dead people rising and walking around...*what's with that?*

Harkening back to the Jewish Holy Word I was reminded of the Egyptian army racing in chariots to destroy the Hebrew children who fled Egypt. *Who can possibly explain in a natural manner the purported escape from their enemies as the Hebrews crossed the floor of the Red Sea on dry ground? How does that momentous occasion in Hebrew history correlate to these unexplainable mysteries—the raising of the dead and such?*

Many among the crowd, stunned by the natural phenomena, fell to the ground. Others were struck dumb with terror. Some thought Jesus would come down from the cross. Others thought the world was ending. Onlookers' faces revealed anguish, redness, puffed cheeks, tears, smirks, triumph, sadness. Some struggled through the darkness from Skull Hill to their homes.

Jesus gathered in enough air to gag out a muffled, "I'm thirsty." A soldier dipped a sponge in posca, the cheap wine of the legionnaires, in this case a concoction of vinegar and myrrh, stuck it on a hyssop stalk and raised it the short distance to the Nazarene's lips. But he did not take it.

No doubt, feeling the effects of their drinking up to now, the soldier's compatriots shouted, "Leave him alone. Let's see if Elijah will come and save him."

Emanating from the ebony, a clap of thunder rumbled across the countryside, followed by a sheet of lightning, lighting the landscape. Like a giant hand overspreading the earth, fingers hop scotched across the horizon and flashed, illuminating all in their path. Backlit by yellowish-white flashes of light the black crosses of the doomed swayed in silhouette.

As the storm spent itself, lightning morphed from lashing the land with staccatoed popping to subdued crackling and hissing. No flash of light; no thunder clap. Silence ruled.

Jesus proclaimed in a loud voice, "It is finished."

In his condition I would have expected a more frail version, wherein he gasped syllables in barely audible, brief intervals, "It...is...fi...finished, Fa...ther. Into...y...your hands...I...com...mit...my spirit." 'Commit my spirit" being not much more than a strained whisper. But his dying breath epitomized his strength and commitment.

At that moment the earth shook. Priests officiating during the evening sacrifice witnessed the Temple veil, a curtain made of pure linen attached with gold, scarlet and purple, rip down the middle from top to bottom. And more than one person mused that the Holy of Holies, once reserved for only the priests, was now vacated by Jesus, the one who had come to replace the old, blood sacrificial "righteousness" with a new holiness available for all men at no cost. His surrendered life replaced rules with love.

You might say the ripping veil brought down the curtain on the evil men who manipulated the Christ to the cross. Perhaps the rending of the material was a metaphor applicable to those who make bad choices. Ironically, reversing the first two letters in veil results in spelling *evil*...perhaps describing those who betrayed the Nazarene.

The literal and figurative falling curtain signaled the last act of the Galilean. Or did it?

The air was filled with a hint of spring-like newly plowed ground and its accompanying sense of the renewal of life...a stunning contrast to this field of death.

Traditionally soldiers broke the legs of condemned men to expedite their inability to breathe and their deaths. Because crucified victims often remained alive on the cross for days, breaking their legs speeds the process by causing a rapid onset of asphyxiation or fatal shock. Once deprived of support and unable to lift himself, the victim would die within a few minutes.

It was common for victims of the cross to be left there, allowing vultures and dogs to devour the remains.

The soldiers broke the legs of the two criminals and proceeded to the Prophet. However when they came to him, discovering he was already dead, the Centurion Longinus thrust a spear into the Rabbi's right side, from which flowed a watery liquid and blood. As I watched, the multitude melted into the landscape, some returned home beating their breasts in mourning; others crowed in jubilation to see the "King of the Jews" destroyed.

Having previously mocked the Nazarene, the soldiers had since changed. They had witnessed his crying out and his death, the earthquake and all that took place. They knew power and authority when they saw it. They were alarmed. With fear in their hearts their lips parted and they proclaimed, "Truly, truly, this man was the Son of God!"

Centurion Manlius Novius Adventus stood near the cross, my friend whose servant Jesus had healed without going to his home. This tough Roman had never witnessed a man die with this kind of grace. Never had he seen an innocent so treated. He spoke from his heart, "This was for certain a righteous man."

I have to agree, this entire event was violent, dark and foreboding.

CHAPTER 20 — Big Surprise

After the Nazarene's last breath, I left Skull Hill and hastily found my way to the home of Gaius. It had been a long day and I wanted to check with him for a number of reasons, not the least of which was his involvement with the flogging of the Savior. I wanted to let him know my mission was complete and I'd be leaving shortly for Rome to report my findings.

Almost before I knew it, I reached my friend's home and was met at the door by Livia. As she welcomed me, I noticed a constrained look upon her face. She quietly ushered me to Gaius. I noticed his complexion seemed paler than I remembered and his eyes displayed a somewhat vacant look.

It was then I learned that Gaius had not inflicted the terrible butchery of the Galilean. After I summarized the execution, he related the events of his involvement as they unfolded. "I can't really explain it. When I saw the Healer and knew it was my task to flog him, I was so confounded by the measure of it all. I was mortified. I can't explain the feeling that came over me. You know that the man who bears the whip must obey the standards or suffer the whip himself. Besides that, how could I bring pain to the one who brought so much joy to my family? Here was the very one who saved Carisia. Yet I was commanded to punish him. To obey orders was my job. But ambivalence overcame me.

"I held the flagrum in my right hand, preparing to swing. Jesus gave me a knowing look and spoke to me, 'Do what you must. We've both been given a task, one of distaste but necessary.' He looked upon me with mournful but merciful eyes. I could not help but recall his words at our first meeting, that we would meet again under less favorable circumstances. So, this was the circumstance. Now I understood. I knew it was my duty to Rome. And, with great regret, I smote Jesus.

"I weakened with each stripe. I'm sure part of it had to do with the look in his eyes when he came before me. A look of pity toward me, yet a look of knowing and understanding…as well as, perhaps forgiveness. His eyes told it all.

"The event became a blur, jammed with stress. A vague humming filled my ears. I knew that something was wrong but I couldn't focus. My mind was a blank. The next thing I knew the Healer was gone. I was gone. I was being attended by medical officers. Seems I blacked out. They put cold cloths on my forehead and behind my neck. One even had a damp cloth, moving it over my legs—I suppose in an effort to cool my body as I was fevered.

"After a while I came around and was led to a room and assisted onto a bed where they monitored me.

"I'm guessing an hour later the doctors rounded up six legionnaires, placed me on a pallet and carried me to my home with strict instructions to stay there and they would come later that night to check on me. They informed me that I was in no danger from my superior officers, that they took my condition as a result of some strange illness.

"They also told me that after I passed out, the man who replaced me flogged Jesus over a hundred strokes. He should have died after such a lashing. How he could have carried a crossbeam is beyond human understanding."

"In all our years together, I know you're a man of conviction and courage. It must have been overwhelming to consider whipping this man."

"My only explanation is that the stress overpowered me…or, perhaps, the Healer caused my collapse."

"I suppose we may never know. At any rate, it is most unusual but, hopefully, will end in your best interests. You had your watershed moment and I'm glad that you survived it. My entire time away from Rome has been a definite experience but I'm not sure I could even compare it to yours. Perhaps in time this will all be a distant memory."

"Maybe it will be a bargaining chip for my release from service. Perhaps my superior will recommend a sort of medical discharge. In spite of my pride, I'd consider it. Maybe my nightmares will finally end."

"If anyone deserves it, you do, Gaius. You've put in your years and earned it outright."

"Thank you, Brachan. I'm honored by your support, your words, your confidence and your friendship."

"It's interesting. As long as I've been here, first following the Baptizer then the Nazarene, it seems like a flash in time. Now with Jesus' arrest and execution, it's as if I were living a dream. Has it really happened? Now it's over. By all accounts my job here is definitely complete.

"Tomorrow I'll report by way of post carrier that the questioned threat to the Empire is dead, literally. At least from the hands of these two men of God. That will just about wrap up my business here. And I'll be on my way home."

"Livia, Carissa and I will be sorry to see you go. But we'll be comforted in the fact that we got to see you a few times and that your duty to Rome was honorable and valuable. Maybe I'll rejoin you in Rome in due time. We won't complain if you take these infernal earthquakes and darkness at midday with you. What do you make of them?"

"You must remember, my friend, I am a soldier not a philosopher, a meteorologist nor a theologian. I don't know just what to make of them. However it seems the timing for such atmospheric or geologic activities was either extremely coincidental…or, perhaps, providential. How else to explain these events occurring at the exact time of the man claiming to be God's son?"

"It certainly gives one pause, alright."

"As for the preposterous things I've heard and witnessed against the Son of Man, I found some of his words and actions confusing and difficult to understand in the moment. However after listening to and talking with others as well as listening to and talking to myself, those words and actions have come to make sense. Even though I can't explain all that I've experienced involving the Nazarene, I'm most impressed and inclined to believe his message."

However, there is confusion. Here I was tracking down opposition to my Republic. But so far, other than the vocal Jews and an occasional Zealot radical, I was unable to put my finger on it. I felt conflicted and told Gaius as much, "In my heart I feel the Prophet was not a threat. The more I think about it, the more I wonder if he was everything he claimed. When he discussed such things as what it profited a man to gain the world but lose his soul, truly he and the Baptizer spoke the same language, shared the same message, served the same God.

"He was not attempting to establish an earthly kingdom, or he would and could have. The Jews couldn't find him guilty because he was telling the truth. He threatened their greedy and hypocritical ways. When I consider the discipline it took for him to remain silent in his defense, to take the path he did to the cross, to surrender his life as he did, he was definitely a lamb taken to the slaughter."

"There's no question he was definitely different. Hard to capture in words."

"It's almost ironic. My mission was to observe the Baptizer and later the Nazarene as a threat. I've looked at this from every conceivable angle—physical, political, social, financial and theological. And I'm closer to understanding the situation.

"My assessment is that both the Baptizer and the Master were revolutionaries but not in the sense of changing the power structure of a country. Both men instructed their followers to love God and to do good toward their fellows. Rather their motivation was against man's effort to self-destruct, against man's desire to fulfill his humanness. Jesus walked among men restoring the sick of physical as well as spiritual health.

"He made no efforts against Rome. I find no fault in this man. But that seems irrelevant now.

"Even though his following and power could likely have given him an exalted position, he spoke of serving others. He fled from the very thought of attaining power while telling all who would listen about the importance of loving their enemies and favoring others over themselves. Instead of seeking power and utilizing his followers to attain a higher position, he renounced all that he could have sought. Even though the government was oppressive, to the best of my knowledge he was honorable in all his dealings with Roman authority. And he attempted no civil reforms."

"You have done your job well, Brachan. Covered miles and months ferreting information about these men. You deserve a break."

"Thank you, Gaius. There's another thing I've been pondering. Man wants freedom. The Jews want out from under Rome rule. In the same manner Spartacus wanted freedom from Rome so much that he rounded up gladiators and fought for freedom. What about this Jesus? He preached freedom. He freed people—not only of their physical 'chains' but other 'chains.'

"Yes, freedom is what he taught, freedom from physical needs and bondage, freedom of mind, freedom of spirit and soul.

"He freed Legion from physical and spiritual bondage.

"He freed Mary of Magdala from her lifestyle, guilt and shame.

"He freed Matthew the publican to a brighter future.

"He freed Lazarus from the tomb."

It did not surprise me when Gaius said, "I wish it had been my lot to be free from whipping the man."

"Yes, it seems there are many things in our past it would have been nice to be free from."

"Don't we all want that freedom, Brachan? I'd like the freedom of raising my little girl to become a shining person, to develop her personality and intelligence in order to be a good person. It seems we should all have that."

"There's much to consider, Gaius. Some say the Nazarene was either everything he said he was or he was a fake! How do you fake what he's done? After my time observing him, how could I doubt who he is? His majesty?

"And another thing. As long as I've been shadowing the Baptizer and him, not a single Roman lifted a finger against either of them. But those who suspected them and wanted them destroyed were their own people, the Jews."

I left Gaius with best wishes to him and his, made my way to my sleeping quarters and jotted a dispatch in my journal anticipating sending it to Flavius:

JOURNAL

In retrospect it appears that during the entire teaching and preaching of the Nazarene he was in total control, control of his activities and his future.

He followed the Baptizer. Taught this unheard of new concept of loving God and man. The concept of forgiveness. He orchestrated his travels healing the lame and encouraging the poor. Then he brought himself full circle, right back to the Temple. He cleared the Temple the first week of his ministry and the last week, inciting the religious hypocrites into action so that his God could fulfill the century old prophecies of the Jews.

1) My mission is complete. I'll put my things in order and head for Rome shortly. I'll write a dispatch to my superior within hours and make way for my departure. It's time for me to return to Rome with my report. There'll be no kingdom of the Messiah for the Empire to worry about. No more worry about the Man from Galilee. He is dead and buried. It should take only a day or two to gather my belongings and wrap up my report. Then I'll make my way overland for a refreshing and well earned sea voyage to Rome.

2) My journey of intervention turned into one of introspection, a journey of rooting out danger to one of witnessing exemplary humanitarian behavior. My mission to monitor the Baptizer and subsequently Jesus seemed a twisted trail at first but upon reflection, evolved into a wide path of enlightenment. I learned that John never planned to overthrow Roman rule. Perhaps the Baptizer was a revolutionary in the sense that he preceded the Savior whom he hoped would deliver the Jews from the Romans. How strange he represented his cousin.

DISPATCH: Flavius Diusus Caldus,

My suspicions that the Nazarene was a co-conspirator with the Baptizer were well founded. The two did work in concert. It must be noted, however, that they did not oppose the Empire.

As per your previous instructions regarding the reduced threat posed by the Galilean, since he is dead, I see no reason to remain here. I will check with the naval detachment to determine the next sailing from Rome and begin my journey to make that voyage. I will deliver my final report to you upon my arrival in Rome. In the meantime, however, I am sending this dispatch in the event that, for some unknown reason, I am incapacitated and/or unable to deliver my report to you in person.

The next day I began preparations for my trip home, giving myself a few extra days to contact the men I'd worked with before returning. Before my departure, however, I learned more about the execution and its aftermath. After the execution word reached Pilate about the King of the Jews's death. He was astonished that the Prophet should have died so soon and summoned the Centurion who confirmed the Prophet's death.

One of my men informed me that Jesus had been taken from the cross and buried by at least two men, perhaps others assisted. I can't imagine the difficulty of removing the patibulum with a dead man on it, then carting off the body. Whether they removed the body or had to remove the crossbeam first is pretty amazing. Two men did this? Surely they must have had help. And what about the complications of wrapping the body involving rigor mortis? Jewish custom required a shroud-like covering and additionally added spices.

After the execution of the Rabbi a rich man and prominent member of the Sanhedrin, a just and upright man named Joseph from the Jewish town of Arimathea in Judaea, had arrived in Jerusalem. He was a godly man and influential member of the Sanhedrin, anticipating the arrival of the Messiah. Because he feared the Jews, he remained a secret disciple of the Rabbi. He was devoted to the Prophet and had approached Pilate as the evening shadows fell across the land, requesting the Nazarene's body.

Pilate respected Joseph and gave him permission to take the Rabbi and honor him with a proper burial.

Joseph approached Calvary. In a short period of time Nicodemus, the man who had come by night long before to discuss spiritual matters with the Rabbi, joined Joseph. They removed Jesus from the stake. They were intent upon saving him from burial as a common criminal. These men were wealthy and wanted a decent "burial" of their Master.

Neither Joseph nor Nicodemus, a prominent Pharisee, had accepted the Savior while he lived, for fear of being excluded from the Sanhedrin. Though neither was present when the council condemned the Rabbi, they had hoped to protect him with their influence in the council. Some say the council acted without them in order to accomplish their deception. And their absence weighed heavily upon his murder.

Nicodemus brought myrrh and aloes weighing about one hundred pounds. The two men took the Prophet's body and wrapped it with the spices in a long, clean white linen winding sheet lengthwise from front to back according to the Jewish burial custom.

Although Joseph had a tomb newly hewn of rock for his own use in a garden close to Calvary, he chose to surrender it for the Rabbi. With the Sabbath rapidly approaching and the tomb nearby, Joseph and Nicodemus carried Jesus to the mausoleum and respectfully placed him in it. They rolled a large stone across the entrance to seal it and left.

Perhaps I can locate either of these two men and their accomplices in order to gain more information, not that it matters now. I wondered what kind of effort it took to carve this grave from rock

I learned that the three women who had come from Galilee—Mary Magdala, the other Mary and the mother of Jesus—followed the bearers of the Rabbi's body to the tomb, sat opposite the sepulcher and took note of where he had been laid and of the position of the body. They then departed, purchased embalming fluids and went home and prepared embalming spices and ointments in order to properly bury him. However by the time they had completed their work it was the Sabbath. Custom demanded they honor it. They determined to complete their task the next day.

On the day of execution the Chief Priests and Pharisees went to Pilate, "Your Excellency, we recall what this imposter said about rising again after three days. Therefore we request you to order the sepulcher kept secure until the third day in the event that his disciples come by night to steal him away and tell the people that he has risen from the dead."

By this time, quite annoyed with the whining priests, Pilate refused them a Roman guard and suggested they select a guard from among their Temple police.

Some time after Joseph and Nicodemus' departure, guards went and sealed the sepulcher with Pilate's insignia and temple guards took their positions. The great stone was in its place and the Roman seal unbroken. Roman guards protected the area.

Throughout Jerusalem a pall of despondency enveloped the Deliverer's followers. Those who knew him and shared visions of greatness in his company found themselves at a dead end. Their Messiah, the one they'd expected to deliver them, was gone. Dead. Sealed away in a burial tomb. What would become of them now? What would they do? By all appearances they would return to their former activities—keeping house, tending orchards, farming, fishing.

That night Jesus' mother Mary lay sleepless, tossing and turning, wondering about the plight of her son. Mary Magdala also suffered despair about her Rabbi.

In the darkness of early morning Mary Magdala, Mary the mother of James, Salome and certain others made their way to the tomb in order to anoint the Rabbi.

Sometime later that morning, a silent, sliver of moon joined me in the affair and watched the tapestry unfold. The day opened its eyes beneath a crimson sky, presenting a scintillating sunrise.

At first glance, a brilliant, red bonnet covered the earth's canopy. It then faded to bright pink, and dissipated incrementally from bright rose to a lighter pink, followed by the palest of pinks. From left to right, a monster slate gray cloud layer sliced the sky in half. Two parallel rosy pink clouds, each adjoined by blue sky, split the dark cloud in half at near right angles, forming two colossal cross shapes of gray, pink and blue.

A panoply of colors and brightness—from the slate gray above, tinted by pinks and partnered with blue, to the silver clad hills below, backlit by soft gold—proclaimed unexcelled beauty.

At the sepulcher guards remained on duty, sworn to thwart any persons from approaching it or even gawking, prepared to shoo them away. Anyone breaking the tomb's Roman seal could receive the death sentence. When daylight dawned, guards wondered what was happening as the earth began to shake. The shaking intensified into a violent earthquake. Suddenly a brilliant, near-blinding presence appeared at the tomb, rolled back the grave stone and sat upon it. The presence wore a robe as white as snow. Guards heard the presence cry out, "Son of God, come forth. Your Father calls you."

Overcome with fear, the guards fell to the ground as if dead.

As Salome, Joanna and others worked their way along the pathway approaching the sepulcher where Joseph and Nicodemus had interred their Master, they did not know a Temple guard had been posted and that the tomb was sealed. Charged with sorrow and shock from their loss, no doubt they had completely overlooked the task of removing the stone. As they neared the tomb, they remembered the stone and discussed who would roll it from the cave. How could they remove it?

By then the guards had awakened and noticed the stone rolled away from the tomb. They arose from the ground and rushed to the burial place, only to find it empty. *He's escaped! Oh, no! What now? We are dead men! They'll have our heads.*

They decided their only option was to tell the high priests. Slowly they trudged down the hill onto the Via Dolorosa. The men wondered what they could do to save their lives—what could they tell the religious leaders who'd hired them? They kicked around several likely stories but finally decided to provide the leaders the facts. Some of them entered Jerusalem, met with the Chief Priests and elders and spilled their story. A guard suggested the shining men "must have been one of those angel things for it sat upon the stone, arms crossed, and we were not hurt."

Unbeknownst to me, I was about to receive the shock of my life. On Monday my contact informed me of rumors on the street—the Nazarene was gone. He'd vanished from the tomb! *How could that be!? Why would someone steal a dead man? And, who would steal a dead man?* This is one for the books. *When I considered his absence, how was I to know that for centuries to come thousands would join me, while wondering "where is the Christ?"*

As rumors ran rampant and reached me that the Nazarene had disappeared, I was dumbfounded. My reaction was Holy Jupiter! What in the world? *Who aided his removal? Where did He go? I must make an immediate report to Superior Flavius.*

The only sense I could make of it was that somehow someone had carried him away. I continued to wonder. But who? How? And why? The only answer I came up with was either Pilate, Ciaphas or the Deliverer's pals…or, possibly someone thinking a ransom might be paid. *Perhaps bar Abbas brazenly secreted the body away?* If it was not the followers of the Nazarene, who, then, stole his body?

In the midst of my wonderment, another possibility presented itself… one I chose to ignore—at least for the moment. It didn't really seem plausible. Nevertheless the thought presented itself,

could it be the Nazarene was born of a virgin,

that his miracles were not sleight of hand,

that he rose from the dead as he'd prophesied,

that, in fact, he is the Son of God?

No man was ever born in such fashion. No man preached as he did nor healed the sick, lame and blind as he did…how could anyone—including me— doubt after all this?

As I considered my next move, I mentally constructed my journal entry:

JOURNAL

Oh, boy! Now what? A wrinkle has developed. Jesus' body is gone. Rumor is that his disciples stole it and secreted it away. Perhaps they've buried him somewhere. Others are saying they've seen him alive. Although this turn of events makes me consider whether I'm dreaming, I'm not. I will get word out to my network to discover where the body is. I don't know what this recent event might portend. However I will persist in this effort until I've succeeded. How am I going to explain this to Flavius?

CHAPTER 21 — Now What?

It wasn't long until I heard from another of my watchmen. He informed me that Pilate had sent a report to Caesar Tiberias about the events of the Prophet's end. In a nutshell the report claimed "An agony such as was never heard by mortal ears blew on the winds from Golgotha announcing an agony. Dark clouds covered Jerusalem like a veil." And he went on to explain his wonderment at the Nazarene's being the Son of God.

Information trickled in to me. After the Temple guards told the Jewish priests of the missing Master, the leaders came up with a plan. They bribed the guards to say "Jesus' disciples came during the night and stole him away while we were asleep. If the governor should hear about this, we'll talk to him and persuade him so that you won't get into trouble." Prepared to lie if asked, the guards accepted the money.

After I heard from my intelligence about the phony guard story and the Jews' deceptive pay off, I learned about the assembly of women arriving at the tomb and their surprise.

Discovering the stone rolled away, Mary of Magdala stood before the entrance weeping. She and the other Mary entered the vacant grave to discover it empty. *What in the world?* Dumbstruck by the missing body, they viewed the grave cloths. *Where has he gone?* Mournful of her Lord, still wondering what had become of him and what she could next do, confused with numerous thoughts tumbling through her mind, Mary of Magdala wondered, *Could someone have taken Him? Why? Where could I find him?*

Suddenly two men clothed in shining white robes appeared before the ladies, one sitting at the head and the other at the foot of the place where the Galilean had been lying. They asked her the reason for Mary's tears.

"They've taken away my Lord and I don't know where they've taken him."

The women shielded their eyes and the younger man said, "Don't be afraid. You're looking for Jesus of Nazareth who was hanged. He is not here. He is risen!" Terrified, the women bowed to the men.

The second man then spoke, "Why do you seek the living among the dead?"

The first then added, "He is not here. He rose as he said he would. Come, see the place where he lay."

The second man added, "Here's the place where they laid him."

Then the other said, "Remember what he told you in Galilee…that the Son of Man must be handed over into the hands of sinful men to be hanged and rise again on the third day? Go quickly and tell Peter and the others that He is risen from the dead and will precede you to Galilee. You will see him there."

Full of fear, awe and great joy the women left the tomb and rushed to tell the disciples, Mary of Magdala rushing foremost. She glanced over her shoulder and beheld a man who said, "Woman, why are you weeping? For whom are you looking?"

Thinking he was the gardener, she said, "Sir, if you have taken him away, tell me where you have put him and I will go and remove him."

The man spoke, "Mary." It was the gentle, reassuring voice she had loved and listened to for so long. The voice of the one who had changed her life forever. But here he was! It was the Master but Mary had not recognized him.

Overwhelmed with joy, yet still confused, she blurted, "Rabbuni!" (My Lord! My Master!")

"Don't touch me because I have not ascended to my Father. Go tell my brothers that I ascend to my Father and your Father and to my God and your God."

When Mary finally reached the disciples, they were weeping and mourning. She told them she'd seen and talked with the living Lord. Coupled with the anguish they suffered from the Savior's death, the disciples were shocked. They doubted her, wondering what kind of tale she'd come up with. Even though the other women arrived and confirmed Mary's story, the disciples did not believe them or Mary.

Regardless, Peter and John rushed toward the tomb, wondering aloud as they ran. Peter asked John, "What in the world is happening? How could this be?"

John responded, "I don't know, Peter. Is it possible the women are wrong? Do you think they really saw what they claimed?"

Peter said, "Maybe the high priests stole the Master? What about the guards, how could they allow this to happen?"

John asked, "I don't know but what could have become of Jesus?"

Though neck and neck when they started, gradually John pulled ahead of Peter and reached the tomb before the big fisherman.

He looked into the opening and saw the linen cloths lying on the ground, undisturbed like an empty cocoon...not heedlessly tossed aside but carefully folded, each in a place by itself. John stood amazed. *The Master is gone.*

Then panting Peter rushed up and pushed his way past John right into the tomb, determined to see what it held. He looked and made the same discovery as John. The head cloth was rolled up in a place by itself.

The words that the Rabbi had spoken about raising the temple in three days finally registered with the two. He would rise in three days! They slowly, but triumphantly turned to leave, wondering where he could be and what would happen.

Later I heard about two men walking the road to Emmaus when they encountered a man brilliantly dressed.

That day Cleopas and another follower of the Galilean traveled the road from Jerusalem to Emmaus, a journey of seven miles. They discussed the recent happenings. Before long they discovered another traveler, a stranger, going their way with them.

The traveler asked, "What are you discussing that makes you so sad?"

Cleopas responded, "Are you only a stranger in Jerusalem and don't know the things that have happened these past few days?"

"What things?"

"The things concerning Jesus of Nazareth who proved to be a great prophet from what he said and did. And how the Chief Priests and Jewish leaders handed him over to the Roman Pontius Pilate to be hanged. We had hoped that he would free Israel. Today is the third day since his death. Some women from our group visited his tomb early this morning. They found it empty and reported their findings to us. They said they had seen angels who assured them that he was alive. Some of our friends went to the tomb and found it as the women described but they didn't see him."

"You foolish men. So slow of heart to believe all that the prophets have spoken. Shouldn't Christ have suffered these things in order to enter his glory?"

The traveler related to them from the time of Moses what the scriptures contained about the Messiah. They neared Emmaus and he acted as if he were going further until they pressed him to stay with them, "Stay with us. It's getting towards evening and the day is almost over."

He went into a house with them and partook of the evening meal. He took bread and blessed it, broke it and gave it to them. And their eyes were opened. Their companion was none other than Jesus. But he vanished from their sight.

They said, "Didn't our hearts burn within us while he talked along the road revealing scriptures to us?" Then they returned to Jerusalem to tell the others.

When they arrived, they found Jesus' chosen ten gathered for dinner with their companions, behind closed doors for fear of the wrath of the Jewish leaders.

Cleopas said, "The Lord has for a fact risen and appeared to Simon."

They recounted their experience with the traveler and as they spoke, the Nazarene appeared and spoke, "Peace be with you."

The disciples and the others were terrified and thought they viewed a spirit.

"Why are you so worried and why are these doubts rising in your hearts? Look at my hands and my feet. It is I. Touch me and see for yourselves. A spirit has no flesh and bone."

They were dumbfounded, still in disbelief but in joy. His body appeared as whole as it had before his flogging and execution.

He asked, "Have you anything to eat?"

They offered him a piece of grilled fish which he ate. He reproached them for not believing the witnesses earlier. "These are the words that I spoke to you when I was with you, that things must be fulfilled as written in the Law of Moses, the prophets and the Psalms concerning me. Because it is written that Christ suffer and rise from the dead on the third day, that had to take place. The same for the repentance for sin beginning in Jerusalem. You are witnesses to these things. I send the promise of my Father upon you. Peace be with you. As my Father sent me, so send I you."

He breathed on them and continued, "Receive the Holy Spirit. Go into all the world to preach the Good News. Whoever believes will be saved. The believers will cast out demons in my name, speak with new tongues, heal the sick."

The Prophet walked with them as far as the outskirts of Bethany where he lifted his hands and blessed them. He departed to heaven. They returned to Jerusalem and rejoiced in the Temple praising and blessing God.

Thomas was not with the group when Jesus came and they told him, "We have seen the Lord."

Thomas was skeptical and said "unless I see the nail holes and put my finger into them and thrust my hand into his side, I won't believe."

Eight days after Jesus' return from the tomb the group gathered in a house. Thomas was among them. Although the doors were closed, the Rabbi appeared to them, "Peace be with you."

He turned to Thomas and said, "Put your finger here. Look here are my hands, put your hand out and put it into my side. Doubt no longer. Believe."

Thomas was aghast, "My Lord and my God."

"Thomas, because you have seen me you believe. Blessed are those who have not seen and yet believe."

Thirty-two days later the eleven disciples set out for Galilee and the mountains where the Prophet had arranged to meet them. When they saw him, they fell down before him, though some hesitated. He spoke to them, "All power has been given to me in heaven and on earth. Go, therefore, and teach all nations baptizing them in the name of the Father, the Son and the

Holy Spirit. Teach them to observe what I have commanded. I am with you to the end of time."

In a matter of days hope evolved from hopelessness and reappeared as hopefulness—the festive pilgrims had welcomed their Messiah into Jerusalem shouting and spreading palm branches and articles of clothing before him; then he was captured, tried and killed, dooming their hopes. But, alas, now he is alive.

Having received reports from all my informants I'm updating my journal prior to leaving for the home of my friend Gaius.

Whereas I had previously journaled of my completed mission and preparation to return to Rome, I'm adding two paragraphs about the Nazarene's disappearance.

JOURNAL

But wait. I must change course and confess just when I thought my mission completed, I discover there's more.

1) My supervisor is going to think I'm totally off my noodle or that I need rescue of some sort. I just dispatched him that Jesus was in a tomb. Turns out he is not to be found. Now I'll have to search for the body and discover what's going on in order to finally complete my mission. Just when I think I have a handle on things, my workload increases.

2) If I'm given the job of shadowing him and his activities (and can't find him), how do I report the Galilean's disappearance after death? And how do I begin to understand, much less report, his appearances after he has been seen walking around? Walking around? I saw him killed!

How can I complete this task? Where do I go from here? Sometimes it would be easier to have declined this assignment. It's a daunting task. It should scare me away but I will see it through...all the more intrigued, and confused, than ever.

Having mulled over numerous details on my way to Gaius' home to compare notes with him, it was pleasant once again being welcomed into his home. I got right to the point, "Remember when I complimented you for surviving your watershed moment?"

"Yes, I do."

"You've heard about the Nazarene's disappearance?"

"Yes, I have. When I left you the other night, I thought my assignment here was completed. Then the Rabbi disappeared. Next he was seen. Which brings me to another point. Now I have to find out what's going on."

"What do you mean?"

"I've heard of miracles. I've witnessed astounding things. Unexplainable things. Even you said he should not have survived. Yet within a few days of his flogging and punishment on the cross at the hands of Rome's best, I've heard this dead man is completely restored to physical health. How could an emaciated-flogged-nearly-dead-person-turned-corpse be restored? Consider this. Even if he never died but his body were stolen…even if he actually reappeared, how could his body recover within hours of his flogging, hanging and stabbing? How could a skeletal mound of flesh and blood be restored to health?

"How can I explain these things to my superior? How do you explain the dark hours and the earthquake and the tombs coughing up the dead? This Jewish man, King of the Jews, the Nazarene, seems to be the embodiment of the Jewish *Tahakh* and its prophecies. What's not to believe?"

"Sounds to me like your watershed moment is here. But since you've informed Flavius of your mission all along, surely it will not be difficult to explain these events. Difficult to understand, but explainable in light of your understanding."

"Maybe so. I have to admit, who can dispute the path of the Savior— from birth to death—born in an obscure village, raised in the Jewish faith and persecuted by the Jewish leaders? The mistreatment at the hands of the Jews, the betrayal by one of his followers, the mock trial, unfair judgment from Pilate and Herod, his death. These are all mentioned in the Jewish religious tradition, actually prophesied hundreds of years previously. The Nazarene fits all of these.

"It's so paradoxical. I have viewed his disciples as pretty stupid. Couldn't understand why they couldn't figure out who he was. Yet, it's taken me nearly three years to get it. I am now beginning to understand. When he alluded to destroying the temple and rebuilding it in three days, he was not referring to the building. Everyone criticized his utter nonsensical concept of rebuilding the temple. However he referred to himself. Rebuilding his body, the true temple of God. No wonder people were mistrustful and doubted him."

"I never made that connection either, Brachan. It makes perfect sense. The immensity of the miraculous nature of it is truly amazing."

CHAPTER 22 — Searching for Jesus

I left Gaius committed to learn the Son of God's whereabouts. Before long I heard he was at the Sea of Galilee and began my journey there… wondering all the more. For instance, *how could the Romans execute the Rabbi based on the accusations of the Jews? How do I explain the empty tomb? I know Jesus died. I watched it. But how am I to understand—much less, explain—that within days of his death he was alive? AND his fatal wounds were completely healed!*

When it looked like things couldn't get any worse, *voila*—they did!

You'll recall my earlier confusion about dead people leaving tombs and walking about? Holy Jupiter! I'm wondering if I'm losing my mind.

You might also recall my visit to the tent maker's to purchase a leather strap for my sandal repair. Remember the Aged One who suggested to me the Nazarene was the Messiah, the one Ariella called Reuven ben Judah? The same man whose funeral I later witnessed. Tell me I'm not going crazy. I saw him walking the street just today! *This is turning into some kind of journey. Crazy! Crazy! Crazy!*

Some time later while I tried to make sense of all this, the Master appeared to the disciples by the Sea of Galilee. Simon Peter, Thomas called the Twin, Nathanael from Cana in Galilee, the Sons of Zebedee and two more of his disciples were together when Simon Peter said, "I'm going fishing."

The others said, "We'll go with you."

They fished that night from their boat but failed to catch anything. The next morning a stranger called from the shore, "Children, have you any meat?"

"No."

"Cast the net out on the starboard side of the boat and you'll find something."

Peter had some ideas of his own about commercial fishing. They'd fished all night, the best time to fish, and had nothing to show for it.

A crusty group, experienced in their profession, they wondered to a man, "Who is this stranger who thinks he can come along and tell us how to fish? He's got some gall!"

Several of them grumbled about the stranger's nerve. Nevertheless Peter hid his disgust and directed his fellow fishermen to drop the net. They had gone where directed and as it turned out completely encircled a school of tilapia. As Peter and his crew pulled their net into the boat, it was nearly too heavy to haul aboard.

Peter called to his partner boat captain that they were into the fish. That boat's crew rowed to Peter's aid and helped them with their task. As the fish piled onto the floorboards, the boats filled and were difficult to propel to the beach—the huge amount of fish nearly swamping the crafts.

In all his years' fishing Peter had never caught so many fish. He and his partners were jubilant with the catch.

Then John said to Peter, "It's the Lord!" It was then that Peter realized the man on the beach was none other than his Messiah. Peter had to believe that even though the Messiah was not a fisherman, he truly was the master of the sea and its inhabitants. He wondered if Jesus purposely repeated his earlier "fish on the other side" trick.

Peter, who wore hardly any clothing, wrapped his fisherman's coat about himself and jumped into the water in his eagerness to see the Messiah.

The men saw a charcoal fire with some fish cooking and some bread. Jesus hailed, "Bring some of the fish you've just caught."

Simon Peter went back to the boat and dragged the net ashore full of big fish, one hundred and fifty three of them. And in spite of the amount, the net was not damaged. The Nazarene called out, "Come and have some breakfast."

None of the disciples asked him who he was because they knew intuitively that it was the Lord. The Rabbi stepped forward, took bread and fish and gave them to the men. This was the third time that he showed himself to his disciples after he had risen from the dead. When they'd finished eating, he spoke to Peter, "Simon, son of John, do you love me?"

"Yes, Lord, you know that I love you."

"Feed my lambs. Simon, do you love me?"

"Yes, Lord, you know that I love you."

"Look after my sheep. Simon, son of John, do you love me?"

And a third time Peter replied, "Lord, you know all things. You know that I love you."

"Feed my sheep. When you were young, you put on a belt and walked where you wanted. But when you are old, you will stretch out your hands and another will put a belt around you and take you where you do not want to go."

He said this because he knew the type of death that Peter would endure would glorify God. Then he said, "Follow me."

Peter turned and saw John following them. Peter wanted to know about that disciple, but the Rabbi said if he wanted that disciple to stay behind it was no concern of Peter's and that the Rabbi wanted Peter to follow him.

Having heard that Jesus was at the Sea of Galilee, I hastened there, eager to see—with my own eyes—the one who had cheated death. I had a lot to chew on while I traveled in my search. I recalled his words about "the way, the truth and the life," "let not your heart be troubled," "if you have seen me, you have seen the Father." I continued wondering about many things such as "where your treasure is there will be your heart."

His heart was to set men free, free from their spiritual bondage and into a life of eternal joy. No prison of any sort.

I wonder if the Nazarene taught a subliminal message with his illustrations? He talked about being a servant. He healed those in bondage. He was a servant, freeing those enslaved yet he was sold for the price of a slave.

I found it hard to believe that in spite of the Master's overwhelming events, the Jews continued to cling to their errant beliefs that purity was something that they could gain in and of their own efforts. And even his friend Judas Iscariot, must have had his doubts as well as an avaricious heart. I wonder if we don't all have a skosh of Judas in us. We all want

purchasing power,

friendship,

relationships,

acceptance and

approval.

But there are various means of attaining each. Perhaps the most sensible means for man is to travel the road of the Galilean—allegiance to his God and obedience to his teaching.

The next thing I knew I was back at the site where I'd been months earlier and heard the old fisherman regale the fishermen about Peter's amazing catch. And before I knew it, there was the brash, big fisherman approaching me with some others. As he neared me, he hailed, "Peace be to you."

"And to you."

As he reached me, he thrust his right paw toward me in greeting and proclaimed, "I'm Simon bar Jona."

I accepted his hand and gripped it tightly. "I know. I am Brachan. Or if you prefer, Aurelius Junius Brachan."

"So... you are Roman?"

"That is correct. I saw you recently at the palace of Caiaphas, early in the morning after the arrest of the Deliverer.

"That was a dark time."

"Yes, there have been very dark times of late. For instance, I learned that your friend Judas Iscariot turned him over to the priests who then enacted his death. It must have been the lowest point of Judas' life. And when he attempted to return the coins, the priests laughed at him. I felt conflicted.

It was a travesty to send his friend to the cross, yet I felt sorry for Judas. I'm assuming he expected the Nazarene to lead the Jews to power over the Romans and when that didn't happen, he chose to seek financial remuneration. It seems unfair that the priests used him then abandoned him. So strangely sad that the priests did not give Judas a second chance. But I understand now that they would stop at nothing to rid them of him."

"You speak truly. What should be the holiest of men turned their backs upon the real Holy Man. And Judas sent Jesus to the gallows as it were. But haven't we all? I denied him three times."

"So you did. I know about the rooster. But just think. You denied him only three times. You acknowledged your error. You can put that behind you. On the other hand there are those who deny him daily, refusing to even consider what he's done. Or who he is."

"To a degree you're right. Initially I followed him from the seashore. But I've failed him more than three times.

"I failed him when he called me across the water.

"I failed him the night before his arrest and the morning after.

"I've failed him since.

"The night before he died he never slept. But my fears and doubts took over. I and the others slept. He endured those days rife with turmoil and stress but I failed.

"Those recent days were the darkest days of my life. I was afraid. I had reason to be afraid. There was every chance the Romans would arrest me. But I'm not afraid anymore. Speaking of second chances. My big mouth got me in trouble again. In my loyalty to serve and protect him, I acted impulsively with my actions and my mouth. I told Jesus I'd never fail him. But I did. Even so, he gave me a second chance."

"That's what I've been told. After Jesus' death, I prepared to return to Rome. But then he disappeared from his tomb."

"It is true. His tomb is empty. The disciples and I first heard the good news when Mary Magdalene came from the tomb and told us."

"I'm told he walks the earth…that numerous people have seen him. What can you tell me about that?"

"Jesus appeared to me. Then he talked and walked with two men just a few miles outside of Jerusalem on the road to Emmaus."

"How did he look? Or, rather, what was his condition?"

"He looked just like he did when he called me to follow him to be fishers of men. Alive. Well. Happy."

"Tell me, Peter, can you explain how a butchered human could rise from the tomb and be made whole?"

"Only if I believe he is God."

"I understand. I am seeking the Christ."

"He is not here."

"Can you tell me where I might find him?"

"You can find him in your heart if you only believe. He visited the disciples and ate with us. The last time I saw him was the third time he visited my fellow disciples and me on the beach just beyond here. Yesterday he blessed us and rose into the sky, disappearing into a cloud and returning to his father—leaving us here."

"What do you mean 'rose into the sky'?"

A look of puzzlement spread across Peter's face, "I don't think I can explain it any better than that. When I first met Jesus, he invited me to follow him, to fish for men, as he called it. I didn't understand him but followed anyway. These past few years have been a wonder to me. So many things I can't explain. I'm thinking his call to follow him was his first indication to me that he is God. I can't explain that either except that he continued to equate himself to his Father in Heaven."

"So, he's not here. Will he be coming back?"

"I don't know when. He said he would return to accompany his believers to Heaven, that he had prepared mansions there for them."

"And what of this 'heaven' thing…what does that mean?"

"Jesus talked about living forever in heaven with him and his Father. It is a place we've never been. It is a place beyond…or as Jesus discussed, 'above us.' Centuries ago our prophet Isaiah prophesied a Savior would come to the Jews…that he must be bruised and afflicted, brought as a lamb before the slaughter, buried like a criminal in a rich man's grave…that he would rise again to bear our sins and save us."

"Well. That takes me back to square one…right back where I started, my friend, at least we both have some questions answered about the Nazarene and how he has affected our lives. It appears now it is our challenge to determine what we're going to do about it."

Peter nodded his head in affirmation. "Yes. You make an excellent point. I've learned some lessons—some the very hardest way—we have but one choice. The greatest decision we face is whether or not to believe that he is the Son of God. We either accept or reject him. That choice will affect our entire lives…and life after death."

"I'm beginning to understand but…"

"Jesus said it was our job to take his message throughout the world and that he was going back to his Father. We were puzzled by his comments. I'm not sure anyone will ever comprehend a physical body going into the sky. However my friends and I have left our nets to fish for fellows."

I was puzzled also. Numerous thoughts and concepts continued rattling around in my head. Jesus presented a major hurdle for the Jewish leaders. He preached a new paradigm, one that didn't fit their perceptions, traditions or agenda. His only fault was in telling the truth. He represented the eradication of their power structure. He died revealing the truth.

During our entire discussion Peter had been holding a stick. He drew an elongated semi-circle on the beach, from left to right. It resembled the top half of a fish viewed from the side. He looked me in the eye and handed me the stick. It was my turn. I put the point of the stick at the left point of his line. Then I moved it in a semi-circular motion to the right below his line, connecting the two points. My line intersected his line just before the end, leaving a mark that formed an "X" and looked like a fish's tail. The completed image resembled a fish.

GLOSSARY

caligla	sandal
capsarri	medics
Corbitas	ship
crucifixion	Crucifixion was not a term used during the time of Christ but later; therefore hanging from a tree or hanging was the proper term for such punishment.
cursus publicus	mail service
flagrum	whip with lead balls
himation	article of clothing
lanista	gladiatorial school manager
ludi	gladiatorial school
medicus collegia	a group similar to a union
novicius	rookie gladiator
optio valentudinarii	hospital operators
phylacteries	strips of parchment inscribed with texts from the Law, worn on the arms and forehead
plumbatae	instrument of punishment; whip with attached bones or sharp objects
rhedae	light carriages
stipes	vertical post of a cross
tunic	outer garment, with or without sleeves, sometimes belted

BIBLICAL REFERENCES

Some scripture referrals are listed below

BRACHAN ORIGIN

This work is historical fiction. It is not my intent to distort history but rather to present an informational and inspirational challenge.

Having heard "Forty Soldiers for Jesus" on radio KTBN in 1989 the thought passed through my mind to re-tell the last years of the life of Christ through the eyes of an objective observer. A Roman soldier seemed appropriate. The name Brachan popped into my head and the next day I looked up a book on Greek and Roman names during my free period in the A.J. Dimond High School library. I was surprised to see the name, or one very close in spelling. More surprisingly the English meaning of the name was "called of God." Goose bumps bombarded my body. I felt strongly I was supposed to write Brachan...that my other books were in preparation for writing this book.

One day my son-in-law Brad Risch volunteered information reminding me about Brachan. He said, "It was a sunny, warm day around 1991 when we pulled into the A.J. Dimond parking lot, probably to pick up your son Ben. You got an excited look on your face, turned to me and said, 'I had a dream about a Roman soldier. His name was Brachan. I looked it up to see if there was such a name.' I really remember when you told me the title, and the different times you shared portions from your novel, your bright eyes and divine inspiration about Jesus."

From inception in 1989 I questioned whether a book of this magnitude could be written—a challenge of questionable achievement. I remained in denial and busy with other projects until I finally began research. I chose to use the voice of first person to tell Brachan's story, supplemented by a journal and dispatches to provide additional information and a break from the narration.

TRANSLATOR

I thought it would be both interesting and fun to write the introduction as though Brachan were the author, and this, his memoir. Since I credited Brachan as the book's author and since I have long considered using the pseudonym J.C. Luvsus, it seemed most appropriate to credit J.C. Luvsus as the translator of this soldier's book. After all, the book's message is that Jesus loves us. This way I could upgrade the text into today's vernacular so that it could be better understood—using different fonts for the narration, journal and dispatches.

It was my intent for the reader to immerse himself in this story, perhaps unknowingly reading segments of the life of Christ found in the *Holy Bible*.

Obviously Brachan is NOT 100% accurate. Even biblical scholars do not agree on many of the Bible's elements. For instance, some say Yeshua cleared the temple once; others say he did so the first and the last weeks of his ministry.

Was a Roman soldier selected to monitor John the Baptist? Perhaps. Research reveals that Herod Antipas feared John's growing popularity. If you were a Roman soldier shadowing John, doesn't it seem conceivable that Jesus was a likely partner in a possible revolution? And wouldn't you be concerned about Jesus and monitor his actions as a co-conspirator until proven otherwise?

I attempted to follow a chronology and to include characters and action that might have happened. My hope was to write descriptively in an effort to capture the scenes and senses, to transport the reader to those ancient days. I also hoped to parallel Brachan's persona and questions to those of the reader.

J.C. Luvsus/Larry Kaniut

ABOUT THIS JESUS

Our history books record past persons and their achievements—Julius Caesar, Johnny Appleseed, Jesus Christ. All lived. Jesus was born, credited with miracle performing acts, died by crucifixion and placed in a tomb and later seen walking the earth, entirely whole within days. How could a person survive crucifixion? Whether he was stolen from the tomb or actually rose from the dead with no human help, how could anyone so physically injured recover from that brutal treatment (and so quickly)?

How do you explain—even if Jesus were kidnapped or "man-napped" by his followers—the fact that within days after his departure from the tomb, he was healthy? What do we do with this knowledge? How do we respond to Jesus?

How do you explain his virgin birth?

How do you explain the healings he performed?

How do you explain his resurrection?

How do you explain his body's complete healing after his crucifixion?

How do you explain his eating after his death and resurrection?

How do you explain his claim to be Savior of the world?

What will you do about your standing before him?

When Jesus healed the leper, perhaps it was a symbolic gesture representing all mankind. After all, we are all lepers of a sort. We're all "unclean." Who among us can claim any cleanliness?

Jesus life proclaimed, "I've got your back." To put it another way, "I've got you covered. In all kinds of weather, in every situation, I've got your number but you can call me if you want."

He did not wish to hang people, rather he was interested in man's hang ups, wanting to restore man to a happy, healthy state. He came to set man free. If you are in bondage, you need but call upon his name.

The Creator of life in the form of man chose to suffer humiliation, anguish and death on man's behalf, the lowly creature who had turned his back on his Creator. God chose to experience the suffering of the cross in exchange and as a sacrifice for man's sin. Now it's our choice—do we accept or reject Him?

Acceptance leads to eternal life—and the unabated loss of guilt, taking the burden of anguish from us. Acceptance of Jesus as your personal savior directs you to a pathway that he has chosen for you, providing guidance throughout your life, and a peace unavailable otherwise.

Rejection results in eternal death. Rejection leads to your personal choices and their attendant consequences, without his divine directions and void of His rewards.

In Jesus' parable about the Prodigal Son, the young man exhausted his inheritance pursuing personal pleasures before he realized his happiness was at home with his father. So it is with man. Until we choose to be with the father, our "happiness" is an illusory vapor.

After years of reflection I've come to the conclusion that the Nazarene was everything he claimed—Son of Man, Son of God, Savior of the world. When he said, "I am the way, the truth and the life," he expressed numerous truths:

1. His is THE way;

2. His life, works and spirituality are THE truth;

3. He IS life.

The Bible tells us Jesus' ministry was to save us from our sin. Another way of saying this is that Jesus came to save us from ourselves. Human nature wants its own way. Our egos know no limits. Where man's ego reigns, man fails. Unless man relinquishes self to his Creator, man loses.

When God tosses a life ring, it is useless unless we grasp it. For man to have a fulfilled life, it requires that he surrender his will to that of Jesus. When he spoke about denying ourselves, taking up our crosses and following him, he meant just that. In order for man to maximize himself, he must first deny his desires. When Jesus condensed the ten commandments into two— loving God and loving man, he meant for us to love with ALL our heart, soul, mind and strength.

All of this was to fulfill Jeremiah 29:11 where Jeremiah tells us that God has a plan for us.

Every man is on a journey, just as Brachan. Until we realize that Jesus is the one to set us free and that his father has a plan for us, we seek in vain.

Brachan realized that the Rabbi was the Passover lamb…that he turned our darkness into light, our red into white—his blood turns us white as snow. As my sister Laura Lee Smothers wrote, "He wrote his love story for us in his blood."

When you choose Jesus, you go from one thing to another:

From	To
guilt	innocence
upheaval	peace
darkness	light
sickness	health
old	new
weakness	strength
night	day
agony	joy
bondage	freedom

Jesus knew who he was.

He knew who his Father was.

Jesus knew what he was about. He didn't have to answer to man.

If you find you are in the need of asking Jesus Christ into your life or of pursuing a closer walk with Him, I suggest you:

Acknowledge your sins (confess to God)… "I am a sinner…

Express your desire to turn from sins… "I desire to be forgiven and…

Ask God's forgiveness… "I ask your forgiveness."

Find a Bible believing and teaching church and begin worshiping there… so that you will grow in knowledge and experience with the Lord. Learn the Bible and pray daily.

You're going to meet Him sooner or later. Why wait?

ONE SOLITARY LIFE

He was born in an obscure village. He worked in a carpenter shop until He was thirty. He then became an itinerant preacher. He never held an office. He never had a family or owned a house. He didn't go to college. He had no credentials but himself. He was only thirty-three when the public turned against him. His friends ran away. He was turned over to his enemies and went through the mockery of a trial. He was nailed to a cross between two thieves. While He was dying his executioners gambled for his clothing, the only property He had on earth. He was laid in a borrowed grave. Nineteen centuries have come and gone, and today He is the central figure of the human race. All the armies that ever marched, all the navies that ever sailed, all the parliaments that ever sat, and all the kings that ever reigned, have not affected the life of man on this earth as much as that One Solitary Life.

- Anonymous

Perhaps it's time for God to take a bow...

Is it possible that Jesus Christ never took a bow? Perhaps as a child. Probably not as an adult. His primary objective was to obey his Father. Through that obedience he opened the possibilities for man's redemption. Surely as the Creator who has accomplished so much in the created and the creation he deserves our utmost honor, praise and obedience...and he is most worthy of taking a bow.

APPENDICES

APPENDIX 1 The History of the Church

The following is quoted directly from the pages of Eusebius' book. If Eusebius' record is accurate, what does the reader do about it?

Because of His power to work miracles the divinity of our Lord and Saviour Yeshua Christ became in every land the subject of excited talk and attracted a vast number of people in foreign lands very remote from Judaea, who came in the hope of being cured of diseases and disorders of every kind. Thus it happened that when King Abgar, the brilliantly successful monarch of the peoples of Mesopotamia, who was dying from a terrible physical disorder which no human power could heal, heard continual mention of the name of Yeshua and unanimous tribute to His miracles, he sent a humble request to Him by a letter-carrier, begging for relief from his disease. Yeshua did not immediately accede to his request, but honoured him with a personal letter, promising to send one of His disciples to cure his disease, and at the same time to bring salvation to him and all his kin. In a very short time the promise was fulfilled. After His resurrection and ascent into heaven, Thomas, one of the twelve apostles, was moved by inspiration to send Thaddaeus, himself in the list of Christ's seventy disciples, to Edessa as preacher and evangelist of the teaching about Christ. Through him every word of our Saviour's promise was fulfilled.

Written evidence of these things is available, taken from the Record Office at Edessa, at that time the royal capital. In the public documents there, embracing early history and also the events of Abgar's time, this record is found preserved from then till now; and the most satisfactory course is to listen to the actual letters, which I have extracted from the archives and translated word for word from the Syriac as follows:

Copy of a letter written by Abgar (*) the Toparch to Yeshua and sent to Him at Jerusalem by the courier, Ananias (Eusebius, *Ecclesiastical History*, Book 1, xiii)

"Abgar Uchama the Toparch to Yeshua, who has appeared as a gracious saviour in the region of Jerusalem —greeting.

"I have heard about you and about the cures you perform without drugs or herbs. If report is true, you make the blind see again and the lame walk about; you cleanse lepers, expel unclean spirits and demons, cure those suffering from chronic and painful diseases, and raise the dead. When I heard all this about you, I concluded that one of two things must be true--either you are God and came down from heaven to do these things, or you are God's Son doing them. Accordingly I am writing to beg you to come to me, whatever the inconvenience, and cure the disorder from which I suffer. I may add that I understand the Jews are treating you with contempt and desire to injure you;

my city is very small, but highly esteemed, adequate for both of us."

Yeshua's reply:

"Happy are you who believed in me without having seen me. For it is written of me that those who have seen me will not believe in me, and that those who have not seen will believe and live. As to your request that I should come to you, I must complete all that I was sent to do here, and on completing it must at once be taken up to the One who sent me. When I have been taken up I will send you one of my disciples to cure your disorder and bring life to you and those with you."

To these letters is subjoined the following in Syriac:

"After Yeshua was taken up, Judas, also known as Thomas, sent to him as an apostle Thaddaeus, one of the Seventy, who came and stayed with Tobias, son of Tobias. When his arrival was announced [and he had been made conspicuous by the wonders he performed], Abgar was told: 'An apostle has come here from Yeshua, as He promised you in His letter.' Then Thaddaeus began in the power of God to cure every disease and weakness, to the astonishment of everyone. When Abgar heard of the magnificent and astonishing things that he was doing and especially his cures, he began to suspect that this was the one to whom Yeshua referred when He wrote in His letter: 'When I have been taken up, I will send you one of my disciples who will cure your disorder.' So summoning Tobias, with whom Thaddaeus was staying, he said, 'I understand that a man with unusual powers has arrived and is staying in your house [and is working many cures in the name of Yeshua.' Tobias answered: 'Yes, sir. A man from foreign parts has arrived and is living with me, and is performing many wonders.' Abgar replied:] 'Bring him to me.'

"So Tobias went to Thaddaeus and said to him: 'The Toparch Abgar has summoned me and told me to bring you to him so that you can cure him.' Thaddaeus answered: 'I will present myself, since the power of God has sent me to him.' The next day Tobias got up early and escorted Thaddaeus to Abgar. As he presented himself, with the king's grandees standing there, at the moment of his entry a wonderful vision appeared to Abgar on the face of Thaddaeus. On seeing it Abgar bowed low before the apostle, and astonishment seized all the bystanders; for they had not seen the vision, which appeared to Abgar alone. He questioned Thaddaeus.

"Are you really a disciple of Yeshua the Son of God, who said to me, 'I will send you one of my disciples who will cure you and give you life?

"'You wholeheartedly believed in the One who sent me, and for that reason I was sent to you. And again, if you believe in Him, in proportion to your belief shall the prayers of your heart be granted.'

"'I believed in Him so strongly that I wanted to take an army and destroy the Jews who crucified Him, if I had not been prevented by the imperial power of Rome from doing so.'

" 'Our Lord has fulfilled the will of His Father: after fulfilling it He was taken up to the Father.'

"'I too have believed in Him and in His Father.'

"'For that reason I lay my hand on you in His name.'

"When he did this, Abgar was instantly cured of the disease and disorder from which he suffered. It surprised Abgar that the very thing he had heard about Yeshua had actually happened to him through His disciple Thaddaeus, who had cured him without drugs or herbs--and not only him but also Abdus son of Abdus, who had gout. He too came, and falling at his feet found his prayer answered through the hands of Thaddaeus, and was cured. Many other fellow-citizens of theirs Thaddaeus restored to health, performing many wonders and preaching the word of God.

"After this, Abgar said: 'It is by the power of God that you, Thaddaeus, do these things; and we ourselves were amazed. But I have a further request to make: explain to me about the coming of Yeshua and how it happened, and about His power—by what power did He do the things I have heard about?'

"Thaddaeus replied: 'For the time being I shall say nothing; but as I was sent to preach the word, be good enough to assemble all your citizen tomorrow, and I will preach to them and sow in them the word of life— about the coming of Yeshua and how it happened; about His mission and the purpose for which His Father sent Him; about His power and His deeds, and the mysteries He spoke in the world, and the power by which He did these things; about His new preaching; about His lowliness and humility, and how He humbled Himself and put aside and made light of His divinity, was crucified and descended into Hades, and rent asunder the partition which had never been rent since time began, and raised the dead; how He descended alone, but ascended with a great multitude to His Father [; and how He is seated on the right hand of God the Father with glory in the heavens; and how He will come again with power to judge living and dead].'

"So Abgar instructed his citizens to assemble at daybreak and hear the preaching of Thaddaeus. After that he ordered gold and silver to be given to him. But Thaddaeus refused them and asked, 'If we have left our own property behind, how can we accept other people's?'"

(Pages 30-33)

(* V) Another source with the same letters www.gods-kingdom-ministries.org

APPENDIX 2   "Can You See Him?"

To my knowledge this is the first published piece I ever wrote, taken from the college literary magazine, 1961 *Pylon*, a production of Associated Students of Warner Pacific College, Portland, Oregon. How was I to know when I was 19-years-old that years later I would expand upon this most precious of all stories?

You, you there, can you see him? Look!

I see, as I stand beneath my load, a man. He is tired. He is bruised and swollen. The picture before me is rather hazy. There he is. He, too, has a burden. He is struggling up a small hill. Easy! Watch out! He stumbled beneath his load.

What is it that he carries? I see. He drags a…cross. Yes, it is a cross he carries upon his back. There are no friends beside him to help him.

It seems as though this man did nothing, and yet he is being taken to the governor, Pontius Pilate, to be tried. Pilate gave this man over to the mob to be crucified.

Maybe, maybe this is…the Christ…Yes! It is the Christ.

See how the mob scorns him. He is mocked and spat upon. The throng laughs and jests. Is it a funny picture?

This man, Christ, goes before the mob to be crucified. He carries that cross upon his back; soon he will be hanging from it.

The crowd assembles around him upon the horizon. Step closer to the cross. Death is imminent. Can you taste it? Can you hear and feel it? Can you smell it? Look, now you can see it.

The atmosphere is sultry. It is like the sea before the storm, as smooth as glass. All is quiet. The spikes are driven!

Your mouth is dry and your lips are parched and cracking. Your throat is swollen. It is hard to swallow.

Listen! You can hear the moans of the two thieves.

You feel the pain. Inch by inch the spikes go into the Master's hands and feet.

Now you breathe the sickening smell of blood. You can smell the "stench" of the mob.

You can see it now. Yes, you can see death. Step a little closer, friend, see the blood? Sweat covers Christ's face. See the crown of thorns upon his head? There, look at the wounded side and the welts, bruises, and cuts upon his back. See the mob snickering, sneering and jeering at Jesus.

Why? Why this? Why did he die? He did no wrong. The people, they have done wrong. They wanted not to hear his preaching.

There it is standing in the distance—the cross. There he is hanging from the cross—the Christ.

Friend, you have overlooked something here. Look again! This he did for you, he suffered all of this pain and agony for you, a poor, sick, wretched sinner. Jesus loved you enough to die for you. He went to that cross to atone for your sins and lift your burdens.

Yes, friend the thing you have overlooked is God's love. You can see, through all this suffering, that had it not been for God's love for us, He would never have sent His only begotten son to atone for our sins, forgive us, and make us whole. God is love.

You ask me how I know all these things? I know, I was there. I was that "other disciple," the one who fled. I witnessed the whole crucifixion from a distance. You must understand that I couldn't get close enough to let the mob know that I was one of Christ's followers. They might have killed me.

I can look back now and see my mistake. Yes, I forsook Christ. I left him when he needed a friend the most.

Friend, don't you forsake him. He went to that cross to atone for your sins and lift the burden from your weary back.

There! Look! See him?

APPENDIX 3 Sunrise-Sunset

SUNRISE (sunrise over Anchorage Monday, January 20, 2014) *

Beneath the crimson sky, the day awakened, presenting a scintillating sunrise. At first glance, a brilliant, ruby red bonnet covered the sky. It then faded to bright pink, and dissipated incrementally from bright rose to a lighter pink, then followed by the palest of pinks. From left to right, a monster slate gray cloud layer sliced the sky in half. Two parallel rosy pink clouds, each adjoined by blue sky, split the dark cloud in half at near right angles, forming two colossal cross shapes of gray, pink and blue.

A panoply of colors and brightness—from the slate gray above, tinted by pinks and partnered with blue, to the silver clad hills below, backlit by soft gold—proclaimed unexcelled beauty as the day opened its eyes.

SUNSET (sunset over Anchorage Friday, January 17, 2014—one of most impressive ever seen)*

It was a strange day in a strange place and a strange event. Highlighted by a bedazzlingly bright rainbow and ushered in by a strong southeast wind, a low weather system enveloped the valley. Wanting to avoid getting soaked, I took shelter beneath the outstretched limbs of a giant oak tree. Every blast of whooshing wind rattled it. Hail pelted the red-brown earth bouncing upward like so much popping corn, turning the ground white.

While the day wound down, the wind worked its magic—orchestrating the dark, ominous cloud cover. It was almost as if one of our storied Italian fresco painters teamed up with Apollo, producing a masterpiece for the ages. While heralding out the day, our god of the sky raced his chariot across the heavens, stopping long enough to dip his finger in a paint pallet. He nudged his horses slowly onward while mischievously running his hand across the canvas of sky, creating a mosaic that showcased the very pageantry of the heavens.

As the sun tiptoed to bed in the west, the passing storm morphed into a dazzling apricot sky, presenting a glorious pattern. Thirteen bands of orange-gold-apricot clouds, bordered on either side by shades of blue sky, paralleled the valley.

Above my head a dark, steel gray lid stretched as far as the eye could see north and south. Touching that dark cloud, a cobalt blue sky embraced an apricot cloud. Beyond that cloud a brighter, lighter blue touched yet another cloud of silver-laced apricot. The pattern repeated itself till the sky met the earth in the west. As if by an out-of-control fire, the horizon lit up, spilling brilliant orange across the sky as the sun sank from sight.

This painted scene, if set to music, would be an anthem to the day. There was a certain wholesomeness—if not holiness—to this masterpiece.

*My wife Pam suggests I footnote these and place comments in Appendix re: how I got the ideas/based on actual sunsets in Anchorage in Jan. 2014

APPENDIX 4 Celebration

One of the most successful leaders to ever walk the planet mastered celebration. He achieved greatness by allowing others to celebrate.

He accepted people unequivocally for who they were—NOT for their superior status, what they might become or how they might benefit him.

His diplomacy and magnetic personality helped people feel good about themselves, thus they felt good about him. His compassion toward them gained their respect and admiration. His influence caused them to change for the better.

He accepted each who sought his help. He honored their requests by rewarding their faith in him. He granted people's wishes and helped them fulfill their desires, even to his detriment

He was loving and caring, considerate and kind. He was humble—not arrogant nor haughty. He was intuitive. And he was selfless.

He molded a dozen misfits into a force that has affected the world as no other person, simply by following the principle that "he that is greatest among you shall be your servant."

We could learn volumes from him.

Celebration benefits everyone, whether CEO, junior partner, receptionist, new hire or client.

Be a genuine friend and good fellow. Place others' best interests above your own. Elevate their importance, helping them to feel special.

Express 100% interest in others. Support and encourage them. Seek their happiness and best interests.

Accept others' worth as equal to or more valuable than your own.

Listen to others. Hear what they're saying. Don't wait your turn to upstage them. Refrain from telling a "better" story than the one just told... rather congratulate the teller.

Understand celebration. Then your allowing others to celebrate will boomerang, multiplying your efforts and rewarding you with vastly more than when you began...not to mention the endless benefits to others.

Larry Kaniut, July 2008

APPENDIX 5 The Christian Fish

Ichthys (Wikipedia)   The **ichthys** or **ichthus** (/ˈɪkθəs/[11]), from the Greek ikhthýs (ἰχθύς "fish"), is a symbol consisting of two intersecting arcs, the ends of the right side extending beyond the meeting point so as to resemble the profile of a fish. It was used by early Christians as a secret Christian symbol[2] and now known colloquially as the "**sign of the fish**" or the "**Jesus fish**".[3

Symbolic meaning

ΙΧΘΥΣ (Ichthus) is an backronym/acrostic[5] for "Ἰησοῦς Χριστός, Θεοῦ Υἱός, Σωτήρ", (Iēsous Christos, Theou Yios, Sōtēr), which translates into English as "Jesus Christ, Son of God, Saviour".

- Iota (i) is the first letter of Iēsous (Ἰησοῦς), Greek for "Jesus".
- Chi (ch) is the first letter of Christos (Χριστός), Greek for "anointed".
- Theta (th) is the first letter of Theou (Θεοῦ), Greek for "God's", the genitive case of Θεός, Theos, Greek for "God".
- Upsilon (y) is the first letter of (h)uios[6] (Υἱός), Greek for "Son".
- Sigma (s) is the first letter of sōtēr (Σωτήρ), Greek for "Savior".

A Modern Day Disciple

My wife Pam received a card in the mail August 29, 2015, which captures the devotion of a true disciple of Christ. I am quoting a portion of it from our family friend Tamie Hollingsworth:

Dear Pam,

I've been in Seattle for 2 days for customer service training for Alaska Airlines. The whole 2 day emphasis was engaging with people and making the extra effort. This is something you excel in! You make every person, every time, every consideration special—you make every day events special…You have perfected the art of valuing people. I have so often benefited from your attention and praise. You have been such an encourager to me and many others. Thank you. And may God continue to bless you as you infuse others with courage and confidence.

Tam

SOURCE NOTES

Websites

www.aish.com   Herod the Great, Rabbi Ken Spiro,

www.anchientrome.com

www.aristotle.net

www.bbc.co.uk/schools/primaryhistory/romans

www.bi.iup.edu/historyofpain/studentcasestudy3.htm

www.bibleplaces.com

http://biblesources.americanbible.org

www.biblicalresources.net or www.brusa.org

www.ccel.org/bible/phillips

www.centuryone.com

www.champlain.edu

wwwchristiananswers.net/dictionary/herodthegreat

www.christiancourier.com

http://christianity.about.com

www.christanitytoday.com

www.crystalinks.com

www.darbar.org

http://en.wikipedia.org

www.galegroup.com (Military Medicine of Ancient Rome)

www.godandscience.org

www.gods-kingdom-ministries.org

www. historylink102.com

www.historylearningsite.co.uk

www.jesuscentral.com

www.jesus-institute.org

www.jerusalemperspective.com

www.konnections.com

www.latter-rain.com

http://library.thinkquest

www.livius.org/helg/herodians/herod_the_great

www.loriswebs.com

www.ludusmilitis.org

http://mb-soft.com/believe/text

http://members.aol.com/donnandlee

www.newlife.net

www.ourfatherlutheran.net

www.newlife.net

www.pagesperso-orange.fr/fira/cadouam/english/.../flogging.htm

www.pbs.org

www.realtime.net

www.romanarmy.net/Military.htm

http//romanmilitary.net/people

www.Sundayschoollessons.com

www.thenazereneway.com

www.vroma.org

www.weather.com

www.weatheronline.com

Books

Barton, Bruce, *The Man Nobody Knows*, The Bobbs-Merrill Company Publishers, Indianapolis, 1924

Bouquet, A. C., *Everyday Life in the New Testament Times*, Charles Scribner's Sons, N.Y., 1953

Brown, Charles Reynolds, *These Twelve*, The Century Company, New York and London, 1926

Brown, Raymond E., SS, *The Birth of the Messiah*, S.S., Doubleday, New York, London, Toronto, Sydney, Auckland, 1977

Brown, S.S., Raymond E., *The Death of the Messiah* (Vols. I and II), Doubleday, New York, London, Toronto, Sydney, Auckland, 1994

Bruce, F.F., *The New Testament History*, Doubleday & Company, Garden City, New York, 1969

Burpo, Todd with Lynn Vincent, *Heaven Is for Real*, Thomas Nelson, Nashville, Dallas, Mexico City, Rio De Janeiro, 2010

Cahill, Thomas, *Desire of the Everlasting Hills*, Random House, New York, 1999

Casson, Lionel, *The Ancient Mariners*, Princeton, 1991

Casson, Lionel, *Travel in the Ancient World*, Johns Hopkins University Press, 1994

Cohen, Shaye J.D., *From the Macabees to the Mishuah*, The Westminster Press, Philadelphia, 1987

Dudley, Donald R., *The Romans: 850 B.C.—A.D. 337*, Barnes & Noble Books, New York, 1970

Dunn, James D.G., *The Evidence for Jesus*, The Westminster Press, Louisville, Kentucky, 1985

Duriez, Colin, *AD 33 The Year that Changed the World*, Sutton Publishing, UK, 2006

Eusebius, *The History of the Church*, Penguin Classics, London,1965

Goodspeed, Edgar J., *A Life of Jesus*, Harper & Brothers Publishers, New York, 1956

Gower, Ralph, *Manners and Customs of Bible Times*, Moody Press, Chicago, Illinois, 1999

Hanson, K. C. and Oakman, Douglas E., *Palestine in the Time of Jesus: Social Structures and Social Conflicts*, Fortress Press, Minneapolis, 1998

Hobbs, Herschel H., *Illustrated Life of Jesus*, B&H Publishing Group, Nashville, TN, 1999

Holy Bible, The, (Authorized King James Version), Harper & Brothers Publishers, New York

Johnson, Luke Timothy, *The Writings of the New Testament*, Fortress Press, Philadelphia, 1986

Johnson, Luke Timothy, *The Real Jesus*, HarperSanFrancisco,1996

Keller, W. Phillip, *Rabboni*, Fleming H. Revell Company, Old Tappan, New Jersey, 1977

Korb, Scott, *Life in Year One*, Riverhead Books, New York, 2010

Living Bible,The, Tyndale House Publishers, Wheaton, Illinois, Coverdale House Publishers Ltd., London, England, 1971

Marshall, Peter, *First Easter*, Chosen Books, Grand Rapids, Michigan. 1959

Marshall, Peter, *John Doe, Disciple*, Mc Graw-Hill Book Co., Inc., New York, Toronto, London, 1963

May, Herbert G. (editor), *Oxford Bible Atlas*, Oxford University Press, New York, Toronto, 1962

McCorkle, Dennis F., *The Book of Jesus*, Writers Club Press, New York, Lincoln, Shanghai, 2002

Meeks, Wayne A., *The Moral World of the First Christians*, The Westminster Press, Philadelphia, 1986

Roberts, Richard, *That Strange Man Upon His Cross*, The Abingdon Press, New York, Cincinnati, Chicago, 1934

Sanders, E.P., *The Historical Figure of Jesus*, Penguin Books, London, England, 1993

Spong, John Shelby, *Liberating the Gospels*, Harper SanFrancisco, 1996

Stambaugh, John E., David L. Balch, *The New Testament in Its Social Environment*, The Westminster Press, Philadelphia, 1986

Strobel, Lee, *The Case for Christ*, Zondervan, Grand Rapids, Michigan, 1998

Throckmorton, Jr., Burton H. (editor), *Gospel Parallels*, Thomas Nelson & Sons, Toronto, New York, Edinburgh, 1949

Vermes, Geza, *Jesus and the World of Judaism*, Fortress Press, Philadelphia, 1983

Vermes, Geza, *The Religion of Jesus the Jew*, Fortress Press, Minneapolis, 1993

White, Ellen G., *The Desire of Ages*, Pacific Press Publishing Association, Mountain View, CA 94042, 1898

Wilson, Ian, *Murder At Golgotha*, St. Martin's Press, New York, 2006

Witherington III, Ben, *The Jesus Quest*, InterVarsity Press, Downers, Grove, Illinois, 1995

CD ROM

Ray Vander Laar, *Life and Ministry of the Messiah*, CD Rom.

Chorus/Song

"How Deep the Father's Love for Us," Stuart Townend, 1995 Thank you Music by worshiptogether.com, 800-234-2446

DVD/VHS

"The Story Begins, Jesus Among the People," *Reader's Digest*

Miscellaneous

literacyjewishhistorycrashcourse#31

Archaeological evidence of Jesus? (Technology & Science News)